HIGH PRAISE FOR JEFF BUICK!

LETHAL DOSE

"Full of action and danger... The author keeps the reader turning the pages long into the night."

—Detective Mystery Stories

"Lethal Dose is a fast-paced, energetic, and relevant read."

—Fresh Fiction

"...a thought-provoking, suspense-filled novel."

—*The Midwest Book Review*

BLOODLINE

"Buick has created an intense, gut-twisting thriller with his brilliant debut. With characters modeled from real-life headlines, he gives the book depth and a life of its own."

—*The Best Reviews*

A GRUESOME DISCOVERY

A scream from behind them, deep in the brush, stopped McNeil mid-sentence. With a reflexive motion, a gun appeared in his hand. He held the other up to silence the porters. The scream came again, this time the location more identifiable. McNeil counted the porters and silently indicated to Sam that one was missing. He held up his fist, a sign for them to stay put, and moved stealthily into the underbrush. All was quiet for a minute, then he reappeared with a shaking porter in tow. He motioned for Sam to follow him.

"I don't think you're going to like this," he said. They broke into a small clearing and Sam gasped, horrified. Before her lay a massacre. Skulls littered the clearing, at least fifteen, perhaps more. Bones, gnawed on by jungle carnivores and partially covered with lichens, interspersed the hollow skulls. McNeil knelt down and picked up a skull, then another, and another. He looked back at Sam and stuck his finger through a round hole in one of the skulls. A bullet hole.

"They were executed," he said. "Each one shot in the head once." He gingerly held up a long bone with a loop of nylon rope hanging off it. "Their hands were tied. They didn't stand a chance."

He kicked at something with the toe of his boot, then bent down and retrieved the object from the moss. He held it out to her. "Do you know what this is?"

"Yes, of course. It's a geological hammer. Standard gear for a field geologist. We all carry them." She stopped and stared at him. "It's them, isn't it?"

He nodded. "It's the expedition that went in a couple of months ago. The bones are reasonably fresh."

Other *Leisure* books by Jeff Buick:

LETHAL DOSE
BLOODLINE

JEFF BUICK

AFRICAN ICE

LEISURE BOOKS **NEW YORK CITY**

A LEISURE BOOK®

April 2006

Published by

Dorchester Publishing Co., Inc.
200 Madison Avenue
New York, NY 10016

ISBN 0-8439-5720-4

The name "Leisure Books" and the stylized "L" with design are trademarks of Dorchester Publishing Co., Inc.

Printed in the United States of America.

Visit us on the web at www.dorchesterpub.com.

Dianne Young
A woman of incredible
courage and strength and moral character.
Who tracked the silverback gorillas through the
darkest and most dangerous jungles of the
Ruwenzori Mountains in Africa.

AFRICAN ICE

ONE

Springtime in New York City.

The promise of summer just around the corner. Winter laid to rest for another year. For Samantha Carlson, spring meant New York at its finest. Trees sprouting green, their new leaves softening the harsh lines of the apartment and office buildings that surrounded Central Park. And the early-morning smells. Pretzels, freshly brewed coffee, and dough rising in the bakeries. And with the longer days came mild temperatures. When the mercury rose to a sensible level, Samantha dug her jogging shoes out and brought them back into active duty. Today was day one of the new year.

She entered Central Park from East Sixtieth Street and began to run—slowly at first, her long blond hair swaying in the breeze—then faster as she settled into a rhythm. She had the park mostly to herself, with only a few other intrepid souls braving the early-morning chill. She checked her watch as she ran—six minutes after five. Her breath misted as she exhaled, then disappeared behind her. She kept an even pace for the better part of twenty minutes.

She rounded the pond and cut north until she hit the

Transverse. Then east toward the park boundary. She picked up the pace as Fifth Avenue came into view, and then slowed to a marginal jog as she hit the sidewalk. By the time Samantha reached her apartment building on East Sixty-third, she was breathing normally. The doorman eased the door open as she approached. She slid effortlessly through, and made for the elevators.

"Morning, Miss Carlson," the building employee said as she passed.

She turned, still moving. "Ernie, I keep telling you, it's Samantha."

"Yes, ma'am." He smiled. They had had this same conversation at least two hundred times. There was no way he would ever call her by her first name. They both knew it. She disappeared into the elevator, and he looked back to the empty street.

The elevator slid open on the eighteenth floor, and Sam exited into the deserted hallway. Her apartment was the third on the left. She unlocked the door and let herself in. She added a bit more hot water to her shower than usual, to take off the chill from her jog. Twenty minutes later, she emerged from the bathroom, housecoat on, hair wrapped in a white towel. She stared at the telephone for a moment, then checked her watch.

Six twenty-four, and her voice-mail light was flashing. Someone had called while she was in the shower. Early for a call, she thought. She punched in her code and hit the speakerphone button. A baritone voice enveloped the room.

"This is Patrick Kerrigan calling for Samantha Carlson. Please call me at my office when you get this message. The number is—"

She grabbed a notepad from the end table and jotted down the number. It was local, somewhere in Manhattan. She considered calling it immediately, to see if he was actually up and at work yet, then changed her mind. The coffee was brewed, and Samantha settled into her favorite couch with the daily *Times*. She skimmed the headlines, then flipped to the business section. The Dow-Jones was up, the Nasdaq was up, but the American dollar was down against the euro. She shrugged, and wondered why she bothered; economics baffled her.

She finished her coffee and stretched. Across the room, a bank of glass overlooked Central Park. She lifted herself off the couch, moved to the windows, slid open the door, and walked out onto the balcony. The view was awesome. She found herself thinking about where she was in her life. For some reason, staring out over the park was a catalyst that triggered memories, and the balcony had become her place for quiet reflection. At thirty-two years old, she held a doctorate in geology—a piece of paper she had used to carve out a remarkable career. Her exploits in some of the most dangerous countries on the planet had earned her the reputation as the female Indiana Jones of the Geological Society. She was no stranger to the ice floes of the Canadian arctic or the steaming rain forests that bordered the Amazon River. Her trips to Africa were too many and too varied to remember. The newspapers and television stations were quick to run a story if it involved Samantha Carlson hunting down a new geological find. She was attractive, athletic, intelligent and accomplished. She was newsworthy.

Her love-hate relationship with the media had started three years ago, when she had discovered a new anticline loaded with oil in northern Texas. The skeptics insisted that the area had been exploited and a large find was impossible. She had responded by throwing the algorithm for her computer program on the table, and letting it go public. The program, she contended, was the crux of her discovery. It allowed the previously unnoticed bulge to be seen through geophysics. She recommended they punch an eight-thousand-foot hole in the ground, and they did.

The anomaly gave way to three million barrels of light Texas crude. Two million dollars to drill the well and almost two hundred million in return. The bonus they had lavished on her had paid for half the penthouse in which she now stood. She winced as she thought about where the other half had come from.

Her parents' estate. It was almost two years to the day since their plane had crashed into the sea just after liftoff from Casablanca. They had been en route to London, to meet her and spend a week traveling through Europe. The news had devastated her. Her mother and father had been young, in their early fifties, and in excellent health. She had never entertained the thought that they wouldn't be there, and the void their deaths left was still unfilled. Her mind relived the memorial service, and once the all-too-familiar tape played through, she let it go.

She'd tried to stop the images for the first year, but her subconscious was too strong. The sight of the two coffins, side by side, being lowered into the ground was indelibly etched into her mind. She watched as the two handfuls of dirt left her hand and splayed across the tops of the coffins as they sat beneath ground level. Empty caskets, lined with a few trinkets and pictures of her with her parents, their bodies never found. She closed her eyes and the picture stopped.

Samantha opened her eyes, feeling the wet tears, and blinked away the moisture. The park was blurry for a few moments, then it came back into focus. She turned away and reentered the apartment.

The coffee was still reasonably fresh, and she poured one more cup. She sat on the edge of the couch and looked at the number she had taken from her voice mail. She picked up the phone and dialed.

"Good morning, Gem-Star," a pleasant voice answered.

"Good morning. Could you put me through to Patrick Kerrigan, please?"

"Certainly. Whom should I say is calling?"

"Samantha Carlson."

The line switched over to Muzak for a few moments, then

Kerrigan's unmistakable baritone voice came on. "Ms. Carlson, thank you for returning my call."

"No problem, Mr. Kerrigan. Except that I have no idea who you are, or what you may want with me."

"That's understandable, Ms. Carlson. Have you heard of Gem-Star?"

"No, can't say I have."

"We're a mining company, specializing in gemstones. Diamonds, rubies, sapphires, that kind of thing. And we need a geologist. Would you be interested in meeting with us?"

Sam Carlson took a moment before answering. She was currently without a contract, but financially, she didn't need to work another day in her life. Then again, not working was boring. "It depends on what you're offering, Mr. Kerrigan," she replied.

"Our offices are in Manhattan. And I'd rather not discuss it over the phone, if you'd like to drop by. Shall we say, one-thirty this afternoon?"

At precisely one-twenty, Samantha Carlson stepped off the elevator onto the sixty-third floor of Gem-Star's building, and into a world of opulence. Cultured Italian marble tiles graced the floors, and original oils hung throughout the foyer of the multinational company. Comfortable leather chairs and couches paired with teak tables furnished the room. The tones were muted teal, and a small waterfall tucked into a feature wall gurgled as the water softly fell onto the rocks.

Sam Carlson took it all in, and stopped at the rocks in the waterfall. She moved closer and almost gasped. Embedded in the stone were small greenish rocks—uncut diamonds. She bent over, admiring the naturalness of the display. A voice drifted over to her from behind, and she turned to face the speaker.

It was a man in his early fifties, and of obvious wealth. His hair was well groomed and dark, with a slight graying about the temples. She wondered if the gray was natural or dyed for the effect. His suit was Armani, his tie silk. But it was the charismatic air about the man that told the uneducated of his position in society.

"You must be Samantha Carlson," he was saying. "Only a geologist would see more than some drab rocks and a waterfall."

"You mean the diamonds?" she asked, and he nodded. She extended her hand and he shook it. His grip was firm, but she caught the slight twitch in his eye as he felt the strength in her grip. That happened a lot. Between the gym and working in the field, she had extreme upper-body strength for her size and gender.

"I'm Patrick Kerrigan." He smiled and motioned past the reception desk toward the hallway. She followed him as he started into the labyrinth of offices.

"Do you always meet your appointments in the lobby?" she asked, curious.

"Almost never," he responded, and waved her into a corner office, shutting the door behind them. "But your reputation precedes you. Plus"—he smiled—"I just happened to be walking by the reception area when you arrived. Please, sit down." He pointed to a cluster of wing-back chairs by the windows. As she moved toward them, she noticed the top of a head barely protruding above the back of the nearest chair. She came alongside the chair, and a man rose to greet her.

"Samantha Carlson, this is Travis McNeil. Travis, Samantha." Carlson made the introductions, and the two strangers shook hands. "He's involved in our latest venture—the one for which we'd like to have you as geologist. I'm getting ahead of myself, Ms. Carlson. Please make yourself comfortable, and I'll start from the beginning."

An employee carrying a tray with light snacks and drinks entered from another door. Samantha took the opportunity to study Kerrigan's office, as he looked over the tray. It was a man's office—heavy in texture and style. The floors were hardwood, with Persian rugs thrown about almost randomly. Numerous statues and large carvings dominated the furnishings. It was an eclectic mixture, and very worldly. She was impressed.

"You like my collection?" Kerrigan caught her surveying the room. She nodded. "I brought back one souvenir from each country I traveled to. Currently, there are one hundred thirty-three different figures in this room, some of them priceless, some of them quite worthless."

"It's quite the collection, Mr. Kerrigan. I especially like the trinket you retrieved from Kenya." She stole a quick glance at the ivory statue tucked back in a far corner. "I'm sure that came out before the ban went on."

Patrick Kerrigan pursed his lips and eyed his visitor as if seeing her for the first time. She interested him.

He knew her background from the file his company had compiled. Born thirty-two years ago in Boston, she had followed her father's footsteps into geology. She had completed her undergraduate degree in Boston, but shifted to New York to attend Columbia University for her master's and Ph.D. Samantha Carlson had excelled in a field dominated by men. Times had changed over the past twenty years, and her gender had made great strides into the field, but the top geologists worldwide were all men, with one exception: her.

She showed no fear, and took on the toughest assignments under the most dangerous conditions. And she consistently came out on top. She successfully negotiated a multimillion-dollar drilling contract with the Russian government after she discovered huge oil reserves in the desolation of Siberia. The Amazon basin had yielded a substantial find of tourmaline, and she had hammered out a working arrangement between her employer and the Brazilian government. Her latest venture was in the Canadian arctic, where she was unable to save the drilling rig, but kept seventy-eight men from certain death by ordering their evacuation.

She was attractive, Kerrigan decided, but not from a

strictly feminine view. Her features were more chiseled than soft, her body tensile and wiry, not spongy. He was surprised she wore her hair so long, but it suited her. But of all her features, it was her eyes that awed him. It wasn't just their color, a shade of teal that danced between green and blue. They had an intensity that told of a quick and alert mind behind them, a mind with a thirst for knowledge. Her eyes probed the person she looked at, gnawing into his soul and taking more from him than the words he spoke. To call Samantha Carlson interesting was an understatement.

He smiled. "Patrick," he said. "Please call me Patrick."

"Samantha. Or Sam. Your preference," she responded.

Kerrigan rose from his chair and moved to the windows that looked out over Manhattan. "We're looking for diamonds. We have a few preliminary scouting reports that indicated there could be good potential for high-quality gemstones in the region. We sent in a team about four months ago, but that didn't yield anything. I think we need a fresh perspective."

"What country are we dealing with?" Samantha asked.

"Democratic Republic of Congo," Kerrigan replied.

Sam Carlson simply stared at the man. "DROC. Nice place." Her tone was sarcastic.

"You know it?"

"I wrote my master's thesis on alluvial diamonds in Sierra Leone, and my doctorate on industrial diamonds in the Congo. I know both countries well." She stood up and walked to the window, peering down on Manhattan as she continued.

"The Democratic Republic of Congo is a wealth of industrial-grade diamonds. The rocks that end up in engagement rings don't come from the Congolese mines. They come from Sierra Leone, South Africa, Brazil, Canada, and a dozen other countries. But not the Congo. Kananga is a major center near the mines, but the town of Mbuji-Mayi, about ninety miles east, is the hot spot. For industrial diamonds, not commercial grade. And diamond miners have overrun

Mbuji-Mayi since the 1950s. So if you want my opinion, you don't need a geologist, Mr. Kerrigan, you need a thousand Africans with shovels."

Kerrigan held up his hand to stop her. "I know you have a great deal of knowledge about the Congo," he said. "But our target is not the alluvial diamonds that scavengers have dug for over the past fifty years. And we're definitely not looking for industrial-grade diamonds. We're looking at a diamondiferous formation to the north, in the Ruwenzori Mountains." Sam started to speak, and Kerrigan stopped her once again. "I know it's been tried before, and the core samples came up empty, but I think we have further proof that such a vein may exist."

"What kind of proof?" Samantha asked, interested but skeptical.

Kerrigan strode across the room and slid a painting to the side, revealing a wall safe. He entered a combination, opened the safe, and pulled out a small bag and an envelope. "These were taken from the vein, at a depth of sixty-two feet." He handed four dull greenish rocks to her.

Sam motioned to the magnifier on Kerrigan's desk, and he nodded. She placed the stones under the scope one at a time, carefully studying them. She lifted her head. "They have all the characteristics of Sierra Leone diamonds. But you say they were found in northeast Congo." He nodded again. "I need a specific test to be sure they aren't simply Sierra Leone diamonds."

"You're referring to the laser ablation method the Canadian RCMP have been working on?" he asked, and she nodded.

"Laser ablation inductively coupled plasma mass spectrometry," she said.

"Done," Kerrigan responded, holding the legal-sized envelope up in his left hand. "We sent the samples to the RCMP about a month ago, and got the results back last week. Have a look."

Carlson took the envelope and let its contents drop onto

the coffee table. She quickly sorted through the analysis, concentrating on the trace elements found in the diamonds. "Ninety-nine point nine five pure carbon, as expected. Point zero five trace elements. Trace elements not found in the mangrove swamps of Sierra Leone." She paused for a moment. "You're positive these are from the Congo?"

"Absolutely. Our team reported back a position close to Butembo, but they weren't precise with their coordinates. We have an idea within about seventy square miles where they were, but it's impossible to pinpoint any closer."

"You're familiar with the terrain around Butembo?" Sam asked, and Kerrigan nodded. "Sticky, sweaty jungle, teeming with every kind of poisonous creature God ever created. Rugged cliffs, hundred-foot waterfalls, dense underbrush, and local tribesmen who would just as soon kill you as say hello."

"It has its moments."

"Not to mention the current political situation. It's a mess over there right now."

"Agreed. And that's why we're paying so handsomely. We're offering one million dollars up front, and an additional five million if you can locate the vein and get that information back to us."

"You mean if I live long enough," she said quietly. Kerrigan didn't respond to her statement. "It's been four years since I was in the Congo, and I have no desire to go back. It's corrupt, and it's dangerous." She took a sip from her tea, then set it on the end table. It was cold. "How does *he* figure into all this?" she asked, gesturing at the man who had sat quietly through the meeting.

"Travis will keep you alive while you explore. He's assembled an elite team of men who are well skilled in protecting people from—other people. The snakes you have to watch out for yourself."

"When do you propose to send the expedition?" she asked.

"Almost immediately. Travis has been acquiring the necessary supplies, and the team is just about ready. Any instruments you require will, of course, be supplied."

"And how long do you think it'll take to unearth the vein?"

"That depends on you, Ms. Carlson."

"Okay," she said, looking him straight in the eye. "Why me? Why offer me the job?"

"Like I said, Ms. Carlson, your reputation precedes you. You are one of the most knowledgeable geologists in the world on the Democratic Republic of Congo. You're resourceful, and you've demonstrated many times a commodity very valuable to this expedition."

"And that is?"

"Your ability to stay alive."

Samantha Carlson rose from her chair and extended her hand to Kerrigan. She offered the same to Travis McNeil. "You don't talk much, do you?" she asked as they locked grips.

"Not today," he responded.

She unclasped his hand and walked to the door. She opened it, then turned back to face Kerrigan. "I'll let you know one way or the other by tomorrow." He nodded. "One more question," she continued. "What happened to the last team you sent in?"

"They disappeared," Kerrigan answered.

"Before they could pinpoint the location of the vein?" she asked, and he nodded. "That's most unfortunate. For them *and* for you." She closed the door behind her as she left.

TWO

Samantha took the same route for her jog she did every morning, but New York had changed overnight. It seemed constricting and crowded. Her mind had shifted gears, and she found herself thinking of Africa. She remembered the landscape of the Congo near Kananga and Mbuji-Mayi, pockmarked by hundreds of thousands of holes dug into the earth in the hope of finding diamonds. The carnage digging inflicted on the surface was the bane of alluvial stones. And the town of Mbuji-Mayi was the center of this madness.

Mbuji-Mayi. The place was a shit hole. At least that was her recollection of four years ago. It was a harsh region, with steep rifts and valleys that overran the area. In the valleys the soil was porous, and tunnels commingled under the mass of corrugated metal shacks that served as houses. The extent of the tunneling was so severe that it wasn't uncommon for a section of hovels to just disappear into a hole. Sometimes, not too many people died.

The town's water came from a central pond, dirty and contaminated. Shady characters lurked everywhere, and the value of human life was measured by how many carats one carried. A lucky day of searching could translate into a death sentence. People didn't walk upright or make eye contact. They hunched over, their eyes ever glued to the soft dirt that held the promise of glittering riches.

Everything in a constant state of turmoil—that was life in the diamond-producing areas of Africa. And now they wanted her to go back. But not to excavate for the industrial diamonds that littered the area. They wanted her to leave any vestige of civilization behind, and venture into the Ruwenzori Mountains—an area that made Mbuji-Mayi look like a five-star resort town. The northern reaches of the Congo were untamed. It was madness to think of entering the virgin jungle, let alone leading an expedition into the uncharted wilderness.

She finished her jog and walked briskly back to her apartment. Nothing seemed the same as yesterday. The city was ugly, the people unfriendly. The aromas from the corner pretzel stand didn't tempt her, and she only wanted her coffee for the caffeine.

She stood on the balcony overlooking the park, and wondered what had happened to the first team of geologists Gem-Star had sent in. They had disappeared in the heart of the Congo. That usually meant the missing persons were dead. It wasn't a forgiving country, and the exploration crew would have had access to radios and satellite telephones. She tried to put it out of her mind, but she knew they had not survived.

A million dollars would be a nice paycheck, but she didn't need it. There were plenty of contract jobs out there if she wanted them, and few would be as dangerous as this one. But something inside her was drawing her into the waiting mystery. And geology, at the best of times, was a mystery.

It was this aspect of geology that had attracted her to the profession, not her father's involvement, as many people thought. She remembered her university instructor in first-year geology, holding up a strangely shaped object as he lectured. Draw it, he told them. Draw it from six different perspectives. If you couldn't do it, quit the course. It took her a quarter of the time the next fastest student took. And her drawings were flawless. Thinking in three dimensions was second nature to her.

She knew that her mind worked as it should to be successful in the field. She could envision any structure, no matter how deep beneath the earth's surface it lay. She recognized the trapping mechanisms for oil and gas, and the "pipes" that often held diamonds. She was a natural, and she excelled. It didn't hurt that she was almost without fear, and would tackle anything that got in her way. It was this part of her nature that landed her the most dangerous jobs on the market. Like this one. But still, she had reservations. She knew virtually nothing about Kerrigan or Gem-Star. It was time to find out.

Samantha backed away from the balcony and entered her apartment. She flipped through her Rolodex and found the name she wanted. She dialed the local number and waited. Seven rings, then eight, and still she waited. She knew her colleague hated voice mail and would not pick up until at least twelve rings—plenty of time to weed out the garbage calls. She had counted the start of the thirteenth ring when it stopped and a man's voice answered.

"Hello." The tone was civil, but curt.

"Farid, it's Samantha. How are you?"

"I'm well." The voice changed, warmer now. "What can I do for my favorite geologist?"

"I need some information on a guy I met yesterday. Patrick Kerrigan. He works for a mining company called Gem-Star."

"Kerrigan rings a bell, Sam," the man answered slowly, as if trying to retrieve a byte of data from his computerlike mind. "Something to do with a divorce. Scandal on the social pages. Give me an hour and I'll be back to you." He hung up.

Sam replaced the phone and poured a fresh cup of coffee, adding a touch of cream and one sugar. Farid Virgi was the one man she couldn't live without, a private investigator who could open any door or pry information from the most closely watched file. She had no idea how he did it and she didn't care. He got results, and *that* she cared about. Samantha Carlson was not a person who entered into contracts with unknown parties. Farid would get the info on Kerrigan and the company he worked for, and she would make her decision accordingly.

Forty minutes later the phone rang. She checked the call display. It was Farid. "That was quick," she said. "What did you find out?"

"All your inquiries should be this simple," he said lightly. "Gem-Star is a private company, owned entirely by the Perth family. Nathaniel Perth founded the company eighty-two years ago and built it into a midsize operation heavy on new exploration in virgin areas. Difficult and tricky, but this guy was a risk taker. When he handed the reigns down to his son, Reginald, thirty-six years ago, the company was valued at just over fifty million. It turned out that Reginald was even more astute than his dad."

"How so?" she asked, intrigued.

"Reginald had the same frontier spirit as his father, but took things one step further. He saw that federal grants were available to American exploration companies, and he learned how to open government coffers. Business boomed, and by the time he retired eight years ago, Gem-Star had an estimated worth in excess of one hundred seventy-five million. Then things changed."

"Let me guess. Reginald's son took over and screwed things up."

"Right and wrong. Davis Perth, Reginald's oldest boy, *did* take over at the helm, but he certainly didn't screw the pooch. He didn't want to have hands-on control like his father and grandfather, so he hired Patrick Kerrigan. Davis Perth enjoys yachting and spends half his life at sea, unreachable. So the responsibility of running Gem-Star lies directly with Kerrigan. And I *was* right about him, he did suffer through a nasty divorce about a year after joining Gem-Star. His wife, ex-wife I should say, took him to the cleaners. She raped and pillaged every penny he'd saved. There are more than a few entries in the social pages on the split up."

"He seems to be doing just fine now," Sam said.

"Yes, he does. His estimated net worth is about sixty million."

"What? How the hell does a guy get cleaned out, then rebuild a personal fortune like that over seven years?"

"Creative financing, shrewd investing, and a lot of questionable entries on his tax return. He's got a secondary source of income, but I have no idea what it is. He certainly didn't replenish his investment nest egg from the salary Gem-Star pays him."

"So he's dipping into something, somewhere," Sam said thoughtfully. "Embezzling from the firm?"

"Doubtful. The company would have noticed. Gem-Star is legit, and word is it has been since ol' Nathaniel started it. Kerrigan's got a sideline somewhere."

"Is Gem-Star still profitable under Davis Perth?"

"Abso-fucking-lutely," Farid said. "That's Arabic for yes, by the way."

"Thanks for the interpretation."

"Welcome. Gem-Star is actually doing very well. They seem to concentrate on major plays and carry the ball from exploration right through to exploitation. The only reason they're not a household name is that they're private. And very low-key."

"Thanks. Send the bill to my apartment. And courier it if you want to get paid inside three months. I may be heading out of town."

"Done," he said, then added, "Take care, Sam. I get the feeling that there's more to Patrick Kerrigan than shows up on his file."

"Okay, Farid. Just for you, I'll be careful." She hung up.

She finished her coffee, checked her watch and placed a

call to Gem-Star. The receptionist answered and forwarded her call to Kerrigan immediately. He picked up on the third ring.

"You've hired yourself a geologist, Patrick," she informed him. "On certain conditions. How about we meet at your office at ten o'clock and go over them?" He agreed. "And please invite our talkative friend from yesterday—Travis."

Samantha arrived at ten minutes past the hour. New York traffic was impossible to predict. The receptionist ushered her into a conference room on the same side of the building as Kerrigan's office. The view was a carbon copy of the previous day. She stared at the expanse of buildings that lay beneath her until she heard the door open. She turned to see Kerrigan and Travis McNeil file into the room.

"Samantha," Kerrigan said, this time without offering to shake hands. "Please have a seat. I've asked Travis to sit in on the meeting, as you requested."

"That's good, because it's Travis I want to talk to," she responded. Kerrigan looked slightly taken aback. "You said it yourself, Patrick. This is the guy who's going to keep me alive. I'd like to find out how he's going to manage that."

Kerrigan relaxed and cocked his head, nodding in agreement. "I understand. Tell her whatever she wants to know," he added.

"I'll try." Travis turned to face her. "Ask away."

She scrutinized the man before beginning. He was older than her by a few years, probably close to forty. His eyes had tiny crow's feet, and he constantly squinted, a conditioned reflex from searching the surroundings for danger. His hair was deep brown, wavy and thick. When he smiled, which was rarely, his teeth were even and white, contrasting with the deep brown of his tanned skin. He was an inch or two taller than her, which put him right at six feet. He was relaxed in the chair, but she could tell there was a great deal of strength and agility in his frame. She liked what she saw.

"Your background. Where are you from, what's your military experience, and have you ever led an expedition like this in the past?"

"San Antonio, Texas. I was born in Houston, but moved to San Antonio when I was ten. I did some undergraduate work in the sciences, but dropped out after two years. It didn't suit my tastes."

"The sciences?"

"No, school. I liked physics, and chemistry was okay, but I hated biology, zoology, and all that stuff. Hated it. Anyway, I left after two years and joined the Navy. They stationed me in Little Creek, Virginia."

"SEAL?" she asked.

"Yes, ma'am, Navy SEAL," he responded.

"Team Six," she muttered. "Where the action is."

"Correct again. I spent six years operating with Team Six."

"And now you're for hire? Mercenary, bodyguard, that sort of thing?"

McNeil's stare hardened as she spoke. "Babysitter would be more like it," he said, between clenched teeth. "And no, I've never led a mining expedition before."

"What armaments are you taking into the Congo?"

"We've detailed a list that will give us flexibility under differing conditions. We'll take in a few Remington 12/26 modified 12 gauges, and some Remington Vent Rib Rangers are good for close-in jungle stuff. I prefer Smith & Wesson handguns. We've got a few AirLite Titanium M337s, and a couple of the new model that Smith & Wesson and Walther cooperated on—the SW 99.40. And a Daisy 600."

"You're taking a sniper rifle?" Sam asked. "I can understand the shotguns and the revolvers, but the Daisy 600 is a sniper rifle. What do you need that for?"

"I used to be a Boy Scout, Ms. Carlson. You know their motto." He tried not to show it, but he was surprised and impressed by her knowledge of guns.

Samantha turned to Kerrigan. "Mr. McNeil seems to know what he's doing. If the rest of his team are equally qualified, they're quite acceptable." She paused for a moment, then continued. "I'll need a spectrometer. The one that can perform laser ablation to determine trace elements. And I'll need a copy of that report you got from the RCMP."

"I'll have photocopies of the file made up for you." He paused for a moment. "Are you sure you need a spectrometer? It'll take some doing to get one away from the Canadian police."

"I need that machine to test the trace elements in any diamonds we find near Butembo. If the tests match, we'll know we're onto the same vein of the diamonds in your safe. If they don't, we've missed it. And we have to be careful, because there could be alluvial diamonds kicking around. I want to be sure we have it before I send the location back through the GPS systems."

Kerrigan nodded in agreement. "Good point. I'll get on it. Anything else?"

"What is the possibility of getting a helicopter to recon the mountains east of Butembo?" she asked. "Can we charter one to fly overhead and take a few aerial shots?"

"I suppose, but it's dense jungle. You can't see anything but treetops."

"The canopy can tell stories," she said. "If you can confirm a chopper is available, I'd also like a BritPix. It's a camera you can attach to an aircraft that gives you 360-degree spherical imaging. If we can arrange for the surface scans to be transmitted to us on the ground, I can use various filters to look for differences in the vegetation. It will be useful in establishing the existence of a pipe."

"What's a pipe?" Travis asked.

She smiled. The ex-SEAL didn't know everything. "It's a geological term for an outcrop of denser rock that hasn't eroded over the millennia at the same rate at the surrounding rocks. It may not stick up high enough to see above the rainforest canopy, but the vegetation that grows on it may vary enough to see the difference. It's a long shot, but it'll give us an area to start in, rather than just combing the area in a grid."

"Who's the manufacturer?" Kerrigan asked.

"Britannia 2000 Limited. The company's head office is in Berkshire, U.K. There's been a lot of talk around the industry about this machine. We think it has incredible potential for exactly this purpose. It's fairly new; they just began production a couple of years ago."

"That could take some time, Sam," Kerrigan said, writing down the information she gave him.

"Then I guess how quickly we leave depends on you, Patrick," she answered.

"Of course, you're right. I'll get on it."

"What's the size of the team?" she asked the team leader.

"Myself, and three other . . ." He paused for a moment. ". . . mercenaries. Ex-SEALs, all of us. We'll pick up a dozen or so locals to help pack the equipment east from Butembo. And you, of course."

"We can fly directly into Butembo?" she asked hopefully.

He looked uneasy. "No. Our route in will be complex. The munitions must come in through Kinshasa, the capital of the Congo. There's no way we could bring that stuff in through Rwanda."

"No one mentioned Rwanda. Why are you bringing it up now?" Sam asked.

"The team is going in through Kigali, the capital of Rwanda." Travis saw the color draining from Sam's face, and hurried to explain. "It's closer. Kigali is only a hundred sixty miles from Butembo. Kinshasa is almost a thousand miles to the southwest of Butembo. The entire trip from Kinshasa is over the Congo River basin. It's too dangerous."

"And you think Kigali is a nice place?" she asked him, memories of time spent there coming back to her.

"I've been to Kigali. It's a nightmare. But I'd rather take my chances with a day or two in the city than a four-hour plane flight over the Congolese rain forest."

Sam looked nervous. "Can we fly into Butembo from Kigali?" she asked. "I'm certain there's a small airport on the south side of the town."

"You might as well advertise in the local newspaper that

we're looking for something new. Flying into Kigali won't raise any eyebrows, but heading directly into Butembo would raise red flags. You'd have diggers and scavengers all over you within hours. When you land in Kigali, inform the customs officials you're looking for highland gorillas rather than diamonds. Mentioning diamonds can trigger people to do stupid things, like following you into the jungle and killing you when you find the vein. I may not have led a mining expedition before, but I know these people. I know how desperate they are." His tone was serious, his message very clear. Sometimes the truth only got you into trouble. "We'll travel in Land Rovers from Kigali to the Ruwenzori Mountains."

She turned to Kerrigan. "What's our budget? Cash in our jeans?"

"Two million, five hundred thousand, with a line of credit at the National Congolese Bank for another five hundred."

"Signing authority?"

"You and Travis McNeil, together or separately."

"Who will be meeting us in Kigali?" she asked.

"Our military contact in the Congo has arranged for an escort to get you safely out of Kigali. Four men, all highly trained and loyal to their commanding officer."

"And their commanding officer is?"

"Colonel Nathan Mugumba. He's reliable—we've had dealings with him before. He's well schooled, spent almost five years in the Boston area in an undergraduate program. He speaks and writes impeccable English, which makes communication a lot easier than dealing with the regional dialects. We'll leave Rwanda and enter the Congo at the Gisenyi-Goma border crossing. Mugumba himself will provide a small military escort from the border to Butembo."

Sam nodded. The plan was not appealing, but Kerrigan was obviously well organized. "Whom do we report back to?"

"You'll relay all information back to me, personally. This entire operation is very tight-lipped, and I'd like to keep it that way. You report only to me."

"What *is* your position with Gem-Star?" she asked, suddenly aware that she had no idea.

"President," he said.

"But not CEO?" she asked.

He stared at her, his eyes searching, but not finding what they were looking for. "No, Ms. Carlson, I'm not the chief executive officer of the company. That title is held by Davis Perth, grandson of the founder."

"Some people are just born into it, aren't they?"

Patrick Kerrigan rose from his chair, this time extending his hand to her. "I'll make sure you have your spectrometer, Ms. Carlson, in addition to any other equipment that would be considered standard. Take care; I'll be in touch later this week."

"Thanks. And please have your accounting department make the initial check out to Samantha, not Sam. The bank still thinks anything made out to Sam is for my father."

"As you wish."

Sam left the office and the building. She glanced about her as she walked, taking in the cityscape—the concrete jungle. It was widely known to be dangerous and difficult to live in New York. It was a cakewalk compared to what lay ahead—the real jungle. Butembo bordered the equatorial rain forest, and to the east it was solid jungle to the base of the Ruwenzori Mountains. On her previous visit she had hiked in a few miles, just to get the feel. It was eerie moving about the ancient forest, surrounded by multitudes of rare and exotic species. And dangerous. The smaller creatures had more enemies, and therefore better defense systems, often poison. The larger animals could simply eat you.

Her mind drifted back to Travis McNeil. He intrigued her. His demeanor was calculated and wary, but she suspected a very different man would emerge once they were on the go. He had never led a mining expedition before, so the chances were good that this was his first business arrangement with Patrick Kerrigan. She had a sixth sense that Travis didn't trust Kerrigan. She could understand why, because she didn't trust him either.

He troubled her, but she couldn't put her finger on why. He came across as a consummate businessman, professional and organized. The firm was successful, and he had achieved the leadership of the company without being born into it. Davis Perth, the CEO, *had* been born with a silver spoon, and that obviously riled Kerrigan. It didn't take a master's in psychology to pick up his body language when she had made the comment in his office. Kerrigan didn't like playing second fiddle. And he had proven his tenacity by bouncing back from a disastrous divorce and rebuilding his financial net worth to sixty million. Quite a feat.

But Patrick Kerrigan was the least of her worries right now. In the next few weeks her skills as a geologist would be tested under the most rigorous conditions. Her ability to survive the deceit of the diamond traders, the corruptness of the military, the constant threat of disease, and the perils of the jungle were foremost in her mind. She swallowed hard as full reality hit her.

She was going back to Africa.

THREE

Travis McNeil swung his 330xi into a parking stall at the end
of the strip mall and locked the car. The trip from Manhattan to Hoboken, via the Holland Tunnel, had been a nightmare. Some idiot had slid the front end of his Porsche under
a five-ton delivery truck and the tunnel traffic backed up,
causing him to be half an hour late for his meeting. Still, the
advantages of having this place in Hoboken, only two
blocks from the dock he used to load his gear onto ocean-
going ships, far outweighed the occasional problem crossing the Hudson.

A menswear store took the last two commercial spaces in
the complex, and he entered, nodding to the desk clerk. He
moved through the retail space into the storage area,
around a few racks of hanging suits, to a steel door in the
rear. The handle had a box attached with five buttons. He
punched in the code and the door opened, exposing stairs
leading to the basement. He took the stairs, ignoring the
heating and cooling systems to his right, and faced the wall
to the left. Just in front of him, a natural gas meter was anchored to the wall. He grasped the glass housing and

twisted. Ten feet to his left, a portion of the wall opened, revealing a hidden room. He replaced the housing to its original position, and entered.

The room was twenty by thirty feet, and well lit. Scores of boxes of differing sizes and shapes lined the walls. The markings indicated they were filled with men's shirts, socks, underwear, and belts. None of them were. Three men sat at a table in the midst of the boxes, and McNeil greeted them as he sat down.

"Alain, everything okay with our communications?" he asked the balding, late-thirties man who sat across from him.

Alain Porter, communications expert with Team Six for his entire eight-year tenure, nodded. He was not a large man, only five-nine in height, and barely more than one seventy pounds, and the best electronics expert the SEALs had ever produced. There wasn't a system he couldn't hack into, jam, or recalibrate. More than once, Porter's knowledge of electronics had saved their skins by reestablishing downed communications with their extraction team.

"All set." He smiled, his thin lips pulling back over teeth that were one size too large for his mouth. "The GPS system is packed, ready to go. I've tested it extensively—no glitches. Smiths Industries makes a NAVPAC unit that has integrated GPS and inertial systems. Once we're in the rain forest, we can pinpoint exactly where we are without a break in the canopy. We're relying strictly on satellite information, not topography."

"Samantha Carlson wants to send a chopper up to take video footage of the canopy. Can your gear receive the aerial footage it shoots?"

"Absolutely," Alain said. "The NAVPAC has a twelve gigabyte memory. Whoever's in the chopper can send them to us in a compressed pulse or real-time."

"Which is better?" Travis asked.

"Either way is fine," Alain responded. "The first few times the chopper goes out, it would be best to let it film the area, return to home base, compress the data, and send it out to us as a pulse. It's much quicker. But once your geologist thinks we're closing in on what she's looking for, it would be better to download the images as they're filmed. That way, she can direct the helicopter to do exactly what she wants."

Travis nodded that he understood. "Did you arrange for portable units?" he asked.

"I went with Panther 5/20W manpack, and 5W minis for person to person. Damn tough to sweep the frequencies and find us. Electronically, we'll be invisible once we're in the bush."

McNeil nodded and turned to the man immediately across the table from him, Troy Ramage, weapons expert. Ramage had spent only five years with the SEALs, but his knowledge of munitions and guns was legendary. He was on call twenty-four hours a day, for any member of the SEAL team to call and ask what equipment was best suited for a specific assignment. The best-trained, most active fighting force in the U.S. military called him for advice. It looked good on his resume when he retired.

"Troy?"

The arms man stood up and walked to the far wall. His six-foot-five-inch frame looked cramped in the windowless room. His hair was closely cropped, military style, and his face was rugged, with a strong jaw and piercing blue eyes. He opened a box and took out a gun.

"In addition to the Remingtons and the Daisy, I've added a few more toys." He held the gun out in front of him. "The Vektor MINI SS 5.56mm machine gun. Much lighter than its 7.62 big brother, and more accurate at close range. Excellent for jungle warfare." He replaced the machine gun and pulled a shorter, more compact weapon from an adjacent box. "Vektor CR21 Assault rifle. Also 5.56mm ammunition. The advantage for keeping to the same ammo is obvious. This little pup is totally nasty at almost any range. Largest caliber slug of any compact assault rifle on the market."

Ramage was enjoying himself. He slid the gun back into its case, and gingerly opened a wood crate tucked in the corner. He held up a device with a long tube, mounted on a tripod, and a small missile-shaped shell. "M8 81mm mortar, by Vektor, of course."

"Was Vektor having a clearance sale?" Alain asked, laughing.

"Hardly. I spent a shitload of money on these things." He grinned as he spoke. "You get what you pay for. This mortar is extremely light, the tube short for the accuracy you get, and the shells are all frags. For those special moments." He carefully replaced the mortar and its ammo, then continued.

"The Daisy 600 is a nice rifle, but I prefer this." He took a briefcase-shaped object from another box. He opened it and began taking parts out, snapping them together. The final result was a long, high-caliber rifle. "The Sako TRG 21/41 sniper," he informed them. "Accurate to within four inches over a half mile. Outstanding." He disassembled the rifle and replaced it, then sat down.

"Impressive, Troy. As usual," McNeil said. He turned to the final man present at the table: Dan Nelson, explosives guru with Team Six for seven years. "Dan, how did you spend your money?"

"Very carefully." Nelson smiled and stood up. Six feet tall, with a linebacker's build, Dan Nelson was a handsome African-American with the most astute mind the SEAL team had ever had on staff. He was notorious for acing the bomb-defusing drills, knocking so many seconds off the previous record that no one could ever hope to better it. It made him a legend in the tight-knit SEAL community, and pissed off a few of the brass when McNeil had talked him into leaving the SEALs and working in the private sector.

Nelson hoisted a wooden crate from the floor and placed it on the table. The top opened easily, and he retrieved a metal object from amidst the packing chips. "Fragmentation grenade, gentlemen. Manufactured by SM Swiss, this baby weighs one pound and has over two thousand fragments. Absolutely deadly inside a fifty-foot radius. Great for the jungle. The shrapnel cuts through the underbrush like it isn't even there. Just remember to duck."

He replaced the hand grenade and pulled out what appeared to be a large-caliber bullet. "Believe it or not, a 7.5mm anti-tank round." He had everyone's attention as he continued. "Up to two hundred and fifty yards, this thing will penetrate almost any armor, including tanks."

"Impressive," Travis said, "if we're up against tanks."

"You never know," his explosives expert shot back. He replaced the shell and pulled out a mortar. "SM 120mm Mortar Cargo Bomb. It's effective up to seven thousand yards, and delivers thirty-two anti-personnel grenades. Much better than the conventional HE Bombs."

"Now *that* we can use," Troy said approvingly.

"And a handful of explosives for our geologist," Dan said, closing up the boxes. "Surface charges, and some down-hole stuff as well. If she finds the vein, we can uncover it."

"Did you get the missiles?" Travis asked. "In case they have helicopters?"

"Certainly," Dan said, prying open the lid on the last case. Inside were three Saab-Bofors surface-to-air missiles. "Laser guided, based on the Linear Quadratic Method, with night devices. Range of just over four miles."

Travis rose and addressed the three ex-SEALs. "Well done, gentlemen. We've been in some pretty hairy places before, but from what I understand, we're heading for hell. I've been to Kigali, but never across the border into the Congo. Kerrigan has, and he says that the Congo is the vilest country on the planet. The government is totally corrupt, the military more dangerous than the criminals, and the climate makes a steam bath feel like a blast of arctic air. Just our kind of place."

The three commandos and McNeil took the next hour to load the van outside the men's store, then Troy Ramage followed Travis as he headed his BMW south on Washington Street. Acquiring the armaments had gone flawlessly so far, and that was worrying Travis. Past experience had taught him that Murphy's Law was bound to surface at some point when guns were involved. Porter had the necessary communications gear, Ramage had the guns, and Dan's cases were brimming with explosives. Each commodity had been carefully chosen for the job. Weight was the primary factor, with performance a close second. Nothing was left to chance.

Each piece of equipment was chosen for a specific task and environment. They would be in the jungle, so weapons with a short killing range were preferable. But he knew from other sorties in heavy underbrush that the occasion would arise when a target would be a good distance off. Thus the sniper rifle. And where military was involved, there would be helicopters. Trustworthy was the last word Travis would use to describe any central African military force, and he needed a weapon to bring down a hostile chopper. That was where the surface-to-air missiles came in.

The more he thought about it, the more he felt the missiles were crucial to the operation. If a heavily armed government gunship decided to take them out, there would be little they could do but hide and hope for the best. With surface-to-air missiles, the playing field changed dramatically. His group could take out an incoming helicopter before it came within range of its missiles or machine guns. He smiled. The man with the best toys usually wins.

A quick five-minute drive at exactly the speed limit took him deep into Hoboken—to the docks. Twelve blocks from the men's store Travis used to stash the mission's armaments was Dock 39. A rusted trawler, small by ocean-going standards, was lashed to the dock. Dusk was quickly enveloping the area, and shadowy figures moved about the deck, making final preparations for departure. The scene was almost surreal. He pulled the BMW up to the gangplank, the van with the weapons immediately behind him. Two men from the ship walked down the plank to meet them. Travis greeted the first man with an outstretched hand.

"Khanh Ng." Travis inclined his head slightly forward, a

sign of respect to the ship's captain. "Always a pleasure, my friend."

"Yes, Travis," the Vietnamese captain replied in perfect English. "A pleasure, and, as always, a bit risky." He smiled.

"No risks involved here. Simply a shipment of auto parts," he said, glancing at the stack of boxes in the back of the van.

The captain nodded. "From New York to Kinshasa." He studied the ship's manifest for a moment, "And we're to deliver these auto parts to a military colonel. Sounds perfectly legitimate to me."

"Agreed. However, just because you're such a respected and highly sought-after sea captain, I'd like to offer you a small incentive to ensure these parts make it to the colonel." McNeil slipped a briefcase from the backseat of the BMW and handed it to Ng. Inside was fifty thousand dollars more than they had originally negotiated for delivering the weapons. What the hell, he thought, it was Kerrigan's money. A bonus to the ship's crew certainly wouldn't hurt. The captain glanced inside the case and smiled, then snapped it shut. The excess money had not gone unnoticed.

"Your parts will arrive, my American friend." They shook hands as some of Khanh's deckhands loaded the missiles on the ship. Travis motioned to his men, and they left the dock. The ship would be on the open seas en route to the Congo within the hour.

FOUR

Nine days had passed since the second meeting with Kerrigan and McNeil, and Samantha Carlson was ready to go. Her bags sat in the foyer of her apartment, her fridge was empty, and the *New York Times* would not appear on her stoop until she returned. Her buzzer sounded, and she pushed the intercom button. It was Travis. She grabbed the two bags from the floor and walked into the hallway, taking one last look at her apartment. He was waiting in the lobby.

"You all ready, Doc?" he asked her.

"As ready as I'll ever be," she replied. "How about you?"

Travis just smiled and held open the cab door. When *wasn't* he ready? he thought to himself. He lived his life constantly on the edge. He had cheated death so many times that the thought of actually dying was becoming more and more foreign to him. Almost as if each escape made him stronger, more incapable of believing in his own vulnerability. He glanced over at Samantha as she leafed through the *Times*. She was engrossed in an article and didn't notice his prolonged look.

Travis watched the New York skyline as the cab wove

through the traffic en route to the airport. Samantha smelled nice, he thought. She looked nice, too. Faded jeans, tight white T-shirt, and sneakers. Sexy like an athlete. And smart. How many attractive, well-toned women held a doctorate in the sciences? Not many. He stole a glance at her as they traveled, wondering how she would fare once they were in the Congo. She'd been there before, so at least she knew what to expect. Much better than landing in a foreign cesspool with a totally dependent client. And he'd had a few of those.

Sam folded the newspaper and rubbed the back of her neck. She was quite aware of his presence beside her in the cab. And she felt safe with him nearby. She had little doubt that he was more than capable of protecting her under reasonable conditions. It was the unforeseen problems she worried about. No matter how good McNeil and his men were, there were only four of them. Against an entire tribe of hostiles, they stood no chance. And that possibility existed. She dropped the *Times* beside her on the seat as the cab pulled up to JFK.

Ramage, Porter and Nelson were waiting at the gate when they arrived. McNeil nodded as they boarded, but kept his distance from them in line and once on the plane. Four men and a woman were too conspicuous. They settled into their business-class seats, and he pulled out a book, Margaret Atwood's *The Blind Assassin*.

"Interesting reading," she remarked. "Especially for someone in your line of business."

"Do you read much Atwood?" he asked her, and she shook her head. "The main character is an eighty-two-year-old woman," he said, settling into reading. Samantha checked out the in-flight movie.

New York to London was one of her favorite flights. Leaving the historical vacuum of North America for Europe always thrilled her. And often, London was merely a stopover en route to more mystical destinations, as was the case this time. They had two hours at Heathrow between the New

York-to-London segment and the London-to-Cairo leg. From Cairo, they touched down in Khartoum, then flew directly into Kigali. All told, it would take twenty hours to reach the capital of Rwanda. She groaned as the first movie lit up the screen. She'd already seen it. As the credits floated across the screen, telling the viewer who was starring, the cameras focused on a young woman walking along a college pathway on a crisp autumn day. She was attractive, her step lively. Perhaps the image Samantha herself had projected so many years ago.

Was it that many years since college? She mentally ticked off the time that had passed since her undergraduate work in Boston. Fifteen years since she'd walked down a similar path as a freshman, eager to learn her father's trade. She faltered. Eager to learn or eager to please? Would she have picked geology as a career if her parents had had no influence? Was her entire life being spent just to impress her father? Christ, even after his death she sought his approval. She shook her head, admonishing herself for thinking so negatively of her innocence; youth was responsible. She vividly remembered her father's face, glowing with pride as he stood next to her at the enrollment desk. She checked off her courses, all predetermined the evening before, then glanced up at him. He grinned back at her, his eyes moist. She knew now that her enrollment into his discipline had somehow justified his existence. An existence that she had never questioned; it had always seemed right. *He* had always seemed right.

Her father had always been her hero. He was a blend of Indiana Jones and Mahatma Gandhi. Adventurous to a fault, but the most skillful negotiator she had ever witnessed. It was probably the latter trait that had kept him alive as long as he had been. And while he was alive, he had loved his daughter. Samuel Carlson had doted on her, showering the young girl with presents and the teenager with countless pieces of advice. He had counseled the young woman on relationships and helped her to understand men better than most women could ever hope to. But one common thread bound together everything he had ever given her—his time.

Time was the most valuable commodity every person on the planet possessed, her father had told her during one of their more esoteric discussions. Do not waste a moment. He lived his life not as a hypocrite, but true to his own words. He cherished his time, never allowing anyone to waste it. Yet as she looked back, she realized he had spent a hugely disproportionate amount of time with his daughter. Had he shaped her into the woman she was today? Yes. Were his efforts in vain? No. Had she become the woman he knew she could? Yes. She smiled and felt a warm tingle run down the length of her spine. She had done him well. She let her earphones slip down around her neck, and drifted off.

Twenty hours and thirty-two minutes later, Flight 3673 from Khartoum touched down on the steaming runway at Kigali Kanombe Airport. Sam grabbed her carry-on from the overhead bin and she and the team followed the line of people onto the runway. The heat hit her instantly, the humidity a few seconds later. She tugged at her shirt as it clung to her, then gave up. The moist equatorial air kept clothes feeling like they just came out of the washer. She walked across the asphalt into the terminal. The customs area consisted of a few worn desks manned by sleepy Rwandans. Sam retrieved her luggage from the baggage cart, and walked over to the nearest desk. The man's eyebrows rose slightly as he looked up at her.

"American?" he asked. She nodded. "Your passport, please," he said in stilted English. He took the document from Samantha and slowly flipped through the pages. He stopped numerous times to check out the stamps of the countries she had visited over the past few years. On more than one occasion he nodded and pursed his lips slightly. He finished perusing the passport and pointed at her luggage. "Open them, please."

Samantha unzipped both of her bags and folded back the top flaps. The security men hovering behind the customs official leaned forward as he began to poke through the first bag. He found nothing of interest and continued on to the second, smaller bag. He stopped when he came to her underwear. He lifted a pair of panties from the suitcase and held them up like a trophy.

"Cotton," she said to him. "They breathe."

He smiled at her and gave the ever-growing group of men behind him a stern glance. "What is your reason for visiting Rwanda, Miss Carlson?" He replaced her underwear.

"Gorilla research. In the Ruwenzori Mountains."

"The Ruwenzori Mountains are in the Democratic Republic of Congo," he said, "not Rwanda."

"I'm aware of that, sir," Sam responded quietly. "However, the less time I spend in the Congo, the better. I would much rather be in Rwanda than the Congo any day."

"Why is that, Miss Carlson?"

"The Congo has a corrupt government. When I pay the expected fees to enter the country, or to travel on a road, the money does not go to the correct people. The men in charge always get the money. I resent that."

"Yes," the customs official agreed. "That is very true."

"In Rwanda," she continued, "your government is freely elected, and your president is a good man. He encourages free enterprise, and is rebuilding your country's reputation and economy. And the entry tariffs are always fair."

"Yes. Agreed. Our rate of," he paused, watching for her reaction, "fifteen thousand francs is very reasonable."

Samantha did the math in her head. With one U.S. dollar equivalent to about three hundred eighty Rwandan francs, the man wanted slightly less than forty U.S. dollars for her to breeze through customs. She nodded slowly, and reached into her suitcase. She pulled a wad of francs she had bought in the U.S. from under her clothes, and tucked fifteen thousand into a half-full cigarette package. She held it out to him.

"American cigarettes," she said. "If you are allowed to accept them."

He opened the package and slipped a cigarette out, quickly closing the pack. "Thank you, Miss Carlson." He stamped a blank page in her passport. "Enjoy your stay in Rwanda."

The remainder of the team followed her lead, slipping the official the obligatory fifteen thousand francs as they passed through. Ramage was the last one to clear customs, and the official took his money, but did not stamp his passport.

"The contents of your suitcase bother me, Mr. Ramage," he said, fingering the stamp gingerly.

"What bothers you?" Ramage asked, irritated at the delay.

"I am a simple man. I own two white shirts. One I wear to work every day, and the other I wear to church on Sunday. I could not imagine owning more than two white shirts."

"So what's your point?" he asked.

"You have six white shirts in your suitcase, Mr. Ramage."

Troy shrugged. "So what?"

"Perhaps you are considering selling these shirts in Kigali. And selling merchandise without a license is illegal."

"What the—" Ramage began, but he was cut off in midsentence by Samantha Carlson.

Sam reached across the table and lifted four shirts out of the bag. She handed them to the customs agent. "Mr. Ramage brought the shirts to give as gifts," she said. "He told me while we were in the air that he hoped he would find someone in Rwanda that would appreciate them."

The official smiled again. "How thoughtful, Mr. Ramage. I'm sure I can find someone who can benefit from these shirts." He tucked them under his desk and stamped Troy's passport. They filed from the relative comfort of the inadequate air conditioning in the terminal out the front door and into the blazing African sun.

"What the fuck are you doing?" Troy turned to Sam.

"Keeping you out of a Rwandan jail," she replied tersely. "If you think any of *this* looks bad," she waved her arm at the squalid slums that bordered the airport, "you should see the inside of the prison. It makes this quite palatable."

"She's right, Troy," Travis said as he scanned the line of cars and taxis for their contact. "They don't need a reason to throw you in jail here. You do what's necessary to keep them happy." He cocked his head slightly to the right. "Those are probably our guys."

About a hundred feet from the doors, two Land Rovers were parked against the curb, their motors idling. One man leaned on the tailgate, and when Travis caught his eye, he nodded. The group turned and walked down the crowded sidewalk toward the waiting vehicles. As they approached, the man smiled and asked, "Travis McNeil?"

"That's me." He extended his hand and the man shook it. "And you are?"

"Philip Acundo," he said. "Personal aide to Colonel Mugumba. We are to accompany you to Goma."

McNeil ran his eyes over the man, evaluating what he saw. The man's skin was typical for the region, very black and stretched tautly over his facial bone structure. No wrinkles. His eyes were deep hazel, the whites in striking contrast to the darkness of his skin. His teeth were white, but in need of orthodontic work. Still, when he smiled, he looked pleasant enough. McNeil's eyes paused at the area near Acundo's armpit. A slight bulge. The man was armed.

Acundo motioned to the four-wheel-drive vehicles. "Please, let's get loaded up and drive into the city."

The group split into two, Travis and Samantha traveling in Acundo's vehicle, and the remaining three members of the team in the other truck. The four Congolese soldiers, all dressed in civvies, split into two per truck. The drive into the heart of Kigali was slow, but hardly boring.

The roads were partially paved, but long overdue for maintenance. Potholes peppered the road and jarred the riders whenever the driver hit one. Both sides of the road were lined with shanties, pieced together with discarded boards and covered with corrugated metal. Scores of natives, dressed mostly in motley clothes, watched suspiciously as the two-vehicle procession motored slowly into the city center. Remnants of the long-past Belgian influence still showed through in places. French signs were as prevalent as English, and the architecture reminiscent of a European culture was now replaced with African influence.

The foliage was thick and tropical. Umbrella and banana trees punctuated the white buildings, and low broad-leafed plants thrived everywhere. Hibiscus, lianas and ferns grew wild, wherever a patch of dirt allowed. Raw sewage, open to the tropical air, fed and watered the shrubbery. Samantha watched the passing spectacle with vivid recollection.

Four years had not changed Rwanda's only city. People still moved about the grimy streets and narrow alleys, eking out a subsistence on whatever they could lay their hands on. Many suffered from diseases unfamiliar to the western world. Signs of AIDS were everywhere—hollow cheeks, sunken eyes devoid of life, and people stricken with viral pneumonia. In such a temperate climate, good health should be easy. But it wasn't.

The United Nations deemed the AIDS epidemic to be out of control in numerous Central African countries, Rwanda and the Congo included. They adjusted the mortality rates accordingly, and the life expectancy had dropped in Rwanda to less than forty years. Contraceptives were almost unknown, birth control a bad joke, and abstinence totally unheard of. Sex was killing these people now, just as the horrific infighting in 1994 had decimated the Tutsi population. 1994.

A year that would live in infamy in Rwanda. Modern-day genocide while the civilized world watched. She had seen the aftermath much more clearly four years ago. The hatred still embodied in the Tutsi people as they strove to live alongside the Hutus, who had randomly killed over 800,000 of their brethren. And the fear in the Hutus. The massive refugee movement had been just returning from the Congo as she worked on her doctorate in geology. Two worlds so far apart, she thought. The other was her life in New York, with the penthouse and money in her bank accounts. Anything she wanted was available, providing she had the cash. But not here.

Central Africa could not provide for its people. And what it did provide often proved deadly. Floods in the rainy season washed away entire villages and poisoned the water supply with human feces. Drought in the dry season killed the cattle and starved the masses that lived hand to mouth. Malaria was rampant in the forested areas, and the temperatures on mountaintops were cold. Even snow was possible. She wondered how anyone could survive here.

They pulled up in front of the Meridien Kigali Hotel Umubano on the Boulevard de L'Uhunganda. The hotel was a testament to what the local business community could do if given a chance. It wasn't a new structure, but was well kept and nicely renovated. The facade was white stucco with adobe brick highlights. Generous arches welcomed the traveler into the foyer, where a fountain gurgled softly with crystal-clear water. McNeil headed straight for the concierge desk, and returned a minute later looking pleased.

"I need a few things, and our concierge tells me there will be no problem getting them. Remind me to tip him well when we leave."

Samantha followed him into the lobby and across the tile floor to the registration desk. The clerk was efficient by Rwandan standards, and they had their rooms in under a half hour. McNeil pointed at the restaurant as they made for the stairs.

"Lunch?" he asked, glancing at his watch. "It's almost two o'clock."

"Sounds great," Samantha responded. "Okay to eat here?"

"You're the one who's been to Kigali before. Didn't you stay here?"

"Briefly. Headed from the airport into the jungle. None of this five-star decadence for me."

He grinned as he pulled a chair back for her. The hotel was okay, but certainly not five-star. She sat and a moment later their waiter appeared. They ordered drinks and Samantha said, "I don't know much about you, except that you were born in San Antonio and spent time with the SEALs when you grew up; being macho and saving the world. Anything else you'd like to add?"

He grinned again. "If I leave it like that, I'll come off a lot better than if I start telling stories," he said. "I'm a bit of a klutz."

"Really," she said, interested. "How so?"

"Oh, like the time I fell out of an airplane."

"Fell or jumped?"

"Jumped. But my parachute screwed up. It folded in on itself at about a thousand feet, and I hit the ground like a lumpy meteorite."

"They usually burn up," she pointed out.

"That didn't happen, but I did break one hundred seventeen bones. And spent the next year in a hospital. I haven't jumped since."

"That's why you didn't want to fly into Butembo from Kinshasa. You're scared of flying."

"Flying doesn't bother me. It's what can happen if the plane stops flying when it's supposed to be flying. Parachuting from a crippled plane into the Congo rain forest is dangerous. In fact, it's probably one of the top ten extreme sports on the planet."

She looked thoughtful. "How about something a bit more personal about the kid from San Antonio—what your parents did, that kind of thing."

He fumbled in his breast pocket for his cigarettes. He tapped the bottom of the package and one popped up. He slid it out and placed it between his lips, then struck a match and puffed once. As he shook the match to extinguish it, he wondered what to tell her. The truth was abhorrent, out of the question.

When his mother had met his father, she held a respectable position as a social worker with the city of Houston. She dealt with the downtrodden, the dregs of the oil-rich city. Mary Lambert had a natural intuition that allowed her to separate the grifters from the needy, and she doled out social service justice with a fair hand. She made a difference in people's lives. Young mothers, their eyes hollow sockets, carried crack-addicted babies into her office every day. She touched the nerve that showed these seemingly hopeless cases there was a light in the darkness. Mary understood the process: clean them up, restore their self-worth and give them dignity in lieu of drugs and disease. She turned people away from life on the streets toward mainstream society by recognizing what natural assets they had, and encouraging them to enroll in courses that made them saleable. She found them employment and stayed in touch, letting her clients know she was there—that she cared. Some failed miserably, but many flourished. Mary Lambert was a jewel in the cracked and broken crown of thorns that was the Houston social service department. Until Joe McNeil walked into her office.

She had instantly recognized him for what he was—a con man looking for an easy ride. A guy who would rather spend an hour lying to Social Services and walking away with some food stamps than get out there and dig around for a real job. But for some reason, she couldn't say no to him. He was an attractive, mid-twenties man, two years her senior, with an easy one-sided smile. Joe had even white teeth and wavy blond hair that framed his boyish face. She was attracted to him even though she suspected he harbored a dark side. For the first time in her six-year tenure at social services, she cheated the system. Joe was the recipient of undeserved public money—money he spent on drugs and booze. Against every instinct, she began to sleep with him. When sober he was a great lover, often bringing her to climax. When he drank to excess, his performance shriveled. Mary began to drink to wipe out the desires that couldn't be satisfied by a drunken partner. More often than not, morning would find them passed out on the floor or the couch, the bed unused. And mornings were becoming difficult for Mary.

In fact, mornings were just the tip of the iceberg. Her entire life began to unravel as she plunged into the same abyss from which she spent her days trying to pull out other addicts. Her work suffered. Travis figured it was about the time he was conceived that she began to use crack cocaine. She started smoking one pipe in the morning to get her going. By the time Travis was born, she was a full-fledged crack addict, living the precarious edge between two worlds. When her baby was eighteen months old, the shadowy world of crack and alcohol finally won the battle. She was fired for embezzling funds and told to go quietly or criminal charges would be filed. She returned home to her alcoholic husband and told him she was unable to support him any longer. He beat her to within an inch of her life. From hospital records Travis dug up later in his life, he knew she had spent thirty-two days recovering from the beating. And it wasn't the last.

Young Travis had watched as Joe McNeil's true colors emerged. He regularly beat Mary, and by the time Travis had reached double digits, his father had turned pimp, selling Mary on the street for pitiful sums of money to buy his booze. They lived in squalor, Travis going to bed hungry so often it became the norm. He would lie awake listening to them fight, praying for a miracle. In a way, he got it. Seven days before his eleventh birthday, his parents began to fight over who should get the last hit off the crack pipe. His father repeatedly hit Mary in her face and stomach as the young boy screamed for him to stop. When he did, Mary was unconscious and bleeding profusely from a gash on her cheek. Travis's father lit the pipe and sucked in the mind-numbing smoke, then sat back contentedly to watch television. When his mother awoke, she staggered into the bathroom to clean up. From there she walked into the bedroom and returned with the family gun. Travis watched as his father rose from the couch and moved toward her, threatening to kill her if she didn't give him the gun. She pumped five bullets into his chest, three of them cutting through his heart. She turned the gun to her temple, said good-bye to her son, and pulled the trigger. The sixth and final bullet tore through her brain, spattering blood and gray matter across the room. He was an orphan.

An aunt in San Antonio, from his mother's side, offered to take the boy, and Social Services agreed. He packed up his meager possessions and moved from Houston to the much smaller center, and to a loving, caring family. What had happened in the past belonged in the past, Aunt Sarah had told him. He had the rest of his life ahead of him, and nothing could be done to right the wrongs he had been subjected to.

He had assimilated into the new environment well, achieving good grades and making whatever sports teams he tried out for. With the sports letters came the girls, attractive ones with developing bodies and lustful desires. He reciprocated, giving the young women what they wanted. He was the hottest commodity in school his senior year, and he took that with him into college. He made the football team as a wide receiver in his freshman year, racking up seventy-one catches for one thousand two hundred forty-three yards and sixteen touchdowns. The scouts were watching as the whiz kid suited up for his sophomore year. Third game into the season, his chances at the big leagues evaporated when an opponent forced his knee to flex in a manner no knee can withstand. The ligament damage was so great, the team doctors told the boy he'd be lucky to walk without a limp. A professional sports career was out of the question.

He finished his second year of college with a dismal two-point-six grade point average. He didn't bother registering for his third year, but enlisted in the Navy instead. His knee had healed, and they saw a healthy body and an alert mind. He was transferred to Little Creek, Virginia, almost immediately. Navy SEALs, Team Six. The rest was history. Except that he took the memories of a horrible youth with him everywhere he went. There was no escaping.

Travis McNeil took another drag on his cigarette and slowly blew the smoke into the humid air. "Not much to tell, really," he said. "Normal family, cute house with a white picket fence on a quiet street. Mom and Dad went off to work each day, provided for us. I made a few sports teams, but never got invited to any training camps. Started smoking early, drank underage, that kind of stuff. Pretty boring, actually."

Samantha nodded and opened a small pouch attached to her belt. She extracted a large pill and looked at it with great distaste. "Three weeks of these things has been hell," she said, swallowing the last of her malarial pills. "Have you ever had malaria?"

"Once. It's not pleasant. How about you?"

"Lucky so far," she answered.

Their drinks arrived and he crushed out his cigarette after ordering lunch. "I'll miss these when they're gone."

"American cigarettes?"

He nodded. "They've got those awful French cigarettes. Gitanes, I think they're called. Quite vile," he said, then turned as three men entered the restaurant. He motioned for his team to join them.

"Careful you don't get your shirt dirty, Troy," Travis goaded his arms expert as he sat down. "You've only got two left."

Troy just laughed and turned to Samantha. "Thanks," he said. "Extra shirts or prison. It's an easy choice."

Sam just smiled. Travis got down to business. "I was talking to Philip Acundo on the trip from the airport. He says the munitions arrived in Kinshasa two days ago. Colonel Mugumba took a personal interest in the shipment. He met with Ng at the docks and offloaded the cargo into a few Land Rovers. Acundo told me the equipment should be en route to Goma sometime tomorrow. If all goes well, we should be armed and dangerous in two days."

"Thank God." Alain Porter breathed a sigh of relief. "I feel naked. All four guys who picked us up at the airport this morning were packing."

Dan Nelson agreed. "We're sitting ducks. It would be nice to pick up a few handguns. Just in case."

"No. I'm sure Mugumba made it pretty clear to these four guys to get us out of Rwanda and into the Congo. If we don't arrive, they might as well not come back. If we get caught with weapons in Rwanda, they could shoot us on the spot. Zero tolerance toward foreigners."

"Nice fucking place," Ramage said.

"That's why you're getting the big bucks for this one, Troy. Let's just stay out of trouble until we get to the border and get our hands on our gear. Then we can kick some serious ass if we have to."

The other three men nodded. Samantha watched them as they interacted. A bunch of overgrown macho men, she thought. And then she reconsidered. What kept these men alive was their ability to kill the other guy before he got them. And without guns, Dan Nelson was right. They *were* sitting ducks. If anyone wanted this entourage to disappear, what better time than before they picked up their guns? She realized the gravity of the situation. And in that, she found a new respect for these men.

They were here to protect her, to ensure she found the elusive diamond formation in the Ruwenzori Mountains. They were ready to lay their lives on the line. That they were being paid for it suddenly became insignificant. These four men brought a commitment to their jobs that few others did. If they had a bad day at the office, they died. She glanced around the table as they continued talking about the upcoming mission. She liked what she saw. And for a fleeting moment, she felt safe.

Then the doubt returned. Could she find the formation? The longer it took her to locate the diamonds, the greater the chance they'd all be killed. Ultimately, the success of the mission rested on her shoulders—her ability as a geologist. She felt a slight curl at the edge of her lips as this thought hit her. Kerrigan was right about two things. She had a knack for staying alive, and she was one damn good geologist.

Things would be okay. Keep her alive long enough and she'd find the diamonds.

FIVE

Samantha was up before the sun. She wriggled out of her clothes and started the shower. A trickle of dusty water spilled from the showerhead into the claw-foot tub. She stepped in and shivered in the early morning heat. The water was freezing. She wondered how in such a sweltering climate, the water could be so cold. Other than the planned stop in Butembo, she knew this would be the last decent shower for some time, and she tried to enjoy it. It didn't work, but she emerged clean and refreshed after ten minutes. She dressed and took the stairs to the main floor.

The front-desk clerk was the only sign of human life. She said good morning and walked into the street. She glanced both ways, then turned right and began to jog. The cobblestone road was rough and slippery under her feet, and she relaxed a bit when she turned off the main road and the stones turned to dirt. She picked up her pace, pressing her cardiovascular system to work harder. She was breathing heavily as she turned right into a narrow street a few blocks from the hotel. This was the Rwanda she remembered.

Shanty housing lined both sides of the lane, many shacks

with broken windows, and few in good repair. Mottled doors infested with termites stood as testaments to the resident's position in Rwandan society. Most in this area were in poor condition, with peeling paint and rusted hardware. An occasional one boasted a new coat of paint, a sign that the owner was doing just fine. She continued along the road for half a mile, then cut left into a darkened alley. She slowed her progress as she approached the end of the street.

Twenty feet from the dead end was a door, similar to almost every other door she had run past in the last ten minutes. She stopped and knocked. Inside, there were scuffling noises as the residents roused themselves. A moment later, the door opened. A short man, just over five feet, with a pug nose and a puzzled expression, looked out. Suddenly he brightened.

"Doctor Sam," he said, grinning widely, his white teeth shining in the low light of dawn. "Doctor Sam, you've come back." He waved his arm for her to enter his house.

"Hello, Hal," she said, grasping the man's hand and holding it affectionately. "You look great." She glanced about the room, where five other people now stood looking at her. "Mauri." She dropped Hal's hand and gave his wife a hug. The woman smiled and nodded. English was not her native tongue, nor had she ever learned it.

"Doctor Sam, what brings you to Kigali?" Hal asked, motioning for her to sit at the lone piece of furniture in the tiny house. She sat at the table and watched as Mauri prepared the morning tea.

"I may need your services, Hal," she said. "You know the Virunga Mountains, near Gisenyi."

"I have led many expeditions into the wilds in search of the mountain gorillas. I know the area very well."

"I need you to know the Ruwenzori Mountains as well. Please tell me you've been there."

"I've been there, Doctor Sam, but not for a long time. The Democratic Republic of Congo does not appreciate Rwandans since our government sided with the rebel forces that are trying to overthrow the Congolese government. The border is shut down. We can't get across anymore."

"Leave that to me," she said. "The important thing is that you know the area around Butembo."

"Oh yes. That's where the upland gorillas live. I've been there many times. I know the area very well." He looked at her suspiciously. "You're not an anthropologist. You're a geologist. Why are you interested in gorillas?"

"I have no interest in the gorillas unless some government type asks. I'm looking for a rock formation."

Hal winked at her. "I understand."

"Then I'd like to hire you, Hal. I'll pay very well, but it will be dangerous. You may not make it back alive."

"Living in Rwanda is dangerous. Some people don't come home from a trip to the corner store. Perhaps, since it is so dangerous, we could arrange for payment in advance. For my widow."

Samantha laughed. The little man was exactly the same as she remembered from four years ago. She dug into her pockets and pulled out five hundred American dollars. She handed it to Hal. "Another one thousand if you make it back. Deal?"

"Deal, Doc," he said. This time his smile lit up the entire room. The sum represented almost four year's wages for an average Rwandan.

Sam spent the next half hour sipping tea with Hal, his wife, and their four children. After arranging for Hal to meet her at the hotel bar within the hour, she excused herself and headed back to the hotel. The sun was up and the streets had changed. Gone were the closed doors and empty laneways. Instead, windows and doors were open, and children hung from them, watching her as she moved through the teeming slums. Street vendors hawked their goods from small carts or off the dirt that served as the sidewalk. She attracted a great deal of attention as she walked, her white skin and blond hair visible from a distance. At times, conversations stopped as she passed, the natives intent on watching her as long as possible. None of it made her feel uncomfortable. Rather, it made her feel special.

And special is not something New Yorkers feel when they walk down a crowded street. But here in Africa, she was a square peg in a round hole. She was different. She was someone to be stared at in bewilderment. She was an outsider, someone who didn't live in the most populated country on the African continent. She was someone who had a life beyond the daily misery that defined Rwandan society. And for that reason alone, they stared at her with envy.

She arrived at the hotel just after eight and found the four ex-SEALs in the restaurant eating breakfast. She sat down and ordered, waiting until the waiter had left before explaining where she had been since before sunrise.

"I met Hal last time I was in Rwanda," she said. "He is absolutely trustworthy and will make an excellent guide. He knows the region we're headed for. He's spent a lot of time in the mountains on both sides of the border between the Congo and Rwanda. And he speaks the language."

"You're sure he's okay?" Travis asked. "There's no way he could be a plant?"

"Impossible!" she responded quickly. "He had no idea we were here, and I approached him, not the other way around. This one is not negotiable—we need this guy."

"Okay," the team leader said, "he's in. But he's on a short leash." She nodded. Travis finished his coffee and continued. "We have two Land Rovers from Kigali to the border. Once we arrive, Colonel Mugumba will have our supplies in two additional vehicles. We get to keep all four. We lose the support team we have now, but pick up a military escort from Goma to Butembo. After that, we're in the jungle, and on our own."

"My geological equipment is with your guns?" Sam asked.

"Supposed to be," he answered. "According to Kerrigan and Ng. They stowed everything you asked for on the boat the night before we arrived with the missiles."

"Missiles?" Samantha asked, intrigued.

He grinned sheepishly. "We probably won't need them. Overkill, you know. When will our guide arrive?"

"I told him within the hour, so he should be here soon. What time do you want to leave?"

"Soon." He brightened as the concierge entered the restaurant. The man carried a small box and looked quite pleased. He placed it on the table in front of Travis and waited as the team leader poked through the contents. A few moments later, Travis thanked the man and slipped him some cash. He held up a mason jar containing a clear liquid, a handful of flowers, and some thin rope.

"Everything you need to keep the creepy crawlers out of your sleeping bag. Diesel fuel," he said, holding up the mason jar. He slipped one of the flowers from the box. "Pyrethrum. Mixed with diesel, this stuff is totally repugnant to any jungle creature."

"What's the rope for?" Alain asked.

"We're going to be on army cots," Travis said. "We'll have mosquito netting over the cots and draped on the ground surrounding the bed. The problem is, snakes and other poisonous things can get in under the netting, unless you stop them. We soak the rope in the diesel and Pyrethrum mixture and then lay the rope around the edge of the netting on the ground. Presto. Nothing poisonous in your bed."

"Fucking brilliant," Dan said.

Philip Acundo entered the restaurant, followed by the three Congolese soldiers assigned to protect Sam's group. He approached the table, smiling broadly.

"Good morning, my American friends. It is a perfect day for traveling. Not too hot, not too cold."

Troy Ramage glanced at the thermometer on the restaurant wall. It was shielded from the morning sun, and it already read ninety-two degrees. "Holy shit," he muttered. "What do they consider hot around here?"

Sam checked her watch as the men threw their overnight bags into the Land Rovers. It was over an hour since she'd left Hal's house. She walked to the corner and peered down the street. She spotted her friend a block away and motioned for him to hurry. He broke into a swift jog and reached the corner a few moments later. They walked to the vehicles and she introduced him to the team. With his easygoing nature, the guys all seemed to accept him. Samantha felt grateful for that.

"Hal isn't exactly an African name," McNeil remarked to the man as they cruised through Kigali. "How did you end up with it?"

"My mother only saw one movie in her life. She wanted me to be smart, so she named me after a computer in the movie."

"*2001: A Space Odyssey*?" he asked, and the short man nodded. "Interesting way to get a name."

"Hal's an interesting guy," Samantha said. "Once you get to know him." She turned away and glanced out the window at the slums that passed for housing. She knew Hal, and she knew exactly how interesting the little man was. Hal survived in a world that killed most. On the surface he was your typical Rwandan, concerned with everyday survival. But under the facade was another man, one Sam would never have known if not for a small indiscretion on Hal's part years ago.

Hal helped people. In a country where greed and corruption controlled almost one hundred percent of the money, he stood tall in the shadows. For years, he had pried money and goods from carefully cultivated sources and redirected it to the people of Kigali who truly needed it, which was just about everybody. No one knew who the clandestine benefactor was and he kept it that way, fearing for his life and the safety of his family. Displays of wealth in Kigali rarely brought anything but heartache and suffering. When destitute people saw something of value, they took it, and often the one driving the car or wearing the jewelry ended up in a pool of blood. Hal was street-smart and kept his identity from those who received the benefits. He could not, however, keep it from the government officials and corrupt businessmen he blackmailed. And that haunted him.

Hal never condoned the use of blackmail as a means to an end, but it was his only avenue. He had worked for the government in a sensitive department for a few years and had seen the incredible corruption that made the rich richer and the poor poorer. And he had documented it. Pages and pages of information that could destroy reputations and land high-level officials in jail. When he left his post within the government, he used that information to skim some of the dirty money off the top. He picked the vilest of the bunch and demanded they funnel some of the wealth back his way, or else. To a man they capitulated, giving him a source of income that he redistributed as he saw fit. Samantha knew he liked to think of himself as an African Robin Hood. Just shorter, and without the bow and arrow. But it was dangerous and he had many enemies in high places. It was only through sheer coincidence that Sam had stumbled onto an exchange one night four years ago, and Hal had come clean with his agenda. She understood what a good man he was, but it remained their secret.

They were on the edge of Kigali, and, to a person, they were disgusted. The northeast portion of the city was a squatter's settlement. The shacks were barely standing, raw sewage was everywhere, and small children picked through heaps of garbage that lay strewn about. The stench was overpowering. They rolled up the windows, but nothing could stop the smell from entering the trucks. Babies suckled dry breasts, and the eyes that stared back at them were tired and haunted. Samantha turned away. This was the side of Africa that sickened her—the starving children, lacking even the simplest of life's necessities. They crested the last of Kigali's four hills, and swung onto the country road heading northwest.

What had been poor road conditions in Kigali became horrendous. It was mid-May, and the February-to-April rainy season had just ended. The road was unpaved and deeply rutted. In places water still pooled, and the drivers took care to skirt these puddles, not knowing how deep they might be. The going was slow, and Samantha calculated they would reach Gisenyi, on the Rwandan side of the border, just before dusk. An entire day to travel sixty miles.

Ahead of them to the north loomed the Virunga Mountains. Drenched in foliage like an undulating green veil, they both welcomed and threatened visitors. From a distance, the rifts and valleys looked peaceful and serene, but when the group began the uphill climb into the hills, the road became a treacherous series of switchbacks. No guardrails protected the Land Rovers from the sheer drops that punctuated the drive, and the muddy road was slick from the recent rains. Numerous times, the four-wheel-drive vehicles came perilously close to sliding off the road and down the steep hills bordering the canyons.

They crested the southern range at Ruhengeri and began the equally tricky drive down the other side of the pass. This time, the trucks had gravity pulling them toward the edges as they inched forward, and Sam simply closed her eyes a few times, willing the truck to stay on the road. It was more than two hours and a few miles from Gisenyi before they reached level ground. They made good time once on flatter terrain, and pulled into the border town of Gisenyi at four o'clock.

Samantha was taken aback by the condition of the town. Once a destination spot for wealthy European tourists, Gisenyi was now a shell of its former self. The beaches bordering Lake Kivu were still rimmed with glistening white sand, but the backbone of the town was broken. The formerly impeccable stucco hotels that lined the main drag were covered with English, French, and Kinyarwanda graffiti. From what she could read, the messages were hateful and reflected the violence that had previously shrouded the country. Garbage littered the paved streets, and poverty, not affluence, now gripped the village.

Their drivers motored through the town center to the border crossing, stopping or slowing on occasion to allow a wayward potbelly pig to cross the road. Samantha dug around in her pack looking for her passport as they pulled up to the shack that housed the border guards. A young soldier, his military shirt unbuttoned to his navel, moved slowly from the shade toward the Land Rovers. A rifle was slung over his shoulder. Two more border guards exited from the shack, both with their rifles horizontal.

"Can I see your papers?" the guard asked. He spoke French.

"Of course," Travis answered back in the same language, one of three other tongues he'd learned while with the SEALs. He gathered passports from Samantha and Hal and handed them over. Acundo and his partner also gave the man their DROC passports. The young guard looked flippantly through the DROC papers and handed them back. He studied the American papers closely, then motioned for the driver to turn the truck off. He moved to the second truck and repeated the procedure. As he took the five American passports into the guard shack, he said something to the other two soldiers, and they moved closer to the trucks, the safeties off their weapons.

Ten minutes passed, then fifteen. Travis grew restless with the wait, and when the elapsed time hit twenty minutes, he opened the door and started for the guard booth. Surprisingly, neither of the guards stopped him. He entered the booth, and a minute later emerged with the passports. He spoke to the guards in French, and they lowered their rifles and lifted the wooden arm that crossed the road, allowing the trucks to proceed.

"What happened?" Sam asked as they moved through a hundred-yard stretch of no-man's land toward the Congo.

"I don't believe these guys. I go into the booth, and the guard's asleep. The passports were just sitting beside him, so I took them. Christ, it's amazing anything gets done in these countries."

"What did you say to the other guys when you came out? I couldn't hear you."

"I just told them that the other guy said it was fine for us to go ahead." He shook his head in amazement.

The border patrol at the Democratic Republic of Congo was not as tired. There were seven of them, their uniforms pressed, and their AK-47s well oiled. The differences did not go unnoticed by Travis or Samantha. Philip Acundo looked relaxed as he steered the Land Rover up to the nearest officer. He produced his papers, and spoke in what Samantha thought to be Kikongo, one of the four official indigenous languages. She recognized an occasional snippet, but couldn't make out the overall gist of the conversation. Everything seemed all right, until the guard looked at Hal's Rwandan passport.

"The border is restricted to Rwandans right now," he said, handing the papers back.

"He is part of our expedition," Acundo answered half-heartedly.

"This man is not entering our country," the guard said forcefully, and began to walk away. Sam started to speak but Travis held his hand up, then pointed to a line of military vehicles parked a hundred yards distant. All six vehicles were manned by members of the DROC military. As they watched, a man exited the armed personnel carrier and strode across the clear-cut area to the crossing hut. He spoke with the official who had refused Hal entry, then the two men turned and walked toward the Land Rovers.

Samantha watched the newcomer as he approached. He was of average height and build, his skin very black, and he sported a small mustache and goatee. A service pistol was strapped to his left side. As he closed the distance, she studied his eyes. She didn't like what she saw. They were emotionless, almost cruel, and she wondered what horrors this man had seen, or perpetrated, for that matter. He scared her.

"I am Colonel Mugumba," the man said as he reached the lead Land Rover. The crest on his shoulder sported a small circle with three underlying symbols that mirrored the shape of a detective's badge—the insignia of an army colonel. "Who is in charge here?"

McNeil extended his hand. "I am. Travis McNeil. Pleased to meet you, Colonel."

The officer shook hands. "Why is there a Rwandan citizen with your team? I was not informed of this."

"He is essential to our success, Colonel. He knows the area well, and will be our guide."

"We have many local tribesmen who can guide your expedition, Mr. McNeil. And I have already assembled a team of twelve porters and guides. You do not need this man."

"*I* need him," Samantha said. She shuddered as Mugumba's gaze fell on her. "I asked him to join us."

"You must be Samantha Carlson," he said, letting his eyes run up and down the length of her body. "Surely you realize we cannot allow Rwandan riffraff into our country. We did so back in 1994, and the result was quite disastrous."

"You're talking about a massive humanitarian issue, Colonel," Sam countered. "Hundreds of thousands of displaced peoples. We're dealing with one man here—one who's essential to our expedition."

Mugumba studied her again, his eyes burning into her. No one spoke for a minute, as the leader of the Congolese military convey weighed the options. Patrick Kerrigan had made it clear to Mugumba that Samantha Carlson was to be treated with kid gloves. Her requests were to be met without resistance. And Kerrigan paid well to have his demands met. Escorting this expedition alone would pay for his retirement. Mugumba shrugged and smiled, pointing at the Rwandan.

"If Ms. Carlson feels this man is that important, then so be it. Issue him an entry visa, good for sixty days," he said to the border guards. Then he turned to Sam. "Sixty days will be sufficient, I trust."

"Yes, thank you, Colonel," she replied. "More than sufficient."

Mugumba turned to Travis. "Mr. McNeil. I have sixteen

crates that recently arrived in Kinshasa loaded on my trucks. The crates have CARLSON GORILLA EXPEDITION stenciled on them."

"Excellent," McNeil said. "The crates are still on the trucks?"

Mugumba nodded, and motioned for Travis to join him. Together they walked over to the transports, Mugumba speaking to the soldiers in a local dialect as they approached. Troops garbed in the dark green uniforms of the Congolese army leapt from the trucks and opened the tailgates, revealing the crates recently arrived from New York City. As Travis carefully scanned the boxes, his facial features took on a deeply concerned look. At length, he turned to Mugumba.

"Every box has been opened, Colonel," he said quietly. There was an underlying harsh tone to his voice.

"Of course, Mr. McNeil," the colonel replied without missing a beat. "Our customs officials check incoming freight for contraband. As do yours."

Travis checked the contents of the final truck the troops had opened for inspection. One more vehicle stood off a few yards, the tailgate and tarpaulin still covering the rear cargo area. He motioned to the truck. "I'm missing three boxes, Colonel. All three are the same—about six feet long by a foot high and a foot wide. I assume they're in the truck?"

"Yes," Mugumba answered. "But those boxes will not be accompanying you into the jungle. We saw no reason that an expedition searching for upland gorillas would require surface-to-air missiles."

Travis was ready to go for the man's throat, but Samantha intervened. "Colonel Mugumba," she said softly. "Let's not play games with each other." The man stared back at her but didn't respond. "We're not here to find gorillas and you know it. We're here to make everyone some money, including you. If the rock formations we're looking for are denser than the surrounding rock, then part of what we're looking for will be visible due to erosion. But our target will be covered by an outcrop of extremely dense rock. These missiles will be used to strip away the face of the outcrop and get to the vein. And they'll do it quickly. Each explosion will blast off about twenty feet of rock. Three shots at it will take us to the sixty-foot depth where the previous expedition hit pay dirt. One hour if we have the missiles," she pointed to the truck, "or three weeks without them. Your choice."

Mugumba said nothing. He stroked his chin thoughtfully for a minute, then called one of his soldiers over. This time he spoke in English. "Unload the missiles and give them to Ms. Carlson. But remove the targeting computers first." He turned back to Samantha. "For such a purpose, you will not be needing the guidance systems."

"I suppose not," she said, meeting his gaze. There they remained for a few moments. Untrusting and wary of each other, their eyes silently relaying messages of the suspicions they harbored. She interpreted his to mean, *You're in my country now, blond white bitch, and I'll do as I wish with you.* Her look was simple: *Don't underestimate me.* She broke the eye contact and said, "I wish to meet my guides and porters, Colonel. Could you please introduce me?"

He nodded and motioned for her to follow him. Close to the line of military vehicles was a group of twelve men lounging on the thin strip of short grass that separated the road from the jungle. As they approached, the men stood. Mugumba spoke to them in a dialect Samantha had heard, but could not place. She picked up an occasional word, but for the most part was in the dark as to what the colonel was saying. One of the twelve appeared to be the leader, and it was this man Mugumba introduced to Samantha.

"This is Faustin Amba. He organized the group you see here." Mugumba waved his hand in the general direction of the other eleven. "They came down from Butembo this morning to meet you at the border. If they are not acceptable, we will find other porters. The choice is yours, Ms. Carlson."

"Hello, Faustin," Sam said, extending her hand. The man reluctantly took it—his grip anemic, almost nonexistent. It belied his physical stature: broad shoulders with powerful forearms. His curly hair was closely cropped along his gently sloping forehead. His eyes were widely spaced, their whites tinged with yellow. His nose was smooth, not pug, and his lips full. His jawline was round and firm, his chin prominent. He wore a sweat-stained, long-sleeved white shirt and faded Levi jeans. She looked directly into his eyes, putting his height at almost six feet. "Do you speak English?" she asked.

"Yes, ma'am."

"The language you and the colonel were just speaking, what is it?"

"Adamawa-Eastern, ma'am," the man replied shyly.

"You are Bantu, with Sudanic heritage?"

He nodded and she continued, this time in French. *"Il faut savoir comment se debrouiller?"*

Faustin looked shocked for a moment, then smiled. "No, ma'am, I don't need to steal. If I guide you into the Ruwenzori, I earn my money honestly. *Servir, oui, se servir, non.*"

She turned to a slightly puzzled Mugumba. "These porters will do, Colonel. Thank you for organizing them."

Mugumba addressed the porters in the Adamawa-Eastern dialect and they picked up their meager personal belongings and shuffled toward the line of military trucks a few yards away. They split up and sat with the troops already occupying the transport carriers. McNeil and Sam returned to their Land Rover and he took the driver's seat. Their escort from Kigali to the border had disappeared, his job done. Ramage took the wheel of the second Land Rover. They fell into a gap between the third and fourth truck as the convoy pulled out and headed north.

The road was in poor condition, rutted badly from the torrential rains that had fallen inside the last month. Once they cleared the treeless section near Goma, a result of the Rwandan refugees stripping the countryside bare for firewood, the jungle closed in on them and depleted the already waning sunlight. McNeil flipped on the headlights but they mostly illuminated the dust churned up from the preceding vehicle. He swore under his breath and eased off the gas, expanding the space between the trucks. He turned to Samantha.

"What do you think of Mugumba?"

"Don't trust him in the least. How about you?"

"The same. And the son of a bitch knows exactly what armaments we brought with us. I don't like it when people I don't trust know too much."

"Will the missiles still be usable without the guidance systems?" she asked, grasping the upper hand grip as the Land Rover hit a deep rut. Even holding on, she still smacked the side of her head on the window. She winced in pain.

"It's going to cut down the useful range by quite a bit, but we can probably still use them," he answered, trying to keep the truck on the smoothest part of the road. "If we miss what we're aiming at, we're screwed. The missile is totally blind. It won't look for a heat source or a denser mass than the surrounding air. It'll just keep going. It comes down to how accurate the shooter is."

"How accurate *are* you?" she asked.

He grinned. "I suck. Troy's the guy you want working the missiles. He's done it before, in Lebanon."

"Did he hit what he was aiming at?"

"No, but he came real close." Travis glanced at her, amused by the concerned look on her face. "Relax; we still made it out."

Samantha kept her grip on the truck to keep from being banged about as she looked out the side window. Dense jungle flashed by in the early evening light, broken by an occasional grouping of wattle-and-daub huts. Smoke curled into the night sky from small cooking fires that dotted the pockets of the most basic civilization on earth. Bantu natives huddled about the flames watched the procession of trucks with trepidation and fear. Samantha knew the local tribes had no use for the military, that they had suffered horrible injustices from the very men who were supposed to protect them. Rapes and beatings often accompanied a visit from the soldiers. Sometimes the machetes came out and then villagers died. No one wanted the trucks to stop at their village.

She lived in a world where the good guys were the cops, and they protected honest citizens from the element of society that would break the laws justly imposed by a functional judicial system. The lines that delineated good from bad were clear, easy to discern. But in the Congo, there were no such lines; nothing was black and white. Everything functioned in a zone of shimmering gray, convoluted by corruption at every level. The viewer was never allowed a clear picture. Just as the African sky was constantly mutated with heat waves rising from the scorched savannahs or the steaming jungles, so was the world between normalcy and horrendous atrocities ever blurred. One moment dinner stewed above the evening fire, the next a group of soldiers or rebels stopped at the small grouping of wattle-and-daub huts. The result was inevitably the same. Young women were raped, sometimes taken. Men who objected were hacked to death with rusting machetes. People died, people mourned, life went on. And there was no justice. There were no courts to punish the guilty, no jails to hold the perpetrators of atrocities so horrific they would sicken even the hardest European or American. It was the way things were. It was life as normal in the Democratic Republic of Congo. It was unbelievable.

So the villagers watched in fear as the trucks motored past, hoping that death passed them by today. And for a moment, as part of the convoy, Sam felt the loathing aimed at her. She dropped her head to her chest and felt the tears start. Tears of sadness that the world could be such a brutal and uncaring place. As she sat in the Land Rover, a world away from the peasants who crouched at their nearby fires, she vowed to try to make a difference. Somehow. She had been brought back to Africa, and she began to wonder why. Was she here for more than locating a trove of diamonds? It *had* to be more. For her sanity.

SIX

The rising sun attacked the crisp morning air with an unrelenting vengeance, heating it wave by wave as its rays advanced over the rain-forest canopy. The equatorial heat pounded the gentle predawn breeze into submission and replaced it with stagnant humidity as the moisture was sucked from the exposed soil into the still air. A family of aardvarks retreated from open ground and found refuge under the prop roots of a nearby umbrella tree. A speckled tinkerbird hovered overhead for a few moments, then nestled into the relative safety of a prosperous breadfruit. Only an occasional duiker braved the intense heat to graze on some fresh shoots. It was still early, but nature's furnace was already on full blast.

Samantha glanced about the small clearing where her military escort had camped for the night. Descending darkness had stopped the convoy from advancing any farther than the southern edge of Rutshunt, a crossroads village thirty-four miles north of Goma. A few tents were pitched, but most of the soldiers slept in their vehicles. The only activity that Sam could see so far was a group of four men hunched over a small fire at the far side of the clearing. Her men. Travis McNeil smiled as she approached.

"You're up early," he said cheerfully. "Sleep well?"

"As well as can be expected, given the amenities," she replied, looking around.

"We're just going over a few things," Travis said. "I want this chance to talk before Mugumba's men are awake. Sit down and listen in." She nodded and joined them. Alain had boiled some water and he offered her coffee. She accepted and sat back, content to let her team do the talking.

"Including Mugumba, they number twenty-three. Each soldier is armed with an older style M-16, probably thanks to the military aid the U.S. government provided to Zaire prior to cutting off Mobutu's aid in November of 1990. And they've got plenty of extra ammunition. One of the trucks has eleven crates of bullets tucked under the seats. If it comes down to a firefight, don't expect these guys to be running out of ammo."

"It's what we can't see that bothers me," Alain Porter added. "The second truck from the rear is tarped over. They could have some pretty nasty stuff in there."

Dan Nelson nodded his head. "Alain's right. Everything else is out in the open, except what's in the back of that truck. It worries me."

"All right, let's see if we can get a quick look at what's inside. Keep on your toes, and if you see an opportunity, go for it. What really bothers me, though, is that these guys have had access to our supplies for the past couple of days. When we unload in Butembo, I want every piece of equipment checked and double-checked for any signs of tampering. Firing pins, mortar fuses, gun barrels, everything. Run diagnostics on the NAVPAC and the portable Panther units. I don't want any problems with our communications. If they've sabotaged any of our gear I want to know now, not later." McNeil quit talking as a member of Mugumba's platoon walked across the clearing toward them. The soldier stopped a few feet short of the group and pointed back to the trucks.

"We go now," he said, then turned and left.

"Quite the conversationalist," Troy noted, rising to his feet and stretching. He watched as the tents collapsed and Mugumba's men prepared to depart, then pointed out to the others that the level of efficiency in dismantling the camp was far greater than normal. "These are crack troops. I've been on enough African missions to know an elite platoon when I see one."

"Mugumba probably hand-picked them," McNeil agreed. "Let's just hope they get us to Butembo and piss off. I think I'd feel a lot safer without them around."

They pulled their Land Rovers in behind the lead vehicles as they left the clearing. A few turns later, they rolled into the center of Rutshunt, a village of two or three thousand that bordered a small tributary flowing south from Lac Rutanzige. The creek water was clear, unsullied by lowland silt or refuse from upstream encampments. They were now skirting the southern edge of the Virunga Mountains. Through breaks in the dense foliage that hemmed in the narrow dirt road, they caught occasional glimpses of the highlands. The tree line extended well past the mountain's highest elevations, and the upper reaches were still cloaked in seemingly impenetrable rain forest.

They continued north, hugging the western flank of a rift valley that sliced through the upper plateau bordering the mountain range. Sixty miles out of Rutshunt they motored through the tiny village of Lubero. After the town the road went from bad to worse, tapering from a questionable two-lane dirt track to a winding goat path, barely passable by the four-wheel-drive vehicles. The army trucks had a wider wheelbase than the Land Rovers, and were struggling with some of the tighter bends. Within a hundred feet of a sign announcing they were sitting directly on top of the equator, a stream had washed out part of the road. Mugumba stepped from his truck to survey the situation, and McNeil joined him. The heavy rains had taken their toll as they coursed down the thirty-foot cliff on the uphill side of the road. The water had gushed over the edge and landed directly on the road, eroding it and cutting a six-foot incise across its breadth. To the left was a sheer drop of three hundred feet to the valley floor.

"The trucks won't make it across that," Mugumba said, eyeing the gash that lacerated the hard-packed dirt.

"Do your trucks have metal ramps for loading items with wheels? Sometimes they slide in under the cargo area."

Mugumba turned to one of his men and spoke in a Bantu dialect. The man nodded, then walked back to the trucks and began sliding the metal ramps out from the hidden compartments. He yelled orders to a group of soldiers, and they hustled over to the trucks parked farther back and pulled those ramps out. A few minutes later, a pile of twelve lengths of high-tensile steel lay on the ground next to the washout. McNeil had one of Mugumba's men retrieve a chain saw from a truck, and he busied himself cutting and stripping four trees to about ten inches in diameter. A roll of three-millimeter wire was brought up, and McNeil and Ramage set the ramps two deep and in groups of threes on top of the poles. They lashed the long steel pieces to the poles, spacing them to the approximate width of the army trucks' wheels. Inside a half hour, the temporary bridgework was finished. They slid it into place over the gap in the road.

"The Land Rovers are the lightest," McNeil said to Mugumba. "Let's get them across first in case the heavier trucks are too much for the bridge." Mugumba nodded, and Alain and Dan slipped the two four-wheel-drive vehicles past the lead military trucks and stopped at the bridge. "Empty the vehicles," Travis said to Alain, the lead driver. "If the truck goes over, I don't want to lose the equipment."

"You're worried about the equipment? What about me?" Alain protested.

"Leave the door open. And if the truck starts to tip, jump. It's not rocket science."

"Easy for you to say," Alain shot back, gingerly edging the truck onto the steel ramps. Troy guided him from the forward side of the bridge, keeping the tires centered. The ramps, lashed two deep, were strong enough to handle the vehicle, and it took only a few seconds for Alain to maneuver across. Dan followed with no problems. They reloaded their gear as the larger and heavier army trucks lined up to cross. The increased weight was going to make it considerably more difficult, and McNeil insisted that Mugumba's men unload the gear they had shipped from New York and carry it across manually. Box after box of munitions, arms and communications equipment came off the trucks and went across on the soldier's backs. To a man, they looked pissed off.

The army vehicles began to ferry across, with one of Mugumba's men directing them as Troy had done for the Land Rovers. The temporary bridge groaned under the weight, but held firm. Four of the trucks were across and being reloaded when the second-to-last vehicle pulled up, still covered with a tarpaulin—and still fully loaded. Everyone stopped and watched as the truck began the crossing. The cab was fine, slightly heavier but still well within the limits of the bridge. The rear axle was another story. As the tandem rear end moved onto the ramps, they began to bend. Slowly the rear of the truck slid toward the edge as the added weight overloaded the span. The driver felt the motion and gunned the truck engine, sending power to the rear wheels. The tires caught and jerked the truck forward quickly enough to hit the dirt on the far side before the ramps folded. Once across, the driver slammed on the brakes and jumped from the cab, swearing loudly in an obscure dialect.

Mugumba briefly inspected the bridge. The ramps were bent, but the structure was still intact. He motioned for the final truck to come across. The front wheels were not a problem, dropping slightly with the curve the previous truck had forced into the steel. The rear of the truck was not so simple. The tandem axle split the weight better than a single, but there was too much stress on the already weakened timbers that shored up the bridge. The first log shuddered for a moment, then snapped. The cracking sound was followed almost instantly by three more as the remaining logs split apart. The backbone of the bridge was compromised, and the metal ramps bent to the breaking point and then collapsed. The rear bumper smashed down onto the dirt, and for a moment the truck seemed stable, hung up on the dirt next to the washout. Then the edge caved in. The rear of the truck slid into the enlarged gap, and then pulled the cab with it as it careened over the cliff. The driver opened the door, but couldn't jump quickly enough. His screams echoed up the canyon as the truck crashed down the incline, rolling end over end until it hit the bottom with a sickening thud. No one spoke for a few moments.

"Finish loading the trucks." Mugumba finally broke the silence. "I want to make Butembo by nightfall." He made no reference to the dead man, nor did any of his platoon. The reloading was accomplished and the convoy moving within a half hour. The road remained treacherous but passable. An hour before sundown they pulled into the bustling city of Butembo.

Samantha jumped from the Land Rover the moment McNeil pulled in front of the Queen Anne, Butembo's premier hotel. She stretched her legs, gathered her hair off her shoulders and headed into the hotel. Reminiscent of the early Belgian influence on the country, the lobby was very European. High ceilings, ornate chandeliers and candelabra, overstuffed easy chairs with dark colonial woodwork, and smooth marble floors greeted her. She padded across the foyer to the reception desk and checked in. Her room was on the third floor and she spent no time getting stripped down and into the shower. Similar to Kigali, the water was ice-cold. By the time she finished washing the day's dirt off her skin, she was shivering. She shut the water off and towel dried. She glanced out the window as she dressed for dinner, scanning the rooftops, then raising her gaze and letting it rest on the distant mountains.

She had a limited knowledge of this remote city. It was

nestled between two national parks and stood as the last civilization for travelers venturing in any direction. To the southwest was the vast, mostly uncharted Congo River basin. Satellite imagery was responsible for humans' understanding of this geography, not hands-on exploration. The major routes through the interior of the country were well known, but the river basin held more virgin land untouched by anyone but an occasional headhunter than the entire Amazon Basin in Brazil. On past expeditions she had marveled at the scope of the river system, the largest in Africa and second only to the Amazon in water flow. And flow it did, refusing to dry up in even the driest season, as it was fed from both sides of the equator.

Northwest Congo was mostly savannah with an occasional woodland thrown in. Easier to navigate, but hotter than Hades. Below Butembo to the south was the route they had come in on, rugged and unforgiving plateaus and rift valleys. But nothing could compare to the volcanic Virunga and Ruwenzori Mountains that sliced down the eastern border of the Congo like a jagged scar on a plush green field. Pic Marguerite, the highest peak in the Ruwenzori, topped out at almost sixteen thousand feet. Their target area was somewhere in the seventy square miles that lay to the south of this monster.

Samantha turned from the window, left the room and joined her crew in the restaurant. They ordered chicken, but from its texture they were pretty sure it was not chicken that arrived at their table. They appreciated that the meat was edible and cooked, and between the five of them cleaned the platter. The sun had slipped beneath the western savannah by the time they finished the last few drops of rye whisky Alain had brought to the restaurant. The trek had taken its toll, and they drifted off to their rooms shortly after to get a decent sleep. Dawn came early in the tropics.

Travis and Troy were engaged in a heated argument when Samantha arrived at the restaurant the next morning. They stopped as she arrived and it took fifteen minutes for her to find out what they had been discussing. Strippers. McNeil held the view that when the woman left a piece of clothing on, it added to the performance. Ramage disagreed. Everything off was better. Samantha just shook her head—she was surrounded by a bunch of schoolboys. Eventually, the conversation touched on securing a helicopter.

"There's a guy in town who rents his machine out by the hour," Dan Nelson informed them. "But the fellow I was talking with told me the pilot will give customers a good break on weekly rates. He's an excellent pilot from what I hear—Billy Hackett. He's on the east side of town, maybe ten minutes in the Rover."

"Okay, after we finish eating, Alain and I will check it out. Dan, I want you and Troy to open our gear and give it the once-over. Strip the weapons down and rebuild them. Run diagnostics on all the communications gear, especially the GPS systems. Sam, you should break open the crates and check your geological apparatus. Make sure everything's operational."

Travis took care of the breakfast tab, then headed out with Alain in search of Billy Hackett and his helicopter. Sam joined Troy and Dan in a compound adjacent to the hotel, where the expedition gear had been offloaded from the military trucks. Five uniformed soldiers stood watch over the crates. The remainder of the military force was nowhere to be seen. Samantha watched the ex-SEALs as they methodically disassembled each weapon, made notes on a pad of paper and then returned each piece of equipment to a workable state. There were no wasted movements, no hesitation as to which piece fit where. She knew from watching them that these men were the consummate professionals—at killing people. Despite the numbing heat, it made her shiver.

Sam cracked open her crates and began to poke through the geological gear Gem-Star had provided her. For the most part, it was her first look at the equipment. She was impressed with what she saw. Gem-Star had spared no expense.

Aside from the usual binocular microscope, hand lens, geological pick and sample bags, was a mobile spectrometer.

The hotel manager, smiling eagerly, approached her as she repositioned her gear. The arrival of the team was a boon to his monthly take, and he wanted to personally meet the attractive woman who headed the team. He held out his hand.

"I am Martine Abouda," he said pleasantly, enjoying the feel of her skin against his. "I am the manager of the hotel. If there is anything you need . . ."

"Sam Carlson," she responded, "and I think we're okay. Your staff has done a wonderful job of making us feel welcome."

"Sam Carlson." He laughed. "You don't look at all like Sam Carlson."

She chuckled. "It's short for Samantha. And thanks for stopping by." She returned to checking her gear, and the man left.

A few minutes later Samantha snapped the final case shut and stood up. She swayed slightly as her equilibrium threatened to leave her, but caught hold of a nearby palm plant. The heat was outrageous and her temples throbbed as she fought to regain her balance. Don't stand up so quick, she reminded herself as everything came back to normal and she let go her grip on the palm. She walked back into the hotel, wondering how Travis and Alain were progressing with the helicopter.

Billy Hackett was laid out on a hammock when Travis walked around the side of the thatched hut that served as Hackett's house and his business address. A half-consumed sun-baked beer rested on his chest and an open package of cigarettes lay on the ground. Numerous butts and burned matches peppered the immediate area. Travis stood over the man for a moment, his shadow covering the pilot's face. He knew exactly what he was looking at.

Billy Hackett was ex-Nam—Travis had seen hundreds of

these guys. Americans who had seen the dark side of humanity and lived to remember it. The war had been a travesty for all the troops, but the chopper pilots had been subjected to every conceivable act of violence on and above the battlefield. Bringing in the wounded, limbs torn from torsos, napalming suspected Cong infestations, knowing full well that innocent people lay below the propellant that scorched human skin and sucked the oxygen from the air. The machine guns that poked out the side of the Hueys rained death on anyone inside the target areas. From a hundred feet up, it took too much time to decipher between a child and a man with a gun. Every pilot had seen atrocities and had perpetrated them. They lived with the memories, none of them pleasant. They did what was necessary to survive—physically and emotionally. And that's what made them the best damn pilots on earth.

McNeil cleared his throat and watched the man's eyes slowly open. He shifted slightly and his shadow moved off Hackett's face. Hackett shut his eyes against the harsh glare of the sun and groaned. He sat up and rubbed his free hand across his face. He still clutched his beer with the other hand. He squinted at McNeil for a minute, then set the beer on the dusty ground and stood up.

"Your wife sent me around. Told me you'd be back here," Travis said.

"Yeah, she does that kind of thing," Hackett said. "What do you want?"

"I need to hire a helicopter and a pilot for some recon work. You available?"

"When do you need me?"

"I've got some specialized gear that needs to be loaded in the machine. Spherical imaging stuff of some sort. I'd like to get that done today and have you running a grid by tomorrow."

Hackett nodded again. "I charge eight hundred American dollars a day. Fifty percent payable in advance. How many days do you need me?"

"I'm more interested in your weekly rate," McNeil replied. "You'll be covering an increasingly small area as we zero in on what we're looking for. The more precise your search becomes, the more time you'll be spending on the ground. But I still want you working exclusively for us. You have to be ready to fly when we need you. What's the weekly rate for that?"

Hackett rubbed his chin and pursed his lips. A minute later he responded, "Four thousand a week. You pay me in advance for the week, a week at a time. If you find what you're looking for halfway through a week, I still keep the money." He paused for a minute. "What *are* you looking for?"

"Differences in vegetation coloring for mining purposes," McNeil said, studying the man. "Do you mind if I ask you a question?" Hackett shook his head. "What's a white guy doing here in the middle of Africa?"

Billy Hackett laughed, and Travis couldn't help smiling with him. It was almost contagious. The pilot was McNeil's height, but quite slender. He was pushing fifty-five and still sported a full head of blond bushy hair. He was unshaven, and gray hairs interspersed the thick five o'clock shadow that covered his prominent jaw line. His teeth were white, but crooked in a few spots—something that might have been easily fixed with rudimentary orthodontics. His eyes were deep brown and devoid of the haunted look so many ex-military pilots wore. They sparkled with a life of their own, telling the observer that a fertile mind existed beyond them. McNeil found himself instantly liking the man.

"What's a white guy doing in the middle of Africa?" Hackett repeated. "I married that wonderful woman who sent you back here to find me. I met her in Kinshasa ten years ago and we were married two weeks later. We went back to the States, but she hated the weather. Montana is just too fucking cold when you're used to this." He waved his arms about as he spoke. "We tried California, but she couldn't stand the pace. So here we are, living happily in the Congo."

"Third-world living," Travis said. "Is your chopper in decent condition?"

Hackett looked insulted. "Most certainly. You want to have a look?" McNeil nodded and Hackett motioned for the ex-SEAL to follow him. A narrow path led into the jungle immediately behind the house, blocking out the sun and cooling the surrounding air. It felt good. Forty yards into the rain forest, they suddenly broke out into a round clearing. Travis stared, his mouth open. A fully functional helipad, paved and night-lit, sat directly ahead. On the circular patch of asphalt sat a spotless Bell 427, the sleekest baby in Bell's fleet. The sun reflected off the highly polished maroon finish covering the twin turbine engines, and all four rotors were buffed and properly tied down.

"Holy shit," he muttered under his breath. "Now that's a helicopter." He turned to Billy Hackett. "How the hell can you afford this thing?"

"It's not that hard," the pilot replied. "I'm the only rotary wing air service for a few hundred miles. I get all the medivac work from the government, tourist flights in and around the Ruwenzori, government VIPs, and lots of commercial work for mining companies out of Rwanda and the Congo. This place is a gold mine." He motioned toward a small Quonset tucked back into the tangle of ferns and vines that bordered the well-kept landing area. McNeil followed Hackett to the shed and waited as he entered a code into the electronic lock. The door opened and he walked behind Hackett into the darkened room. A motion-sensor light activated a ceiling-mounted bulb and the structure was suddenly illuminated.

McNeil stared around him. The building was a fully stocked repair shop, complete with additional rotors, a spare turbine, and all the necessary tools to maintain the million-dollar machine. He whistled softly at the sight.

"Okay," he said, turning to Hackett. "You're hired. I'll bring over the gear we need affixed to your machine later today. It shouldn't be too hard to install; I think it's manufactured for exactly this kind of thing."

"I'm sure we can make it work," Hackett said, accepting

Travis's outstretched hand. They walked back to the front of the house, where Alain was sitting in the Land Rover, watching for activity. "See you later, then," the pilot said as McNeil jumped into the vehicle and Porter pulled away.

"Did we get a chopper?" Alain asked.

"Yeah, Alain, we got one," McNeil said, smiling.

Samantha finished overhauling her gear and wiped the back of her hand across her brow. It left a dirty smudge on her tanned skin. She sat down heavily on a low stone wall, her breathing shallow. Unpacking the exploration gear and checking it was an onerous task, one made even more rigorous by the heat and humidity. She looked up as Travis and Alain pulled the Land Rover into the hotel compound. Travis smiled at her as he got out of the vehicle.

"Finished, Doc?" he asked.

She nodded. "How did it go? You know, getting the helicopter?"

"Perfectly. If there's one part of this mission that's totally acceptable, it's Billy Hackett and his machine."

"Mission?" Samantha repeated. "You make it sound like a military exercise. We're just here to find some diamonds, not to get in a fight."

He slipped a cigarette from his pocket and crushed the empty package in his left hand. He lit the smoke and took a long, deep drag. "Whether you want to admit it or not, Samantha," he said, "this *is* a mission. We're surrounded by hostile jungle and escorted by twenty-some soldiers about whom I have grave concerns. Dan got a quick look inside that truck they keep tarped over. It's loaded with Bofors Carl-Gustaf CGA5 assault rifles."

"So?"

"The M-16s the guys are carrying around with them are just for show. The real firepower is in the back of that truck. If and when they come gunning for us, they'll have the CGA5s loaded and the safeties off. And trust me, Sam— they're coming. Dan and Troy finished checking the gear and gave me their findings just before I stopped in to see you. The sights on our guns had all been tampered with. Nominal changes, but adjustments that would make hitting a target at any distance over thirty feet very difficult. And they both think that the inside of some gun barrels have been scored. It's tough to tell, but if they have been, it'll throw off the trajectory of a bullet enough to miss the target. These guys sabotaged our gear, Sam. Only people who think they may end up facing off against us would do that. It's not a very comforting thought, but it certainly makes me think that this is beginning to resemble a military mission more than a mining one."

"Jesus, Travis, this is getting scary."

"Scary is *not* seeing the signs—not knowing your equipment was sabotaged until it's too late. That's scary."

Samantha stared straight into his eyes as he spoke. She saw an iron resolve behind the blue facade. She saw a man who had been in this situation before and who had survived. She saw a man she trusted. And she liked what she saw.

SEVEN

The Land Rovers led the way as the team departed Butembo and headed into the jungle. Behind them trailed the twelve porters, each leading a loaded pack animal. The animals were split evenly between horses and donkeys, each heavily laden with supplies and armaments. Travis, with Samantha and Hal in the lead Rover, kept the pace slow. This was more for their own benefit than that of the porters, as the road they were traveling was a series of tangled roots and exposed rocks that threw the occupants of the trucks about. They headed almost due east, cutting across a couple of ridges before joining up with a slightly better road leading south. They made better time for about two miles before Troy waved for Travis to stop and pointed at a tiny, almost impassable road leading back into the jungle.

"That's the quickest way," he said as they scanned the topographical map together. "If we stay on this road we'll make better time, but we'll end up too far south. We'll lose time backtracking."

"Okay," Travis said reluctantly. "We're not going to have the vehicles for much longer by the looks of this. This upcoming low-lying area looks like it could be swamp."

Troy Ramage agreed and took the lead as they left the road for the narrow jungle path. Umbrella trees and mangos dominated the upper foliage, while thorny lianas interspersed with broadleaf ferns provided the ground cover. An occasional almond or breadfruit tree, laden with produce, punctuated the forest. Trailing vines hung from the taller oil-palm trees that stretched high above the shorter trees and formed the canopy. Epiphytic orchids colored the underside of the palms. The humidity covered the lush greenery with a fine mist, giving the forest an ethereal quality. Samantha stared out the window into the ancient world as they slowly moved through the rain forest.

"You know," McNeil said as he drove, "I hardly know anything about you. Just what Kerrigan told me, which wasn't much. Feel like talking?"

She glanced over at him. "Sure," she said. "Why not?" She unscrewed the cap on her bottled water and took a long draw, then wiped her lips on her sleeve and replaced the cap. "I'm originally from Boston, born and raised. Dad was very successful as a field geologist, which meant two things: He was never home; and we had tons of money. I never wanted for anything when I was growing up. Maybe that's why I'm so spoiled."

"Haven't seen that side of you yet," he said.

"You may. After high school I went straight into geology in Boston. It seems I had a natural ability in the field. Maybe a learned thing from my father, maybe it was just what I was meant to do—who knows? After I finished my undergraduate degree, we moved to New York."

"So you could continue your education?"

"No, not at all. My mom was a literary agent and she outgrew Boston. If you want to excel in the industry, you have to be based in New York. Dad didn't care where we lived because he was hardly ever home anyway. So when they moved I went with them. I was twenty-two and probably could have gotten my own place if I'd wanted, but I liked living at home. They bought a huge flat on the Upper West Side, so I could be close to Columbia. Mom opened an office down on Third Avenue, just a few blocks from Union Square. She was really successful, almost cornered the thriller market for new talent. The editors at the publishing houses were calling her to find out what new writers she had in the wings. Usually it's the other way around."

"It's a tough business from what I'm told," he said. He lit a cigarette and threw the match out the window. "Why did you choose central Africa for your master's and your doctorate? Surely there were more hospitable places."

"Africa has always intrigued me," she answered slowly. "And I'm not sure I've got a much better reason than that. I'd studied so much soft rock geology in my undergrad years that I wanted to work with hard rock stuff, which means mining of some sort. What better than diamonds? And Africa produces a lot of the world's diamonds. But it was more than that. At least I think it was." She sat quietly for a minute and he remained silent, letting her collect her thoughts. "Something about Africa excited and repulsed me at the same time. It represented the epitome of both good and bad. The people I met had next to nothing, yet they offered me whatever they had. They wanted nothing but to be treated well and a chance at something better for their lives. Or their children's lives. And that's the scary thing. I know their lives won't change and that their children will be sentenced to the same subsistence living that every previous generation has endured. I looked into their eyes and saw desperation and despair behind the vacant stares. And I wanted to make a difference. But I couldn't."

"So you came back—perhaps to finish what you wanted to do?"

"Perhaps," she said. "But now that I'm here, I see the same wall I ran into last time. Too many people in dire need and no way to help. I've got about four million dollars in mutual funds, real estate and other investments, but throwing money at the problem isn't the answer. And four million wouldn't even begin to make a difference. These people need proper housing with clean water and education for their sons and daughters. They need medical facilities and trained doctors and nurses to staff them. They need the basics, and they don't have them. I feel so . . ."

"Helpless?" he offered as she let the sentence trail off. She nodded, and he watched a tear slowly roll down her cheek. She didn't try to wipe it away, just let it trickle down until it reached her jaw and spilled onto her shirt. He reached over and lightly grasped her hand. "If there's another reason for you being here, you'll find it." He saw the corner of her mouth curl up almost imperceptibly before he turned his attention back to driving.

A few moments later he changed the subject. "I've got Billy Hackett watching Mugumba and his men. Promised him an extra ten-thousand-dollar bonus for him to arrange a team of locals to keep an eye on what they're up to—especially if they leave the city and follow us into the jungle. We also secured the BritPix to Hackett's helicopter this morning and gave him the first two grids we want him to fly. He's got a radio tuned to our frequency and will call in once he's covered the area. He can download the video images to your computer this evening when we stop moving. Kerrigan seemed pleased with our progress when I spoke to him."

Samantha glanced over at him, her eyes dry. "You checked in with Kerrigan today?" He nodded. "What else did he have to say?"

"Not much, just wondered how things were going. When we expected to start looking for the formation."

"What did you tell him?"

"That we were leaving Butembo and heading into the jungle. That's all I know, so that's all I told him."

Samantha decided to go out on a limb. "I don't trust him. I didn't like the man when I met him, and the more I dealt with him the less I wanted to."

Travis kept his eyes on the trail, threading the Land Rover through the overgrown trail. A minute passed before he slowed almost to a stop and turned to her. "I don't trust him either, Sam. This is the first time I've worked for the guy. I was referred to him by a mutual colleague who gave me a glowing review, and Kerrigan offered me a deal I just couldn't turn down. And the bonus if we make it back is enough to retire on. But I've really got some concerns about the way things are going."

"What do you mean?"

"Kerrigan arranged for Mugumba to meet and escort us to Butembo. Mugumba has a truck full of very expensive, and very deadly, guns. And he sabotaged some of our gear. Keep in mind that this is the guy Kerrigan hired. What does that tell you?"

Samantha was silent. He was right. If Kerrigan had hired Mugumba, which he had, then the man most likely knew exactly what his Congolese colonel was up to. The hidden guns, the sabotaged gear and the creepy feeling the diminutive man had given her all added up to bad news. Yet the soldiers had not accompanied them any farther than Butembo. They were alone in the jungle, just the five of them and Hal, and the twelve porters. If Mugumba wanted to keep them close at hand, why wasn't he with them?

"At least the soldiers aren't with us," he said, reading her mind. "I suppose that's good and bad."

"I can see how that's a good thing, but bad?"

"Mugumba is going to stay in touch with what we're doing. If he's not physically with us, then he has some other way of tracking our progress. My first guess is the porters. At least one of them is a plant." He paused for a minute, a troubled look on his face. "But there may be another way." Another pause, then, "Shit."

"What's wrong?"

"Something I just thought of. The GPS systems. I'll put money on it that he's tampered with them. We'll get Alain to run a full series of diagnostics on the instruments when we camp tonight. Let's just hope we can find whatever he did to them."

The Rover hit a particularly large root and the front end dipped violently, smashing the grill into the ground and throwing him and Sam into the windshield. Hal flew over the front seat and hit the dash before sliding onto the floor, unconscious. Travis rubbed his chest for a moment, sore from hitting the steering wheel, and then checked his head. His hand came away with a tinge of blood on it, cut from hitting the edge of the windshield. He grasped Samantha by the arm, and slid her back into the seat. She was only partially conscious, and shaking her head to clear the cobwebs. She nodded that she was okay, and they both grabbed Hal and lifted him off the floor and onto the seat. A four-inch gash across his forehead poured blood onto his face. He groaned as he began to regain consciousness. Sam spilled some of her bottled water onto a cloth and dabbed the wound.

"Sorry," he said. "I have no idea what we hit. Are you okay?"

Samantha nodded. "Hal's pretty shaken up, though. Let's get some antiseptic on this." She rummaged through the medical kit, then unrolled her window as Alain Porter appeared. "We're okay. Hal's got a cut, but that's about it."

"Jesus, you should have seen you guys. The truck just nose-dived into that rut and stopped dead. You're lucky you didn't go through the windshield."

"No shit," McNeil said sarcastically. He got out of the truck and surveyed the damage as Samantha attended to Hal. He walked ahead with Alain and Troy about a hundred yards and they quickly made a decision. "Unload the Rovers; we're on foot from here. It's too swampy in the low-lying areas, and we'd never make it up the other side of this cliff anyway." He pointed to the wall of jungle that confronted them, a few hundred feet on the other side of the swamp.

"I'll get something rigged up to probe the water and see

how deep it is," Ramage said. "The bottom is probably mud, and we don't need to lose any animals."

"Watch out for water moccasins," Travis warned him. "They're fast and they're deadly."

"I think I know enough to get out if I see a snake," Troy shot back, then grinned. "Hey, wasn't it you who got bit in Angola?"

"Piss off, Troy." Travis grinned as he spoke. "Just find a way across the swamp." He left them at the water's edge and returned to the Land Rovers. Samantha was halfway through stitching the gash on Hal's forehead, and he watched her as she finished the final two stitches. She clipped the suture and returned the instruments to the kit.

"How's that feel?" she asked Hal.

"It hurts, Doc, but I'll be okay. It's my fault; I should have been holding on."

Travis shook his head and lightly grasped Hal by the shoulders. "No, my friend. It's my fault; I should watch where I'm driving. You okay to walk from here?"

Hal indicated he was fine and McNeil turned his attention to the porters as they unloaded the trucks. They already had the gear lashed onto the pack animals, the loads evenly distributed. He motioned for Faustin Amba, the lead porter, to join him away from the rest. They walked a hundred feet down the path before he spoke.

"Faustin, how did Colonel Mugumba hire you?"

"By reputation, Mr. McNeil," he answered. "Mugumba asked the village elder for the most experienced guide who also spoke English, and that was me. When I talked with the colonel, he agreed to hire me and asked me to prepare a team of porters for an expedition into the Ruwenzori. I had ten days to prepare. Mugumba paid me half the money up front, and the other half is due when we return."

"You hired the entire team?"

"Except for three, yes. Mugumba had some top Ruwenzori guides come in from another village."

Travis turned his head sharply. "Three of the men on your team are unknown to you?" Faustin nodded. "Which ones are they?"

"Manou, Koko and Beya. Manou wears the red shirt with the white sleeves. Koko has the Miami Dolphins T-shirt, and Beya has a black shirt with light-colored trousers. They have no change of clothes, Mr. McNeil, so you can always recognize them by this."

Travis studied the man for a moment, then continued walking. Faustin kept pace. "Do me a favor. Keep a close eye on the three men who are not from your village. I suspect at least one of them is feeding information back to Mugumba. And I don't exactly trust our military escort."

"Yes, sir. I will have all my men watch them closely."

"And Faustin," Travis added, "stop calling me Mr. This and Mr. That. Call me Travis."

Faustin grinned and headed back to the trucks. Travis walked ahead a few hundred feet and met up with Troy and Alain. They had marked a passage through the swamp with broken branches stuck into the muddy bottom, which now protruded above the slime covering the stagnant water. They were just burning off the leeches when he arrived.

"Everything okay?"

"Yeah, it's passable. Deepest part is about six feet and the bottom isn't too soft. The horses should make it all right. Full of fucking leeches, though."

He watched as Alain seared the last one from Troy's back. They were a nuisance more than anything else. Painful if they got a good grip, and very painful if one didn't wear underwear. Burning a leech off one's groin area was not a lot of fun. He turned and motioned to the approaching line of porters to keep coming. Samantha walked a few feet ahead of the lead horse and she arrived first.

"Can we make it across?"

"Easy. It's going to get a lot tougher than this," Travis said. They both looked ahead to the obstacle. The bottom of the ravine was approximately two hundred feet across and was mostly stagnant water. An occasional mangrove poked above the water line, and lilies and floating grasses covered much of the surface. To the left was a bend in the valley, obscuring the source of the water. To the right, the direction the water slowly drained, was a long area of open water truncated by a pile of uprooted trees some hundred yards downstream. He pointed to the lead porter to continue once he hit the water's edge, and the man led his horse into the slough, following the branches Troy and Alain had used to mark the safest route. One after another the team forded the swamp. McNeil and Samantha crossed with the seventh man, about halfway through the caravan. They waited on the far side. Trouble hit when the final porter was only thirty feet from safety.

A ripple creased the still water moments before the man screamed and disappeared beneath the surface. A stream of bubbles marked the direction the man was moving underwater. It led downstream toward the logjam. His horse bolted and surged ahead to the shore, knocking down two men in its panic. Numerous shouts and panicked screams rose from the porters grouped along the shore. Samantha turned to Travis, who was ripping off his shirt.

"What's happening?" she screamed above the din.

"Crocodile," he yelled back, slipping a hunting knife with a ten-inch blade from its sheath and breaking into a run through the loose undergrowth near the water's edge. He was almost at the far end of the slough when he veered sharply right and dove into the water. A few ripples extended from where he entered, then the water went calm again. There was no indication of two men and a crocodile somewhere under the surface.

"What the hell is going on?" Samantha screamed in disbelief.

Troy grabbed her arm. "With a croc, you've only got one chance, Sam," he said. "Get in quick and kill it while it's busy with its catch. Crocs are predictable. It's going to try to stuff its dinner under a log somewhere down at that end of the swamp. Travis knows what he's doing."

"You've got to be kidding! Two guys and a crocodile underwater and I'm supposed to be calm. To hell with that." She pulled away from Troy's grip and grabbed his gun from its holster. She snapped off the safety as she ran toward the far end of the water. She stumbled as she ran, almost falling, but managing to remain on her feet. As she got closer she could see the water was stained red. She reached the area where Travis had gone into the water just as a figure burst from beneath the surface. She stopped and leveled the revolver. Then lowered the gun. Travis, holding the porter across his shoulder, stared back at her.

"Unless there's another croc in here, I don't think you need the gun," he said. "That one's dead. Here, give me a hand." He shrugged hard and the man fell forward. Sam had only a second to react, but dropped the gun and caught the unconscious figure before he hit the ground. She immediately checked to see if he was breathing. He wasn't. She tilted his head back and began applying CPR. Travis worked the man's chest, pushing gently. A few breaths into the prone figure and he gagged, spitting out a mouthful of water. She tipped him sideways and patted him on the back. He started breathing normally. Travis was already stripping away the man's pants and checking the bite wounds.

"How is he?" Samantha asked.

"Not bad. The croc never let go of its initial grasp. There are only a handful of puncture wounds and no tears. He's going to be okay, won't even lose his leg."

"Quick thinking," she said. "I'm impressed." They both stood as the group of porters and McNeil's team arrived. They stared at each other. Samantha let her eyes drop from McNeil's face to his broad shoulders, then down his v-shaped torso. His chest was well-defined and his stomach rippled. His musculature was pumped and his biceps swollen from the physical exertion. Not the body of an average thirty-something male. She looked back into his eyes. "Travis McNeil, croc killer," she said. The sexuality in her tone surprised even her.

He just smiled and dried off with a ragged towel one of the porters offered. Alain and Dan sterilized and bandaged the stricken man's leg, and other than the bite wounds, his condition had stabilized. Travis waved to Faustin and the lead porter came over.

"He has to be taken back to Butembo," he said. "Get one of the three men that Mugumba assigned to your team to take him in the Land Rover. The vehicle is useless to us anyway. And that takes one of Mugumba's men out of the equation."

"Consider it done," Faustin said. He spoke to the group of porters surrounding the wounded man, and they split up, some of them fashioning a stretcher by thatching palm fronds and attaching them to lengths of wood they found nearby. Some of the others moved back to the crossing area and settled the animals. Three men waded into the water and pulled the now-visible croc carcass onto land. They set about skinning it.

One hour later the injured man was loaded into the rear of the Land Rover and the chosen porter backed the four-wheel-drive up the jungle path and out of sight. Everyone met on the far side of the swamp, and they resumed their trek into the foothills of the Ruwenzori. Travis showed Faustin where he wished to go, then let Faustin pick the guides to lead the group into the jungle. The going was slow. There was no path, and the lead men hacked at the ferns and thorny lianas that covered the dank dirt of the forest floor. The lead porter changed every half hour to avoid overexertion and McNeil kept close track of his compass as they progressed. At six o'clock he called Faustin over and told him to find a suitable spot to camp for the night. Twenty minutes later they were setting up their tents.

Travis was kneeling with Alain when Samantha showed up at his tent. The GPS system was sitting on the ground in front of them, and the unit for receiving data from the helicopter was only a few feet away, attached to a quietly purring generator. Travis waved her over. Alain was pointing to something in the guts of the GPS unit and explaining what he had found.

"They tampered with the GPS." Porter filled her in quickly as she settled in beside them. "See this board tucked in under the main memory cache?" She nodded and he continued, "It's a second transmitter, set to a different frequency. It's feeding someone, we can't be sure whom, our exact position."

"Oh, I think we have a pretty good idea," Samantha said. "What can we do about it?"

"Well, we can make a small adjustment to it when the time is right." Samantha looked puzzled and he explained. "Once you think we're close to the vein, we'll switch the polarity on their transmitter. That way, when we move the last mile or so, their positioning will show us moving one hundred eighty degrees from the direction we're actually moving. If we move one mile due east after we change it, they'll end up two miles west of the actual location. And two miles in this mess," he looked about the dense foliage, "is forever."

"Okay," she said. "When I think we're getting close, we'll leave the GPS at the base camp. When we're sure we've located our diamonds, you can make the adjustments and then we'll take it with us."

"Excellent," McNeil said. "Give us at least a half mile." She nodded. A small red light suddenly glowed on the unit set up to receive the signal from Billy Hackett's helicopter. "We've got information incoming." They collectively moved to the machine. The light shone for four to five seconds, then flickered and went out. "Billy must have compressed the data and sent it as a pulse."

Alain checked the unit and nodded. "We've got almost three gigabytes of data stored on the hard drive. At normal transmission speed that would take more than an hour to download. He compressed it, all right."

Samantha watched as Alain hooked the field computer up to the liquid crystal screen and clicked on the play button. The monitor showed a picture-in-picture display, the main screen showing a sea of green as the helicopter flew over the forest, while the smaller image relayed the position of the chopper against an underlying land-based grid. The latter was a feature Hackett had included without being asked and it looked to be an excellent idea.

"This is going to make my job a lot easier. I won't have to print promising-looking areas and overlay them on a precisely scaled map. I don't know how he did it, but it's brilliant."

She spent the next three hours carefully digesting the aerial video footage and marking possible hot spots on her field map. When she had finished, she reviewed the results and reported them back to Travis. She told him she'd have a more definitive list of possible targets after Hackett's second pass, scheduled for the next morning.

She returned to her tent and adjusted the mosquito netting and poison-laden rope. As she lay atop her bedding in the tranquility of the night, she thought about Travis McNeil. She pictured him standing knee-deep in the swamp, breathing heavily and dripping with water after rescuing the porter. She saw his perfectly honed body, his handsome face and sparkling blue eyes. She remembered the relaxed manner in which he held the knife in his right hand and how he'd made the prone body draped across his shoulder seem weightless. She sighed and closed her eyes, shutting out the dim starlight that filtered through the canopy. She saw him smile, and then she watched as their bodies came together and they kissed. It felt good to dream, and the last thought she had before drifting off was that it didn't have to be just a dream. She slept very well.

EIGHT

The limousine pulled up in front of the marble and glass building, and Patrick Kerrigan stepped out into a light afternoon drizzle. His driver sped around the car and held an umbrella above the president of Gem-Star as he walked across the expanse of sidewalk to the lobby doors. Kerrigan nodded to the security officer and proceeded directly to the bank of elevators servicing floors fifty through sixty-five. He punched the button for sixty-three and stood patiently waiting as the high-speed elevator sped up its narrow shaft. Thirty seconds later, he stepped into the reception area of his company, said a perfunctory hello to the receptionist and walked directly to his office. He had his secretary bring in coffee and then secure an overseas line to Belfast. A moment later, a second man entered the room. Kerrigan motioned for the man to take a seat, and sipped on the coffee while waiting for the connection to Ireland. When a voice answered, he put the call on speakerphone.

"O'Donnell here," the distant voice said.

"Hello, Liam," Kerrigan answered. "How are things in Belfast?"

"Things are fine, Patrick. What's up?"

"I'd like to book your services again. Same deal as last time—you'll remain on standby until I need you. Same rate of pay we agreed on before. Just be ready to move if and when I deem it necessary."

"When?" Liam O'Donnell asked.

"Starting immediately, and for at least the next three weeks."

"I'll give you a month, but that's it. I have another job scheduled after that. Do you need the same size team in place?"

"Yes, if you can arrange it. Six men plus yourself. I'll wire half the funds to your Swiss account this afternoon, and the other half two weeks from today. Eight hundred thousand English pounds in total."

"Sounds good. I'll get the team together and ready to move inside an hour of hearing from you. What's our target this time?"

"Same as before—Africa." Kerrigan pushed a button and terminated the call. He turned to the man sitting a few feet from him. "They're the second team, Garret. You're the third."

Garret Shaw nodded. He knew exactly what Patrick Kerrigan meant. Liam O'Donnell and his team of ex-MI5 operatives were a backup in the unlikely event Mugumba was unsuccessful in wiping out the mining expedition once they had located the diamond formation. From Belfast, they could be in the Ruwenzori Mountains within twenty-four hours. Two years ago, Shaw had personally overseen planting a cache of weapons in an underground dugout on the outskirts of Butembo. If O'Donnell and his men were needed, they would be given the location of the stash; if not, the guns and missiles would remain safely tucked away for future use. Shaw knew Kerrigan left nothing to chance.

"Brandy?" Kerrigan asked, and Shaw nodded. Kerrigan poured liberal servings into the snifters and handed one to him. "How many years is it since you quit working for the government and joined our little organization?"

"Seven years, Patrick," he answered. "Seven very good years." He lifted the brandy glass slightly to toast the longevity of their relationship.

"It's been more profitable killing people for me than it was when you were with Delta Force. And not nearly as stressful."

"It's certainly more relaxed," Garret said, thinking back to the life-or-death missions he had routinely run when he commanded an elite counter-terrorism squad. Life with the army's most prestigious unit, the Delta Force, was demanding and dangerous, but not well paying. He had defended the United States from terrorist attacks, had often gone on the offensive and taken out perceived threats before they materialized, and had killed countless people in the process. And every two weeks, he had received a major's pay for his efforts. When Kerrigan had approached him seven years ago, he had jumped at the chance to move from Fort Bragg and ply his considerable skills in the private sector. Kerrigan paid very well, as a healthy overseas account attested to.

"Why did you pick McNeil to accompany Samantha Carlson?" Kerrigan asked the ex-soldier. The recommendation to hire McNeil had come from one of his SEAL buddies, but Shaw, unknown to McNeil, had planted the seed. He thought his only connection to Kerrigan was his former colleague. And it was best to keep it that way.

"McNeil is resourceful, enough to keep your geologist alive until she finds the formation. And he's expendable. He has no real family—they were killed in a murder-suicide when he was about ten years old. An aunt and uncle from San Antonio raised him, which means McNeil can disappear without a lot of rocks being overturned. After he does his job, he'll just go away quietly."

"I hope you're right, Garret. Perhaps this guy will prove more resourceful than even you think. That could ultimately leave you and him staring at each other down gun barrels."

"Impossible. Mugumba has over twenty men, all crack

troops armed to the teeth. He has an inside man with the expedition, and a good working knowledge of the terrain. The chances of McNeil surviving Mugumba's attack are zero. And even if he does, you have Liam O'Donnell and his crew standing by in Belfast. You worry too much, Patrick. And," he paused for effect, "it's hardly as if this is the first time we've done this."

"I hope it's the last," Kerrigan said hotly. "I'm getting tired of sending geologists into the jungle and then getting screwed on the location of the diamonds."

"The last team was quite slippery," Shaw acknowledged. "We know they found it, but they never told us where it was. I think we may have taken them out a little prematurely."

"We should have had the location from the first team." Kerrigan literally spat the words. "We've wasted four years and millions of dollars since then. God damn him."

"You still netted quite the profit from that, Patrick. You should look at the upside of things every now and then."

"Quite the upside, Garret. If anyone ever found out what we did, there'd be a public lynching. You're trained to kill people and you may sleep well, but I still have nights when the memories of what we did keep me awake."

"It's over," Shaw said, rising from his chair. "Forget about it. Okay?"

Patrick Kerrigan stared at the man. His hired killer was right; this was no time to suffer an attack of conscience. He had deviated from the straight and narrow path so many years ago that it now seemed forever since he had performed his duties as president of Gem-Star within the law. But it wasn't always so. The notion of straying into covert acquisition of gemstones under the guise of a legitimate businessman had come upon him innocently enough.

Eight years ago, he had been appointed to the top position in Gem-Star, reporting to Davis Perth, the grandson of the company's founder. A half-million-dollar bonus and a yearly salary of eight hundred thousand dollars signaled the end to any mediocrity his life had held and his arrival at the top. The next six months had been glorious. The prestige of position, the wonder of wealth, and the glamour of high-society invitations were his. He reveled in his achievements, playing the power hand he had been dealt to the max. The New York social pages contained the comings and goings of people who mattered, and it was as often as not that Patrick Kerrigan's picture graced the pages. His life was perfect, his dreams fulfilled. Until the divorce.

The bitch he had dragged up the social ladder with him suddenly decided her life would be better with his money, but without him. She hired a top-notch matrimonial lawyer and proceeded to rip his financial life apart. She went for the jugular, and got it. The bonus was gone, as was half his yearly income. Along with the financial ruin came a pariah effect. The beautiful people didn't wish to be seen with a loser. They knew, they always knew somehow, who the winner was when a couple split up. They sided with his ex and expelled him from the group. He was relegated to watching the goings-on of the select few, including his ex-wife, from the sidelines with the masses. He was close to a breakdown when Davis Perth stuck his head in one day. He threw a file on Kerrigan's desk and told him to wrap up the exploration; they had hit nothing but dirt on this one.

He had opened the file and lightly perused its contents. The more he read about the Brazilian property, the more he believed Davis Perth was wrong. There were gemstones to be had in the formations, and the geologist had made mistakes. But instead of having Gem-Star reopen the dig, he took some time off and visited the site personally. After three days of concentrated digging in the area, he knew he had uncovered stones of great value. Sapphires by the dozens, perfect in color and clarity, were his for the taking. And take he did. The vein provided him with an additional three million dollars in untraceable income. He opened a numbered Swiss account and applied for Caymanian citizenship. He funneled the ill-gotten wealth into the Caymans and Switzerland, protected by the secrecy of the banking institutions. He paid no taxes and was asked no questions. It worked well, and he looked for other plays to pilfer. He did not have to look long to find more.

Gem-Star was a large corporation, looking for large deposits to exploit. They deemed numerous smaller plays to be unprofitable and abandoned them. Kerrigan went in later and cleaned out whatever wealth was trapped in the rocks. As time progressed, he got bolder. He began to change the essayer's reports on the new properties, masking potentially prosperous veins. When Gem-Star decided the play was not worthy, he took over and plundered it. His personal wealth grew at an astronomical rate. But the path was dangerous. The mines often fell inside political boundaries that were hazardous to his health. Central and South America were dangerous if you strayed off the beaten path, and that was exactly where the mines were. So he hired Garret Shaw to do his dirty work—a move that had paid enormous dividends for seven years now.

He continued to stare at Shaw as his mind regressed. It was sheer coincidence that they had met. Shaw had been in New York for a two-day layover before departing for North Africa with the Delta Force, and he had stopped at a small bar for a couple of scotches. The driver's side front tire on Kerrigan's Audi had suddenly gone flat, and he had entered the bar looking for a telephone. Shaw overheard Kerrigan asking for a phone to call AAA, and had offered to change the tire just to keep from getting bored. As Shaw worked, they had talked. And the conversation finally drifted around to what he did for a living. With three malt scotches down the hatch and another one waiting on the counter, he had divulged more information to Kerrigan than he should have.

As they parted, Kerrigan gave him his business card and told him to phone if he wanted to become very rich. Shaw had called and set up an appointment. The rest was history. Shaw had resigned from the army to take care of the shadowy details of Kerrigan's profitable mining adventures. The allegiance between the two men was solid, with each knowing enough to send the other to prison for two or three life-times. Shaw joined Kerrigan in the small percentage of Americans who are independently wealthy, and gave his boss complete loyalty in return. There was only one act the two had perpetrated that Kerrigan wished they had handled differently. But, as Shaw had said, that was in the past and now was not the time to develop a conscience.

He continued to stare at the ex-soldier, this time seeing the man and taking in the image. Garret Shaw was six-foot-four-inches, two hundred fifty-five pounds, without an ounce of fat. He wore faded jeans and a loose plaid shirt, but Kerrigan knew that under the clothes was a finely tuned body, trained to kill. Shaw worked out two hours a day, every day. He bench-pressed over three hundred pounds and ran the fifty in under six seconds. His face was tight skin over chiseled steel and his eyes burned a bright blue. He still wore his hair in a military crew cut, and he often reminded Kerrigan of a huge GI Joe doll.

"Tell me, Garret," Patrick said. "What's going to happen if McNeil manages to survive Mugumba and O'Donnell? You and him, face to face. Who would win?"

Garret stared back at Kerrigan. "Why, I would, of course." He turned abruptly and left, leaving Kerrigan with the feeling that no man could face off with him and live. It was a good feeling, very reassuring. What was even more reassuring was that the chance of McNeil ever going toe-to-toe with Shaw was nil. McNeil would die in the jungle, along with that uppity bitch, Samantha Carlson.

NINE

Samantha rubbed her eyes and splashed cold water over the nape of her neck. She stood up and walked around for a minute, then returned to the computer monitor and stared at the images of the rain-forest canopy. She scrolled the video feed ahead a few frames, then paused it again. She was right; there was another possible spot for the kimberlite outcrop. She noted the exact coordinates of her find in her field notebook and shut off the computer. Her latest find brought to seventeen in total the number of possible locations for the pipe. She called it in to Hackett, and then headed off to find Travis.

"I've finished the second video feed from the helicopter," she told him when she located him having a beer on the far side of their base camp. "It's down to seventeen possible locations."

"And one of those is our target?" he asked, sitting up in the hammock and finishing his beer.

"Not necessarily. I used the video footage from the two perpendicular grids that Billy ran in his chopper. Most of the distinct color changes in the canopy were caused by shadows. What appeared to be a darker section of forest from one view was often eliminated when I looked at it from a ninety-degree angle. The seventeen areas I've got locations for are ones that appear darker on both passes. The reason they're darker is unknown. The vegetation could be spring fed, which would cause different coloration than the surrounding trees that rely solely on rain for water. Or they could be fertilized by something that brings out a deeper green shade. Or," she smiled, "they could be sitting on a kimberlite pipe."

"Ahh, the kimberlite pipe you talked about in Kerrigan's office," Travis said, toasting her as he opened another beer. Then he looked puzzled. "That's where the diamonds are, right?"

She motioned for him to follow her back to the equipment, and they talked as they walked. "Right. The pipe is a rock formation that brings the diamonds up from deep inside ancient geological formations to the tertiary, or current, rocks. Without kimberlite pipes, the diamonds would remain trapped far too deep to ever find or mine."

"But you talked a lot about alluvial diamonds in Sierra Leone and the Congo. They're not the same, are they?"

"No," she said. "Alluvial diamonds are found on the surface. Somehow, usually through erosion, they've made their way to ground level. It's common for them to get caught in the flow of a river or a stream and end up hundreds of miles from where they initially surfaced. What the old prospectors would do is follow the rivers to the source and look for the pipe. If they found it, they'd stake it out, then try to mine it or sell it to De Beers."

"Makes sense. De Beers is the big boy on the block."

"Huge. They control the market. They have since 1888, when Cecil Rhodes consolidated a bunch of smaller companies to form De Beers Consolidated Mines."

"Who's Cecil Rhodes? I thought it was the Oppenheimer clan that controlled De Beers."

"Ahh, very good, Mr. McNeil," Samantha said, raising an

eyebrow. "He kills crocodiles and understands the intricacies of the diamond cartels as well. Impressive. The Oppenheimers have headed De Beers since 1929, when Ernest Oppenheimer was appointed chairman. He lasted until 1957, and then his son Harry took over. They were the brains behind controlling production and keeping global sales channeled through the Diamond Producers' Association. It was brilliant marketing. Hell, it still is."

"Okay, Doc, enough history. We're not following any rivers back to their sources, are we?"

"We don't have to. According to Kerrigan, the last expedition narrowed the area where the pipe is located to the seventy square miles we're having Billy Hackett recon. And look at this," she said, unrolling one of the numerous topographical maps that seemed to accompany her everywhere. She stabbed the atlas with her finger. "This region to the northeast is the most promising, with nine of the seventeen targets in this four-square-mile block. And you'll notice that there is no river originating farther up the mountains and flowing down through this area. So that would explain why no alluvial diamonds have been found below the pipe. There's no water to wash them out of their formation and push them down onto the flats."

"So the diamonds have remained undiscovered over the centuries because there've never been any clues to their existence," Travis said, and she nodded. "They must be well hidden."

"Nature is a master of disguise. You've probably walked on or over more money in rare stones or oil and gas in your life than you could ever imagine. What appears to be a simple hill to the average person is an anomaly of some sort to a geologist. We always question why it's there." A beep interrupted her, and Sam turned quickly to the bank of equipment behind her. She slipped on a set of earphones and flipped a switch. "Go ahead, Billy."

Travis could barely hear the helicopter pilot's voice over the static. "Hi, Sam. I'm set up to start transmitting if you're ready." She okayed the download, saying all was ready at the base camp. "I'm sending in blue-six."

"Roger," she answered, then turned to Travis. "Billy and I divided the seventeen targets into three areas, and then numbered and color-coded them so I know which one he's filming. He's sending me the images live now, not prerecorded." She watched the monitor as it came to life, filling the screen with the lush green of the rain-forest canopy. Hackett kept the progress of his machine slower now, as the grid was much smaller. After about thirty seconds, the camera swung up for a moment, showing only sky as Hackett turned the chopper around. Then he was back on the grid again, moving parallel to the first swath, one hundred feet to the west. Sam watched the feed intently.

"Shit," she said, reaching for the transmit button on the Panther unit. "Billy, drop the grid; this one's being fed by a spring." Acknowledgement came across the unit a moment later and the pilot headed for the next set of coordinates. She replayed for Travis the portion of the second pass the chopper had made. "Watch the left side of the screen. Right here. You can see a spring bubbling up through this gap in the canopy. The spring water is mineral-rich and that would cause the difference in the color of the canopy. That one is off the list."

"That's not so bad," he said. "It's better to eliminate them from base camp than to hike through the jungle for nothing."

Sam agreed. "What are Mugumba's guys up to?"

"I talked to Billy before he went up this morning. He's got a handful of village kids watching the soldiers and reporting back to him. They've accounted for eighteen of his men as of this morning. They're just lying about town, taking it easy. Mugumba is checked into the best suite in the hotel and spends most of his time there."

She did some quick math. "When we were in Rutshunt, you said his force numbered twenty-three including him. Then he lost one man when the truck went over the cliff. That leaves twenty-one soldiers, and you said the village kids know the whereabouts of eighteen. Where are the other three?"

He shrugged his shoulders. "Who knows? I'm not too worried about three guys. I'll get worried when the lot of them leave Butembo en masse."

They both looked back to the communications station as Hackett's voice came over the Panther. He was in position to start the grid for the next location. Sam watched as the real-time video began to play. She was engrossed in the footage and didn't notice Travis leave. Ten minutes later, she radioed Hackett that she had successfully received the information and he could head to the next location. She logged the time and location into her notebook, flipped the CD from the write drive and labeled it. This was the part of mining exploration she hated—the tedious, methodical grunt work that laid the foundation for the real prospecting.

It was pointless to head into thousands of square miles of dense jungle and hope to find a target that could be as small as fifty feet across. Sheer lunacy. Sam knew this all too well, and although she hated the dull nature of the work, she realized its importance. The glory that came from announcing a major geological find was always backed by countless hours bent over maps, core samples and essayer's reports. Proper groundwork paid off, and she suspected that if they could locate this play, it would pay off big.

She turned her attention to the Panther as Hackett checked in again. She radioed back for him to begin the new grid, then cross-checked the location against her list of seventeen possible targets. They were making progress. Two hours later, Travis showed up again to see how things were going. The live feed from Hackett's helicopter was beginning again. The earphones crackled and Samantha slipped them on, giving Hackett the okay to start his transmission. Travis waited until the feed was downloaded before he spoke.

"Are you getting anything concrete from this?" he asked, indicating the bank of electronic equipment sitting in stark contrast to the primitive jungle surrounding them.

"It's going well. I've managed to eliminate almost every target in the south; they're all fed by springs. The ground must be quite porous to the south and the west. I think our formation is going to lie up in this area." She traced her hand across the crest of the Ruwenzori Mountains, letting her finger rest on the leeward side of the range. She looked thoughtful for a moment. "It's up there somewhere, Travis. I feel it."

"You'll find it," he said confidently. "And when you do, I think things will get very interesting very quickly."

TEN

Fifteen of the possible seventeen locations were out of the running. Over the past twelve days, Samantha had led the expedition deeper into the primordial jungle, and ever closer to the base of the Ruwenzori. They had covered the shortest possible route as they crisscrossed the western flank, eliminating zones as they moved. One porter had fallen prey to a forest cobra, the bite from the slim brown and black snake fatal within seconds as it shut down the man's nervous system. The antidote, administered within thirty seconds of the puncture, was too late. A somber grouping had lit the funeral pyre and danced the Ezengi for the dispatched soul. The man's Zengi, or spirit, was released by the dance of the dead, and they departed quickly after the service so his soul would be left in peace. It was on the thirteenth day they ran into the pygmies.

Samantha was huddled over the Panther unit as Hackett zeroed in on the final two formations, when a pygmy scouting party broached the perimeter of the camp. Their faces were painted, the bright colors contrasting sharply against the black of their skin. The advance party totaled six men, serious-looking and heavily armed. They carried crossbows and blowguns, both loaded with projectiles tipped in deadly poison. Hal met them face to face as they reached the center of the encampment.

He exchanged words and gestures with the leader of the pygmies, their voices rising on occasion, their hands aping the verbal confrontation. At a seemingly crucial point, Hal acceded to the pygmy negotiator by kneeling and inclining his head slightly to the man. He returned to his feet, spoke a few more words, and then turned to Sam and McNeil, who had gathered, along with the entire crew, to watch the show.

"They are the scouts for a war party," Hal informed them. "These guys are not to be trifled with. They're Zande, from the Haut-Uele region—very independent and quite savage when provoked. And someone has recently provoked them. A neighboring tribe attacked their village when they were out hunting and stole three of their women. When they find the people responsible, they will kill them and take their Zengi. The last thing we want to do is get in their way."

"Okay," McNeil said. "Why did you kneel in front of him?"

"He was getting very upset with us being so close to their village. He was beginning to talk of attacking us. It seemed the logical thing to submit. I'm sure you don't want to fight these guys."

"No, of course not," McNeil agreed. "Did he give you any idea of how large their war party is?" Hal shook his head. "Alain, when Hal gets rid of these guys, set up a tighter perimeter. Keep the main body from advancing any closer than three hundred yards. Break out the Remingtons, one per man. Leave the assault rifles packed. It looks like Hal can probably handle this diplomatically, but I just want to be prepared. Keep in mind that they're not after us; it's some other tribe that's got them pissed off."

"We're vulnerable here," Dan Nelson said, his forearm resting comfortably on his pistol stock. "I've scouted outside our perimeter and there's a grove that backs onto a sheer rock wall about six hundred yards east. We could make it in three or four hours."

McNeil eyed him. "Three or four hours to go six hundred yards, Dan. What are we going to do, crawl?"

"There's a slight obstacle in the way," he answered.

An hour later, the team leaders stood on the edge of "Dan's Precipice," as they had decided to call it. Plunging hundreds of feet straight down, the bottom of the gorge was invisible to the naked eye. The distant sounds of rushing water indicated a stream coursed through the narrow gap. The jagged gash in the earth was only thirty yards across, but it may as well have been a thousand miles. The crevice was impassable.

"Well, this is fucking great," Troy Ramage said, giving Dan an evil look. "Now we've got our backs to a bottomless pit. Any other equally brilliant ideas?"

"There's a bridge," Nelson replied, pointing to the thick underbrush to the left. "About sixty yards or so. Let me see if I can find the path Hal and I hacked out yesterday when we were poking around."

Dan Nelson found the cut marks in the dense jungle and slipped his machete from its case, slashing the residual undergrowth as he made his way toward the bridge. Travis followed immediately behind him, then Samantha, Troy and Hal. Alain remained with the porters at the chasm edge. It was slow going through the tangled mess of vines, and the humidity was intense, drops of water forming on the plant leaves. A family of mangabeys watched the procession from their position halfway up a giant phrynium. The monkeys chattered relentlessly, irritated by the disruption to their daily schedule of gathering bananas and mangos. A few minutes later they broke into a small clearing next to the rift.

"The bridge," Dan said, pointing at it triumphantly.

McNeil just stared. "That's not a bridge. That's a quick way to die." The v-shaped bridge connected the edges of the gap, but the structure looked anything but sturdy. It was a variation on a suspension bridge, made entirely of vines. Small tree trunks recklessly lashed together formed a narrow base to walk on, and a few interwoven strands created handgrips. The vines were wrapped around nearby trees on each side, securing the entire framework from dropping into the chasm. The knots that anchored the vines appeared loose and the vines themselves frayed. Travis turned to Dan.

"How the hell can you call that thing a bridge?"

"It meets the definition of a bridge." Dan defended his find. "It crosses the gap; therefore it's a bridge."

"It is a pretty shitty one," Samantha said. She looked to Hal for an alternate solution. "Are there any other ways of crossing?"

"About twelve miles south, there's a real bridge. It's wooden, with footings and a roadway. But it's a long way through the jungle. Perhaps two or three days."

"Which direction is the pygmy village?" Travis asked. Hal pointed back, away from the chasm. "So if we cross here, we'll be putting distance between us and the war party." Hal nodded. Travis turned to Samantha. "The final locations you've mapped out from Billy's info, are they on the other side of this thing?"

"Yes, and almost due east of here. If we head south to the more stable bridge, we'll be losing four or five days, not just two or three. And we'll risk running into the pygmies."

He surveyed the bridge again, this time studying the structure carefully. Maybe it would work. With some modifications to strengthen it, the bridge might hold. He sent Hal and Dan back to wrap up the camp and move the men forward. Troy and Samantha stayed to help him shore up the span as best as possible. They found a good source of fresh vines close to the clearing, and cut them into useable lengths. Travis secured himself around the waist with a thin but strong vine, and inched his way onto the bridge. He began wrapping the fresh lengths of vine at the suspected weak points, entwining the new over the old. By the time

Hal and Dan showed up with the camp in tow, Travis's hands were knotting up from the tedious task of reinforcing the bridge, and Troy and Samantha were dripping sweat from cutting and stripping the vines. Hal looked beat from the trek, and collapsed on the edge of the clearing with his pack still strapped to his back.

Samantha unpacked the rudiments of her communications system, and had it online within a few minutes. Travis finished shoring up the suspension bridge and returned to the clearing, untying the primitive safety line from his waist as he approached her. She motioned for him to be quiet as she tied into the satellite uplink and connected with Billy Hackett, whose voice was devoid of static, but tinged with anxiety when it came over the line.

"Where the hell have you guys been?"

"Moving base camp. Why?"

"Mugumba's men are on the move, Sam. You better tell Travis right away."

"He's standing right beside me."

"When did the soldiers leave Butembo?" Travis asked the pilot.

"Early this morning. About six hours ago now. They headed south, toward Mutwanga."

McNeil traced the path on the map he had spread out atop Sam's Panther unit. "Shit," he said. "They're heading for the bridge to the south. The one that crosses this goddamn ravine. They know we're heading into the Ruwenzori. Sam," he turned to his geologist, "how sure are you of the final two locations you've identified?"

"Reasonably sure that one of them is our formation. Why?"

"Mugumba must know we're getting close or he wouldn't have started moving his men. That confirms someone inside our camp is advising the colonel—someone who knows we're down to our last two targets. We've got to get across this bridge and establish a new base camp in a safe location on the other side. Show me the final two locations on this map."

She pulled her map out and transferred the coordinates to McNeil's map. Their position at the gorge was less than a mile from both locations. According to the closely grouped topographical lines covering the map, a major ridge separated the two possible sites. He stroked his chin thoughtfully. He lit a cigarette, then flicked the match into the dank grass at his feet.

"Troy, get across the bridge and find a suitable location for a base camp in this area." He drew a small circle on the map. "Switch on your 5 W mini and radio the location back to us. The jamming technology in the Panther 5 W mini is irrefutable; we'll be invisible once we switch over. It's time to get technical and stop giving these guys a fix on us. Except for the GPS, and we're only going to feed them what we want them to know. When we're sure we've got the formation, we'll reverse the polarity on the transmitter they hid in the GPS and send them on a wild goose chase."

Troy nodded and left, taking two porters with him to help clear a path through the jungle. Travis watched as they traversed the bridge, noting that the extra strength from the repairs seemed to hold the weight well. When they were loaded with gear it might be a different story. He turned back to Samantha.

"How quickly can you run the necessary tests on the formations once we get you there?"

"Less than a day for each one," she estimated. "There's substantial outcropping on both formations, so I should be able to test for trace elements without having to dig."

"That's good news. And it should take Mugumba at least a day to reach the southern bridge. From there, he's looking at a minimum of two days' trek northward through the jungle to meet up with us. That gives us a buffer of three days before he's within striking range. We'd better be ready by then."

"You're pretty sure he's going to attack us once we find the diamonds, aren't you?" Samantha asked.

"On a scale of one to ten, that's a ten. The only advantage we have is that we'll be ready for him. If he caught us unaware, there's no doubt in my mind he would wipe us out before we had our guns drawn. Those are top-notch troops with him, not the average underpaid, low-moral soldiers that make up the Congolese army."

"You really know how to sweet-talk a girl," she said.

"I thought that was rather diplomatic, considering we've got a hostile tribe of pygmies behind us and a platoon of crack troops flanking us. And not to mention a huge crack in the earth right in front of us."

"There you go again," she said. "Making me feel warm and tingly all over." She smiled at him and he grinned back. But behind the calm facade, she saw a man tensed and ready for battle. And she knew that soon they would be fighting for their lives against formidable odds in a hostile terrain. And the pressures came back—she had to find the diamonds, and she had to find them soon. Their lives depended on it.

ELEVEN

Patrick Kerrigan was lining up a twelve-foot putt when his caddy approached him with the cell phone. He motioned for the man to back off, finished calculating the left-to-right break, and stroked the ball. It rolled into the center of the cup for a birdie. He smiled as the rest of his foursome congratulated him on a well-played hole, then exchanged his putter for the phone.

"Kerrigan," he said quietly.

Static filled the line, and he struggled to hear the caller speak. "It's Colonel Mugumba." The distant voice was commingled with white noise, but decipherable. "We're moving up to intercept the team. We think they're within a day or two of discovering the diamonds."

"Is the location where we thought it would be?"

"Almost exactly where you said. I'm sure she's located it from the information the helicopter provided."

"Excellent. Stay on top of them. For Christ's sake, don't let the same thing happen again."

"Yes, sir," Mugumba said; then the line went quiet.

Kerrigan turned off the cell phone and snapped it shut.

There were no other calls of enough importance to disrupt his golf game. He jumped into the cart and his caddy hit the gas and headed for the next tee box. He allowed himself a small smile as they drove. He had known from the onset that the diamondiferous formation they sought was within a two-square-mile target, tucked against the rugged footings of the Ruwenzori. The seventy-square-mile grid he had given Samantha was a red herring mixed with the real thing. He could easily have given her the smaller two-square-mile area, but that would be admitting he knew more than he was letting on. And he wanted to test her abilities. She hadn't let him down—she was leading the team exactly where she should. This time the expedition wouldn't keep the location from him.

The previous team had kept him in the dark as to the exact location, without him being aware. By the time he found out they had tricked him, the last of the team was dead and the secret died with him. He cursed the secretive nature of geologists and wondered why they continued to deceive him. He was positive that he portrayed the correct image: a businessman committed to the highest level of integrity in his search to open new geological territory. But if his team leaders bought the front he put on, why did they consistently try to keep the true location from him? Somehow, they must suspect he had another agenda. But how?

He arrived at the seventh tee and accepted his driver from his caddy. His birdie on the previous hole allowed him the honors, and he teed the ball up and then looked down the fairway of the monstrous six-hundred-yard par five. He addressed the ball, but his mind was on diamonds, not golf. The first team he had sent in, years ago, had been the most prolific to date. They had provided him with immense personal wealth, but the head geologist had refused to disclose the source of the diamonds for fear the area would be ravaged by improper mining methods and vast acres of virgin jungle destroyed. He had refused to divulge the location and had paid dearly for his treason. The next two years had proved frustrating as Kerrigan had tried to locate the source himself. He had finally quit the exercise, admitting that he was not a field geologist of any merit. Another team was created and dispatched to the Congo, given the seventy-square-mile grid that the first team had offered. Two months of intensive prospecting had resulted in a phone call. The chief geologist told him that they had found the source. But then the man had pulled the same crap the first team had, by refusing to reveal the exact location. Kerrigan had gone ballistic on the man, insisting that he cough up the information immediately.

The geologist insisted that the area was environmentally fragile, and that he did not want it destroyed by haphazard mining practices. He wanted assurances from Gem-Star that the excavation would be handled with kid gloves. Kerrigan had insisted he would personally work with the production crews and the Congolese government to ensure the safety of the find, but with each word he spoke, the man grew more withdrawn and untrusting. Finally, Kerrigan had made a choice. He ordered the team back to Butembo and dispersed the guides. He flew into the African city and tried to talk directly to his team leader. It went nowhere. Garret Shaw was called in and the geologist suffered a fatal accident. That was the end of his second team. Again, he spent time in the jungle trying to locate the vein himself. Nothing.

He returned to New York a possessed man. Incredible wealth was so close, yet he could not get his hands on it. And the CEO of his company, Davis Perth, was getting suspicious. Gem-Star was active in seven different countries worldwide, but only one of those was Africa. He was spending a disproportionate amount of his time in Africa and the home office was asking why. He couldn't risk elevating Perth's suspicions any further by returning to the Ruwenzori, so he put together a third team. This time, he chose the head geologist carefully. High ideals and integrity were out the window. He wanted someone who would quickly trade the location for a decent payoff.

Everything went well until the unethical team leader located the vein and realized what it was worth. The slimeball had insisted on fifty percent, and was unwavering. Kerrigan spent a day agonizing over what to do.

He knew the location of the team's final base camp, and the approximate distance they were traveling each day to reach the diamonds. He could narrow it down to less than two square miles. Surely to God, he could find the pipe in such a small section of jungle. In a fit of rage, he unleashed Mugumba's troops and the team had ceased to exist. Once again, he traded the concrete of New York for the jungles of the Congo in his search for the diamonds. But again, the formation continued to elude him. He seemed destined for failure, and after three weeks of intensive searching, he left the wilds and returned to New York to put together a fourth team. The one that now stood on the threshold of perhaps the richest diamond strike ever.

He kept his eye on the ball and started into his backswing. The last thought he had, before he crushed the ball three hundred yards straight down the center of the fairway, was that this team would provide him what he wanted. Then they would die.

Liam O'Donnell surveyed the eclectic group of mercenaries that filled the small room in the rear of the Belfast pub. The curtains were drawn, and a bit of ambient noise was all that filtered in from the busy barroom. The seven hired killers were invisible to the good Irish folk who enjoyed their nightly pints only a few feet away. What O'Donnell saw, he liked. Five of the six he knew from his stint with British intelligence and the sixth came highly recommended through an IRA friend he trusted explicitly. He raised his pint of bitter and toasted the men.

"Gentlemen," he began, "for the next month, we're a team. To a man, we are guaranteed at least five thousand pounds. That's what I'm paying for you to be on call. If we need to leave Ireland, the sum doubles. If we travel to Africa, tack on an additional five thousand. And if we see any action while there, an additional ten. As well, all your expenses will be covered, including travel costs, hotels, meals, drinks and even women, if we have time. If we are successful in terminating our target, an additional five." O'Donnell saw the faces and knew the men were doing the math—he saved them the trouble. "That's thirty thousand quid if it goes all the way and you make it back alive."

"What's the target?" one of the men asked. He looked almost disinterested.

"Four men and one woman. There may be some collateral targets, but nothing of any talent."

"Where in Africa?" another man asked, his finger tracing a jagged scar that ran the length of his right cheek.

"Democratic Republic of Congo," Liam answered, then raised his hands to the groans that permeated the room. "We'll charter in and land close to the target at a small city called Butembo. Three days in from there, providing our people aren't on the move."

"Why don't we sit back and wait for them to leave? That place is a shit hole. I spent some time there on a job for Andres the Frenchman."

"That's a possibility. They may get out before we can fly in. Our employer is keeping good tabs on them. I don't think we'll lose them. We hope they'll head back for Europe or at least northern Africa and we can take them out somewhere a bit more hospitable."

"Weapons?" a third man asked.

"Taken care of. You bring nothing but your talent to this one."

"You mentioned four men and a woman. What level of skill are we up against?"

"The guys are ex-SEALs. The woman is a nobody—a geologist." O'Donnell withdrew some glossy pictures from a large brown envelope and pinned them to the wall. Each eight-by-ten featured a facial shot of McNeil and his team. The photo of Samantha was taken from a distance with a zoom lens, and showed her entire body. She was standing on a street corner in New York waiting for a light, dressed in her morning jogging clothes. Most of the men stirred in their chairs when O'Donnell pinned up her picture.

"If you can take her alive, you can have her for a day or two. Then she dies." A contented murmur stole across the room, and O'Donnell knew from their expressions that these men wanted the battle. Collecting money to sit around and wait was okay, but each ex-MI5 member in the room preferred to earn his money the old-fashioned way— by killing people. He wrapped up the meeting and the group joined the regular folk in the front of the pub. Drinks were ordered and put away in record time. The thought of killing four highly trained Americans and raping a beautiful woman was enough to work up a real thirst.

TWELVE

Half the equipment had been ferried across Dan's precipice when the bridge began to fail. McNeil could see the vines he had interwoven with the original structure starting to slip. The knots were still tight and holding, but the added weight of the armaments was too much for the freshly cut strands. He stopped the flow of porters and tested the span's strength. He identified a few crucial weak spots, ordered the porters to cut more vines, and lashed them to the bridge where necessary. The repairs took a while, and it was almost two hours before the trickle of men and equipment restarted the short but arduous trek.

Samantha lounged in the shade of a giant Phrynium, pulling gently at the fresh shoots emanating from the gnarled trunk. This was gorilla country; they loved the new growth on the ancient trees. She had seen signs of recent gorilla activity in the area as they moved steadily east into the more rugged highlands bordering the Ruwenzori. Actually seeing a gorilla was another story; they were incredibly secretive and able to move through the jungle with hardly a sound. She jerked slightly, startled, as Travis appeared around the tree.

"Hi," he said, his tone upbeat. "What are you doing over here all by yourself?"

"Thinking." She smiled back. "Just thinking about how beautiful this country is, and what a tragedy it's so poorly managed. If just once a government that wasn't totally corrupt could come to power and stay in power, this country could be prosperous. Aside from diamonds, they've got gold, cobalt, copper and zinc. Christ, back when the Congo was called Zaire, they were the largest producer of cobalt in the world. Gecamines was a huge mining company that ran at a profit for years, but eventually government greed collapsed it and the military looted the mine sites. Expatriates took off, and without skilled labor the whole industry collapsed."

"Sounds like they shot themselves in the foot."

"No kidding. But it all comes back to the government. If they hadn't put such a financial drain on the company, Gecamines would still be around. They were far from lily white, but at least they employed people."

"You really love Africa, don't you?" he asked, handing her a bottle of water.

She accepted the offering and took a long drink. "I guess I do," she said slowly. "It *is* beautiful. Sometimes I think I feel more at home here than I do back in the States. I just wish I could do something, anything, to help." She smiled at him— not a happy smile, but a resigned one. She held out the water and as he took it their hands touched. Neither moved for a moment and energy seemed to flow between them. She withdrew her hand. "How are things at the bridge?"

"It's holding for now, but I don't know that we'll get everything across. I separated out the most important things, like your communication equipment and mining gear, and had the porters take that across first. Then the weapons. I should get back and see if everything's okay."

She nodded and stood up with him. They walked together

back to the bridge and he surveyed the scene. Only six boxes remained on the near side of the chasm, the rest successfully moved across. Three of the six were ammunition and extremely heavy. He reinspected the bridge, giving careful attention to the vines that attached the span to the anchoring trees. He nodded his approval and motioned for the next porter to cross. The man hoisted one of the ammunition boxes and gingerly stepped onto the narrow cut of wood that served as the walkway. The entire bridge dipped precariously with the heavy weight, and a few vines strained at their moorings. Travis divided his attention between the cross bracing and the anchors, watching both for flaws that would cause the bridge to collapse. When the man reached the midway point, the weight was better distributed, taking the strain off the anchors. As he neared the far edge, the stress again began to pull hard on the anchoring vines. Travis kept his hand on the thickest vine, feeling the amount of strain. A few moments later the man stepped onto the far lip of the crevice and the tension went slack. McNeil breathed easier.

"Five more boxes and we're across," he said quietly, as if worried that a loud noise might cause the shaky structure to collapse. He turned sharply as Hal came running from the forest into the clearing.

"The war party is only a few hundred yards out," he gasped. "And they look pretty serious. I think we should get across here as quickly as possible."

McNeil sized up the situation. "How long until they get here?"

"Half an hour, tops," the guide answered.

"Shit. Get another man on the bridge," he said to Faustin. "Have what's-his-name in the Miami shirt and the other guy, Beya, cross last."

Faustin began chattering at the porters huddled around the remaining boxes. A man jumped to his feet, shouldered a box and started across. McNeil broke open one of the rectangular boxes and pulled out two Remington Vent Rib shotguns. He loaded them, and handed one to Samantha. She accepted it tentatively.

"Targets and crocs are one thing, but I'm not exactly practiced at this," she said. "Shooting people, I mean."

"I'm glad. I'd be worried about you if you were. Just point the gun and pull the trigger. Easy." He gave her a forced smile and turned his attention back to the bridge. It was still holding, but barely. The footings on the near side were pulling out from the bank, and the anchoring vines were stretched almost to the breaking point. Another porter began the crossing and a vine snapped, sending him to his left and into the handrail. He tottered between safety and certain death for a moment, then regained his balance and continued across. Once he was on solid ground, another man rested a box securely on his left shoulder and held the right handrail tightly. The bridge tried to force the man to the left, but he counterbalanced the force and made it across. Two boxes to go.

That left the man in the Miami Dolphins shirt, Koko, and his colleague, Beya, as the final two porters aside from Faustin. McNeil told Faustin to cross now, without a box, and the man obeyed. The bridge held well without the added weight. Koko was next, and he shouldered the second-to-last box and began to cross. Midway, one of the main support vines let go. It came apart with a loud snapping sound and the right side of the bridge collapsed. Koko dropped the box, but grabbed the broken vine as he started the tumble into the void. Travis watched as hundreds of rounds of ammunition disappeared into the blackness. He swore softly under his breath at the loss.

Koko hung by the shredded vine ten feet below the broken backbone of the bridge. One hand was clamped vise-like on the vine while the other flailed helplessly. Travis grabbed a length of previously cut and stripped vine, and tied one end to a nearby tree, the other around his waist. He gave it a quick tug to check the anchoring knot and started onto what was left of the bridge. The structure was totally unstable, rocking back and forth with every step he took. Koko was in dire straits, his grip slipping as his strength ebbed. McNeil reached the center of the bridge, directly above Koko, and lay prone on the wood planking while reaching his hand down. Two feet separated the rescuing hand from the stricken one. He stared into the man's eyes and saw death. He'd seen it before, many times, but it was something he never got used to. He kept eye contact with the man.

"Do you speak English?" he asked, and the man nodded slightly. "Do you understand what I'm saying?" Again, a nod. "I'm going to save you, but I need you to understand what I'm saying. Tell me in English that you understand."

"Yes, I understand. You will save me. But quickly would be good; my grip is slipping."

"Excellent. I'm going to let go of the bridge, and as I fall we'll grab each other. I have this vine," he indicated the one around his waist, "wrapped about a tree."

"We will smash into the side of the cliff," the man said, looking at the rock wall.

"Yes," Travis agreed. "You'd better hang on." He looked back to where Hal, Beya, and Samantha watched from the edge. "Grab the vine I tied to the tree, and hold on!" They scrambled to get a good grip on it, and Hal waved once they were ready. Travis let go and began to fall. A split second later he felt Koko grab him as he angled downward into the gap. He got the man in a bear hug and hung on for dear life as they arced toward the sheer rock face. A moment later they hit. McNeil was on the outside, away from the wall when they crashed into it, and Koko's body shielded him from the impact. Koko wasn't so fortunate. The shock of being sandwiched between McNeil and the wall knocked him unconscious and he relaxed his grip. For a moment, everything seemed okay. Then the vine started to snap.

McNeil heard it first, before the two groups that watched from either side of the crevice. He looked up and watched as, strand by strand, the vine unraveled. He had seconds to live. He yelled up at Samantha to throw down another vine, and seconds later one appeared. He quickly wrapped it under Koko's armpits and knotted it. He yelled to the team on the near side of the gap to grab the vine Sam had thrown over, and let go of the first. He heard a voice yelling they had it, and he released the excess weight.

Koko remained stationary for a moment, then began to move upwards. A foot or two at a time, he was hoisted toward the rim of the gorge, unconscious and totally unaware of his predicament. Without Koko's body weight, the vine holding McNeil frayed less quickly, giving him a chance to get good hand and toe grips into the rock seconds before the vine snapped. He watched as his safety harness drifted past and then hung below him. He was stuck against the wall, with nothing but the strength in his fingers keeping him from a long drop to his death. He took a few deep breaths and began to climb.

Every finger hold was a life-or-death decision. The tips of his boots searched out tiny juts or cracks and kept some of the weight off his hands, but it was his fingertips that controlled his destiny. Inch by inch he worked his way up the cliff side, knowing that one wrong move was the end. A small outcrop crumbled under his left hand and he gasped in air sharply, for a moment not knowing whether he could compensate in time. He curled the fingers of his right hand deeper into the crack and tensed his back muscles to keep his body from swinging. A moment later he was stationary and stable. He found a new finger grip for his left hand, tested its strength and continued. He briefly caught a glimpse of the team members on the far side of the chasm as he arced his neck to search for a new handhold. To a man, they watched intently without making a sound. He swept his gaze back to the wall and upward. Anxious faces stared back at him. He locked eyes with Samantha, and mouthed *"It's okay."* She nodded, almost imperceptibly, and he looked back to the ten feet of wall left before he reached the top.

This was the trickiest part. The uppermost rocks of the cliff face were the least compacted and most subject to erosion. Although they appeared solid, they were easily dislodged, and each time he looked for a new hold McNeil pulled out numerous rocks before finding a well-anchored one. The minutes dragged on and his strength began to wane. He was less than four feet from the top, and within inches of Samantha's outstretched arm, when both his finger holds crumbled at once. He stayed prone to the wall for a split second, then his body began to fall away. He pushed with his toes, willing them to give him the vertical lift he needed to grasp Sam's hand. He made it, barely, and caught her wrist with his right hand.

He saw the pain course through her as her torso was pulled tight into the rough rocks atop the gorge. She grimaced and clenched her teeth, and tears appeared at the edges of her eyes. He knew the pain must be excruciating. He prayed that the men behind her, holding her legs, could take the added weight. Slowly, he hoisted himself up, using only the lessening strength in his arm. He grasped her above the elbow, then pulled upward again until he could hook his loose hand under her armpit. His eyes were level with the rock edge, and he could see Hal and Beya, their faces drenched with sweat as they strained to keep Samantha from plunging into the gorge. He saw the fatigue, and he knew that they were finished, that they could hold her no longer. He made a move that would either save him or kill him.

With every shred of strength his well-honed body had left, he jackknifed hard left, then kicked his right leg out and up. The momentum of the slight pendulum gave him the added lift he needed, and he rolled atop the edge. He lay there for a moment, panting, then looked to Samantha.

"Are you okay?" he asked quietly, his breath coming in gasps.

"No," she said. "I think you pulled my arm out of its socket. You should lose some weight."

He laughed. He looked her in the eye and laughed like he had never laughed before. And she joined him. He cradled her smiling face in his hands, and when they had finally stopped, he said, "Thanks. You saved my life, you know."

"Uh-huh, I know. You owe me one. And I wasn't kidding about my arm. It's really screwed up."

He rose to his feet and pulled her up by her good arm. He gently grasped her damaged limb and tried to lift it. She winced when it reached about halfway, and screamed when he tried to move it a fraction farther. He slowly lowered it, and shook his head.

"It's dislocated," he said. "You weren't kidding. It's pulled right out of its socket. Shit."

Hal tapped him lightly on the shoulder. "Mr. Travis, I can fix this."

The diminutive man spoke the words without pomp or arrogance, simply with confidence. The same confidence that emanated from him as he guided the expedition through the dense jungle.

"Have you ever done this before?" Travis asked.

Hal laughed. "Many times. My brother played professional football for a few years, and there were numerous players with dislocated shoulders. It's quite common—that and gashes from cleats."

"Your brother played in the NFL?" Travis asked.

"No, no, of course not. Not American football—soccer. We call it football. Which makes sense, being that the game is played with the feet. Where you Americans ever got the idea to call your game football, I'll never know. Passball or runball would be better. Anyway, I have had experience with popping dislocated shoulders back into place."

"Will you two shut up and do something? My arm is killing me," Samantha said, still standing, but barely.

Hal had Samantha lie on her side, her dislocated shoulder away from the ground. He sat perpendicular to her and placed one foot under her arm on her ribcage, the other against her neck. He grasped her with both hands by the forearm, and before she had time to tense up, he jerked her arm toward him, sharp and quick. A sickening sound, akin to bones breaking, snapped through the air a split second before Sam screamed. Hal stood up and helped her to her feet. Samantha slowly rotated her arm, wincing slightly at the residual pain. She had full movement in the limb, but once she tried it and felt the discomfort, she lowered it to her side and held it still. She gave Hal a wide grin and then a hug with her good arm. She rested her head on his shoulder and watched as McNeil used a machete to hack into the trunk of a tree with a ten-inch diameter. With every blow, wood chips flew into the air. It took less than two minutes for him to fell the tree, and then he set to stripping the branches from the lower third of the trunk.

"What's that for?" she asked him.

"The bridge is useless, and we've still got five people and a couple of boxes to get across. I'm going to rig up another way to get over. Grab the portable Panther unit, and get someone on the other side of the gap on the line. I don't feel like yelling in case the war party is getting close enough to hear. It'll give away our position and allow them to find us sooner."

Samantha grabbed the lone Panther unit that remained on their side of the gap and held it up. Alain saw what she was doing and grabbed his portable unit. A moment later she heard his voice. She relayed McNeil's order that they keep quiet, then passed the unit to him.

"Alain, find a tree with at least a ten-inch diameter and strip an eight-foot length off it. Bury it three feet into the ground about ten feet in from the edge. Get Dan to tie a rock to one of the nylon ropes and throw it over to us. We're going to glide across. You can anchor your end by having the porters throw their backs into it; we'll have to tie ours into a tree."

"I'll send a rope long enough for you to anchor it to your post and then the tree," Alain said. Travis radioed okay and resumed digging a hole for base of the tree trunk.

Samantha helped dig the hole, but asked him about the arrangement. "Why don't we just tie the rope to that tree?" She pointed to a large tree some thirty feet back from the precipice.

"Once we get a person's weight on the rope, it's going to sag quite a lot. To compensate for that and to give us enough slack to clear this edge of the gap, we'd have to tie the rope almost twenty-five feet up that tree. Try getting these boxes up there. Plus the speed at which you'd be moving when you hit the other side would be far too great. You'd be lucky to land without breaking both your legs. This way the angle is far less, you move at a reasonable speed, and the chances of hitting either this edge or the far one are greatly reduced."

"Question answered," she said, continuing to dig.

They reached three feet into the tropical soil before Travis lowered the stripped trunk into the hole. They backfilled it and then attached the rope that Dan had thrown across to both the pole and the anchor tree. They pulled the rope tight, and Travis nodded his approval at the downward angle it formed. Gravity would do the rest. Travis cut a few short pieces of vine, tested them for strength and lashed them to the side of a box. Then he looped the vine over the rope and tied it to the other side of the box while Hal and Beya held it up off the ground. Once he was finished, they slowly lowered the box and let it rest on the rope.

Travis spoke into the Panther. "Okay, here comes the first box."

Alain nodded quietly and Travis let go his grip. The box began to slide, slowly at first, then with increasing velocity as it traversed the gorge. Just before it hit the pole on the far side, Dan yelled to the porters to release their grip. They let the pole fall and the box crashed into the soft earth just shy of them. They untied the box and lifted the pole back into place. Travis sent across the final two boxes in the same manner. Then it was Beya's turn.

"They won't let go of the pole this time," Travis told Beya.

"They will keep it upright and break your fall with their bodies. Okay?" The porter nodded that he understood, then allowed Travis to lash his wrists with the vine. One hand was on each side of the rope, the vine looped over the top. Beya tucked his knees up into his chest area, and then Travis and Hal let go. The body weight caused the rope to sag immediately, and the man's feet barely cleared the edge. A split second later, he was suspended over the abyss, his speed increasing as he slid along the angled rope. He cleared the far lip of the crevice with a couple of feet to spare, then crashed into the waiting glut of bodies near the far pole. The impact knocked a couple of men down, but the group held, and seconds later Beya was on his feet, waving.

"Nothing to it." Travis turned to Koko. "Your turn." He lashed the man's wrists and repeated the procedure with the same result. Hal was next. He was fairly light and the rope didn't sag as far, allowing the man the smoothest trip of the three. Then it was Samantha's turn.

"Tell me if the vines are too tight around your wrists," Travis said, as he knotted the short length to her left wrist, then threw it over the rope and started on her right.

"That's fine," she said as he finished. She was suspended in air, her body pressing against his as he tied the vines. After he finished he stood there for a moment, just holding her. "I'm ready if you are," she said.

"You don't have to do anything," he said softly to her, his face only inches below hers. "Just keep your knees tucked up against your chest and let the guys catch you at the other end. Okay?" She nodded and he stepped out from in front of her. Instantly, she was moving.

She felt the wind begin to pick up as her velocity increased. Her eyes watered slightly and the group of men at the far end became blurred. Her arm ached from having been dislocated only half an hour earlier. She moved faster and faster, the far edge coming up quickly now. For a moment she thought there was no way she would clear it, but would instead crash into the rock edge and plunge into the darkness. She pulled her knees up with all her strength and skimmed the edge, crashing feet first into the tightly bunched group of porters that awaited her. Bolts of pain shot down her injured arm and she screamed. Then all was quiet. Too quiet.

The jungle had taken on an eerie silence. A lonely cormorant cried in the distance, but even the ever-present swallowtails had suddenly vanished. Travis stood rigidly, listening for the sounds that he knew were coming but he didn't want to hear. A fern rustled; then the bushy top of a bamboo swayed, almost imperceptibly. The jungle seemed to part on command, and fifty faces covered with war paint suddenly stared out at him. He stared back for a moment, then reacted.

With a speed Samantha had never seen in a man's movements, Travis grabbed a length of vine from the ground and ran toward the edge of the gaping crevice. At the last possible second, he threw the line over the rope and grabbed it with his loose hand. His momentum shot him out over the empty void as darts from the pygmies' blowguns flew past him. His hands began to slip on the vine and he slid down, his sweat making the already slippery vine impossible to hold on to. His grip gave way just as his body cleared the far edge and he crashed into the rocks and dirt at full speed. He rolled with the impact and came out of the roll on his feet. He waved at the men to disperse, to get into the safety of the trees. At a full run, he slipped his machete from its sheath and spun sideways, his arm arcing out and severing the rope that linked the two sides of the chasm. Then he hit the tree line and dove into the brush. Once again, all was quiet.

A line of pygmies rimmed the far side of the gap, staring into the jungle but saying nothing. A minute later they tucked their blowguns into their loincloths and retreated back into the darkness of the rain forest. Then they were gone.

Travis raised his head above a bank of ferns and watched

the last of the war party disappear into the jungle. He looked down, checking for punctures from poisoned darts. Satisfied there were none, he turned his attention to the remainder of the expedition. Samantha was a few feet away, still hidden behind a capsized umbrella tree and nursing her damaged limb. Dan and Alain were both up and trying to get a head count on the porters. After a minute they had accounted for everyone, and began checking the equipment. With all that had happened in crossing the gorge, they had lost no men and only one box of ammunition. Dan reported this news back to Travis.

"I thought we'd lost you for sure," he finished. "You were losing your grip on that vine awfully quick."

"Yeah, there was a second there that I wasn't sure. I'm just lucky the little guys were such shitty shots. One nick from a dart and the fat lady's singing."

Samantha was standing off to the side and Travis walked over to her. She looked bruised but in good spirits. "Nice move on the vine there," she said, motioning back to the gorge. "Especially the heads-up on cutting it so they couldn't get across."

"Thanks," he said. "You okay?" She nodded. "Why don't you give me an azimuth so we can get moving? Let's try to make the first of your last two targets before dusk."

Samantha pulled out her compass and map. She lined up the compass and pointed to the solid wall of foliage. "Eighteen degrees off magnetic north," she said. "That's your route. I'll let you know when we're close so we can stop short of the actual location. That way you can recalibrate the GPS system to misdirect Mugumba and his men."

Travis checked his own compass and gave the instructions to Alain, who took four heavily laden porters with him and started hacking through the underbrush. He noted the time and distance, then worked out an ETA to the first target. Two hours. They should be there about an hour before the daylight faded. He put a call through to Billy Hackett before stowing the communications gear. He asked the pilot to stay on call in case they needed him to scout a location. Given the money they were paying, Hackett was most agreeable.

Mugumba's men were on the move. Travis knew his team's escape from the pygmy war party was only the tip of this iceberg. The closer they got to the vein, the tighter the noose was going to draw around their collective throats. He broke open a box and pulled out a Remington Vent Rib Ranger. He loaded the gun and slipped another twenty rounds into his vest pockets. He checked his Smith & Wesson revolver, and slid it back into his belt. The tighter the noose, the bigger the weapons. He watched Samantha from behind as they started into the jungle along the path Alain had carved out. And for the first time, he wondered. He wondered if he *could* keep her alive. He hoped so. By God, he hoped so.

THIRTEEN

One hour and forty minutes of tough slogging brought the expedition to a suitable campsite. The surrounding terrain was rugged, with the towering Ruwenzori immediately to the east and north, and a series of heavily foliated foothills west and south. In the midst of this, Hal led them to a group of waterfalls cascading down to the valley hundreds of feet below. Another handful of smaller falls littered the hilltops, and crystal-clear pools formed beneath the gentle roar of the falling water. They chose a medium-sized pool, with a substantial clearing next to it, for their tents. Samantha pitched hers, put the mosquito netting and poisoned rope in place, and cracked open a bottle of water.

She was absolutely exhausted. Crossing the gorge had terrified her and stimulated her adrenaline to record levels. The trek through the jungle had worn off the last of the adrenaline, and now she found lifting the bottle to her lips to be hard work. She slipped out of the camp and wandered back down the path two hundred yards to another waterfall they had passed. She veered off the path and pushed her way through to the water. It was beautiful.

The falls were no more than thirty feet in height and not overly wide. But the ledge the water spilled over was surrounded on both sides by lush green ferns. The falls curved, forming a small amphitheater around the glistening pool of gently rippling water that lay at her feet. She set her bottle of water on a nearby rock and slipped off her shirt.

She knew that someone would have followed her from the camp—they always watched to be sure nothing happened to their geologist. As she continued to undress, she hoped it was Travis. She pulled her sports bra over her head and dropped it by her shirt, then did the same with her pants. She paused for a moment, sweeping her hair back off her shoulders and curling it into a bun. She reached down and slid her panties off, testing the water with her toe. It was cold, but cold felt good. She walked carefully into the water up to her waist, then stretched her arms overhead and dove in.

The shock hit her immediately and she almost yelped in pain. The water against her sore arm was painful at first, then soothing as she acclimatized to the coolness. She swam slowly, her natural buoyancy keeping her afloat and reducing the pull of her arm on the damaged socket. It felt great—healing. She dove, only a few feet at first, then deeper. On her fifth trip underwater, she reached the bottom. She flipped over and looked skyward, thirty-five feet beneath the surface. Outlines of slow-moving black catfish punctuated the deep blue that merged water into sky. She breathed out slowly, watching as her expended air bubbles rose through the almost invisible water. She had dived many times before, both with and without compressed air, but this was perhaps the most relaxing experience of her life. She felt the carbon monoxide begin to build in her system, and her body told her it needed fresh air. She pushed off the bottom and glided to the surface.

Samantha broke the surface with hardly a ripple, breathing quietly and slowly. A duiker had arrived at the water hole while she rested on the bottom, and was satisfying his thirst, unaware of her presence. He was magnificent, the typical conical shape of his body made even more prominent by his muscular stature. A jet-black stripe ran from his crown to the tip of his tail, contrasting against his dark brown-red coat. The antelope finished drinking, stood silent a moment with his head erect, then bounded back into the bordering jungle. Sam swam to the edge, pulled herself from the water, dried off and slipped back into her clothes. She felt wonderful, and she let her thoughts drift ahead.

Tomorrow would be important. They would tackle at least one of the two remaining possible locations, perhaps both if time permitted. The trace elements Kerrigan's tests had produced were the key. She had tested each viable formation for them, but to date had come up completely dry. However that particular combination of minerals had come together, it had been one in a million, and very identifiable. If the readings on the spectrometer matched, she would know they had hit the formation. Providing she had time to run her tests, that was. Travis was concerned about Mugumba's men moving into the jungle, and rightly so. His force was five times the size of McNeil's, and equally well armed. She hoped Travis and his crew were worth what Kerrigan was paying them.

Sam tilted her head forward then flipped it back quickly, her long wet hair arcing through the air and smacking against her back. She stood up and stretched; her arm felt much better after the swim. But as she walked back to the camp, she couldn't shake the nagging doubt that no matter how good Travis was, he was up against insurmountable odds.

Travis kept to Samantha's left as he tailed her from the campsite, twenty yards off the path, twenty yards behind her. Hardly a twig moved as he glided through the damp ferns that covered the forest floor. He stopped as she branched off the main path and cut left into the underbrush on his side of the path. The angle at which she moved was still taking her away from him, so he resumed tailing her. He came to the edge of the jungle that surrounded the waterfall just as she set down her water and unbuttoned her shirt. It was obvious she was going in the water, and he knew he should avert his gaze as she undressed. He didn't. She slipped out of her sports bra, and he took a long slow breath. Her pants fell to the ground and he felt his breath coming quicker, shallower. Samantha Carlson was one very hot lady.

Her breasts were firm, round with perky nipples barely a tone darker than her skin. Her shoulders were broad and well toned, sloping gracefully down through her rib cage to her narrow waist. Her hips were slender, her buttocks tight and rounded. The kind of body *Playboy* paid top dollar to photograph. She slipped off her panties and waded slowly into the water. His breath was shallow as he watched. She dove into the clear waters of the tropical pool, and he felt his senses begin to return to normal. Jesus, what a woman. Her head broke the surface and he leaned back into the moss that covered the piece of jungle floor he rested on. If there is a God, he thought, let us both live through this and end up in bed together. He smiled and thanked his mom. She'd made him go to church when he was a kid. Maybe that counted for something here. Brownie points of sorts.

Colonel Nathan Mugumba waved his driver ahead onto the bridge and the convoy followed. They had reached the bridge in good time, less than nine hours, but the hardest part of the journey lay ahead. He checked the map. For five miles, the road would be passable as it cut north through the jungle, but what followed then was seven more miles through some of the toughest country in the Congo. He folded the map and told his driver to stop at the next spot that would afford them water and a clearing to pitch their tents. When they found a suitable bivouac, he set up communications and used the satellite to place a call to Patrick Kerrigan in New York. The line was surprisingly clear.

"We are two days from their latest known position," he informed Kerrigan. "I'm sure it will be their final base camp.

According to my inside man, they are down to only two possible locations."

"Excellent, Colonel Mugumba." Kerrigan sounded pleased. "The GPS is still working?"

"Yes, it's relaying their position every sixty seconds, as programmed. It hasn't missed a beat so far. We are in the perfect position. It will take Dr. Carlson at least two days to run her tests on the final locations, giving us ample time to move within striking distance. I'm sure that McNeil will set up a standard perimeter defense around his camp. We can breach it and cut his force to pieces inside an hour once the battle starts. I may lose one or two men, but that's the worst case."

"You impress me, Mugumba. Your ruthlessness is second to none. Please make sure the bodies are hacked up and the bones thrown about. I don't need some explorer finding them two years from now and people asking questions."

"I will take personal pleasure in cutting the bitch into very small pieces. You have my word on that, Mr. Kerrigan."

"And Mugumba." Kerrigan's voice was slightly threatening. "Find the fucking diamonds this time." The line went dead before Mugumba could answer.

"Oh yes, Mr. Kerrigan," Mugumba's soft voice was tinged with sarcasm as he dropped the satellite phone. "I'll find the diamonds, and I'll take many before I tell you where they are. But you'll never know, now, will you?"

Samantha strolled back into camp and scanned the personnel in the advancing twilight. Dan Nelson oiled a weapon, Alain Porter crouched over the communications console, and Troy Ramage rested in a hammock, his eyes closed. She smiled. Travis had followed her into the forest. She hoped he had enjoyed the show. She startled Alain Porter slightly as she came up behind him.

"Hi," she said, and he grinned as he returned the salutation. "What are you doing?"

"Resetting the GPS coordinates in your field computer. I

want to be sure you're exactly where you think you are when you power this thing up tomorrow. The last thing we need right now is to waste time. Travis has got Hackett ready to fly in a minute if you need him."

"Is he always this uptight?"

"Not usually. The only time he gets this anal is when we're heading into a firefight. He's pretty sure we're going up against Mugumba in the next day or two."

"What do you think?" she asked.

He eyed her for a moment before he answered, searching to see if she should be told the truth. "I think he's right. And I think a lot of people are going to die. Let's just hope it's them."

They both jerked around as they heard Travis calling for them. He was standing close to where Troy lounged on the hammock, and waved them over when they looked. They arrived at almost the same time as Dan, still clutching the freshly oiled Vector. Travis had them sit in a tight circle and he spoke in a low voice.

"Koko is Mugumba's guy," he said, opening with a zinger. "When I grabbed him in a bear hug on the bridge today, I felt something taped against his skin. I got a quick peek as you guys pulled him back up to safety. He has a tiny transmitter taped just under his armpit, left side. If the technology is recent enough, it might transmit voice in addition to location. They may have had ears in our camp the whole time."

"So they've got two sources for our location," Troy said. "The secondary transmitter in the GPS system and the one taped to Koko."

Travis nodded. "Now that we know, we can manipulate this to our advantage. The GPS is easy—we'll reverse the polarity. Koko is another story. We've got to get this guy to go where we want, when we want. And we don't even know where that is yet. How we work Koko to our advantage is strictly on the fly." The entire group nodded. "Timing is crucial on him. Anyone who sees the right opening is authorized to move him. Just keep in mind that wherever he goes, Mugumba will be close behind. There's always the possibility of using Koko to lead Mugumba into a trap. Remember the strong points of our perimeter defense."

"We're all set there, Travis," Troy said. "Standard perimeter is in place."

"I'm feeling adventurous today, guys," Travis countered. "Let's make a few changes to that." He leaned over and began detailing his ideas to his men.

Liam O'Donnell knew of only one person who would call him on his private line at three in the morning: Patrick Kerrigan. He was correct.

"Liam, Kerrigan. Things are moving. The first team will be in place within thirty-eight hours. We'll know whether they are successful five fours later, tops. Be ready."

"We'll be in the air inside one hour of your call if the first team misses," O'Donnell confirmed. Kerrigan hung up. O'Donnell checked the clock again and did the math. Team one would be ready to attack the target late afternoon the day after tomorrow. If they missed and his team had to react, they would be flying into Africa in the darkness. He frowned. Africa was inhospitable enough without adding darkness to the equation. He rose from bed and padded down to his modern kitchen. His estate home on the outskirts of Belfast was three hundred years old, but inside it was totally renovated. He put on some coffee and whipped up some scrambled eggs—he wouldn't be sleeping any more tonight.

He took his coffee back up to his en suite bath after finishing the eggs, and had a quick shower. The cool needles that drove out of the showerhead and into his hardened body felt good. He stepped from the shower and looked at himself in the mirror. Thirty-six years old and in peak physical condition. At six feet, he was tall for an Irishman. His thick shoulder-length hair had a reddish tinge and his eyes were a bitter blue. He spoke English with remnants of an accent when he was sober, but with a thick Irish brogue when the Guinness was flowing. Three other languages spilled from his tongue, all fluently and without accent. His knowledge of Russian had saved his skin on numerous occasions, while French and Spanish were convenient. But it was weapons training at which he excelled.

Liam O'Donnell knew weapons. It didn't matter if it had a trigger or a blade, he could inflict injury or death on his opponent with it. A simple length of chain became lethal, a sharpened object as simple as a pencil was all it took to snuff out a human life. He had been formally trained by the Special Air Services and had spent twelve years in the employ of the British government. The SAS molded and shaped him as a lethal weapon and for six years he was on the first team, Special Ops. He loved the fieldwork and excelled at covert operations. Then politics intervened and he began spending more time working with MI5 and MI6. He spent his days gathering information for his former teammates to act on. New Scotland Yard welcomed him because of his hate for the IRA. They felt safe that this Irishman, Catholic or not, would favor them over the militant arm of the Irish desire for independence. That his allegiance would be without resolve. How wrong they had been.

Liam O'Donnell served Liam O'Donnell first and foremost—everything else fell a distant second. Money and power motivated him, not pride in or allegiance to his country. He couldn't have cared less. His position inside MI6 had proven advantageous on numerous occasions, giving him the code names and locations of undercover British agents working abroad. Agents who had often been compromised and found dead under suspicious circumstances. Treason paid well.

But the finger began to point in his direction after a few years, and O'Donnell felt it best to leave Her Majesty's service before someone put a bullet in the back of his head. He resigned and lived the life of a country gentleman, wealthy but low-key. He liked the comforts, but missed the danger.

When the opportunity to embark on a freelance career had arisen three years ago, he had welcomed the opportunity and had thrown himself into his newfound line of work with a vengeance. The correct people had died, and his employers had always been happy with his work. His reputation as a man who got results, at whatever the cost, coursed through the clandestine community, and he became in high demand. It was through this pipeline that Garret Shaw had found him and introduced him to Patrick Kerrigan.

O'Donnell sipped on his lukewarm coffee and stared into his own eyes in the mirror. Somehow, he felt that this time was not going to be a trial run with Kerrigan. He didn't just feel—he knew—that there would be confrontation; that there would be death. He continued to stare into his intense blue eyes, pitying the enemy that saw what he now saw. Because it would be the last thing they would ever see.

Patrick Kerrigan called his travel agent and booked a midday flight to London. Rather than head back home to the suburbs, he picked up a few items at a nearby department store and headed for the airport. The shit was going to hit the fan, and he wanted to be a lot closer to the action than across the Atlantic. He was positive Mugumba's troops would clean up McNeil's tiny force of mercenaries, though he felt the colonel's estimate of one or two dead was a bit low. But in all honesty, he didn't give a shit. Let them completely wipe each other out.

He thought about the teams he had sent to find the elusive Ruwenzori formation. They had been world class, each one of them. And each one, with the exception of the one that now stood on the threshold of discovery, had found the diamonds. And they had died. It was a pity he wouldn't be on hand to see Samantha Carlson die in the steaming jungles of the Congo. He would have enjoyed that.

He arrived at JFK and breezed through customs, smiling at the ticket agents as he boarded the flight. Just another polite American businessman on his way to the U.K.

FOURTEEN

Samantha glanced at the printouts for the third time, then looked up to Travis and shook her head. The laser ablation had come up empty again. The trace elements she needed to confirm that they were sitting on the vein were missing. She sighed and began packing up the gear. She had chosen the most promising of the final two locations and had drawn a blank. The likelihood of the final target being the one was considerably less than this one, and that bothered her. They were running out of time. They had left base camp at dawn and hiked for almost two hours to reach the spot. It had taken her the better part of three hours to secure suitable rocks and run the tests. All for nothing. And Mugumba's men were moving inexorably toward them.

She finished stowing her gear and consulted her topographical map. The direct route to the final location would take them over some extreme terrain, but the indirect route would add hours to the trek. She gave Travis an azimuth and they began to move through the jungle. He altered their course slightly to follow a ridge that ran parallel to their desired route. A small stream trickled along the bottom of the incline and he led the team through the shallow water rather than the thick underbrush. They made much better time not having to hack through the foliage, and just before two o'clock they were closing in on the final location. He signaled for the three porters hauling Sam's geological gear to rest for a minute, and he sat on a felled tree and motioned for her to join him.

"How close are we?"

She studied the lay of the land intently before answering. To their immediate right was a towering ridge, covered with thick vines and totally impassable. It was incredible that anything could grow on such a steep incline, but somehow the thorny lianas and creeping vines managed a foothold. About a hundred feet along the crest of the six-hundred-foot-high ridge was a substantial outcrop, reaching an additional two hundred feet into the air. She placed her finger on the map exactly where the outcrop occurred, then cross-referenced the data from Billy Hackett's helicopter. She pointed upstream and right to the ridge.

"Two hundred fifty to three hundred feet farther," she said. "It's going to form part of this ridge we've been following."

"Excellent," he said, checking his watch. "We should have time for you to set up—"

A scream from behind them, deep in the bush, stopped him in mid-sentence. With a reflexive motion, a gun appeared in his hand. He held his other hand up to silence the porters. The scream came again, this time the location more identifiable. McNeil counted the porters and silently indicated to Sam that one was missing. He held up his fist, a sign for them to stay put, and moved stealthily into the underbrush. All was quiet for a minute; then he reappeared with a shaking porter in tow. He motioned for Sam to follow him.

"I don't think you're going to like this," he said, walking back along the same route he had used moments before. They broke into a small clearing, less than twenty feet square, and Sam gasped, horrified. Before her lay a massacre. Skulls littered the clearing—at least fifteen, perhaps more. Bones, gnawed on by jungle carnivores and partially covered with lichens, were interspersed with the hollow skulls. McNeil knelt down and picked up a skull, then another, and another. He looked back at Sam and stuck his finger through a round hole in one of the skulls. A bullet hole.

"They were executed," he said. "Each one shot once in the head." He searched the carnage for a while longer as Sam tried to grasp what she was seeing. He gingerly held up a long bone with a loop of nylon rope hanging off it. "Their hands were tied. They didn't stand a chance."

"Who would do such a thing?" she said, sickened.

"I think this would answer that question," he replied, digging a piece of metal from a nearby tree. He held it out for her to inspect. It meant nothing to her. "It's a bullet. From a Bofors Carl-Gustaf CGA5."

She shuddered and went wide-eyed. "That's the make of gun Dan saw in the back of Mugumba's tarped-over truck."

He kicked at something with the toe of his boot, then bent down and retrieved the object from the moss. He held it out to her. "Do you know what this is?"

"Yes, of course. It's a geological hammer. Standard gear for a field geologist. We all carry them." She stopped and stared at him. "It's them, isn't it?"

He nodded. "It's the expedition that went in a couple of months ago. The bones are reasonably fresh."

"Mugumba killed them," she said slowly, and he nodded slightly. "He must have thought they found the diamonds or he wouldn't have killed them. In fact, they *did* find the diamonds."

"How do you figure that?" he asked, grasping her by the elbow and gently leading her from the clearing.

"If they had rough, uncut diamonds with them when he intercepted them, he would have known they found the vein. But if they suspected Mugumba was going to kill them, they would have held back the location. Mugumba thought he could locate the vein, it was so close, so he slaughtered them. Then he looked but couldn't find it. He reported his failure back to New York, and Kerrigan hired us to finish the job. Kerrigan and Mugumba knew all along the formation was close to here, and that's why Mugumba's men didn't leave Butembo until we started moving our team into this area. He's waiting for us to find it, and then . . ." She let the sentence trail off.

"I wish you were wrong," he said, as they rejoined the team of porters. "But you're not. How quickly can you find this thing?"

"Let's move up to where the last formation is. I'll be able to tell you better once I'm set up and running the laser ablation." He agreed and the small team began to move. Twenty minutes later Sam was collecting rocks from the base of the formation. She chiseled the most promising stones, keying in on variations in color and texture that would give her the trace elements she so desperately needed. She took twenty-three pieces from the formation and then began testing. Half an hour later, she reported the results to McNeil.

"We've got it!" she said. Her voice was excited, but tinged with some reservation. He picked up on the hesitation in her voice.

"You don't sound totally convinced."

"I'm not. And that's the strange thing. What I'm looking for is there, but in the wrong quantities. I'm lacking two elements almost completely, exactly on with six, and in excess with the last three. It doesn't make sense."

"What about diamonds? Keep it simple, you know. Just find the diamonds and to heck with all this trace element stuff."

She shook her head. "It's not that simple. Diamonds don't look like much before they're cut and polished. They blend in with the surrounding rocks, and most times are found buried deep inside the formation. You need to be sure you're looking in exactly the right spot before you start ripping the rock apart."

"It's not always like that," he retaliated. "You said so yourself." She looked at him inquisitively and he continued. "Two weeks ago, you talked about diamonds you sometimes find sitting on the surface. There's a special name for them."

"Alluvial diamonds. And that was in Sierra Leone, not the Congo. The northeastern region of the Congo has never yielded one alluvial diamond. Not one, Travis." She stopped for a second, then grabbed his arm, staring straight into his eyes. "And yet, we know the other expeditions found diamonds close to where we're standing." She looked up from his eyes to the huge ridge next to them, following the cliff to its peak. "Unless . . ." She stared at the top of the ridge.

"Unless what?"

"Unless we're on the wrong side of the ridge," she said quietly. "That's why there has never been a diamond found in any stream or river anywhere in the northern regions of the Congo. The Ruwenzori Mountains, including this ridge, control which way the water flows. The water in this stream," she pointed to the rivulet they had trudged through earlier in the afternoon, "empties into the Congo River basin and drains into the Atlantic. On the other side of the ridge, the water flows into the Shilango, a small coastal river that's part of the Nile River basin. No wonder no one ever found it."

He looked at the towering cliff with trepidation. "How the hell do you propose we get over this thing?"

"I don't think we have to," Sam said. "The other team found the diamonds, and they weren't geared to climb something like this. I think there's another way—a way through the wall."

"A tunnel," he said.

"Exactly. We just have to find it," Sam said, checking her watch. "We've got about two hours until darkness. I suggest we start looking immediately."

He nodded and began organizing the porters. Samantha divided the rock wall into five seventy-foot lengths, one for each of them. From the ground to twenty feet up the wall, they were to poke and prod through the dense vines and lianas for an opening, no matter how small. It took only twenty minutes before one of the porters began to chatter excitedly in his native Bantu tongue. Travis and Samantha arrived at the same time and the man backed off to let them see his find. Travis pulled aside the heavy curtain of vines, then looked at the porter, perplexed. The man waved his arms excitedly, motioning for him to push farther into the damp growth. Travis turned and wormed his way a few feet upward and inward. All that was left showing was his hiking boots when Samantha heard him say, "Holy shit" softly under his breath. A moment later he extracted himself from the tangled mess and shook his head.

"If I'd been looking here, I would never have found that," he said. "There's a round opening about six feet in diameter that burrows right into the rock face. It's pretty smooth inside, like an ancient river carved it. Hand me up a heavy-duty flashlight and I'll have a look inside."

Samantha checked the battery strength on the largest light they had and handed it up to him. "Watch out for snakes and tarantulas," she said encouragingly as he started into the tunnel.

The walls were reasonably smooth and covered with slimy green lichen. An occasional sharp rock protruded from the ceiling, but Travis could walk upright as long as he crouched a few inches. Anyone a few inches shorter than six feet wouldn't need to duck. He made good progress, encountering nothing living that threatened him, just a few harmless spiders and worms. The footing was tricky, slippery rocks with very little growth on them. He estimated he had traveled slightly over a hundred and fifty feet when the flashlight beam illuminated a wall of vines ahead. He pushed his way through the tangle and into the filtered sunlight. What he saw was unbelievable.

He was inside a huge crack in the mountain. The base of the crack at the mouth of the tunnel was only fifteen feet across. But the walls that rose above him on all sides were hundreds of feet high. Little sunlight filtered down into the crevice, and not much grew on the rocky walls. But the top of the crevice was engulfed by the rain-forest canopy, making the fissure in the rock impossible to see from above. He stared for a couple of minutes, marveling at the freak of nature. He reentered the tunnel and went back for Sam. She was waiting, along with a thousand questions.

"Did you get through okay? What's on the other side?"

He held up his hand. "Whoa, take it easy. It's no problem. Let's grab your gear and get you through to the other side. You can decide whether we've found the diamonds." He grinned at her. "You're the geologist."

Travis got on the radio to Alain at base camp while the porters readied the gear. Travis advised him to reverse the polarity on the GPS system, then move camp by a few hundred yards. That would send Mugumba's troops in the wrong direction, for a while at least. Travis told Alain to have Dan set charges around the area the soldiers would be approaching, and to have the camp on highest alert; Mugumba was coming. They should strip Koko of his transmitter and leave it pinned to a tree near the GPS. That would give Mugumba the confirmation of their location. Or rather, their trap. And then he told his team about the discovery of the previous expedition's bones, just to ensure they realized Mugumba was serious. He cut off the transmission and joined Sam at the mouth of the tunnel. He motioned for the porters to scatter into the bush and wait until they returned; then he and Sam entered the dank confines of the underground passage.

Travis led the way, carrying the heaviest of Sam's prospecting gear. He checked back on occasion, but she was having no trouble keeping up with him. They reached the far end of the tunnel and he pushed through the vines, then set the gear down gently on the other side. He jumped out and grabbed her hand as she came through the tangle that hid the opening. He watched her as she took in the spectacle.

"Oh, my God," she whispered. "This is unreal."

The rock face towering hundreds of feet above her was streaked with varying hues of yellow and blue. Muted shades, barely visible in the dim light that struggled to reach the depths of the chasm, mutated and slowly changed color as she moved along the bottom of the cliff. She stared upward at the spectacle, her feet unsteady on the loose rock that littered the ground. She slipped once, almost falling before Travis caught her, but her gaze never left the smooth rock face. Finally, she turned to him, her eyes more alive than he had ever seen.

"Unbelievable," was all she said.

"Do you need your equipment set up?"

"No," she said quickly. "No, that's not necessary." She took a lingering look at the surrounding walls and continued. "I don't need to run the tests. This is it. We're standing in the center of a kimberlitic pipe. This is the diamondiferous formation we've been searching for."

"You can tell that by just looking?"

"Oh, yes. This is a geologist's dream, the mother lode you search for your entire life and never find. Geology at its simplest, yet its grandest. Mother Nature giving us a glimpse of how she can transform coal into diamonds." She moved to the far end of the aperture, about forty feet from the hole in the wall where they had entered, and pointed up. "See where the rock juts out on one side; there's an indent on the opposite side. This is a giant crack in the mountain. And that crack split a massive kimberlite pipe right in half. We are standing inside a rock formation that is millions of years old, once under intense heat and pressure. Enough pressure to squeeze chunks of coal into diamonds." She scanned the wall in front of her intently, then pulled her hammer from her belt and chipped away at the rock. A few moments later, she held a greenish tinged rock up for him to see.

"This is a raw, uncut diamond," she said. "Probably ten carats, give or take. It would be a rare find in a fully operational diamond mining operation, yet commonplace in these walls. I could dig out a million dollars in stones in twenty minutes. Ten million in less than two hours."

Samantha handed the stone to him, knelt down and began sifting through the rabble that covered the ground. A minute later she held up a small rock, another diamond.

"This explains why there were never any alluvial stones found in the riverbeds on either side of the Ruwenzori," she said. He looked confused and she elaborated. "As the diamonds eroded from the rock, very slowly because they were so well protected from wind and water, they fell to the ground and stayed exactly where they fell. There were no water currents to wash them downstream, no pools for them to sink into, no chance they would be discovered by a native washing her clothes. Unless you found the tunnel we used to get in here, you would never know this place existed." She stopped and stooped down, pushing aside a tiny fern and lifting a small object from amidst the loose rocks. It was a time-worn, rusted geologist's hammer. She rubbed the metal head and squinted at the engraving on the side.

"It's hard to read, but I think it says DSC," she said, handing it to him. He studied it for a minute, then nodded.

"It has more engraving on the other side," he said, wiping the rust and moisture off. "AIPG—1994. What does that mean?"

"The AIPG is the American Institute of Professional Geologists," she answered. "Whoever dropped this hammer was a professional geologist, and an American. I guess they got the hammer in 1994. Who knows?" She shrugged.

They both froze where they stood at a sudden distant sound—the rapid staccato of automatic gunfire. Travis motioned to her not to move, slipped his revolver from his belt and pushed through the vines into the tunnel. He removed the safety and kept the gun pointed ahead as he moved through the darkness. He reached the curtain of vines that covered the tunnel entrance and carefully pushed a few strands aside until he could see out. What he could see was not good.

Three of Mugumba's soldiers stood over one of the porters who had accompanied them through the jungle. The man lay on his side on the jungle floor, alive, but bleeding badly from a gash on his head. Beside him, a few feet away, lay two bodies contorted in death—the other two porters. McNeil watched in horror as one of the soldiers yelled at the still-alive man and continuously beat his head with a rifle butt. The language was indistinguishable, but the meaning was not. The soldiers wanted to know where Mc-Neil and Samantha were. McNeil's mind raced as he tried to sort out what to do.

His line of vision was severely restricted by the size of the opening and the shrouding vines. There could be more soldiers nearby, and he wouldn't know what he was up against until he left the safety of the tunnel. Taking on three highly trained soldiers armed with automatic weapons while he was armed with only a revolver was risky, perhaps even stupid. If he was lucky enough to kill all three but more soldiers were nearby, he would be gunned down and Samantha's position compromised. He took a couple of deep breaths as he pondered the best course of action. A few moments later, the decision was made for him. The soldier smashing the porter's head suddenly turned the gun around, pointed it at the man's temple and pulled the trigger. His body jerked for a moment, then fell sideways to the ground, lifeless.

McNeil gripped his revolver tightly, his temples pounding with pressure as his blood coursed through his body. He knew the moment to act and save the man's life had passed, and only his professional training kept him from bursting out of the tunnel, gun blazing. He felt the pressure in his head subside as he remained motionless, watching the aftermath of the execution. He wanted desperately to avenge the three deaths, but instead waited and listened. A few minutes later, from the left of the tunnel opening, two more soldiers sauntered into his line of sight. He took a long deep breath, knowing that his decision to remain hidden had been the right one. Had he taken on the three soldiers he could see, he would have been cut down by the two he couldn't. It was a small consolation.

The soldiers eventually dragged the bodies a few yards into the jungle. Dusk was approaching, and they lit a fire and began preparing dinner. He backed away from the tunnel entrance, now reasonably sure that at least five of Mugumba's men were on the other side of the vines. He retraced his steps and found Samantha sitting on a narrow ledge, her back to the rock wall. She started as he appeared from the quickly darkening hole.

"What's going on?" she asked apprehensively.

"Five of Mugumba's soldiers are outside the entrance to the tunnel," he said. She didn't ask, and he finally volunteered the bad news. "They killed the porters."

Samantha's face went red with anger; she clenched her teeth and took a few deep breaths. "What do we do now?"

"We've got a couple of options. We can call in to the expedition and have them come to us. I think that's extremely dangerous. It'll just lead the remainder of Mugumba's force to our location."

"He must have known the location, Travis," Samantha countered. "How else do his men suddenly show up here? And a lot quicker than you expected. You said they would need at least two days, maybe three, to get this far north of the bridge."

"You're right. The only explanation is that Mugumba has at least one helicopter at his disposal, perhaps more. The five guys camped out there must have been dropped fairly close by and then they hoofed it in from the drop zone. Shit. I suspected he'd have a chopper, but I was hoping not."

"It also means that Mugumba knows almost exactly where this place is. To within a few hundred yards. He just can't find the tunnel." Sam was quiet for a moment. "You said we had a couple of options. What's the other one?"

"Simple. I sneak out of here in the middle of the night and kill the five guys while they sleep."

Samantha stared at him. "Get a grip, Travis. You may be good at what you do, but nobody is that good."

"It's our only other option, Sam," he said. "I'm not all that happy with it, but unless you can think of some other plan, it's the one we'll have to use."

"We can wait it out. The rest of the expedition will come looking for us."

"That would be *really* stupid," he said, his voice matter-of-fact. "If they survive Mugumba's men moving up from the south, they'd run into these guys. And we can't warn them."

"Why not? We've got one of the Panther units with us. Alain said they were untraceable."

"Absolutely untraceable. But any energy surge is going to be detected. They won't be able to pinpoint where we are, but they'll know for sure we're here. Right now, they must suspect we're close by, but firing up one of these things would just confirm their suspicions. It's not a good idea."

They sat in silence for a few minutes, watching as the dusk turned into night and any residual light filtering from above disappeared. They sat in absolute darkness, only feet apart but completely invisible to each other. She knew he was right. Their only chance was for him to sneak out and try to eliminate the five while they slept. She also knew that the chances were good that Travis would die trying. And that she did not want. Finally, she reached out her hand in the blackness and grasped his.

"Do what you have to, Travis," she said quietly. "But for God's sake, please come back." She felt pressure on her fingers as he lightly squeezed. Then he was gone. She wiped away a tear that formed in the corner of her eye and briefly wondered why she'd chosen such a bizarre career. Most women, and men for that matter, lived normal lives. They had houses in the suburbs, jobs in the city, and kids in Little League. But not her. She had taken an interesting vocation and turned it into a daily struggle to survive. Crocodiles, snakes, bottomless gorges, angry pygmies, and now corrupt government soldiers. Christ, what a month. She rested her head against the billion-dollar rock wall and, surprisingly, slept.

Travis reached the tunnel opening and peered through.

His eyes acclimatized to the absolute blackness, and the pale moon that shone above the rain-forest canopy lit up the jungle floor. The soldiers' fire was reduced to a smoldering heap of embers, and he kept his eyes from looking at the red glow and thus reducing his night vision. He slowly parted the vines and slipped from the opening to the root-covered ground at the base of the cliff. He crouched, heading away from the lightly glowing fire and into the jungle. He counted three bodies scattered around the fire, leaving two on sentry duty, somewhere nearby in the underbrush. He desperately hoped they were dozing.

He surveyed the layout, trying to think of where he would station his men. The west side was completely dominated by the mountainside. All other directions were covered by dense jungle. The only passable route into the location was from the south. And Mugumba must know that McNeil's team was camped to the south. Therefore, one man positioned south. He thought of where they had discovered the previous expedition's bodies, and made a guess that the second sentry would be west, covering that area in case he and Sam were to suddenly appear. He moved south, not a twig or a leaf moving in his wake. Twenty yards distant, he saw the first man, awake, but barely. His head kept nodding down, then jerking back up as he forced himself to stay conscious. Travis waited.

Half an hour later, the head stopped jerking back and the man's chin rested on his chest. Travis began to move, quietly but quickly. He covered the distance in less than a minute, his knife in his right hand. He came up behind the soldier, slipped his hand over the man's mouth and drove the knife into the back of his neck, severing the spinal cord. The body instantly went limp. He lowered the body to the forest floor and pulled his knife out. He cleaned the blade on a leaf and then moved back to the north and a bit west. The second man was much more difficult to find. He had fallen asleep and was prone on the ground. Travis almost stepped on his leg before he saw him. The tiny rustles Travis made did not wake the soldier. He took him out in the same fashion as the first sentry, then headed back toward the fire.

He neared the grouping of men, then froze. Only two of the three men remained bedded down and asleep. One of the soldiers was up and on the move. Travis felt the hairs on the nape of his neck rise and his senses go into overdrive. Every sound, every fluttering of a leaf could mark the presence of the missing soldier, and possibly a violent death. He crouched low, pondering whether to take out the two sleeping men or quietly scour the area for the third man. After a few minutes, he decided to do neither. The position he held, close to the waning fire, allowed him to keep the remaining two soldiers in sight, and he felt after this much time that his location had not been compromised by the missing man. Waiting and watching seemed the best course of action. He didn't have long to wait.

Five minutes later, the man reappeared. He showed no signs of alarm and Travis knew the two corpses had not been discovered. The soldier had probably needed to relieve himself. Travis settled back and waited to see what the man would do. His target poked a stick into the fire, stirring up the embers and effectively ruining his night vision. He kept his gaze averted until the gently licking flames had subsided and the area was once again dark. Then he moved.

His pupils remained tiny, affording him excellent vision even in the low light level of the forest. He moved silently to his left, circling the man until he faced the man's back. He crept forward, his knife comfortable in his grasp. He reached the soldier without alerting him, clamped his hand over the open mouth and cut left to right across the windpipe. A low gurgling sound emitted from the slit trachea and the dead man's feet made slight scuffling noises as he kicked out involuntarily. Then quiet again returned to the small clearing. He lowered the body to the ground and turned to the remaining two soldiers. And froze.

One of the men had awakened and was staring at him, stunned for a moment. Travis acted without hesitation, drawing his revolver from his belt and pumping two bullets into the man's face. He swiveled and rolled to his right at the same time. A loud explosion went off and a bullet cut through the air where he had stood milliseconds before, missing him by inches. He came out of the roll with his finger squeezing the trigger. The first shot missed the last man and for a second it appeared his adversary might get off a killing shot. But Travis's reaction time was a split second faster, and he managed to squeeze off a second round before his prey. This bullet did not miss. It hit the soldier in the neck, crushing his larynx and ripping through his spinal cord. The man went limp and crumpled.

Travis swore lightly at the noise. He had wanted to take out the men without resorting to gunfire, but that hadn't happened. He reloaded his revolver, checked to ensure the three were dead, and then returned to the tunnel and to Samantha. It was still pitch black, and he spoke to her as he exited the tunnel mouth, so she would know it was him and not one of Mugumba's men. She answered, relief evident in her voice.

"I don't know if more of Mugumba's troops are within earshot. I kind of doubt it," he said as they sat beside each other in the blackness. "The only way those five guys arrived so quickly was by helicopter. The rest are probably slogging through the rain forest toward what they think is our camp. We should be okay. I was being overly cautious more than anything else, trying to keep the noise down."

"I'm dead tired," she said, yawning. The tension had evaporated over the time they talked, and she suddenly felt unable to stay awake. "Can we get some sleep?"

"Sure." He smoothed out a few vines and palm fronds and then guided her to the makeshift bed. She lay down and was asleep within seconds. He listened to the rhythmic cadence of her breathing, enjoying the soft sound. He reached out and tenderly stroked her hair. Then he sat back and made himself a vow. He would keep this woman alive, no matter how tough things got. He would die to keep her alive. That surprised him. He had never thought that way of any other person. Ever.

FIFTEEN

"African ice."

McNeil rose to one elbow and tried to focus. It was daytime, barely. Streaks of sunlight fought their way through the tangled canopy hundreds of feet above them, but the foot of the crevice was still shrouded in darkness. He squinted, bringing the figure in front of him to a clearer image. It was Samantha, and she held something in her hand.

"What?" he asked, his mouth thick and dry. "What did you say?"

"African ice. African diamonds." Samantha extended her hand. Numerous greenish rocks sat in her palm. "The stuff we came for. I've just dug out a few more specimens. Big specimens. This is quite the find, Travis."

He shook his head a couple of times to clear the cobwebs, then accepted the bottled water Samantha held out to him. He drank deeply, the liquid replenishing his body and bringing reality back to him. He watched the woman standing in front of him and found himself wanting her. Badly. Her lips were moving and he concentrated, trying to decipher the words as they came at him.

". . . that old saying about diamonds being a girl's best friend is bullshit. Diamonds are a guerilla's best friend. Violence and death are often the companions of these stones, hardly the rich and glamorous lives De Beers portrays in their commercials. People are tortured and murdered, lives destroyed, children orphaned, all so rich women in America or Europe can look good in evening wear." Samantha's eyes burned as she spoke, her voice rife with emotion.

"The African people don't benefit from the diamonds. At least, not the ones I've met. They still live in abject poverty while some corrupt government asshole steals the country blind. The guerillas that roam about, terrorizing innocent villagers, are financed almost exclusively with diamond money. Christ, I hate precious stones. I honest to God hate them, Travis.

"African ice." She mouthed the words once more, this time with contempt, then dropped the handful of wealth into a small suede bag and slipped it in her pocket.

Travis watched her tuck the diamonds away. "If you hate them so much, why are you taking them?"

"They're worth a lot of money—and I'm a realist. We may need them."

"I see. What time is it?" he asked.

"Just after ten," Sam replied. "You've been sleeping like a baby."

"Well, this baby just got up," he said. "Let's get our stuff together and get back to the base camp."

They packed only the necessary gear and traversed the tunnel. He scanned the immediate area around the vine-covered entrance to the hole in the wall. Once he was sure no more of Mugumba's men were present, he jumped out and helped Samantha down. They set an azimuth on their compasses and headed out, after quickly checking in with the camp on the mobile Panther unit. The passage through the jungle was difficult and Travis finally let Sam take the lead after two hours of hacking a path with the machete. He was surprised when Sam lasted over an hour before asking him to spell her off. Most women, or men for that matter, wouldn't have had the strength or endurance to last an hour. They continued on, calling in to the camp more frequently as they got closer, until he clipped the mouthpiece back on his front pocket and pointed to a ridge of trees two hundred yards to the southwest.

"Troy and the boys are set up over there," he said. "Let me lead from here, and watch where you step. Try to follow exactly in my footsteps. The guys will have every access to the camp, except one, booby-trapped."

Samantha nodded that she understood and kept tight behind him as he moved. He kept his strides short, making it easy for her to mimic his steps. He stopped about a hundred fifty yards from the camp and pointed to the left side of the path they were following. She stared at the ground for a few seconds before she saw it—a trip wire extending across the path. He lifted his boots over the wire, then held out his hand to steady her as she crossed it. They passed one more trip wire before they hit the camp perimeter. Samantha was sweating profusely as she doffed her pack, and she knew it wasn't just from the heat. Moving through booby-trapped jungle was something she had never experienced before.

He surveyed the new base camp. Troy had chosen the position carefully, and as Travis looked about, he was pleased with the choice. A small clearing, less than twenty by thirty feet, held the communications console, stacked armaments boxes and tents. One side of the clear-cut hugged an almost vertical wall covered in dense foliage, impossible for an opponent to attack from above or rappel down. The opposite side from where they had entered bordered a small river, eighty feet in width. This formed exposed ground, making the enemy easy targets once on the water. The river split just after the clearing, with a small tributary snaking along the third side. It was less than twenty feet across, but still provided the defenders with a clear shot at anyone trying to cross. The fourth and final access to the camp was from the north, the route they had used. It was booby-trapped, not only on the path but also in numerous places in the jungle. Also, any attackers coming from the south would have to circle the camp first in order to reach the northern side, giving the defenders both advance notice and an additional chance to take them out as they moved past.

"Well done, Troy," McNeil said, patting the man on the shoulder. "Let's you and I have a quick look at the dummy camp." He referred to the mock encampment that held the GPS gear and Koko's transmitter. Ramage led the way, heading west across the wide part of the river. There was little current and the water was only waist deep, making the crossing quite easy. They hit an obscure path on the far side, moving hastily through the ferns and lianas. Six minutes from the real camp, they arrived at what appeared to be a fully functional jungle encampment. Radio and GPS equipment sat on a portable table, wedged between two tents. Evidence of a recent fire, complete with a spit for roasting meat, sat in the center of the clearing. A few articles of clothing hung on branches. McNeil nodded to Ramage.

"Excellent," he said. "You've given them two good sides to attack from. Once they storm the camp from those two sides, we'll counter-attack from here, then fall back to the river. We should get at least half the force, assuming the platoon is intact and there are still seventeen of them."

"Seventeen?" Ramage asked, the numbers not making sense.

"Five of them must have been dropped off by chopper near the mine site. They interrupted us, and killed the porters. The soldiers are dead."

Ramage may have been impressed, but he didn't show it. "Taking out five bad guys is good, but them having a chopper is bad news. You can bet they'll bring it in once they walk into our trap."

"Guaranteed. The trip back to the real camp will be dicey. They'll be right behind us and overhead as well. Let's hope the chopper's not equipped with heat-sensing equipment, or we're in trouble." If Mugumba's helicopter could see through the rain-forest canopy by picking up the heat from their bodies, they could follow them to the real camp, all the while firing heavy-caliber bullets at them. Whether they would be successful in surviving Mugumba's attack came down to one thing—their ability to disappear into the jungle and not be detected from above.

"What should we do with the porters?" Ramage asked as they humped back.

"Get them out of here. They're target practice for Mugumba's men. No way do we stick rifles in their hands and tell them to hold off crack government troops. They're gone as soon as we get back. We'll send them north, away from Mugumba's little army." The river came into sight as he finished speaking and they called over to Dan and Alain, letting the men know they would be coming out of the bush in a few seconds.

Back in camp, they immediately told the porters to pack and leave. McNeil paid the men, including the pay for the three porters who had died at the mine site and a healthy bonus. The only native who remained was Koko, and he was securely tied to a tree. A bandana, which could quickly become a gag, hung around his neck.

Samantha pulled Hal aside as the porters prepared to leave. She gave him a hug, refusing to hear his pleas to stay. "No one questions Travis on this, Hal," she said softly. "Just go home and enjoy the money you made. You did your job, and you did it well. I'll be in touch with you later." He acquiesced and, after bundling up his belongings, trudged off into the jungle.

Travis set out the game plan and the men requisitioned the necessary gear from neatly stacked boxes. They went over the plan again, then split up. Travis and Alain Porter moved across the river and took up positions bordering the dummy camp. Dan Nelson also crossed the river, but he stayed back, closer to the real camp. Troy Ramage remained at base camp with Samantha, with a stern warning from Mc-

Neil that nothing was to happen to her. McNeil expected Mugumba to arrive early the next morning.

He wasn't disappointed.

Just after dawn, slight rustlings disturbed the growth on the far side of the camp. McNeil clicked twice on the Panther and received the same number back. He slipped the safety off his Vektor CR21 Assault rifle and readied additional clips. A few moments later, all hell broke loose.

Seven of Mugumba's men burst from the jungle into the small clearing, spraying the tents with automatic fire, then diving to the ground. Additional muzzle flashes a few yards into the dense foliage lit up a semicircle in the jungle, exactly where the ex-SEALs were watching. Both McNeil and Porter targeted the muzzle flashes and opened fire. Their pinpoint accuracy silenced four of the hidden assailants; then they turned their lethal fire onto the exposed soldiers. Only a few seconds had elapsed since Mugumba's men entered the clearing, and they had no time to retreat into the relative safety of the surrounding jungle. One by one their bodies shuddered from the impact of the 5.56mm cartridges as death rained down on them. Three men lay unmoving in the clearing and a fourth crawled slowly into the nearby brush, his wounds fatal.

Travis stopped firing and spoke quickly into the Panther. "Back off, Alain. Now! Dan, we're coming back down the path." He let the mobile unit drop to his side, shouldered the CR21 and slipped a clip into the MINI SS machine gun. He leveled it and backed out of his position, watching for any sign of troop movement in or near the camp. It remained quiet. In his peripheral vision he saw Alain moving in his direction, crouching as he backpedaled through the brush. They joined up and began moving down the path. Seconds later, a withering crossfire erupted from either side, chewing into the trees and ferns that hid them. Lightning reflexes saved both men as they immediately hit the ground and rolled into the thick ground cover.

Bullets screamed inches above their heads as Travis and Alain stared at each other from opposing sides of the path. They were totally pinned down. Travis managed to unclip a fragmentation grenade from his belt, and held it out for Alain to see. He made a slight motion to his partner that his intention was to take out the guys on Alain's side of the path. Porter slid a grenade out and readied himself. He pulled the pin, held up one finger, then two, then three. Both men lobbed the grenades and hugged the ground. The explosions sent jagged shards of metal slicing through the jungle at a phenomenal speed. The ex-SEALs heard screams as the hot frags cut into their foes. Travis waved to Alain and they leapt up simultaneously and sprayed the bush with automatic fire. The screams were reduced to whimpers, then died off completely. They cautiously worked their way back into the underbrush, finding only corpses on both sides of the path. No one had survived.

McNeil mentally tallied Mugumba's casualties as he and Alain ran for the camp. Four in the bush, three more in the clearing, plus one badly wounded. They had taken out a further four on the path, for a total of twelve. From seventeen, that left five nasties. The odds were becoming favorable. For the moment.

A swath of heavy-caliber bullets raked the vegetation beside them as they came abreast of the river. Overhead, the thumping of helicopter blades broke the jungle silence. The gunfire stopped and the sound of the rotors diminished as the chopper veered off and headed north. Travis breathed a sigh of relief, then sucked the air back in. Through the break in the jungle cover that followed the river, he could see the chopper as it hovered some three hundred yards distant. From the machine came figure after figure: low-altitude parachutists. He counted eight before the machine stopped hovering and came back toward his position.

He motioned for Porter and Nelson to dig in close to the riverbank while he waded back across toward the camp. He called Troy on the Panther as he sloshed through the water.

"They had a line on us while we were still under the canopy," he said as he approached the camp. "They must have heat-sensing capabilities. Get under something cool to mask your heat."

"Roger," Ramage shot back into his mobile unit and started moving. He grabbed Samantha by the arm and pushed her under a fallen log, scooping out some of the surrounding damp earth and throwing it on her. She understood without being told, and smeared the mud and moss on her body as best she could. She watched as Troy raced across the tiny clearing and yanked one of the Saab Bofors RBS 70 missiles. He activated the manual sighting mechanism and aimed it skyward. Seconds later the ground all around him exploded with the impact of hundreds of rounds of machine-gun fire as the chopper let loose on his position. Ramage squeezed the trigger on the missile at the same moment he took a slug in the shoulder. He jerked violently right, throwing the missile off course. The machine gun on the chopper went silent for a moment as the pilot saw the missile trail and went into evasive maneuvers. When the guidance system on the Bofors didn't kick in and the missile shot harmlessly skyward, the pilot returned to his vantage point and began laying down more fire.

Troy Ramage rolled to his left and grasped the top of a second missile box. He jerked upward with all his strength, sending the lid flying into the ferns. He armed the missile and propped himself on the empty box as he took aim through the canopy. The gunner zeroed in on him, but not before Ramage squeezed the trigger, firing the second missile. Milliseconds later, Troy took two high-caliber bullets, one in his leg, the other through his right side just under his lung. He collapsed and passed out.

The pilot saw the vapor trail as the Bofors surface-to-air missile broke the canopy and streaked toward him. He hit the throttle and pushed forward on the stick. But there simply wasn't enough time to accelerate the machine out of the missile's path. The tip pushed into the helicopter's underbelly, then exploded, reducing the machine to a flaming chunk of airborne debris. It dropped straight down, smashing through the canopy and the underlying forest, then hitting the forest floor with a thunderous explosion. The sound dissipated, and once again, aside from the flames lapping at the blackened shell, silence engulfed the jungle. Samantha moved to Troy.

He was critically injured, but still breathing. She dug through the nearby supplies and found a medical kit. She ripped open a field dressing and pressed it against the wound in his torso. The sulfa drugs and salves on the bandage began to coagulate the blood. She covered him with a blanket and waited.

McNeil saw the missile hit the chopper just as he cleared the river and broke for cover next to the camp. They had at least five soldiers coming up behind them, and eight more fresh paratroops to the north. He had to get around the camp and position himself between the fresh troops and Samantha. He thought for a moment of joining Samantha and checking on Troy, but that would just waste precious seconds. As he jogged, he reset the Panther unit to a different frequency and hit the send button. Moments later, Billy Hackett's voice merged with the static.

"Billy, we need an extraction," he shouted, spouting off the exact coordinates to the base camp. "At least one wounded. At present, four healthy. You'll be coming in hot. We've got at least thirteen of Mugumba's men on the ground and heavily armed."

"Tell me you'll pay for my retirement," Hackett said. "If I save you from government troops, I'll never work in the Congo again."

"Yeah, one million dollars. Just get us out of here."

"Two million."

"Two is fine, but one in cash and one in raw diamonds. Deal?"

"Deal. I'm twenty-five minutes out. I'll bring a ladder for

the healthy ones and a sling for the wounded. Get to the edge of the river. I'll hover at sixty feet. I know the area, and that's the best I can do."

"Roger," Travis told him and cut the connection. He switched the Panther back to person-to-person and got Porter on line. "Alain, you and Dan have got five coming in behind you. Try to get across the river and help Sam with Troy. I saw him take at least two hits from the chopper guns."

"No can do, Travis," the reply came back a few moments later. Gunfire punctuated his words. "We're pinned down here. And we're still on the wrong side of the water. If we try to swim, we're dead."

"Okay, just stay cool. How entrenched are they?"

"They've got the good ground. We were ready to make the crossing when Sam got us on the Panther and told us that she thought she saw something moving behind us. We waited and they opened up on us. If we'd moved into the water, we'd be dead."

"Roger that. Keep cool. I'm heading for the drop zone, maybe try to cut off the fresh troops before they get to Sam and Troy. Twenty-five minutes 'til Billy's here with the chopper. Hang in there." He let the Panther unit fall to his side and slowed his pace. He had circled the east side of the camp, but had not caught another glimpse of Sam or Troy. She must be keeping him low and under cover. He approached visual distance to the first set of trip wires and stopped moving. He slipped the smaller MINI SS over his shoulder and set up the larger CR21 Assault rifle. Then he waited.

His mind was racing with what was happening. They had expected Mugumba to attack, but what benefit could there be for the colonel to kill the entire team? Surely they wanted Samantha alive, if only for the location of the diamond vein. Yet they had sprayed the tents with automatic fire—reckless abandon if you wanted to take someone alive. It didn't make sense. Then a motion off to his left caught his eye and he wiped his mind clean, concentrating on what he did best—surviving.

A solitary figure, silhouetted black against the tropical green, crept slowly along the path, almost at the trip wire. McNeil steadied the CR21 and waited. He could almost feel the man's boot snug up against the wire and he certainly saw the result. Two fragmentation grenades exploded simultaneously, shredding the surrounding fifty feet with a lethal wall of jagged metal. The victim was sliced almost in two by the razor-sharp shrapnel. It took a few seconds for the smoke to clear and Travis kept his eyes focused on the area, watching for a second soldier to fill the dead man's steps. The path remained vacant. He felt a cold shiver run down his spine. There were still seven highly trained soldiers hidden in the jungle, yet not a branch moved. He wiped away a lone bead of sweat as it threatened to drip into his eye. This was not good.

Troy Ramage was critically injured, perhaps dead. Dan and Alain were pinned down on the wrong side of the river, and he was face to unseeing face with seven elite paratroops. It was a waiting game; the first to move would draw the fire. He checked his watch. Sixteen minutes until Billy arrived. Twelve hostiles within range of their extraction zone. The logistics didn't work; he had to change the odds. They could rely on covering fire from the chopper once they had one man in the bird. The remaining two, probably he and Dan, could pin down five or six of the enemy from a position next to the extraction zone. Realistically, they needed to eliminate at least five of the ground troops before even attempting to board the chopper.

McNeil mentally reviewed the defenses they had at their disposal. Aside from the one wire already tripped, three more lay in wait, well camouflaged and deadly. But he needed the soldiers moving to trip them. Then the answer hit him. He grabbed the Panther and called for Samantha. A moment later she responded.

"Is Troy conscious?" he asked.

"Yes. He was out for a couple of minutes but he's awake

again. I've given him a shot of morphine but he's still in a lot of pain."

"Okay, here's what I want you to do. There are four small brown boxes next to you. Inside are mortar shells. The larger green box holds the launcher. Get Troy to show you how to set it up, and target two hundred and thirty yards on an azimuth of eighteen degrees. Then lay down a barrage twenty-five yards in every direction. And hurry, we've only got ten minutes."

He leaned back against a hollow stump and waited. Precious minutes ticked by. He knew Troy and Sam were doing their best to get the gear set up and targeted. Then he heard the low thump of a mortar leaving the tube. Moments later the jungle exploded as the shell crashed to earth. The targeting was off by a few yards, but close enough to be effective. He picked up movement close to the explosions that were now raining down with regularity. He targeted the movement and squeezed his trigger. The assault rifle coughed and a stream of bullets tore through the ferns and thudded into the soldier, who gasped as the air was forced from his lungs. McNeil heard the killing sound between mortar blasts, then reverted his gaze back to finding another target.

A swift movement from McNeil's left to right ended with the soldier tripping a second booby-trap and falling prey to the fragmentation grenades as they exploded. Three down, five to go. More motion to his far right; he aimed and fired. Another hit. Bullets suddenly tore through the bush that obscured him and ripped chunks of wood from the tree behind him. He threw himself hard left and rolled numerous times, coming to rest behind a fallen tree. He looked down for blood but came up empty. They had missed. He checked his watch and noted two minutes until their ride arrived. He slowly raised his head above the horizontal trunk, searching for enemy. Nothing. He slipped the assault rifle over his shoulder, cradled the more maneuverable MINI SS, and beat a retreat back toward the camp.

He called in to Alain and Dan as he hit the clearing, motioning to Sam to keep the mortars coming. He could hear sporadic gunfire from the far side of the river. Seconds later Alain came online.

"We've nailed two of them for sure. The other three have dropped back a bit. These CR21s are fucking great; they chew through everything. We should have enough time to get across if you can set up some cover fire."

"You got it," Travis yelled back over the din. "Move now; I'll cover you."

He slipped a fresh clip into the assault rifle and waited. A few seconds passed, then movement on the far bank. Alain and Dan burst from the tree line and hit the water running. McNeil aimed into the thick darkness of the jungle and waited. A slight movement at one o'clock caught his eye and he pummeled the area with hot lead. He let the trigger go, waiting for another clue to the enemy's location. Muzzle flashes at ten o'clock. He swung about, aimed and fired. The thudding sounds changed as the bullets stopped hitting plants and dug into human flesh. Another kill. He stopped again, his breathing rhythmic, his focus intense. His men were almost across. Another muzzle flash and he retaliated. The enemy fire stopped, but he wasn't sure whether the man was hit. Alain and Dan hit the near bank and ran the few feet into the trees and safety. He breathed deeply. Just the extraction now.

Travis looked skyward as the distant sounds of helicopter rotors floated down to him. Then he spotted Hackett, on target and coming in fast. The ladder was already hanging below the bird, and as it dropped to sixty feet, Travis could clearly see Hackett's wife in the copilot seat. She looked scared. Travis waved and Hackett returned the signal. It was time to move.

Travis motioned for Sam to leave Troy and get on the ladder. She hesitated for a second, then saw the look on his face. It told her to not question him, just move. She left the injured man and climbed onto the wooden rungs, placing foot over foot as quickly as possible. She was halfway up when Travis waved to Alain. Porter made a mad dash for the ladder and began climbing. He and Dan stayed back to back, guns leveled into the surrounding bush, ready to give cover fire. So far, so good. As he looked back to the chopper, he saw the sling being lowered. He shouldered his rifle, yelling at Dan to cover 360 degrees, grabbed Troy and hoisted him onto his shoulder. He beelined for the river and arrived just as the sling reached ground level. In seconds, he had Troy in the sling and gave the signal to begin raising it. Troy moved upward as the first enemy fire targeted in on them.

Hackett immediately pulled the chopper up, taking Troy out of range as the pulley winched him in. Travis and Dan dove for cover and returned fire. They were taking hostile fire from two directions as the paratroopers moved into the skirmish. Travis turned north and laid down covering fire until his assault rifle clicked, the hammer hitting empty space. He threw it down and leveled his MINI, strafing the underbrush again and again. He looked skyward as the chopper dropped back into place, then yelled at Dan to make a break. The firing behind him stopped as Dan sprinted for the ladder. He counted to four, then broke off firing and started to the chopper. His MINI was almost out of ammo, and he grabbed the Sako sniper rifle on the run. He reached the lowest rung and began to climb.

Dan was twenty feet up the ladder and moving fast. Billy angled the chopper away from the river and began to climb. Just as Travis thought they were home free, Dan Nelson took four direct hits, the bullets slamming into his back and drilling into his heart and lungs. He hung on the rung for a second, then his grip slackened and he fell earthward. Travis tried to grab him as he careened past, but already the momentum was too great. He watched as his friend's body plummeted to the earth, landing almost in the center of the slow-moving river. Travis closed his eyes for a moment, knowing from what he'd seen that Dan was dead before his fingers let go of the ladder. Travis resumed climbing as the helicopter rose far above the trees. He reached the top and pulled himself in.

Travis looked back to the battleground. Numerous troops were wading through the water to where Dan's body had landed. He watched as they manhandled the corpse, then motioned to Billy to level the chopper out and hover. He slipped the sniper rifle off his shoulder and uncovered the scope. He sighted on the figures, their features recognizable through the highly magnified lens. Then he stopped.

Colonel Nathan Mugumba strode from the jungle and stood at the river's edge. Travis drew a bead on the corrupt leader, and chambered a round. He looked quickly to Billy Hackett, who instinctively knew to keep the machine as level as possible for the next few moments. He rested his right cheek against the rifle stock, his eye to the scope, and slowly squeezed the trigger. The gun jerked back with the recoil and for a moment it pointed skyward. He brought it back down and saw the results of his single shot. The short, arrogant Mugumba clutched at his chest as blood spurted out into the muddy water. He stood for a moment on shaky legs, then collapsed. The bullet had torn right through the center of his heart. Travis snapped the safety on the gun and closed the door. He nodded to Billy and the pilot headed for safety.

McNeil turned to face what was left of his team, his eyes filled with a strange mixture of sadness and anger. He bent over Troy, gingerly lifting up the bandage Samantha had placed over the stomach wound. He breathed a sigh of relief. The bullet had hit at a sharp angle, and he could see that the exit wound was more to Troy's right side than on his back. No major damage was evident, and Samantha had curtailed the bleeding and already had an IV in him, the bag dangling from the far side of the chopper. He looked at Sam and nodded, thanking her for saving Troy's life. He looked out the window and watched as the rain-forest canopy spread out below him in all directions.

The jungle had taken another man. How many times had he escaped only by the grace of God? Why did he continually live while others died? And who decided? He pondered briefly on the possible existence of God, and wondered what the Almighty must think of him: a hired killer. He swallowed, and looked back into the cabin. Samantha was tending to Troy, keeping him warm and watching the fluid levels on his IV. God, what a woman, he thought. She had found the diamonds, a feat that only the most skilled geologists had managed. She had kept her cool through the hellish firefight and saved Troy's life with quick thinking and even quicker actions. And she had done all that without ego.

He continued to look at her. The usually shiny hair, flowing gracefully over her shoulders, was not so pretty. It looked bedraggled, dirty and dull. Her face was covered with streaks of mud and moss, and her clothes sweaty and ripped. But the beauty was still there. Her chiseled features, high cheekbones, and intelligent eyes all shone through the dirt and grime. To him, she was even more beautiful. She turned to face him, and for the first time he sensed something that had not been there before—the adoration and love that he felt for her being returned.

And it felt good.

SIXTEEN

Patrick Kerrigan ripped the cord from its socket and hurled the phone across the room. It hit the far wall and shattered, spraying sharp pieces of plastic across the hotel furniture. He clenched his hands into tight fists and moved his lower jaw back and forth, grinding his teeth. He took a few deep breaths and then walked over to the window, looking out through the London fog. His breathing returned to normal; he slackened the pressure on his jaw and straightened his fingers. He willed himself to relax.

He glanced at the ruined phone, then walked into the bedroom and placed a call from the one on the night table. He knew the number and dialed it, including the area code for Northern Ireland. Liam O'Donnell picked up on the third ring.

"The wheels have totally come off our African operation," Kerrigan said. "Our colonel is no longer with us, and the targets have left the area."

O'Donnell was equally vague with his response. "That's not good news, but the family is ready to leave anytime. Give me your number and I'll call you back."

Kerrigan gave his Irish hit man the hotel number and hung up. He knew that O'Donnell would head for a public phone, eliminating any chance of the authorities overhearing their conversation. Five minutes later, the phone rang. He answered it immediately.

"What happened?" O'Donnell asked.

"Mugumba was sure he had the location of the mine pinpointed to within a hundred square yards, so he went in and tried to take out the entire expedition. He fucked up and got himself killed. They eliminated one of Carlson's team, but she's still alive. And she knows where the vein is."

"Did Mugumba give you the location?"

"No. The team he sent ahead by chopper radioed back the location, but Mugumba cleared everybody away from the radio before they gave him the coordinates. He's the only one who knew, and now he's dead."

"So we need Carlson alive."

"Yes. The bitch knows where the diamonds are, and this time I want the location. I want that fucking location." There was unbridled fury in Kerrigan's voice.

"You'll get it. Where are Carlson and the rest of her team now?"

"I don't know, but I've got feelers out. I'll have their destination for you in seventy-two hours, give or take. They can't go so deep that I can't find them. Just have your guys ready to move."

"Not a problem. I'll be waiting for your call." The line went dead.

Kerrigan replaced the handset in the cradle and sat in a chair next to the bedroom window. From this angle he could see one corner of the British parliament buildings. The cornerstone of Britain itself, and the birthplace of the laws that governed the country. The laws that determined how justice was applied. Justice. He silently mouthed the word, enjoying the syllables as they spilled out mutely over his lips. Justice. Exactly what he would dole out to Samantha Carlson and her motley crew of mercenaries. He had hired them, paid them to perform a service for him and they had stabbed him in the back. Success was theirs, but they chose to hide the information from him, and in doing so, they signed their death warrants. He was through playing games. They had betrayed him, and they would pay.

His carefully cultivated network in Washington, D.C., and Langley, Virginia, was electronically combing the globe as he sat in the Victorian wingback and looked out over London. There could be no escape from the moles he had bought within the CIA and the NSA. They had never failed him, and he knew that given enough time, they would locate Samantha Carlson or one of the remaining three ex-SEALs. And they would feed that information to him. Then on to Liam O'Donnell, and they would die. All except Carlson.

He had special plans for Ms. Carlson. She would endure a horrific fate at his hands. The pent-up anger and frustration he harbored needed an escape, and the traitor geologist would suffice nicely. He wanted to personally torture her, to watch her suffer and hear her scream. Once he knew precisely where the richest source of diamonds discovered in the past hundred years was, then he would really turn up the heat. Torturing the bitch would no longer be business; it would be pleasure.

Liam O'Donnell hung up with Kerrigan and immediately placed another call. His men would be ready to move on a moment's notice. He vacated the public phone booth and entered a nearby pub. He knew the owner well, and the man delivered a frothing Guinness without being asked. O'Donnell paid the man, including a substantial tip, and sat back in the corner booth, mentally conjuring the upcoming mission.

His men were anxious to go head-to-head with the ex-SEALs, but O'Donnell knew full well that these men would be worthy adversaries. They were not to be taken lightly. They were on the run from the African skirmish, but unaware of what was coming at them. They would be wary, suspicious perhaps, and most certainly on edge. They would try to disappear into a sea of humanity, so the battleground would be a major city—which one, he could only speculate. Paris was a possibility; the French authorities were slack about foreigners entering the country as tourists. London was equally attractive, perhaps even more so. They spoke English and could blend in even better.

There were many other ports of entry into Europe. Athens, Rome, Madrid, Berlin, Vienna, the list was long. Perhaps rather than think of where they would arrive in Europe, he should concentrate on where they would leave Africa. Two cities, and only two, came to mind: Tangiers and Cairo. Most of northern Africa was in a state of political upheaval. Algeria was a mess; fair-skinned people were targeted and murdered indiscriminately. Tunisia was almost as bad. Libya was off limits for Americans without valid work visas. That left Morocco and Egypt—Tangiers and Cairo.

O'Donnell wanted the advantage of knowing their African exit point. Rather than wait for them to hit the vast number of available European cities and disappear, he could pin them down before they left Africa. He mentally weighed the two remaining cities. Egypt was far more lax than Morocco in allowing weapons to cross its borders. If his targets came through Cairo, they could theoretically bring automatic weapons with them. Morocco was a different story. The border patrols were always watching for illicit hashish shipments, and they tended to catch anything larger than a breadbox. Hell, a lot of the illegal drugs people tried to bring through were the size of a cellular phone, and when the authorities were looking for something that size, they were bound to find a machine gun. And an ex-SEAL would know that. Cairo. That would be their exit point.

O'Donnell drained his Guinness and waved for another one. What to do? He briefly thought of heading for Cairo without advising Kerrigan, but then thought better of that. Kerrigan held the purse strings, and he didn't want to piss the man off. Besides, talk around the grapevine pegged Kerrigan as a man you did not want to cross. Revenge killings ate up a good portion of Kerrigan's budget. Or so O'Donnell had been told. Another course of action was to call Kerrigan and see if he had arrived at the same conclusion: that their prey would be in Cairo. Or he could do nothing. Just let Kerrigan's intelligence-gathering personnel do their job and follow up once they had a European location. He took a long draught of beer and mulled his options. Suddenly, he stood up, dumped some money on the table and left the pub. He found a different pay phone than he had used earlier and put a call through to Kerrigan's London hotel. The man was in his room.

"I have an idea," he said, and filled Kerrigan in with his thoughts on Cairo.

"Okay," the distant reply came back. "Take three men with you, leave the other three in Belfast. I'll alert my intel sources in the States to keep a close eye on Cairo. I'll be here for a week or so, in case you need me."

"What do you want me to do if I find them?"

"Call me first thing. Then keep them under close surveillance. If they look like they're ready to move, kill the SEALs. Take Carlson alive. I don't care if she's shot up a bit; just don't kill her."

O'Donnell hung up the phone and stepped into a light afternoon shower. The clouds covered part of the sky, but directly above was brilliant blue. He looked upward, squinting to keep the water from his eyes. Several mini-rainbows danced about as the sunlight bent through the airborne moisture. The effect was intriguing, almost surreal.

But one thing was not surreal, he thought. He had been given the green light to track down and kill McNeil and his men. And to capture Samantha Carlson. His heartbeat picked up a bit as he envisioned the upcoming mission. Ferreting out the enemy amidst the dirty, teeming Cairo streets, then methodically eliminating them. He smiled. He really enjoyed working for a living.

* * *

Kerrigan placed a call to his mole in the CIA and advised him to keep Cairo under a magnifying glass. Watch for Internet connections, credit card authorizations, and hotel or car reservations for Travis McNeil, Alain Porter, Dan Nelson, Troy Ramage and Samantha Carlson. He placed a similar call to his inside connection at the NSA, and then poured some room-service tea. He put a dab of milk in the tepid drink, took a small sip and replaced the cup in the saucer. Fucking Brits. He hated tea and there wasn't a single person on the entire island who could brew a proper pot of coffee. He despised London, but knew that New York was too far removed from the current action. He needed to be here. His thoughts returned to Africa, and to what had happened.

Mugumba had screwed up. He had managed to locate the diamondiferous formation, then lose it when he lost his life. Not that Kerrigan gave a flying fuck about that greedy little turd. He cared solely about the diamonds. And once again the location had eluded him. He knew the extent of the wealth that existed inside that vein, and he wanted it. And he would get the precise location from Samantha Carlson's lips just before he killed her. And then once he had it, he would fill her in on a little secret. He would watch the disbelief, the hatred build in her eyes. Then he would finish her off.

"Bitch," he said softly to the empty room. "Will you ever be surprised."

SEVENTEEN

Samantha clutched the lamb close to the robes that covered her upper body, and moved away from the street vendor in search of Travis. She spotted him two stalls down, haggling on some black lentils for their daily kushari. She joined him, pulling the veil down over her blond hair. She couldn't hide all of her face though, and numerous Arabs stared at her fair skin and blue eyes. Travis paid for the food and they walked briskly through the Khan El Khalili Bazaar back toward their Cairo apartment.

The Friday prayer hour was over, and the ancient bazaar teemed with midday activity, just as it had since the four-teenth century. The stones that passed beneath their feet were worn, grooved from countless millions of hooves and sandals. Crumbling concrete replaced the original hand-cut stones that formed the walls lining the narrow, winding paths. The constant barrage of sights and sounds inundated the mind, but the pungent odors arising from food left in the afternoon heat assailed the senses. At times the aromas were sweet, almost pleasant, but mostly they carved a harsh path through the sinuses, leading an all-out assault on the brain. One shop ran into another, then ten, then a hundred and a thousand. They seemed unending, and Sam slowed her pace and rubbed the tip of her nose, trying to suppress the smells. Her eyes burned from the thick industrial pollution that hung in the air, the crud she ingested with every breath. She felt a tug at her elbow and turned to look at Travis, pointing at a break in the upcoming wall. A way out. She nodded and they moved toward it. She recognized the architecture, and thought back to what she knew of Egyptian history, if for no other reason than to diminish the horrific odors.

The land of the Pharaohs. Or so was the common misconception, Sam thought. Cairo, in fact, was never a Pharaonic city; that honor belonged to the much smaller city of Memphis, which lay just south of the Giza Plateau. But it was Cairo that had grown, mosque by mosque, house by house. The Romans founded the city and were the first in a string of non-Egyptian rulers. Muslim Arabs replaced the Romans in 640 AD, rejected Babylon and built Fustat, a tent city on the northern extremes. Then came a series of governors, appointed by the caliph in Baghdad. Followed by the Fatimids, Mamluks, Ottomans, French, and eventually the British. When an Egyptian finally seized power in the person of Colonel Gamal Abdel Nasser in 1956, control of their country reverted back to the Egyptians for the first time since the Pharaohs. And it was then that Cairo's population exploded, making it the most densely populated spot on the planet. Egypt had a colorful history, even before one took into account the pyramids—a history that Sam had studied in depth while in university. She blinked a few times to acclimatize her pupils as they left the bright sunlight of the bazaar and entered the shadows that clung to the passageway.

The high but narrow archway led through a decrepit building dating back to the era of the brutal Mamluks. An era of wonderment and excess. Trade and prosperity followed the rule of the Turkish slave-soldiers as they opened the canal linking the Nile to the Red Sea. But typical of

Egypt's violent history, a price was paid. The rulers reaped the riches that flowed from the trade route, with little but their brutality filtering down to the Egyptian masses. Even Qaitbey, a slave boy who rose to sultan, tortured and maimed the commoners as he built monuments to himself that stood today. Legend recalled the instance when a chemist was unsuccessful at transforming lead into gold: Qaitbey ripped out his tongue and eyes as punishment. As Samantha remembered the details from her college classes, the odors haunting the bazaar seemed muted, almost tolerable. She shuddered at the ability of man to inflict pain and suffering on his fellow man.

Sam trailed Travis from the narrow confines of the passageway into a wider, more modern street and recognized where they were—one block from their apartment. Travis quietly opened and closed the outer doors and walked through the enclosed courtyard, pausing briefly at the fountain to splash some water over his face. Sam set the lamb on the dusty cobblestones and followed suit. The water felt wonderful in the arid May heat. She let the cool liquid drip from her face onto her chest and loosened her robes so the droplets fell on her breasts. Travis seemed not to notice the slight indiscretion. They took the stairs to the second floor where Alain Porter rested on a velvet couch.

"Any word on Troy?" Travis asked, dropping the sacks of lentils, onions and noodles on the table.

"Doc Adamson called about ten minutes ago. Troy's strength is returning quicker than he thought. He said he'd be arranging for a flight back to America in about a week's time."

"Excellent. Thanks." Travis had limited connections in Cairo, but one had proved invaluable. Travis and Greg Adamson, a medic stationed briefly in Little Creek and now living a quiet life of retirement in Cairo, had stayed in touch over the years. Once Travis figured out that Cairo was the best route back to civilization, he called the doctor and put him on alert. They were incoming with a severe casualty.

Billy Hackett had flown the surviving trio into the Ugandan city of Masindi, where for the appropriate amounts of cash no questions were asked. They chartered a Lear, usually used for moving packages, and flew eight hundred miles nonstop into Khartoum. More money crossed palms, and they refueled without incident. Khartoum to Cairo was about the same distance but entry into Egypt was more difficult. The plane sat on the runway for almost three hours before Travis finally talked to an official who could help them bypass customs. More money, a lot more, and they were in. But by now, Troy Ramage was in rough shape after the long haul from the wilds of upper Congo.

Greg Adamson was waiting, having received Travis's call from Masindi some nine hours earlier. Adamson looked haggard from the wait, knowing a desperate situation was only being made worse with each passing hour. When the officials finally released the plane and its contents onto Egyptian soil, Adamson whisked Ramage off to his residence without saying more than two sentences to Travis.

"Here's my address. Be there in three hours." Then Adamson and his assistant were gone. Three hours to the minute later, Travis was standing on the doctor's doorstep, at a striking home in the fashionable district of Mohandiseen, and he was taken aback by its opulence. Egyptian artifacts adorned the pedestals and tables, while more contemporary art graced the smooth white walls. An interesting mixture, but one that worked. The money to purchase the house and all its trimmings had been generously donated by the American government, Adamson informed Travis, after assuring the ex-SEAL that Ramage was out of danger.

"One very high, and I mean very high, ranking government official had a mistress. He got pissed at her one night and beat her up pretty badly. They called me in to fix her up—save her life actually—then paid me off afterward." The young doctor waved his hands around, gesturing to the expansive house. "And this is what I bought with the money." He escorted Travis from the main living area of the house to an interior room in the basement. Travis was impressed with what he saw. A complete operating theater with equipment some cash-strapped hospitals only dreamt of having was laid out in front of him. Off to the right was a recovery room, where Troy Ramage lay quietly on clean linens, breathing regularly.

"How bad was he?"

"Almost didn't make it. The slug through his abdomen wasn't the problem, nor was the one that ripped through the muscle in his leg. The one in his shoulder was a different story. It lodged in such a way that when I took it out, it severed an artery. If he had been anywhere but here or a hospital, he'd be gone."

"Thanks, Doc," Travis said. "What do we owe you?"

"I take donations, Travis. Whatever you can afford."

He thought back to the man footing the bills: Patrick Kerrigan. The man who had unleashed Mugumba and his troops on them. Travis still had access to the funds Kerrigan had made available for the team. He wrote a number on a piece of paper and held it up for Adamson to see. The doctor grinned and nodded.

"I'll bet charities get in fistfights to land on your doorstep. In fact, for that amount, I'll take care of getting Troy back to the U.S. when he's able. That way you can concentrate on whatever it is you're up to."

McNeil thanked the doctor and returned to their modest apartment, to wait and regroup. It was not a short wait. Three days passed, and Travis, Alain and Samantha began to adjust to the climate and the food of the Egyptian capital. With the exception of visiting the Banque Masr to secure Adamson's fee, they hadn't ventured far from the safety the villa-style apartment provided them. The Lear pilot who had flown the final leg from Khartoum into Cairo owned the apartment and used it when he deadheaded in Egypt. His flight itinerary had taken him on to Venice the day they arrived, so he'd flipped them a key in consideration of twice the rent he could ever have hoped to garner from the villa. A win-win situation that gave what was left of the team safe quarters for a few days while they tested their options. And at present their options were limited.

Kerrigan had set them up, of that they were sure. But he had failed, and in doing so had lost both Mugumba and the location of the formation. The only people still alive who knew how to access the diamonds were Samantha and Travis. And they were reasonably sure that Kerrigan knew that. Which meant he would be coming for them. Cairo was a huge city, its population base immense. But keeping under cover from someone of great wealth and resources, even in a city as densely populated as Cairo, was tricky. That Kerrigan was wealthy was a known fact, and if he was involved in shady deals to uncover hundreds of millions of dollars in precious stones, the chances were pretty good that he was well connected enough to eventually ferret them out. It was a waiting game, and the longer they stayed put, the greater the chances were that Kerrigan would find them.

"We've got to lay down a plan of action of some sort," Travis said, pacing the main room of the apartment like a caged animal. "We can't go home, and we can't just stay here indefinitely. Either way Kerrigan is going to find us, and I'd rather have the element of surprise on our side, not his."

"I've been monitoring the business section of the *New York Times* via the Internet in case Gem-Star makes an announcement of a major find in Africa. Nothing so far. If he's managed to figure out where the diamonds are, that will take some of the pressure off us. If not . . ." Samantha let the sentence trail off.

"Let him come," Alain Porter said sharply. "It's not like we're helpless here." He walked over to the far wall and yanked open a crate. He lifted a Vector MINI from inside and held it up. "We managed to get two of these and a CR21 Assault rifle onto the chopper. And Travis had the Sako sniper rifle with him as well. We can take care of ourselves."

"We're short on ammunition, Alain," Travis reminded him.

"We've only got the clips that were in the guns, plus what we had strapped to our belts. And that's not much. Two hundred rounds, tops."

Alain looked thoughtful. "That's not enough. A firefight lasting less than two minutes will chew that up. We need to find more bullets."

Travis nodded, then turned to Samantha. "You brought some diamonds out with you. Can I see them?"

"Sure," she said, disappearing into her bedroom for a moment, then returning with the small suede bag. She carefully shook the contents onto the coffee table. "There are forty-seven in all," she said, anticipating the next question. "Thirty-two stones, nine shapes, two cleavages and four macles."

Travis looked bewildered. "They're all diamonds, right?" She nodded. "Then they're all stones, aren't they? That's what they call diamonds—stones. Like that movie with Michael Douglas and Kathleen Turner."

"*Romancing the Stone?*"

"Yeah, that's it."

"Hollywood takes liberties with things when it's convenient. And the stone in that movie wasn't a diamond. It was sapphire or topaz or something like that. Anyway, stones, shapes, cleavages and macles are names used when sorting roughs, as we refer to uncut diamonds, for size and value." She grinned as Alain reached over and picked up the largest diamond on the table. "That's a cleavage. One of the least valuable roughs in the lot."

"But it's the biggest," he protested.

"Ah, the male thought pattern that size means everything. Well, in diamonds size is important, but not necessarily the crucial element in determining value. If you look at that particular diamond under magnification, which I have, you'll see that it has no crystallographic features. It's imperfectly formed, and has numerous fractures running through it. If you tried to cut this diamond, it would likely shatter. You'd be left with plenty of tiny diamonds for engagement rings, but nothing of real substance."

GET UP TO
4 FREE BOOKS!

You can have the best fiction delivered to your door for less than what you'd pay in a bookstore or online—only $4.25 a book! Sign up for our book clubs today, and we'll send you FREE* BOOKS just for trying it out...with no obligation to buy, ever!

LEISURE HORROR BOOK CLUB

With more award-winning horror authors than any other publisher, it's easy to see why CNN.com says "Leisure Books has been leading the way in paperback horror novels." Your shipments will include authors such as RICHARD LAYMON, DOUGLAS CLEGG, JACK KETCHUM, MARY ANN MITCHELL, and many more.

LEISURE THRILLER BOOK CLUB

If you love fast-paced page-turners, you won't want to miss any of the books in Leisure's thriller line. Filled with gripping tension and edge-of-your-seat excitement, these titles feature everything from psychological suspense to legal thrillers to police procedurals and more!

As a book club member you also receive the following special benefits:
- **30% OFF** all orders through our website & telecenter!
- **Exclusive access to** special discounts!
- **Convenient** home delivery **and 10 days to return any books you don't want to keep.**

There is no minimum number of books to buy, and you may cancel membership at any time. See back to sign up!

*Please include $2.00 for shipping and handling.

YES! ☐

Sign me up for the Leisure Horror Book Club and send my TWO FREE BOOKS! If I choose to stay in the club, I will pay only $8.50* each month, a savings of $5.48!

YES! ☐

Sign me up for the Leisure Thriller Book Club and send my TWO FREE BOOKS! If I choose to stay in the club, I will pay only $8.50* each month, a savings of $5.48!

NAME: _____

ADDRESS: _____

_____

TELEPHONE: _____

E-MAIL: _____

☐ **I WANT TO PAY BY CREDIT CARD.**

☐ **VISA**   ☐ **MasterCard**   ☐ **DISCOVER**

ACCOUNT #: _____

EXPIRATION DATE: _____

SIGNATURE: _____

Send this card along with $2.00 shipping & handling for each club you wish to join, to:

Horror/Thriller Book Clubs
20 Academy Street
Norwalk, CT 06850-4032

Or fax (must include credit card information!) to: 610.995.9274.
You can also sign up online at www.dorchesterpub.com.

*Plus $2.00 for shipping. Offer open to residents of the U.S. and Canada only.
Canadian residents please call 1.800.481.9191 for pricing information.
If under 18, a parent or guardian must sign. Terms, prices and conditions subject to change. Subscription subject
to acceptance. Dorchester Publishing reserves the right to reject any order or cancel any subscription.

JOIN NOW!

"What about this one?" Travis lifted a triangular-shaped diamond from the bunch.

"That one is a macle, even more useless than a cleavage. The problem with macles is they usually have a seam running through the twinned octahedron. That one is thick enough to cut into a decent-sized brilliant, but only if it doesn't split when the cutter makes his first point cut."

"I'm getting confused," Alain said, setting the cleavage back on the table. "What's a brilliant?"

"It's a method of cutting the rough to produce a finished stone. There are lots of ways to cut a diamond. Venetians have been cutting diamonds since the early 1300s. Most of the cutting and polishing is done in Antwerp now. They've been at it since sometime in the fifteenth century." She picked up an average-looking rough from the pile and held it up for Travis and Alain to see.

"Now this stone has value, great value. A talented cutter could probably fashion a brilliant square cut, or Barion cut as we geologists refer to it, from this rough. It will have twenty-five facets on the crown," she pointed at the top of the rock, "and an additional twenty-nine on the pavilion. The cutter will lose very little of the original weight, and the fire will be absolutely stunning. This, gentlemen, is a million-dollar diamond."

"A million dollars? Are you serious?" Alain asked, taking the stone from her outstretched hand.

"Minimum. And the majority of the diamonds in that pile are comparable in quality and size. You're looking at over twenty-five million dollars in diamonds, once they're cut."

Both men sat in silence. In less than three hours, Samantha Carlson had picked up or chipped from the exposed rock face a fortune in precious stones. In less than three hours. The enormity of the find staggered the imagination. What could a fully equipped mining operation glean from the find? Five hundred million, perhaps a billion? Enough to destabilize the world diamond market? Possibly. Probably. No wonder Patrick Kerrigan was relentless in his search for the holy grail of the diamond world. The possibility for one man to dictate terms to the Diamond Trading Company was unheard of, until now. Travis sighed and shook his head in disbelief.

"Is this formation capable of affecting the world market?" he asked.

Samantha didn't answer immediately. She rose from her chair and walked softly to the window that looked over the inner courtyard. Travis's question was a tough one, and not one she took lightly. She was a geologist, not an economist, but the tightly controlled diamond trade was well known to those involved in the industry. And as she mentally presented the arguments, one important question shot to the forefront. What was Kerrigan's ultimate plan? Did he intend to flood the market with high-quality stones, driving the price into the toilet? Doubtful. Or was it simply the money he was after? Perhaps. Or did he want it all? Was his quest to control the world's most lucrative natural resource, with the possible exception of oil? A market that had resisted every parry and thrust of a hostile takeover since the inception of De Beers in 1888. It was ludicrous, but the more she dwelled on it, the more real it seemed.

Kerrigan was already a very wealthy man; Farid Virgi had confirmed that. It made sense that his quest would be more for power and control than simply for money. But that line of thought ran into a major snag. It wasn't Kerrigan who controlled the expeditions, but Gem-Star. Kerrigan drew a healthy salary and bonuses for managing the operations, but the real benefit was to the corporation. Sam thought back to the meetings in New York at Gem-Star's corporate headquarters. Kerrigan's corner office with the eclectic décor of more than fifty countries, the waterfall with the rough diamonds in the reception area where Kerrigan had met her on her first visit. Meeting Travis, and the three of them discussing the mission. Then suddenly it hit her. Maybe there wasn't a snag. Maybe it *was* Kerrigan who controlled things in New York. She turned back to Travis and Alain.

"One thing before I answer." She leaned on the sill as she spoke. "Did you ever meet Davis Perth, Gem-Star's CEO?"

"No. He was sailing in the South Pacific, somewhere near Borneo."

"All your dealings were directly with Kerrigan?"

Travis nodded.

"Did you ever get an expense check or plane tickets, or anything from any other Gem-Star employee?"

"No. I dealt with Kerrigan, no one else."

Sam nodded. "Then the answer to your question is yes. I think the formation we discovered could not only affect the global market, I think it could give Kerrigan control over it."

"What are you saying?"

"I don't think Gem-Star has any knowledge of this expedition, or the last one, for that matter. I think this is Kerrigan's baby. Neither you nor I had any contact with any Gem-Star employees, other than through the main switchboard. He even met me in the reception area the first day I came in to see him. He financed our expedition, and looked to the rewards as personal gain, not corporate. And it doesn't make sense for a successful, private corporation that's been profitable for decades to kill their contract geologists. I think it's Kerrigan, and I doubt it's the first time he's done it." She went on to explain what Farid had discovered about Kerrigan, from teetering on the brink of financial disaster to multimillionaire within seven short years. All while on a fixed salary.

"That bastard," Travis vented. "He's running his own operation under the guise of an established mining company. So it was definitely Kerrigan who gave Mugumba the orders to kill us and to wipe out the previous expedition."

"Or expeditions. Who knows how long this prick has been looking for this formation. We could be his third, fourth, tenth, who knows?" Sam added.

"We know one thing for sure," Alain said quietly. "He's a cold-blooded murderer who will stop at nothing to achieve his goal." He paused for a moment, intent on his fingertips.

"And you two," he said, looking to Sam and Travis, "are the only ones who know where they are."

"Is there anything we've done since we arrived in Cairo that could lead him to us?" Samantha asked, moving away from the window. "The money you gave Greg Adamson for piecing Troy back together, was that from Kerrigan's account?"

"Yes, but I eliminated any paper trail. I withdrew the funds from the Swiss account, but routed them through the Caymans, then the Bahamas before making the deposit into Greg's account. The things you can do with satellite technology and a Chase Manhattan customer card."

"Smart thinking, Travis." Sam smiled at him. "Anything else?" Both men shook their heads. The trio had spent most of their time in Cairo sequestered in the apartment, and a few thousand dollars in cash had enticed their Lear pilot to file an erroneous flight plan, leaving that as a dead end. Any trail that Kerrigan and his men could pick up in the Congo would go cold long before it showed the way to Cairo.

"You mentioned using the Internet to watch for an announcement by Gem-Star in the *New York Times*," Travis said, motioning to the computer that sat on the desk only a few feet away. "Can Kerrigan get a fix on the location where you're signing on to the Internet?"

"He could if I hadn't spoofed my IP address in case Kerrigan put a sniffer out," she responded.

"What the hell did you just say?"

"I set up a proxy; it's a kind of firewall that protects my Internet signature from anyone who knows my IP address and is looking for me."

"Without it, they could track you here?"

"With the right tools, yes," she said. "Kerrigan probably has a person somewhere monitoring things electronically, and the first thing he'd do if he's looking for us is put a sniffer out on all our IP addresses."

"What are the chances they pick Cairo off the map as the most likely place for us to go?" Alain asked Travis.

"That's a possibility. The choices coming out of northern

Congo are limited. Casablanca, Tangiers, Abu Dhabi, or Tripoli. And Cairo, of course. If they're smart, they'll make an educated guess."

"And where would that put them?"

Travis shrugged. "Most likely Cairo." His eyes met hers and the words did not need to be said. They were in a precarious situation. Armed, but short on ammunition. Waiting to be ambushed without knowing whom their attackers would be. Unable to access their private bank accounts or use their credit cards. Waiting. Just waiting for Kerrigan to make his move.

EIGHTEEN

Flight 843 from London touched down on Cairo's steaming tarmac just before noon. The business-class passengers deplaned first and Patrick Kerrigan led the way. He scanned the crowded terminal, knowing a driver from the hotel would be present to pick him up. The sign was in Arabic, but he recognized the characters that formed his name, introduced himself and slipped into the limo. The car was air-conditioned and quiet, blocking out most of the omnipresent horn honking that greeted every visitor to Cairo. He watched the city through the windows, marveling at what a cesspool it had become. Sixteen million people jammed into a space large enough to fit one million could produce nothing but a disaster. The air was heavy with the acrid stench of diesel and gas fumes, mixed with the fetid exhaust from the factories. Kerrigan kept the windows tightly closed as they entered the congested quarters of Al-Abidin and neared the Semiramis Hotel. It was a moderate defense against the toxic air, mostly ineffective.

The limo swung south onto Sari Kurnis an-Nil and then turned away from the river toward the Semiramis Inter-

Continental Hotel. The driver waved to the security guards and cruised up the sweeping drive to the front entrance, jumped from the car and opened the passenger door. Kerrigan tipped the man and entered the hotel lobby. A friendly blast of cool air hit him as he strode through the foyer, glancing at the terraced fountains and huge pillars that stretched thirty feet to the sculptured ceiling. He checked in and was shown to the most luxurious of the hotel's seventy-three suites. He flipped open his laptop and connected to the net. Six new messages awaited retrieval. Four were from Internet companies that somehow managed to breach his firewalls with their stupid giveaway offers and he immediately deleted them. One was from Gem-Star's corporate office, the other from Liam O'Donnell. He ignored the Gem-Star e-mail and opened O'Donnell's communiqué.

His hired killer was en route from Ireland with three of his men and would arrive at six o'clock Cairo time. They constituted the first of two teams; the second group of three mercenaries were to remain in Belfast until needed. Kerrigan checked his watch—five hours until their arrival. He phoned down to the front desk and checked on the reservations for Liam and his men. One suite and three additional rooms were confirmed. He opened the Gem-Star file and perused it. His secretary was wondering why she couldn't contact him at his London hotel, and could he please phone in? He placed an international call, knowing he'd get her voice mail as Cairo was seven hours ahead of New York, putting the Big Apple time at six A.M. His secretary was dedicated, but not *that* dedicated. He let her know he'd call in later and hung up. He placed another overseas call, this time to the Washington, D.C., area. A man answered on the second ring.

"It's me," Kerrigan said. "Anything yet?"

"Wait a minute while I scramble the call," his contact at the National Security Agency said, and for a moment the line went blank. "Okay, we're clean on this end, you okay over there?"

"Hotel phone, but no one's interested in what I'm up to over here. It should be all right."

"Okay." The voice sounded hesitant. "I traced the latest debit from your Swiss account to a branch of the National Bank of the Cayman Islands. The money was forwarded from that account fifteen minutes later to the Bahamas, but I've run into some snags. I've got the transit number, but I can't access the actual account information."

"Why not?" Kerrigan asked, already irritated.

"They used a Canadian bank, the CIBC, and their security measures are state of the art. It's going to take a while to hack into their system."

"I pay you a lot of money to get information for me. Please get it."

"Yes, sir. As quickly as possible."

"Any hits on her e-mail?"

"No. She's either not signing on to the Internet, or she's put some sort of proxy in place. Either way, she's invisible right now."

"Keep monitoring her IP address and concentrate on Cairo. Get a list of every local server and plug into them. If she comes online, I want to know when and where."

"Yes, sir."

Kerrigan hung up and dialed an inside line at the Central Intelligence Agency at Langley. He received the same information from his CIA mole as he had from the man employed with the NSA. Kerrigan reiterated the instructions about tracing Samantha's IP address and terminated the call. He stood in the center of the room for a few minutes, trying to place himself in Carlson's shoes. What would they do? Where would they go? He felt reasonably sure that Liam O'Donnell was correct in his assumption that they were in Cairo. But where? He strode over to the window and looked down over the madness that stretched almost to the pyramids of Giza. Sixteen million people, and he was looking for three or four. Needles in the haystack, and this was one mother of a haystack.

He turned from the window and changed out of his business casual into a black tux. He slipped a thin billfold into his breast pocket and took the elevator to the main floor. The casino entrance was just off the lobby and he entered, asking for the baccarat tables. One of the casino managers appeared from nowhere and insisted on personally escorting him to the private gaming rooms and seating him opposite the dealer. Kerrigan extracted his billfold and placed a note on the table. The pit boss nodded at the new player and placed the equivalent of two hundred fifty thousand U.S. dollars in Egyptian pounds on the table. He slid the money across to Kerrigan.

"Good luck, sir," he said politely. Kerrigan just nodded and looked to the cards being dealt. He had at least five hours to kill, and a quarter million dollars would either carry him through or make him some serious money. He didn't care which.

Liam O'Donnell and his men were scheduled from London to Cairo aboard a British Airways A-340 Airbus. The flight was rough, with violent turbulence at 35,000 feet. The pilot opted to try 31,000 feet, but that almost proved disastrous. As the warm air rising from the Mediterranean collided with the cold Atlantic breezes, it threatened to tear the plane apart. Cabin service was suspended, then oxygen masks dropped from the overhead consoles, sending frightened passengers into a frenzy. Liam watched in bewilderment as act after act of extreme cowardice confronted him. The woman beside him screamed hysterically until he gave her a stiff elbow to her temple, knocking her senseless. A few of the calmer, more rational passengers actually clapped when he shut her up. They were midway through the flight before the pilot managed to drop below the opposing air masses and get the plane back under control. His seatmate slept until they began their descent into Cairo.

Once on the ground, O'Donnell moved efficiently through customs. The remainder of the first team joined him at the luggage carousel. They retrieved their bags and left the airport in a Mercedes taxi, giving the driver the address to the Semiramis Hotel. His watch, corrected to Cairo time, read just after seven P.M. when they checked in to the hotel. The desk clerk informed Mr. O'Donnell that Mr. Kerrigan was at the baccarat table in the casino and to please change into something formal and join him. O'Donnell found his room, threw his luggage on the bed, changed into some freshly pressed dress pants and headed out.

He found his boss easily enough. A small crowd had gathered at the entrance to the baccarat area, watching the high-stakes action. Kerrigan sat at a forty-five degree angle to the gateway, allowing him a peripheral view of the gawkers. He noticed O'Donnell immediately, and waved for him to enter. The guard posted at the break in the ropes hesitated for a moment, reluctant to let the Irishman in without a tux, but a quick flick of the pit boss's wrist and he moved aside. O'Donnell moved to Kerrigan's side and watched the hand play out. Kerrigan held eight and a half points, a winner unless the banker drew nine. He slid a pile of chips into the betting area and closed his bid. The banker declared eight and he raked in the pot. He motioned to the pit boss to cash him in and credit it to his room. He tipped the banker handsomely and left the room with O'Donnell.

"It looked like you had about one hundred thousand dollars in chips," O'Donnell said as they walked through the jumble of slot machines toward the door. "Not bad."

"Unless you consider that I started with two-fifty. Chump change." They didn't speak again until they reached Kerrigan's suite and both men settled into the easy chairs with a scotch in hand. "Who did you bring with you?"

"Brent, Tony and Paul," Liam answered. "They have better skills for close-in fighting. Street to street—the kind of stuff you get in a congested city. They're out picking up their weapons."

"Brandt came through okay?" Kerrigan asked, referring to

a nefarious German they had used on numerous occasions to arm themselves in foreign countries.

"As usual. He has a depot in the Masakin Al-Waila Al-Kabir district, in the northeast section of the city. It's two blocks from the Meteorological Services, and get this—one block from the National Guard headquarters."

"Brandt's got balls all right," Kerrigan said. "He should for what we pay him."

O'Donnell nodded. "Any hits on Carlson's location?"

"Not yet, but it won't be long. We've traced a withdrawal she made from the expedition's Swiss account three days ago to the Cayman Islands and then to Grand Bahama. The Canadian bankers on the island are rigorous, almost impenetrable, in their security. Almost. My men in Washington will find out where the money was transferred to when it left the Bahamas."

"So it's just a matter of time," Liam said.

"Yes. Once your men are armed, keep them ready," Kerrigan answered. "And speaking of being armed, the feedback I got from the soldiers who survived the jungle firefight was that our targets left with nothing but a few guns. No boxes of any sort."

"No ammunition." O'Donnell saw where Kerrigan was leading. "I'll check with Brandt as to where Carlson and her team will most likely find someone to sell them ammunition, and have my men watch for them to show up. There probably won't be more than a handful of places to buy clips for automatic weapons."

Kerrigan nodded and watched his team leader leave the upscale suite. He finished his scotch and poured another one, this time decanting the liquor until the ice cubes began to float. He sipped it slowly, enjoying the burning sensation on his throat. He moved to the window and stared out at the Nile River. It was murky, almost dark brown, and seemed stagnant, incapable of supporting life. Yet from this overused, exploited river an entire nation thrived. Millions of people and animals, crops and trees existed in the harsh desert environment that typified northern Africa for one reason only. The Nile. But it was an enigma. It gave hope, then took it away. It receded, then flooded. It was alive, an entity that knew it held the power of life or death over the living organisms that amassed on its banks as it meandered through the wastelands to the Mediterranean Sea. From the dark liquid, at first disgusting and putrid, came life. The silt and crud suspended in the water could be filtered and the water purified. Appearances were indeed deceiving.

Where the Nile had appearances of malodor, it truly benefited humanity. He, on the other hand, was presented to society as a man of good intentions—wealthy and giving. Nothing could be further from the truth. In his own mind he was dangerous and cunning, striving beneath the calm exterior for power and control—the power that came from capturing the global diamond market. And he was close. Closer than any one man or woman in history. Rhodes and Oppenheimer had toyed with control, but the very companies they created ultimately tied their hands: the Diamond Trading Company and De Beers. The two companies had stood the test of time, and had flourished by keeping tight control on global production and distribution. Now he stood poised to throw them into turmoil, and to rock the very foundation of the network they had created. And rock it he would. He had garnered diamonds from each of the first three expeditions to the Ruwenzori, but never the location. And from the rough he held or had sold, he knew the quality and quantity of the find was beyond anything previously discovered. It rivaled the legend of King Solomon's mines, yet this was no legend. It existed, and he would have it. And once he had it, he would use his trump card to either gain control or destroy De Beers. It would be their choice.

Kerrigan stared at the river, knowing greatness was at his fingertips. He felt the presence of the Pharaohs, of Cleopatra and Anthony, of the Egyptian gods. And he knew that history would remember him as a man of incredible vision, a man of action. And all he needed was the location of the diamonds. And to get that, he simply needed Samantha Carlson. And her, he *would* have. Soon.

NINETEEN

Roland Janus swung his Volvo S80 into the bank parking lot, switched off the ignition and sat for a moment, looking at the palm trees that surrounded the building. He adored palm trees. They personified everything he loved about life and disliked about his native country. A transplanted Canadian, he had never grown used to the cold weather and snow that descended every year between November and February. When the opportunity to head up the offshore investment banking division of the Canadian Imperial Bank of Commerce on Grand Bahama had dropped in his lap, he couldn't say yes quick enough. His wife and kids had been slightly less enthusiastic, but it was a career move, and they had tagged along out of necessity.

He slid out of the Volvo and headed for the building, without question the most impressive structure on the entire island. Fronted with massive pillars and coated with acrylic stucco, it had more the appearance of a Southern plantation than a bank. He entered through the front doors, nodding to staff members as he wove his way to his corner office. His secretary appeared with a steaming cup of coffee a few moments after he sat down. He powered up his computer, and immediately began to have a very bad day.

Someone had hacked into the secure system CIBC used to protect its international clients. He felt sweat forming in his armpits, dripping onto his silk shirt. He isolated the files the intruder had accessed and printed them. Seven wire transfers, all from the Caymans, and all within the last week. He switched programs and downloaded the client information, again sending it to the printer. Three transfers were for the same client, one who regularly used the tax-free conduit between the islands. He ignored them and looked at the remaining four.

The first was a nominal amount, just enough to cover the bank's fees for overseeing the offshore activity of a Pittsburgh company. The second was a transfer-in of funds for one of the staff members. He ignored them. The third was a sizable amount, over three hundred thousand dollars, that had been rerouted from their branch to a Cairo affiliate almost immediately after it arrived. He set that one on his desk. The final transfer was for over twenty million dollars, bank to bank. He discarded that and picked up the sole paper from his desk. Three hundred twenty thousand American dollars, wired in from the Caymans, then wired out inside one hour. Someone was trying to hide a money trail. But from whom? He kicked the program out and booted up a new one, this one capable of tracing an intruder's location. They had entered through the Internet, and he isolated the IP address of the user. He stared open-mouthed at the response.

The CIA had illegally tapped into their system and stolen information. What had been a slight perspiration problem became two large rings of wetness, soaking his shirt and ruining it. He didn't care. His problem was, what to do with this? If he filed a report, the big brass in Toronto would be all over this. A breach of security in an offshore bank, one that held over five billion dollars in tax-exempt money, was a major issue. What if it was drug money? One mandate the

CIBC was adamant about was that the money entering the pipeline was to be clean. They would not be a conduit for illegal funds. And one aspect of his job was to ensure the bank never laundered money.

Christ, what was going on? The implications of this were far-reaching and ugly. If the CIA was looking at wire transfers, they were there for a reason. And if that reason was dirty money, he could kiss his Bahamas posting good-bye. In fact, he could probably say good-bye to his career with the CIBC and any other reputable Canadian bank. He looked at the information that glowed at him from the screen. Then he looked at the keyboard, at the delete button. He sat unmoving for a minute or two, then reached out and pressed delete. The screen went blank, the CIA connection lost forever. He finished his coffee and changed his shirt. And said a silent prayer that the bastards would never hack into his system again.

TWENTY

Travis glanced back at Alain, waiting for the signal. One last car pulled away from the curb and Alain motioned to Travis that things looked clear. Travis shouldered the box and quickly moved down the stairs of the Angel Gabriel church to the waiting taxi. He dumped the box into the trunk and slammed the lid. Alain jumped in the rear passenger door and Travis joined him. The driver pulled away from the curb onto Harat as-Saqqayin and blended into the afternoon traffic. Both men watched the surrounding cars and vans closely to see if anyone was paying special interest to the cab. None were.

"That wasn't so bad," Alain said, relief obvious in his voice.

"I can't believe these guys. They pick a church to do the deal. Fuckers have no respect."

"Like you're a church-going guy, Travis. Maybe when pigs fly out of my butt."

McNeil grinned at his partner. "I think there's a god, and that he's got something special lined up for me." Vivid recollections of Samantha at the jungle pool came flooding back to him. "At least, I hope so."

The taxi pulled up to the villa and the driver jumped out and opened the trunk. Alain paid the man while Travis manhandled the heavy box from the trunk into the apartment. Alain closed the doors and by the time he reached the second floor, Travis and Samantha were inspecting the contents of the small crate. Row after row of bullets, 5.56mm and a perfect fit for the Vektors they had rescued from the jungle. He breathed deeply, feeling the cool touch of the metal against his fingertips.

"They wouldn't let us open it in the church," he explained to Samantha. "And they were well enough armed to not argue with."

"We weren't too worried," Alain added, "as Ali was referred to us by Greg Adamson. But still, you wonder."

Greg Adamson had come through again for Travis. The doctor had called to let them know Troy was recovering well and should be on a plane home within a day or two. While Travis had him on the line, he asked the doctor if he had connections that could net them ammunition for automatic weapons. Not surprisingly, he did, and two hours later Travis was having coffee with a cheerful Arab named Ali at a nearby coffeehouse. Ali informed him that 5.56mm ammunition was a piece of cake, it was becoming increasingly popular, and that he kept a few thousand rounds on hand all the time. The price would be significant, of course, as they didn't have the necessary paperwork to legally buy the munitions. Travis agreed and the next day they met at an address. An address that turned out to be the Angel Gabriel church.

Samantha rolled off the couch and stretched. "I want a real coffee," she complained. "Let's go to a coffeehouse."

Travis slid a handgun into his belt and pulled the loose Arabian garments over it. They walked, heading away from the center of the Khan El Khalili and its horrific odors. Three blocks east, bordering on the fringe of the popular bazaar, was a small cybercafé with four online computers.

The three westerners seated themselves at a table up front, just out of the ever-present sunlight. They ordered the house specialty and mint tea, and Samantha slipped in behind an older model Compaq computer and brought up the Internet. She quickly set up a proxy, then logged on and pulled up her mail. Three pieces, two from friends, and one from Patrick Kerrigan. She pointed to the name of the sender and both Travis and Alain leaned over to read the e-mail he had written.

Samantha Carlson,

It appears that things have not gone exactly as either of us would have predicted. You and the remainder of your team have left the Congo, and in doing so have violated one term of our contract. You were to stay in touch at all times, and to let Gem-Star know of your whereabouts. This is not the case at present, and thus voids our agreement.

I am reasonably sure that you know the precise location of the diamonds and the value of the find. To think that you can exploit the find is ludicrous. You have neither the resources nor the connections within the government necessary to take diamonds from the source into the world market. I, however, have both of these. So I suggest a compromise.

Contact me by sending a reply to this e-mail, giving me your current location, and we shall meet. For the information that leads me to the mine site, I will entrust to you ten percent of the net profit from all operations the find produces, over its entire life span. You do the math, Ms. Carlson. That's a lot of money. But first, we must meet.

Patrick Kerrigan

Samantha typed out a reply and looked to Travis and Alain for their approval. They both gave it the thumbs up and she hit *Send*. The message sat in the outbox for a few seconds, then disappeared on its way to Kerrigan's computer. She logged off, but the smile on her face dissipated quickly as the computer acknowledged her signoff.

"Oh, no," she whispered, more to herself than her table-mates. "Shit, shit, shit!"

"What's wrong?" McNeil asked.

"When I sign off, it should register me as an 'unknown user' because of the proxy. It didn't," she said, pointing to the screen. "It gives my e-mail address. I must have mistyped something when I set up the firewall on this system, or it may be so old it didn't recognize some of the commands. At any rate, we're in trouble."

"Define *in trouble*," Alain said.

"For the two or three minutes I was signed on to the Inter-net, my IP address was visible to the world. If Kerrigan has someone watching, they'll find it."

"Can they trace it back to this computer?"

"It's unlikely they could get that precise a hit on it, but I'm sure they'll know we're in Cairo."

"Okay," Travis said, sitting back in his chair and sipping his hot tea. "We've got to get out of here. Alain, we're going to need a car, truck, van, something that runs. I don't want to try flying. We don't have enough cash on hand to bribe the officials or charter another private plane, so we'd be forced to go through customs using our passports. I think we can get through a border checkpoint easier than the airport."

Alain nodded. "How much cash do we have left?"

"Just over ten thousand U.S.," he replied, not bothering to check his wallet. He finished his tea and stood up, looking down at Sam. "Let's go, just in case they traced your Internet connection quicker and more accurately than you think."

They paid the tab and left the cafe, Samantha and Alain following about a block behind Travis. Both men were armed with Glock A-17 pistols, their safeties off. Once back at the apartment, Alain laid out a plan of action to secure a vehicle. They called Adamson, who gave them the number of an Arab who always had something for sale, and if he didn't he'd know where to find it. One hour later, Travis and Alain had a meeting set to look at a fifteen-year-old Jeep. Samantha opted to stay in the cool of the apartment. She locked the outer doors behind the two men, then returned to the upper floor and powered up the computer.

This computer was secure, she was sure of that, and she wanted to stay up with her e-mail in case Kerrigan sent her another message. She signed on and checked her inbox. Just the two unopened messages from her friends. She sat back and stared at the screen, unseeing. What did she expect? Kerrigan to send her an e-mail saying that he'd been bad and now wanted to atone by giving himself up to the police? Hardly likely. He had them trapped like rats in a maze, except there was no exit to this labyrinth—it encompassed the globe. Kerrigan had money, and with money came power, the power to hire a small army to track them no matter where they hid. She swept her hair back from her face and flopped back into her chair. How the hell had she let herself get into such a mess? A million-dollar paycheck? The lure of unearthing a virgin diamond discovery? Returning to Africa? She mentally nodded to each one. She had been duped into working as Kerrigan's pawn for all those reasons, and at least one more—her interest in Travis McNeil. She switched her attention to the computer screen.

The Nasdaq was up, the Dow-Jones down, and the American economy moving back into a higher gear as people gained confidence in the Bush administration. A Palestinian terrorist had driven a bus loaded with explosives into an Israeli checkpoint, but the charges had failed to explode. A key word caught her attention and she clicked on a headline that read, "Families of Cranston Air Flight 111 protest continued search for diamonds." The full story leapt onto the screen and she read on.

HALIFAX, Nova Scotia (AP)

Embattled families of the 229 victims of Cranston Air Flight 111 that crashed into the Atlantic Ocean in September 2002 are again protesting the possible desecration of their loved ones' final resting spot by treasure hunters.

Ari Kryptostolis, a professional treasure hunter operating out of Athens, has confirmed his company will anchor a suction dredge ship above the wreckage site and comb the area for $300 million in missing diamonds.

Although 90 percent of the wreckage has been recovered, a stainless steel tube containing the diamonds has never been found. Experts speculate the tube was driven deep into the seabed on impact, and sits buried under a layer of sand. It is Kryptostolis's intention to strip away that sand and expose the tube.

It is this proposed action that spokesmen for the families are calling "crass" and even "illegal."

They may have a point, according to the law courts of Nova Scotia. Shortly after the crash, an exclusive application to search the area was granted to Lloyd's of London under the Treasure Trove Act. It appears Kryptostolis is in direct violation of that mandate.

However, Kryptostolis has also discovered a clause in the Act that may open a legal loophole for him to begin his search within the limits of Canadian law. And it is based on this loophole that he is bringing his ship and crew into the area, ready to begin salvage operations.

Lloyd's of London refused to comment on the latest development in what has been a public relations nightmare for the company since they first made their application shortly after the crash. Bowing to pressure from the families, Lloyd's did not proceed with its proposed search for the diamonds. Instead, they paid out the claim to the owner, Gem-Star, a privately owned company operating out of New York, and wrote off the loss.

For now, the grief and suffering of the families has

again been brought to the forefront as a dredge ship
prepares to hover above the burial site. Only time will
tell whether Kryptostolis will be successful in his search
for one of the richest treasures resting on the seabed.

Samantha read the second-to-last paragraph over and
over. Gem-Star had owned the diamonds on Cranston Air
Flight 111. What the hell was going on? This was too much
coincidence to *be* a coincidence. She stood up and paced
the room.

Three hundred million dollars in missing diamonds.
Gem-Star. Cranston Air Flight 111. Kerrigan. The diamonds
in the Ruwenzori. Her intuition was in overdrive—somehow
all of these were related. But how? She slowed her mind
down, and analyzed each thought as it came to her. If Kerrigan, and subsequently Gem-Star, had garnered those diamonds from the Congo, then there should be a record
somewhere of an expedition preceding the Cranston Air
crash by a few weeks or months. He had to send someone
in to find them, and if she could tie that team back to Gem-
Star, then she would know for sure that the diamonds on
that plane were from the find she had just unearthed. Christ,
how long had Kerrigan been looking for this vein? And a
better question was, why was Gem-Star mixed up in this if
Kerrigan was pulling the strings independently?

Sam clicked on the Internet search engine and entered
"geologists." The American Institute of Professional Geologists, AIPG, came up as a hit, and she double-clicked on it.
She scanned through its website until she came to the com-
memorative section, focusing on famous members who had
passed away over the years, and geologists who had died
while working in the field. She scrolled down to the year
2002. Two geologists had been killed while working abroad
that year, one in a traffic accident in London, and the other
in Africa. She concentrated on the latter, a Dr. Anthony
Leeds.

According to the article, Leeds had headed an expedition

into the southern region of the Congo in May 2002. His team had been set upon by hostile natives, and all twelve members killed. Funeral services were in the form of a memorial, as the bodies had been mutilated beyond recognition. She mentally calculated the time line. The expedition went in sometime in April or May, probably to northeastern Congo, not the south as reported. Kerrigan got core samples from the vein, but not the location. He analyzed the rough diamonds, knowing that he was onto an incredible find. But then he made his first mistake. He wiped out the team before he knew exactly where the diamonds were. She nodded to herself—that made perfect sense.

Now that she knew how difficult the kimberlite pipe was to find, she could assume that Kerrigan had felt he could find it if he knew its approximate location. Leeds must have seen through Kerrigan, as she had, and withheld the information. And so Leeds had been killed. Then Kerrigan had tried unsuccessfully to find the diamonds. But for how long? When was the next expedition he sent in? She went back to the AIPG site and continued looking.

The next prominent geologist to die was more than familiar to her. Dr. Samuel Carlson, killed in a plane crash off the coast of Morocco in the spring of 2004. She swallowed hard and fought back tears. She knew the story, and skipped over the details of how both her parents had died when the twin-engine commuter plane had lost altitude and crashed into the Atlantic. She scrolled down further, finally stopping at an entry from late 2005. Dr. Phillip McCullagh, a highly respected hard-rock geologist from Hartford, Connecticut, had disappeared without a trace while leading a team into Sierra Leone. What a pile of bullshit that was, she thought bitterly. The bones Travis had discovered only a few hundred yards from the diamonds were the remains of McCullagh and his team.

So Kerrigan had sent in at least three teams over the past eight years, including hers. He must have spent countless hours between the time he killed Leeds and finally gave up trying to find the diamonds himself and hired another geologist—almost four years. Then he got impatient and hired McCullagh. If McCullagh's crew was the second team, and they had also found the pipe, that meant Kerrigan had repeated his first mistake all over again. And while Kerrigan was the mastermind, it was Mugumba who pulled the trigger. The son of a bitch. He deserved what he got. The man had used his position within the Congolese army to lure innocent people into the jungle and then slaughter them when he got the word from Kerrigan. It was coming together now, but there was still one thing that she didn't get. Why was Gem-Star noted as the owner of the diamonds? If, in fact, Kerrigan was running this show on his own, that was the one piece of the puzzle that didn't fit.

A noise in the courtyard below startled her, and she peeked out the window. Travis and Alain were back.

"How did the car shopping go?" she asked.

"Marvelous," Alain said, smiling. "We landed ourselves a real beauty. And for half the price the prick was asking."

"It's a piece of shit," Travis said, laughing. "And we probably paid twice what it's really worth. But it's a truck, sort of, and it'll get us out of here. How are you? Everything okay here?"

"More than okay. Listen to this." Samantha took the next ten minutes filling in the men on her speculations. Once she finished, the room was silent. Travis rose and poured some of the tea Samantha had brewed while she talked. He sipped it slowly, and no one spoke, waiting for the team leader to agree or disagree with her conjecture.

"Sam, the diamonds that were leaving New York, en route to Geneva, were they rough stones or cut?"

"Rough," she answered. "Once they arrived in Geneva they would be sent on to Antwerp to be accurately appraised, then cut and polished."

"So the three-hundred-million-dollar price tag they placed on the stones could have been just an approximate estimate," he said and she nodded. "Perhaps far below their actual value."

She nodded again, then suddenly sat bolt upright. "Christ," she whispered. "You're not suggesting . . ."

"It's just speculation, Sam," he said.

"There's a way to find out if we're right," Sam responded, moving to the keyboard and typing a couple of words into the search engine. A response came back almost immediately. Twenty-seven matches found for "diamond sights." She clicked on an icon to arrange them chronologically, then looked at the results. She opened numerous files, looking at the contents, then glanced back to him. She nodded.

Alain looked confused. "I'm sorry, guys, I don't get what's going on. Would someone like to tell me what you two are thinking?"

Samantha started. "Kerrigan never introduced Travis or me to anyone inside Gem-Star, so we suspected the company had no idea of what Kerrigan was actually doing in the Congo. Yet Gem-Star showed up as the owners of the diamonds on the Cranston Air Flight 111 manifest. There's a good chance that those diamonds came from the kimberlite pipe we just uncovered."

"How do you know that?" Alain asked. "That's a hell of a stretch."

"Not really," Sam countered. "Only a small percentage of the yearly diamond production is of the quality of our find. And that makes them easily tracked, sort of. The legitimate diamonds come through London, with very few exceptions. The illegitimate stones pass through Switzerland, and believe me, there's a lot of illegal rough floating about. Whichever way the stones enter the pipeline, they eventually head to Antwerp to be cut and polished."

Alain's eyes lit up as he started to get the drift. "So even if someone steals a bunch of diamonds from a mine in, say, South Africa, and smuggles them to Switzerland, they end up going through the same process as legitimate diamonds. With De Beers and the Diamond Trading Company controlling production."

"Exactly. De Beers knows that it can't control all the

roughs from every mine in the world, but what they can control is the diamond auctions, or sights, as they're called in the industry."

"So what did you get from looking on the Internet under 'sights'?" Alain asked.

"We know that three hundred million dollars in diamonds belonging to Gem-Star went down with Cranston Air Flight 111 on September 2, 2002. We also know that hostile natives killed a prominent geologist, Dr. Anthony Leeds, in the Congo in May of 2002. It's not that much of a stretch to guess that he found the pipe and brought a good deal of rough out with him. Kerrigan had him killed and kept the diamonds, but couldn't find the pipe. Now this is where it gets interesting. Somehow, someone at Gem-Star found out about the diamonds. I have no idea how. But they must have, because in September the company loaded an indestructible steel tube onto a plane bound for Geneva. From there the diamonds would have been shipped to Antwerp to be cut and polished, and their true value established. But something happened. The plane crashed."

"So Kerrigan didn't *want* the diamonds to reach Geneva," said Alain. "Once they reached one of the sights, the quality of the gems would be revealed and Gem-Star would know that the three hundred million dollars they thought they had put on the plane was undervalued. And a mining company would pick up quite quickly on an error like that. Davis Perth would be asking Kerrigan a lot of questions."

"Precisely," Sam said. "And what's the best way to be sure the diamonds never reach Geneva?" She waited a moment, then answered her own question. "Don't put them on the plane."

"I didn't see that part of it," Travis said softly. "I thought they were in the cargo hold, just as the manifest said."

"No, and the reason I know for sure are the sights that followed over the next ten months. Look here," she said, pointing to the screen. "Extremely high-quality Sierra Leone stones reached nine of the next sixteen sights. Except they weren't from Sierra Leone, they were from our kimberlite pipe in the Ruwenzori. Kerrigan never loaded those diamonds onto the plane. He kept them and then sold some of them over the next few months at these sights. I'm positive of that."

"But when the plane arrived in Geneva," Alain began, "they would find out that the tube was empty...." He stopped, open-mouthed.

"Exactly," Samantha said, her face dark. "It makes you wonder what brought down Cranston Air Flight 111."

TWENTY-ONE

Patrick Kerrigan reached for a towel, then stepped from the shower onto the thick mat the hotel provided for its premier guests. He rubbed the plush towel across his head quickly, drying his hair enough to comb it out, and put in some gel to hold it. He stood in front of the mirror, admiring what he saw. Fifty-three years of age and in peak physical condition. Rich and powerful, and still filled with the driving ambition that had brought him this far in life.

The phone rang and he walked into the living room and answered it. A hushed voice spoke to him from across the Atlantic.

"We've found her," the man said from his office deep in the CIA headquarters in Langley, Virginia.

"Where is she?" Kerrigan asked, his pulse quickening.

"She's in Cairo. Her IP address popped up for a couple of minutes on the Internet, then went down again. But it was long enough to get a pretty good fix."

"Where in Cairo?"

"Somewhere near the Mausoleum al-Husain. The service provider she signed on with is quite small. They only cover the area south of the Sari-Ramsis to the northern tip of the City of the Dead. I'll try to get the exact address, but it could take a while."

"How long?" Kerrigan asked, impatient.

"One, perhaps two days," his informant responded.

"Okay," he said, pondering the time delay. One day was fine, two was stretching it. "Try to be back to me within twenty-four hours."

"I'll do my best," the voice said; then the line went dead.

Kerrigan rang Liam O'Donnell's room and asked the man to join him immediately. Less than fifty seconds later, there was a soft knock on the door. Just as O'Donnell entered, the phone rang and Kerrigan motioned for O'Donnell to sit down and wait. He picked up the phone. He nodded a few times to the caller, said a few terse yeses, then hung up. He turned to O'Donnell.

"The NSA," Kerrigan said, pointing to the phone. "You won't believe the audacity of Carlson and her little band of mercenaries. They withdrew three hundred twenty thousand dollars from the Swiss account I set up for them to use while in the Congo, and funneled that money through to guess where?"

O'Donnell shrugged.

"Cairo. And guess where in Cairo?"

"I have no idea," Liam said.

"There's a Banque Masr in the narrow street that runs between the Halnan Shepheard Hotel and the Semiramis. They picked up the money, *my* money, less than a block from this hotel. The arrogant bastards."

"When?"

"Four days ago. They routed it from Geneva to the Caymans, then through the Bahamas into Cairo. It took days for my contact at the NSA to get the information from the CIBC bank on Grand Bahama Island."

"Four days is a long time in a city this large," O'Donnell said. "They could be anywhere."

"True. But I had another call from my source in the CIA. Carlson signed on to the Internet somewhere near the Mausoleum al-Husain."

"I know where that is. It's close to the Khan El Khalili Bazaar. That makes sense," O'Donnell said, and continued as Kerrigan made a motion with his hand. "If they're near the bazaar, they can get pretty well anything they need without moving around much. And I'm sure McNeil would prefer moving around Cairo in the darkness whenever possible."

"Move your team in from Belfast. Carlson and the SEALs are here, and I want to trap them before they can escape. Set up some sort of surveillance on the area around the Khan El Khalili. If they so much as stick a nose out of a doorway, I want it shot off. Just remember, don't kill Carlson. I need her alive."

O'Donnell nodded and left the room to make arrangements. It suddenly dawned on Kerrigan that if Samantha had signed on the Internet, there was a good chance she had opened his e-mail. He flipped open his laptop and signed on. He connected to the net and checked his inbox. One new message, and it was from Samantha Carlson. He hesitated for a second, then opened the file.

Patrick Kerrigan,

The very fact that I had any agreement with you, at any time, leaves my stomach in knots. I really don't care if I'm in violation of anything to do with you.

As to the location of the diamonds, you're absolutely correct. I know precisely where they are. And guess what? It's the mother lode.

As far as my location is concerned, piss off.

SC

Kerrigan's teeth ground together as he clenched his jaw. His breathing became increasingly deeper and his temples throbbed as his blood pressure rose, and his face took on a crimson glow. He strived to keep his cool, but the facade snapped and he grabbed the laptop and tore the connections from the wall. He hurled it at the window and watched in amazement as the computer smashed through both panes of glass. He stood fixated, trembling with rage.

The woman had survived what the other expeditions had not: the jungle and the murderous Colonel Mugumba. She had located the diamonds, and now she mocked him. Perhaps he had picked the men to guard her just a little too well. He knew that McNeil was good; hell, he had insisted on better than good. He needed a team to keep his geologist alive until he wanted her dead. But when he decided it was time for someone to die, she should die. Yet that hadn't happened. McNeil had rescued her from Mugumba and had brought her to Cairo. And now, somewhere in the sprawling city, he had hidden her.

Kerrigan regained his composure as he concentrated on the question, where would they hide? O'Donnell was probably right; they would try to assimilate, disappear into the sea of humanity that was Cairo. The closer they were to something like the Khan El Khalili the better. For them, and now, perhaps, for him. Yes, a sixth sense told him that O'Donnell was on target, that they were close.

He moved toward the door as the anticipated knocking began. The hotel manager would be wondering what had happened, and if his prize guest, who was paying enormous sums of money for the room, was all right. He would assure the man that everything was fine. He had simply lost his balance and the laptop had slipped from his grasp and hit the window. Just add it to the bill. But the last thing that Patrick Kerrigan envisioned before he opened the door was not the manager; it was Samantha Carlson, on the floor and pleading for her life.

And he knew what his answer would be.

TWENTY-TWO

Travis stowed the Vektor MINI under the driver's seat after checking that the clip was full. He stared at the tips of the bullets for a few seconds, marveling at how perfectly sculpted each one was, how harmless they looked crowded into the magazine. Until the shooter pulled the trigger and they flew from the muzzle at a speed that defied the imagination, wreaking havoc on anything in their path. He gently patted the gun, praying it wouldn't be needed to escape Cairo. Samantha appeared in the doorway, her arms laden with the last of their food. She dumped it in the back of the Wagoneer and jumped in. Alain slipped through the entranceway to the apartment, locked the door, and slid in the front seat beside her.

The plan was simple. Exit Cairo on the northeast-running number three highway, skirt the international airport, and then across the desert to the Sinai Peninsula. They would follow the coastal highway until a few miles from Rafah, then cut inland and cross the Israeli border just south of the Gaza Strip. But the first thing was to escape the horrific traffic that clogged the main arteries and small side streets alike.

"Where's the sniper rifle?" Travis asked Alain, sliding the keys into the ignition.

"It's under some blankets in the box. There's no way we're getting through a customs inspection like this. We'll have to dump the guns before we hit the Israeli border."

"Yeah, but let's keep them until then. Just in case." He gunned the ignition and the old Jeep motor sputtered to life, deep blue smoke belching from the exhaust. The truck was a piece of junk, but decrepit vehicles on their last legs blended into the Cairo traffic much better than a newer model. And anonymity was exactly what they were striving for.

Travis pulled ahead slowly, and the morning sun hit the cracked windshield, momentarily blinding him. Three city buses surrounded them in seconds, the giant red and white vehicles choking them with diesel fumes. Travis slowed, letting the buses pass. He headed west, the ancient walls of the Mausoleum al-Husain crowding them on the left side. At the House of Qadi, he hung a right and headed north on Bab an-Nasr. The bumper-to-bumper traffic crawled through the gritty haze of the morning heat. The only vehicles making any time were the mopeds that darted between the stalled cars and trucks. He swore under his breath, cursing the traffic.

"Try to keep in mind the Egyptians built this part of the city back in the eight hundred to eleven hundred AD range. There weren't a lot of cars then," Samantha said. She saw a tinge of a smile on his lips, but he didn't respond. She knew both the men sitting next to her were on edge, ready and watching for anything that could spell trouble. She concentrated more on the sights, trying to enjoy the ride.

"What exactly have we got for guns?" Travis asked as traffic began to move.

"Two Vektors, the Sako sniper rifle, two Glock A-17s, and the Panthers for communications. Plenty of ammo for the Vektors, lacking slightly on the Glocks."

"How many Panther units made it back from the Congo?"

"Two," Alain replied. "I've checked them and they work

fine. Batteries are a bit weak on one, but the range should still be over a mile, even in the city."

"Excellent, but we do *not* split into three separate groups." The accent was hard on "not." "Sam, you'll have to stay with either Alain or me. I don't want one of us without communication, and with only two mobile radios, that means we'll have to team up."

"That's fine," Sam said. "We're just driving out of Cairo anyway, so what's the big deal?"

"Yeah," Alain said. "Stop being such a pessimist. We're out of here."

Travis grinned. The traffic opened up a bit and he surged ahead with the flow. Bab an-Nasr threw off its shackles once they cleared the northern edge of the Khan El Khalili. He shifted into third gear and leveled off at twenty-five miles an hour. Ahead and to the left was the backside of the ancient walls of old Cairo. Constructed of tightly formed blocks of sandstone, the walls rose over thirty feet from the dusty ground. They were punctuated with two massive gates, the closest being the Bab al Futuh, or Gate of Conquests, with four separate towers rising above the walls and culminating in square turrets some seventy feet high. A quarter mile to the west was the Bab el Nasr, or Gate of Victory. It sported a single, intricately carved round pinnacle the same height as its non-identical twin, and was equally as impressive, although much smaller. He stole a quick glance at Samantha as he drove, watching her reaction to the thousand-year-old monuments to man's abilities. She was impressed, staring at the wall with the true admiration of a history buff.

"Unbelievable," she said under her breath.

"The walls?" Travis asked and she silently nodded. "You can almost visualize the battles that have been fought here over the centuries. Hot oil pouring down on exposed attackers as they crawled up skinny ladders. Rocks, spears and arrows pelting down on them, anything to keep the Mongol hordes from breaching Cairo's walls."

"Very descriptive, Travis," Samantha said. "But today, it's just another quiet day in a modern city."

He looked grim. "Let's hope it stays that way."

From the darkness of an alley entrance, Brent Hagan scanned the nearly stationary traffic as it inched past him on the Bab an-Nasr. Beneath his loose-fitting western-style clothes lurked a Smith & Wesson 9mm pistol. The ex-MI-5 operative slid his hand under his vest and felt the reassuring coolness of the aluminum and stainless steel alloys that formed the barrel of the gun. He wrapped his fingers around the back strap handle, cradling the weapon gently. The safety was on, but it took only a split second to release it.

His radio sputtered briefly as the Cairo traffic began to pick up a touch. He slipped his hand into his trouser pocket and clicked the talk button, speaking and listening on hands-free. It was Liam O'Donnell checking in. He reported back that he had seen nothing yet, but was still watching the main street a block from the cybercafé where Carlson's Internet signal originated. He killed the call and let his eyes roam over the mass of beat-up cars and trucks that typified Cairo traffic. A white Benz caught his eye, the rear windows darkened, but the passenger was an Egyptian woman and the driver in the midst of a heated argument with her. Little chance there would be foreigners huddled in the rear of that car listening to a husband and wife squabble. He rubbed his eyes, the airborne grit irritating his corneas and drying out his eyes almost to the point of pain. He blinked a few times and stared. Two vehicles from the curb and rolling slowly by was a dilapidated Jeep Wagoneer, driven by Travis McNeil. A woman sat next to him, and another man had the window seat. Brent Hagan turned slowly from the street and moved into the shadows of the alley. He was positive neither McNeil nor his passengers had spotted him. He clicked the send button on his radio.

"It's me," O'Donnell's voice responded to his call.

"I've got them," Hagan answered. "On the Bab an-Nasr,

near the edge of the Khan El Khalili. One block east of the restaurant where she connected to the Internet."

"What are they driving?"

"A Jeep. I'd estimate about 1985, give or take a year or two. It's white, with wood-grain side panels and red primer showing through on both front fenders. All three of them are in the front. I can't see anyone, or anything, in the back."

"Is there a second vehicle?" O'Donnell asked.

"No. I looked for one, but I'm pretty sure they're alone."

"Okay. Keep them in sight, but don't try to take them. Paul and Tony, are you guys online?" The remaining two members of the first team responded that they had been listening in and were up to speed on things. "Brent, watch for Paul and Tony. They'll be coming up Bab an-Nasr from the south in a Fiat. The second team is here from Belfast as well. I'll grab them and head over from the hotel. We'll come in from the north and try to cut them off."

"Roger that," Hagan replied. "They're heading north right now, but they're not making much progress. The traffic's pretty bad. You've got time, but I'm not sure how much."

"We'll be there inside half an hour. Tony and Paul should be about five minutes away. Call in if you think they're going to get too far north for us to cut them off. And don't lose them."

O'Donnell grabbed the phone and dialed the room his men had just checked into. They'd be tired from their flight from Belfast, but he didn't care—work came first. He instructed them to meet him outside the main lobby in three minutes. He left his room, then reconsidered and went back, putting through a quick call to Patrick Kerrigan. Voice mail picked up and he left a quick message that they were off to meet the Carlson party. He took the elevator to the parking garage, and jumped into the rented Mercedes, squealing the tires as he sped out into the bright sunlight. His second team was waiting at the front entrance as he pulled up. They climbed in and O'Donnell opened the frequency to Brent Hagan as he tore down the hotel driveway.

"I'm with Tony and Paul in the Fiat, and we've still got a visual on them," Hagan answered, "but they're moving quicker now. The traffic thinned out once they left the Khan El Khalili. What do you want us to do?"

"We're just leaving the hotel. How far north will we have to be to get in front of them?"

"There's no way you'll get across in time to cut them off, Liam. They're moving way too fast for that. They're almost at the old city wall."

"Shit!" O'Donnell said tersely between clenched teeth. He thought for a brief moment, then gave the first team the go-ahead. "Once they hit the wall, take them out. But for Christ's sake, don't kill the woman."

"Yes, sir." The radio went silent.

Alain picked the Fiat out of the traffic as it tailed them toward the wall. He watched the car for a few moments as it jockeyed about the dense traffic, closing the distance without drawing attention. Still, to the trained eye it stood out. Once he was positive, he turned to Travis.

"We've got company. The white Fiat about one hundred fifty feet back. They've been moving up on us, trying to stay behind vehicles as they shift lanes. I think there's three guys in the car."

Travis divided his time between driving and watching the car in the side rearview mirror. After a minute or two he nodded. "Yeah, I'd say we've got a tail." He switched lanes, moving closer to the curb. When he spoke, he wasted no words. "As we reach the east edge of the wall, I'll take a sharp left. We'll be out of their sight for a minute or so. Get out, take Sam and the sniper rifle with you and head for high ground. I'll pull in at the second gate, it's about a quarter mile down. I'll move to the right, away from the wall and draw them into the open." He turned to Alain, his eyes riveted on the man. "Get at least one. I can't handle all three."

Alain simply nodded and grasped Samantha by the elbow. A few seconds later, Travis reached the easternmost edge of the old wall and cranked a quick left. A few cars slammed on their brakes to avoid them and the traffic quickly jammed up behind. The second they cleared the wall and were out of sight, Alain and Sam jumped from the vehicle. Alain leaned into the back and yanked out the Sako and a blanket to cover it. He pointed toward the Bab al Futuh and Sam broke into a quick run for the ancient gate. They reached the massive stone structure and Alain headed up the series of stairs that led to the walkway atop the wall. By the time they reached the top, Travis was nearing the second gate a quarter mile to the west. Except for them, the walkway was deserted. Alain slipped his Glock from his belt and handed it to Samantha.

"Watch the top of the stairwell we just came up. If a white guy pokes his head through, shoot him. Try not to kill any innocent Arabs."

She nodded and watched as he slid the blanket off the sniper rifle and flipped open the tripod. He chambered a round and sighted on Travis as he leapt from the truck. Puffs of sand exploded around Travis as he charged into the nearest building. Seconds later, the Fiat screeched to a halt and three men piled out, heading for the doorway Travis had just entered. The lead man didn't make it ten feet. Alain's shot tore through his right lung, spinning him violently and slamming him into the coarse brick building. He slid down the wall to the dusty ground, clutching his chest for a moment before going limp. Alain moved the barrel slightly and sighted on a second target. He squeezed the trigger, then swore in disgust as he watched the bullet dig into the stone as the man disappeared into the building. He grabbed the Panther and held the send button down.

"Got one," he whispered. "Two hot on you, already in the building."

Travis heard the staccato burst of automatic gunfire as he leapt from the vehicle and ran for the three-story building. Bullets zinged past him as he crossed the threshold into temporary safety. He surveyed his position. A small brass plaque denoted the business that occupied the building as an architectural firm. Stretching directly ahead was a brightly lit hallway. A long glass wall lined with offices and a reception area lay to the left, a textured interior wall to the right, unbroken but for a stairwell leading up and down. He chose the hallway and jogged quietly down its length, adjusting the Vektor MINI so the gun dangled across his chest from the shoulder strap. He heard a vehicle come to a sudden stop outside the front of the building just as he reached the rear entrance. He pushed open the fire door and burst into a heavily foliated atrium. The sharp crack of the sniper rifle touched his ears as he closed the door behind him. Seconds later, his earpiece crackled with static and Alain's voice. "Got one. Two hot on you, already in the building." Travis raced around the pond and fountain in the atrium's center, dove behind a bank of dwarf palms and waited.

Slowly, the door from the hallway swung open. Travis lowered the Vektor and his finger tightened slightly on the five-pound trigger. He waited. The door swung back and clicked shut. He cursed under his breath. His adversaries knew where he was, but were professional enough to know that if they stepped through the door they were dead. He reevaluated his situation, scanning the atrium and the four walls that contained it. The building he had entered was square, with the entire center of the structure dedicated to the atrium. Four doors, one on each wall, exited the atrium back into the building. Windows from the interior offices looked down on the atrium and a few concerned faces were staring down at him from the third floor. They must have heard the gunfire from the front of the building. He had to act quickly; the police would be arriving, and at this point, he would just as soon take his chances with Kerrigan's men as spend time in a Cairo jail. Travis chose the exit door to his left, opened it and found himself in a hallway similar to the one leading from the front doors.

This hall was dimly lit and he hugged its edges as he moved stealthily toward the far door. If he was correct, it should lead out on the side of the building closest to where Alain and Samantha were dug in on the wall. Halfway down the corridor, he realized he'd made a bad decision. He heard the soft click of a pistol's hammer cocking, and only his lightning-fast reflexes saved him. The bullet slammed into the wall exactly where his head had been only milliseconds before, as he rolled hard across the hall and smashed open an office door with his feet. He continued rolling, his momentum taking him out of the hall and into the room behind the door. It was a dentist's office, and a stunned patient in the chair, the dentist and his assistant all stared at him as he came crashing through the door. The assistant started screaming as Travis jumped to his feet and ran from the dental room through the reception area and into another hallway that serviced the front of the businesses. He turned left, his legs pumping hard as he made for the exterior door some fifty feet away. He touched the send button on the Panther as he ran.

"Alain, I'm coming out the side door closest to you. They're on my ass." The radio clicked and he knew Porter had received the message and was sighting the gun on the exit door away from the main street. He burst into the sunshine, ducking as he heard gunfire in the confines of the hall behind him. Bullets ricocheted wildly off the door and slammed into a nearby palm. He kept moving, running across the open space between buildings, giving his attackers a target. If they could see his back, they should exit the building to sight on him, and when they did, Alain would be ready.

Less than ten seconds passed; then the unmistakable crack of the Sako sniper rifle shot across the empty lot. Travis immediately dove to his right, rolled, and swept his submachine gun up and aimed at the door. His finger tightened and bullets spewed from the gun even before he had stopped sliding on the smooth sand. He watched as one of the men took hit after hit from the Vektor, the bullets jerking his body like a life-size rag doll. Travis eased the pressure on the trigger and the gun went quiet. The body he had raked with automatic fire teetered for a second, then crashed face first into the dust, unmoving. Travis waited for a few seconds, then rose, walking hesitantly back toward the building.

Two bodies lay near the door. The man he had shot was dead before he hit the ground. The second man must have taken a bullet from the Sako. Travis approached warily, unsure of whether Alain's bullet had killed the man or just disabled him. As he neared, he saw a slight movement. He let the Vektor hang from its shoulder strap and slipped out his pistol. He took off the safety and chambered a round. He extended his hands in front of him, targeting the man's head. Twenty feet out, he saw a two-way radio lying next to the prone figure. The man's finger had the send button depressed and he was talking into the mouthpiece as best he could, considering the extent of his injuries. Travis could see both hands, but not a gun. He rushed the last fifteen feet and kicked the radio from the man's grasp. He stared into the eyes that glared back at him from the ground.

"Who did you call?" he asked.

"Go to hell," the man answered, his breathing labored.

Travis knew the longer he stayed, the greater the risk he'd be dealing with the Cairo police. He left the man as he lay, injured but not dying. Alain's shot had crushed the man's shoulder and clavicle, probably collapsed his lung. Some emergency-room doctor could patch him up, but the man wouldn't be a threat for some time.

Travis ran back to his vehicle, slipped into the driver's seat and slammed the old Jeep into gear. He cut a wide U-turn and clicked on the Panther, telling Alain to get back to ground level. He sped back down the Sari al-galal, the historic old wall looming over the road to the right. In the distance, the sound of sirens cut through the late morning heat. He slid to a stop directly in front of the massive Gate of

Conquests just as Alain and Samantha hit ground level running. They jumped into the Jeep and Travis floored it, cutting hard left into the bordering Bab an-Nasr cemetery. He slowed as he entered the graveyard, the vehicle hidden from the main road by the trees and headstones that marked the graves. The sounds of sirens diminished as they drove farther into the burial grounds. After three minutes, he stopped and opened the map.

"The second guy you hit was still alive," Travis said.

"Shit. I thought I hit him a bit high and to the left." Alain wiped some perspiration from his forehead. He looked distraught.

"Don't worry about it. He *did* have a radio, though, and I'm pretty sure he called someone before I got it away from him."

"That's bad, isn't it?" Samantha said, still shaking.

"Oh, yeah," Travis said quietly. "It's bad. The radio he was using has a maximum range of a few miles, so whomever he called is close. And these guys are professionals. They're not going to keep missing."

Samantha sat quietly as the men discussed which route to take. This had become a nightmare, except the corpses were real. She had unleashed a chain of events with no upside. The diamonds she had uncovered in the depths of Africa were responsible for the death and suffering that was now clinging to her. She'd known going in that the bane of precious stones was misery and now that misery had become a real, tangible thing.

Sometimes, diamonds weren't a girl's best friend. Sometimes they were just plain ugly.

TWENTY-THREE

The two-way radio was filled with static, but the voice was discernable. Two men dead, the caller badly wounded and without a weapon. McNeil was approaching, gun outstretched. The voice again gave the location and a quick description of the Jeep McNeil was driving. Then silence. Liam O'Donnell listened for a few moments, then handed it off to the man in the front passenger seat of the van.

"How far are we from the old wall?" he asked. A map of Cairo sat on the passenger's lap.

"Only two or three minutes. Take the next right," the man replied.

O'Donnell drove on in punctuated silence for the next couple of minutes, taking directions from his navigator as they approached the old wall. Two blocks away, they saw a congregation of police and emergency vehicles outside a low-rise office building opposite the wall. O'Donnell kept his speed low and stole a quick glance as they passed the carnage. Directly in front of the main entrance, a sheet covered a prone figure. The Fiat his men had been driving was parked nearby. On the far side of the building, he saw two bodies lying on the dry earth just outside the exit door. Emergency crews were working on one; the other was covered with a sheet. O'Donnell took in the angles as he cruised by, then stopped four blocks farther up the road. Immediately opposite them sat the old wall of Cairo, and the Gate of Conquests. O'Donnell stepped from the van and looked around for a minute, then got back in and turned to his men.

"Brent reported them moving north toward the wall. That would bring them out just ahead of us." He engaged the transmission and pulled up another hundred yards to the intersection just past the massive gate. "If McNeil turned this corner, that would put his vehicle out of sight for almost a minute. Lots of time to dump off whoever's with him." He pointed to the gate. "If I were in his position, I'd send a shooter up to higher ground, then try to draw whoever is following me from their vehicle and have the sniper take them out. That would explain the body in front of the building."

O'Donnell's mobile phone rang and he punched the send button. Kerrigan's voice filled his ear.

"What the hell is going on? And don't tell me you guys are behind all this shooting at the old wall."

"It was us," O'Donnell admitted. "The first team had no choice. They had a visual, but the targets were moving too quickly for the second team to cut them off. They had to act."

"It's all over the news. Who's under those sheets?"

"Two of team one are gone, one is still alive."

"Where's Carlson?"

"We're close to them. I hope to have them back visually within the hour. They shouldn't be too hard to spot. They're driving a white '85 Jeep Wagoneer. There's not a lot of those around Cairo."

Kerrigan exploded. "You lost them? Where are you?"

"Just down the street from the media covering the shootout. Beside the old wall."

"I'm coming," came the terse reply across the phone line.

"Keep your cell on and call in with your location as you move. And Liam . . ." O'Donnell didn't respond for a few seconds and Kerrigan finished the sentence. "Find them."

O'Donnell hit the end button. His mind was already on the task of deciding which way his prey would have moved. "Okay, McNeil's got a shooter on the wall, and he ducks into the building. Team one pulls up, empties the car, and one guy takes a slug in the back. Two follow McNeil into the building. Eventually, he comes out the side door. Why?"

He turned the ignition off and got out of the van. He stood on the side of the road for a few minutes, judging the angles, trying to reenact what had happened. "They've got radios," he said suddenly. Now everything made sense.

"McNeil calls to his sniper that he's coming out the side door. The shooter targets it and takes out the second figure that exits. McNeil hears the shot, turns and fires. Three men down." He snapped his fingers as the sequence became clearer and clearer. "That leaves McNeil at the building and his sniper in the tower. He returns to his vehicle, turns around and picks up his sniper right here." He turned to look at the gate. "That puts him almost where I'm standing. Now where would I go?"

He immediately ruled out returning on the road they had taken to get to the old wall. And turning around and driving by the dead bodies was completely out of the question. That left the cemetery. He pointed to the north, at the gate into the graveyard. He knew for sure McNeil would have taken that way out. Now he just had to find them. He jumped back into the van and crossed the road, slowing as he entered the cemetery. And he *would* find them; it was just a matter of time.

Kerrigan had driven less than a block after terminating his call with O'Donnell when an idea hit him. He called the police emergency line from his cell phone, finding an operator who spoke broken English. He informed her that he had seen a vehicle leaving the area near the old wall only moments after the shootings. He described the Jeep Wagoneer to her exactly as Liam had to him, then hung up. The two-way radio sat next to him on the seat and he switched the frequency over to the police band. It was partially obscured by static, but he could make out individual voices as the police checked in to command central. He stopped his car at a nearby corner and called out to the group of men hanging around the corner.

"Anyone talk English?" he yelled above the din of the traffic. One man stepped forward, eyeing the Mercedes with longing.

"I speak English," he said, a tinge of a British accent to his voice.

Kerrigan surveyed the man for a moment. Reasonably dressed, with nicer shoes than most. His hair was well groomed and clean, as were his western-style clothes. "I need you to translate," he said, waving for him to get in the car, holding an American one-hundred-dollar bill in his outstretched hand. The man did so without hesitation. "Listen to what the police are saying and translate it for me. I want to know everything about the shootings at the old wall, and especially if they locate the Jeep they're looking for."

The Arab nodded and began to interpret. Most of the calls to and from the dispatch were about the shootings, and Kerrigan began to get the story straight. Liam was correct. Two of his men were dead, and one wounded. Nothing about the Jeep, but that would change with time. He continued driving in a northeasterly direction, sure that a police cruiser would spot the Jeep soon, and then the chase would be on.

Samantha watched the tombstones slide past as they cruised through the cemetery at a reasonable speed. She knew Travis wanted as much space as possible between him and the fiasco at the old wall, but speeding through a deathly quiet cemetery was not the way to stay incognito. She had opted for the backseat, and could hear the two men discussing their options as they drove. Travis favored a run straight out the number three highway, past the airport and on to Israel. Alain wanted to head north until they were well out of the city, then cut sharply to the east en route to the border. Travis eventually won out, his logic being that their adversaries would expect them to circumvent the obvious route. Because of this, they would be watching every major road they could, with the exception of the number three. At least, that was the logic. Alain disagreed, but finally caved.

Travis neared the northern edge of the cemetery and turned slowly onto the main east-west road. He accelerated into the traffic and kept at an even fifty miles an hour. It was bordering on noon and the lunch hour brought even more Cairo motorists onto the thoroughfare. They passed a traffic cop parked on the shoulder, who seemed to take a special interest in their vehicle. Travis shrugged it off as paranoia. He concentrated on driving and slowed at the traffic circle that controlled the intersection of Sari-Ramsis and Sari al-Abbasiya and checked his rearview mirror. The police car that had spotted them three or four miles back was only a few cars behind him.

"Shit," he said quietly, entering the circle. "We've got a cop on our tail." Samantha started to turn and look, but his voice stopped her dead in her tracks. "Don't look, Sam. The last thing I want them to know is that we're on to them. Check the map, Alain. What's the best option?"

"Go three quarters on the circle, then right into the university. The grounds look pretty extensive. We should be able to get lost in there somewhere."

"Got it," Travis responded, seeing the exit sign for Ain Sams University. He took the off-ramp, looking even more serious as the police car followed them off the main road and into the campus. "Alain, there's a map on the side of the road a hundred feet up. Try to get a feel for what options we have as I drive by." He slowed, but didn't stop as he passed the giant board that showed the layout of the institute.

"Two main roads in and out," Alain began. "Clusters of

buildings to the northeast and northwest. Medical faculty across the road to the south, dorms up past the sciences buildings. I'd say take the next right and head toward the northeast."

"Holy shit. Your Arabic must be improving. I'm impressed."

"Don't be. The sign was in Arabic and English. Take the next turn."

Samantha sat quietly as Travis wove his way through Cairo's premier campus. Its striking beauty, with trimmed lawns and gurgling fountains, was not lost on her. The campus wasn't crowded; the parking lots only half full. Samantha caught a glimpse of the trailing car as they entered a lot opposite the earth sciences building. Two apprehensive-looking officers sat in the front seat. She snapped around as Travis slid the Wagoneer into a parking spot. He cut the ignition and they exited the truck. He had a jacket over his right arm and Sam knew that one of the submachine guns rested under the coat.

The three Americans walked briskly into the treed gap between the chemistry and physics buildings. The police did not follow, but she knew they would be on their radio. They ducked in behind some potted plants and then through the side door of the chemistry building. The hieroglyphics adorning the exterior walls continued on the interior, interspersed with modern Arabic writing. Travis pointed down a long hallway leading away from the door where they had entered, and they moved swiftly along. They reached the far end of the corridor and he took one last look back before turning the corner into the organic chemistry wing. The hallway remained vacant. The police had not followed them.

"The truck is gone; they'll be watching it," he said as they continued to move through the secondary ell of the building. "And we've lost everything we left in it. Alain, what have you got for weapons?"

"The Vektor with one clip and my Glock with three extra clips."

"Pretty well what I've got. Vektor MINI and my Glock, and

extra magazines for both," Travis said. He turned to Samantha. "Got the diamonds?"

"Of course," she answered, digging down into her bra and slipping out the small suede pouch where she kept the stones. She slipped it back into her shirt. "Now what do we do?"

"I'm not sure. But if it comes down to firing on the Cairo police or giving up, we give up. Understood?" Alain nodded and pushed through the fire door as they neared the end of the wing. They exited the building and looked about. Directly ahead was a grassy area centered with a fountain. Angling off from the water in each direction was another building. The faculty names were noted in Arabic and English. Archeology lay ahead of them, geophysics to the left and geology to the right. Travis pointed at the latter.

"You wouldn't happen to know anyone in there, would you?" he asked Samantha.

"Funny," she said, then reconsidered. "Actually, who knows? I've been to tons of conventions. Maybe I have met someone that works out of Cairo. Let's take a look—they should have the staff list posted somewhere in the building."

They moved across the central square briskly, but without running, and entered the geology annex from the south end. Sam found a student who spoke English, asked him a few questions, then returned to where the men watched to see if anyone was on their tail.

"You," she said, pointing at Travis, "are brilliant. It seems there is a research professor here on a two-year stint from Concordia. Adel Hadr. He's a transplanted Egyptian who's spent the last ten years in the States, but returned on a very generous grant to cover a geological dig near Alexandria. He teaches here in the summers."

"So the good doctor is in?" Travis asked, and smiled when Samantha nodded. "Then let's find him."

Kerrigan listened intently as his interpreter spoke. A police cruiser had spotted a car that might be the 1985 Jeep Wagoneer, but the patrolmen were not sure. They were following the vehicle, and it was just entering the university grounds. They reported it moving slowly through the grounds, then parking in lot G. The reply came back from dispatch to wait for a backup car. Things were busy, so it might be a while. The patrolmen watching the Jeep acknowledged, and other calls took over the police band. Kerrigan reached down and switched the frequency so he could communicate with O'Donnell.

"They're at the Ain Sams University. Parking lot G. How far away are you?"

"Nearby." O'Donnell's voice was quick, excited. "I thought they would head straight out of the city, so we stayed close to the number three highway. We're only a couple of minutes away."

"There's a patrol car parked in the lot. Take care of the police before you look for Carlson. Disarm or kill the SEALs, but keep the woman alive and call me."

"Roger that."

Kerrigan looked across to the man he had picked up as a translator—he looked terrified. Kerrigan slipped his pistol from under his coat and pointed it at the man's head. He looked even more terrified. "You do exactly as I say and you'll be fine," Kerrigan said as he drove toward the university. "If you don't . . ." He cocked the hammer back on the pistol.

Ahead and to his left, O'Donnell could see the group of high-rise buildings that comprised Cairo's university. He took the off-ramp and entered from the southern reaches of the campus, stopping briefly at an information board to locate parking lot G. He drove slowly through the grounds and pulled up a few spots away from the stationary patrol car. He screwed the silencer onto his pistol, tucked it under his shirt and walked over to the waiting police.

"Good morning, gentlemen," he said politely. "Do either of you speak English?"

"I am speaking some," the driver responded.

"Excellent," O'Donnell said, withdrawing the silenced

gun from his waistband and pointing it into the car. "Give me your guns. Now!" Both police officers, terrified, complied. O'Donnell set the service revolvers on the ground beside the car, unclipped the two-way radio from his belt and called Kerrigan. "The patrol car is secure. What now?"

"Get them to call in to dispatch and tell them it was a false alarm and that they're leaving the campus. And make sure they listen to this." O'Donnell could hear Kerrigan giving his interpreter instructions on the other end of the radio. Seconds later, a voice came across in Arabic. Then Kerrigan again. "Keep the radio channel open as they call in. My passenger will be listening to ensure that they say what we want them to."

Liam turned to the driver. "Do you understand? There's a person on this radio who will understand every word you say. If you try to call for help, I'll kill you." The man swallowed hard and nodded. He took the radio hand piece from its mooring, depressed the send button and spoke rapidly in Arabic. A response came back from dispatch, and he spoke again. Another response and he slipped the hand piece back into its holder.

Kerrigan's voice came across Liam's two-way. "Okay, that situation is defused. Now take care of Carlson. I'll be there in a few minutes."

"Roger," O'Donnell said. He looked at the cowering police. What the hell to do with these guys? They probably had families who would be devastated if they didn't come home from work. Then again, they had seen his face and could identify him. He squeezed the trigger twice, pumping one silent bullet into each cop. He looked around, and satisfied that no one was watching, motioned for his men to join him. They opened the police car's trunk and dumped the bodies in, securely latching it afterward and locking the car doors. It would be some time before they were discovered.

"Each of you is armed and has a radio," O'Donnell said to the three mercenaries as they moved from the parking lot into the campus. "We'll split into groups of two. Call in immediately if you locate them."

They split up, with only one thought in mind: Find Samantha Carlson.

TWENTY-FOUR

Dr. Adel Hadr was between classes, marking assignments, wondering how some of his first-year students had graduated from Cairo's public school programs. He hated working with freshmen. Most of them were spoiled rich kids who didn't know what they wanted to do with their lives. And so they wasted part of his as he graded the slop they slapped together and handed in. A sharp knock split the silence in his cramped office and he peered up over his reading glasses at the door.

"Enter," he said in Arabic.

Samantha Carlson poked her head into Hadr's office. She recognized the middle-aged man immediately; he hadn't changed much since his stint at Concordia. Thick-framed glasses sat on the tip of his ample nose, and his intelligent eyes looked into hers. The professor's hairline had receded slightly and a few extra wrinkles crowded together at the edge of his eyes. He broke into a wide grin, revealing uneven but very white teeth. Hadr stood, set the reading glasses on his desk and held out his arms.

"Samantha Carlson," he said warmly. "My God, what are you doing in Cairo?"

"Well, that's a bit of a story," she said, moving across the small room and embracing the man. "We're in a little bit of a pickle here, Adel."

"I see," he said, his face turning serious. He motioned to Travis and she watched as the men shook hands. "We need to get out of Cairo as quickly as possible. And quietly."

"So this isn't a social call," he said, pushing a stack of papers back and sitting on the edge of his desk. "I'll do what I can. What do you need?"

"A vehicle that's reliable enough to get us to the Israeli border. Some food and water would be appreciated."

"The only car I have is my Chevy Malibu. I had to get the local Chevrolet dealership to order it specially. It took six months for it to arrive."

"We only need it to get across the border. We'll leave it at Magen, which is about ten miles into Israel, and pick up an Israeli vehicle." Her voice was soft, almost pleading.

Adel Hadr peered into her eyes, seeing the sincerity. He smiled and nodded. "It's like my first-born, Samantha. I love that car. Please try to leave it in one piece."

She grinned. "I'll try, Adel."

"Here," he said, grabbing his jacket and pulling keys from a breast pocket. "I'll walk down with you to where it's parked."

Travis intervened. "I'm not sure that would be a good idea, Professor. I suspect we may have some company."

"It could be dangerous?"

"Very."

"I rather like danger," he said, turning to Sam. "Remember when we were excavating on the edge of that cemetery and the police threatened to shut us down?"

"Not the same thing, Doc," he said, taking the keys from the man's hand. "These are guys with guns, and they'll kill you if you get in their way."

The professor paled, then regained his composure and addressed Sam. "The car's in lot E, stall 36. It's at the north end of the building and over one lot. There's a case of bottled water in the trunk. Always a good thing to carry when you live surrounded by desert. And Samantha," he hesitated, "please don't get hurt."

Samantha took Hadr's hands and squeezed. "I'll be okay. Travis is quite good at watching over me," she said. "Take care, Adel. I'll see you soon."

They left the second floor office and rejoined Alain where he stood watch at the end of the hallway. They took the stairs to the first floor, and Travis cautiously opened the fire door and peered into the main foyer of the geology annex. He clicked the door shut and backed away from it. "Two guys," he whispered to Sam and Alain, "moving this way, and I don't think they're students."

They moved quickly into an intersecting hallway, and Alain pried open the first door they came to. He waved them in, and Travis and Samantha followed him into a deserted classroom. A blackboard ran almost the full width of the room, and forty to fifty desks sat in seven neatly arranged rows. A long counter ran across the back of the room, close to where they were standing. Rock fragments were scattered across the laminate top, leftovers from a geology lab. Sam was the last to enter and shut the door behind her. Travis was already across the room working on opening a window. He spent a few seconds on it, then turned and shook his head.

"It's bolted," he said quietly. "We'll have to break a window to get out this way."

"The door," Sam said, pointing to a door at the front of the classroom, tucked into the corner next to the blackboard. "It's either that or back into the hallway."

Travis moved quickly to the door. He tried the handle with no success, then withdrew a thin piece of metal from his belt and slipped it into the keyhole, working on the lock's tumblers. A few moments later the handle turned and he opened the door. They ducked into the room and he relocked the door from the inside. They were in an office, used by the professor who taught in the classroom they had just exited. It was dimly lit by one small window mostly blocked by piles of books. A cluttered desk sat amidst the piles of papers and research tomes that littered the room. There was an additional door on the opposite side of the room, and Alain stepped over the papers to try the handle. It opened to his touch, revealing a set of stairs descending into a darkened basement. Alain didn't hesitate. He started down, the others following closely.

The stairwell was dark, lit only by the ambient light that filtered down from the office. Fifteen concrete stairs took them to the basement level and another door. This one was steel, and secured with a dead bolt and a handle lock. Alain moved aside, giving Travis access to the locks. The dead bolt was top of the line and required a few minutes to pick, but Travis finally felt the tumblers click into place. He worked on the door handle lock for less than ten seconds, then swung the door open. He entered the pitch-black room, his hand sweeping across the adjacent wall searching for a light switch. His fingers found one and he clicked it, flooding the room with light. All three stared in disbelief.

Ahead of them was a cavernous underground chamber filled with shelves and boxes. Ancient Egyptian artifacts lined the walls, casting eerie shadows against the drab concrete. Dusty tomes of Egyptian history were stacked carefully on the shelves, each one numbered sequentially. Eight ornately carved limestone sarcophagi sat upright in the center of the room, all properly supported to keep from tipping. The sight was spectacular. They closed and locked the door behind them, then crept forward and moved quietly through the myriad of archeological pieces.

"This is incredible," Alain said softly. "This room has more stuff in it than most museums."

"The museum exhibits probably come from this room,"

Samantha said. "But why the hell is this room attached to the geology building? This isn't geology, it's Egyptology."

"This room probably runs underground and attaches to the archeology building. It would also give us a way out."

Samantha nodded vigorously. "That makes sense. When we entered the sciences complex, geophysics was to the left of the central park, geology to the right, and archeology directly ahead. That would put the archeology annex to our left, as we're directly below geology right now." She pointed to the far corner. "Let's try it and see if we can find another door."

Samantha swung around and headed for the distant corner, her shoulder brushing the edge of the closest sarcophagus as she moved past. She felt a distinct pain in her arm and glanced down, wincing from the sudden unexpected agony. A tiny speck of red showed on her shirt, then spread as the blood poured from the wound. She touched it, unable to comprehend how such a light brush had caused so much damage. A now familiar sound reached her as she stood transfixed—the *pufft* of a bullet being fired from a silenced gun. Travis and Alain caught the same noise and all three dropped to the ground, scrambling for cover. Samantha leapt in behind one of the vertical mummies and huddled close to the floor. She looked over at Travis. He was staring at her arm. She made a quick thumbs-up gesture and he nodded.

She was shot, but how badly she didn't know. She tried to pull her shirtsleeve up to assess the damage, but she couldn't get it past her elbow. The stain was still spreading, wet and sticky. She leaned against the cold stone sarcophagus and forced herself to breathe deeply as she watched Travis and Alain peering cautiously around the edges of their cover. Both men were concentrating on the entrance they had used to gain access to the basement. The gunman must have followed them from the classroom on the upper level. More sounds of silenced guns and chips of limestone flew across the room as bullets chewed into the sarcophagus.

Travis opened the radio frequency to Alain and spoke softly to his partner, only a few yards distant. "I've seen two flashes," he whispered. Alain concurred by nodding and holding up two fingers. "Eleven o'clock and two o'clock. I'll give them a quick headshot, you take the guy at eleven. Okay?" He watched as Alain nodded again, and steeled himself against the sarcophagus he was crouched behind. Travis motioned with his fingers, counting down from three. On one he flashed his hand out from behind the left side of the mummy, then on zero he stuck his head around the right side for a brief moment. He pulled back to safety as two bullets flew past the stone edge. The sharp report of an unsilenced pistol split the room, the sound almost deafening. Travis looked over to Alain, who made a thumbs-up sign. He had a hit—one shooter down, one to go.

"Switch to the Vektor," Travis mouthed quietly to Alain. "He's behind those shelves at two o'clock. Ready?" Again, Alain nodded, sliding the machine gun from across his back and hooking the strap around his right elbow, pulling it tight and sighting. "Three, two, one." On the one count, Travis stepped from behind the sarcophagus and began pumping round after round from his Glock into the shelving units. A split second later the Vector MINI opened up, shredding everything on the shelves and cutting through the concealed mercenary at chest height. He was dead standing up. Alain eased off the trigger and they heard the sound of a limp body hitting the floor. Travis raced across the floor, pistol outstretched, then relaxed. The Vektor had sliced the man almost in two. He quickly checked the first victim Alain had taken down. Blood trickled from a solitary wound in the center of his forehead. Travis moved back to where Samantha had sat motionless throughout the ordeal.

"We'd better move," he said, grabbing her good arm and lifting her from the floor. She winced in pain at the movement. He carefully slipped her shirt down over her shoulder and wiped a bit of blood away from her wound. It was starting to congeal and they could both see the inch-long gash the bullet had left as it cut through her flesh. All layers of skin had been sheared off, exposing the underlying muscle. She grimaced as Travis wet his sleeve with saliva and cleaned the surrounding area. He scanned the cut intently, then glanced up at her and grinned.

"No muscle damage," he said lightly. "It's going to sting like a son of a bitch, but it just took the skin off. *You* are one lucky lady."

He kept hold of her arm as they wove their way through the relics that cluttered the underground chamber. They reached the far end of the room, under the archeology annex, and Travis and Alain searched for a stairwell. They found a heavy steel door tucked in behind a stack of sandstone tablets covered with hand-carved inscriptions. They were on the inner side of the security door and no key was required to open it. Travis simply turned the dead-bolt latch, unlocked the door handle and slowly swung open the door. It creaked under the heavy weight and lack of recent use. He peered into the darkened stairwell until his eyes adjusted to the light. The stairs were empty and he motioned for Alain and Samantha to follow him up. The staircase truncated in a small vestibule, with doors leading into the archeology building or to the outdoors. They chose the latter and exited into the sunlight, immediately beside a huge map of the campus. It showed where they were in relation to lot E. Travis stared in amazement.

"Check this out," he said. "Parking lot E, this way. What are the chances? Maybe our luck is changing." He headed for the lot and Adel Hadr's prized Chevy, with Alain and Samantha in tow.

O'Donnell heard the muffled sound of gunfire. He stopped, almost in the entrance to the math sciences building, and listened. He heard nothing for a moment, then the sound of another volley of pistol shots followed by the unmistakable sound of automatic gunfire drifted across the campus. It was impossible to tell where the gunfire originated. He clicked on the send button and asked for his teams to report in. Only one did. He had assigned the missing twosome to the geology ell. He called back to the remaining team and had them head for the main doors. Then he stopped in his tracks. Two hundred yards from where he stood, he saw three figures exit a side door of the archeology complex and turn north, moving quickly across the grass. He opened up the radio channel again, this time instructing his men to bypass geology and head northeast.

"There are three of them," he told the men as they jogged. "Both men are carrying automatic weapons. Could be Vektors. Fire at will, but don't kill the woman."

"I hear you," the staccato reply came back, the man's voice clipped from jogging.

Liam waited until the three figures disappeared behind a small knoll, then started out at a brisk run. He sprinted across the center courtyard that separated the numerous science buildings, and reached the near edge of the archeology annex without being spotted. Carlson and the two ex-SEALs were moving quickly toward one of the far parking lots. They were either intent on stealing a vehicle or they'd managed to get their hands on some keys. He suspected the latter. The last thing he needed right now was for them to pile into a car and take off, leaving him in a cloud of smoke with his vehicle on the far side of the campus. He began moving again, trying to stay inconspicuous. He had narrowed their lead on him to less than one hundred yards when his two-way crackled and came to life. It was Kerrigan.

"I'm inside the campus. Where the hell are you?"

"Just north of the archeology building," he responded, slowing and ducking behind cover. He motioned for the man accompanying him to get undercover. "McNeil and one other SEAL have Carlson with them and they're heading for a parking lot. It looks from here to be E."

A few moments of silence overtook the radio as Kerrigan got his bearings. "Got it. I'll circle around from the east and come in the entrance to lot E. There's only one, so if that's what they're heading for, we should be able to trap them. Give me about two minutes."

"Sounds good," O'Donnell said.

He linked up with his remaining team via the radio. "Did you guys catch that?" An affirmative answer came back. "Okay, don't let them see you. We've got them cornered. Continue to the northeast on foot, and Kerrigan will block the east entrance with his vehicle. We're coming up from behind, to the south of them. Keep low and out of sight."

Travis spotted the professor's car first. He pointed to it and they angled across the lot, checking around for signs of hostiles. Nothing. About halfway to the parked vehicle, he noticed two students walking toward them. Both the young man and woman looked nervous and stole an occasional glance behind them. They walked quicker than the average young couple moving between classes. They had seen something that had spooked them. Men with guns? Travis motioned to Alain to split off to the right and hug the bushes surrounding car lot E. He grabbed Sam by the elbow and steered her between two rows of parked cars. Moments later gunfire erupted, shattering the midday calm of the campus. They ducked behind a late-model Mercedes as its windshield exploded. Bullets ripped into the driver's side of the car, tearing through the corrugated side panels and shredding the leather interior. Samantha hugged Travis as they felt the slugs thud into the door they were leaning against. The safety panels in the passenger door were too much for the bullets to penetrate, and they could hear the mutilated chunks of lead dropping harmlessly onto the rocker panels. Samantha was terrified.

He slipped the Panther from his belt and called Alain. "What have you got? We're totally blind over here."

"I'm not in a good position," came the breathless reply. "There are two on the other side of Hadr's car, and at least one behind me. I'm caught between them."

Alain's voice crackled, then went quiet as more automatic gunfire cut through the air. Travis pushed Samantha hard against the sandy grit that covered the asphalt and motioned for her to stay put. He duck-waddled his way to the rear of the Mercedes and peeked out, looking forward toward the shooters who crouched near Hadr's Chevrolet. A blond head popped up over an adjacent car; then the man's shoulders and a submachine gun appeared. It spit fire briefly, then the shooter quickly retreated to safety. Travis flipped a toggle on the Vektor, switching it from automatic to single-shot status. He looped the strap tightly around his right elbow and tucked the gun butt into his shoulder. He steeled himself, then slid cautiously around the rear fender until he had a sight on the shooter's location. He counted silently to himself, second by dangerous second. At six, the head appeared again in exactly the same spot, a fatal mistake. Travis gently squeezed the trigger, sending one bullet to its target. The man jerked violently and fell behind the car. Travis slipped back to safety as a barrage of bullets tore into the already chewed-up Mercedes. He looked to Samantha. She hadn't moved, and he held a cautionary finger up to her.

"One down, two or three to go. We just may make it out of this." He depressed the send button and called over to Alain. "You okay over there?"

"Damn, Travis," the reply came back. "I'm hit, buddy." Silence engulfed the radio and then the university grounds as the shooting stopped for a moment. Travis reacted to the news with tempered anger. He flipped the toggle on the Vektor, putting it back to automatic status. He lay prone on the ground next to Samantha, his eyes searching the far end of the parking lot. Through the tangle of parked cars, he saw what he needed—feet. Some fifty yards distant, the second gunman was concealed behind an older model Volvo. But beneath the vehicle were his feet. Travis took careful aim, the Vektor resting on the asphalt, then fired. The stream of bullets ripped through the man's legs, shattering the bones and destroying the muscle. He fell to the ground screaming.

Travis pulled the trigger again and this time the deadly stream of lead cut into the man's torso, killing him. He sat up from his prone position and leaned against the Mercedes while he expelled the empty magazine and snapped in a new one.

"Two down," he whispered to Samantha. "Stay here. I'm going to try to get across to Alain. Don't move." His tone was firm and she nodded, quite intent on not moving. Travis steadied himself against the rear bumper for a moment, then took off at a full run, weaving back and forth as he closed the distance to his partner. About halfway across, bullets started flying. Car windshields shattered and tires flattened as the spray from the automatic weapons tried to cut him down. He kept low and dove behind a vehicle just as the shooters caught pace with him. Bullets punched jagged holes in the trunk, puncturing the gas tank. Fuel poured onto the ground and he knew he had scant seconds before the shooter noticed the leak and fired again, this time to ignite the car. He jackknifed his taut body back onto his feet and again hit the pavement at a dead run. He was twenty feet away when the car exploded, showering everything within a fifty-foot radius with chunks of burning debris. The force of the blast threw him violently to the ground and he slid along the pavement for another fifteen feet before smashing into a parked van. He rolled under it as pieces of fiery metal rained down. He looked out from under the van and found a target. One of the shooters was visible. He wrestled the Vektor from under his body, took aim and fired. Nothing happened. The gun was jammed. He swore under his breath and slipped his Glock from his belt, chambering a round. His target picked up on his movements and swung his gun around. Too late. The Glock A-17 coughed twice and the man collapsed, clutching at his throat. Travis pumped one more bullet into the form as it fell. That was three—he was positive there was one more.

He moved slightly to his left and brought Alain's position back into view. His partner was down, but from the heaving of his chest, Travis could see he was still alive. Travis surveyed the scene, trying to locate his final adversary. The parking lot was a disaster. The car that had exploded was still burning and at least two bodies were visible. The time he had to finish this off, get Alain, and escape before the police arrived in droves was fast approaching zero. From the first shot, less than ninety seconds had passed, but it had been a very violent and noisy ninety seconds. He tensed as his peripheral vision picked up a figure moving quickly toward Alain's position. Seconds later the unthinkable happened. The fourth man, still moving at top speed, whisked by Alain, pumping two bullets into the ex-SEAL. The wounded man convulsed for a moment, then went limp.

"You fucker!" Travis screamed, leaping from behind the van and emptying the remaining fourteen bullets at the killer. "You son-of-a-bitch piece of shit!" He ducked once the Glock started to click as the hammer hit an empty chamber. Again, a torrent of bullets strafed the van, rocking it back and forth. He squeezed out the clip and slapped in a new one. Shit. Seventeen shots. One full clip on the Glock was all he had. And the Vektor was jammed. If he didn't take out this guy before he emptied his gun, he was dead. He knew by this time that these guys were pros. It had come down to a final twosome, and neither man would quit until one of them was dead.

He looked over at Samantha, still visible to him from the angle he held. He gave her the thumbs up. She looked more terrified than he had ever seen anyone look. He turned his attention back to his final opponent, hidden from sight now behind a small foreign car. Travis estimated the distance to be about sixty yards. Certainly within the range of the Glock—if he could get a clean shot. His eyes again drifted back to the woman crouching behind the vehicle. This time he locked eyes with her. He felt a new resolve creep through his very being, empowering him to do whatever was necessary to keep this woman alive.

Sixty yards, mostly open ground with a few cars sporadically parked between them. The archeology annex loomed large to his left, and he turned his Glock on the building and sighted on a third floor window. He pulled the trigger and the window shattered. He leaped from behind the van and started running toward the car. The distraction worked, and for a split second the man turned and sighted on the window, thinking a sniper had taken position above him. By the time he realized Travis's slug had smashed the window, it was too late. He tried to spin around and aim, but already his body was being slammed again and again with hot lead. Travis pumped round after round into the falling figure as he raced across the hot asphalt. By the time he covered the sixty yards, Liam O'Donnell lay dying in an expanding pool of blood. Travis kicked the mercenary's gun from his hand and stood over the prone figure.

"You bastard," he spat at the man. "You killed my friend."

"Don't be so pissed off," O'Donnell managed to gasp. "You've got your revenge." His eyes and mouth remained open, but his life was over.

Travis jogged over to Alain's body and tried for a pulse. Nothing. He hoisted the corpse onto his shoulder and started for Hadr's car. Samantha joined him, jogging alongside. They reached the Chevy, a Malibu Classic, and he struggled with the keys for a few seconds before opening the trunk and dumping Alain's body in. He slammed the lid and jumped in the driver's seat. Samantha waited for a second as he leaned over and lifted the button to unlock the door, then slid in beside him. Travis slipped the car into gear and pulled forward, angling toward the exit, some fifty yards away. The opening from lot E onto the main road was bordered on both sides by leafy trees, blocking out any view of the traffic outside the lot. Just as the Malibu reached the entrance, a Mercedes cut in from the main road, sliding sideways as the driver brought the car to a quick stop. The vehicle covered both lanes, effectively blocking the Malibu from exiting. Travis started to swear at the driver, then stopped.

Staring back at them from the driver's seat of the Mercedes was Patrick Kerrigan.

TWENTY-FIVE

Travis locked eyes with Kerrigan for less than a second before slamming the Malibu into reverse and flooring it. The car careened backwards through the lot, smashing into a curb and bouncing up onto the grass. He grabbed Samantha and dragged her out, ducking as Kerrigan unloaded a fifteen-shot magazine in their direction. He kept Samantha ahead of him, shielding her with his body as they ran at breakneck speed through the campus. An unattractive building, squat and drab amidst the fine Egyptian architecture, was the closest structure and Travis shouted to Samantha to head for it. A small sign, UNIVERSITY MAINTENANCE, was posted on the side. They reached the outer doors with Kerrigan only a few yards behind. The doors were locked and Travis jumped onto an adjacent loading dock, hoisting Samantha up behind him. A large metal door blocked their way into the building. He hit a green button on the wall close to the door and it began to open, the top half sliding into the ceiling and the bottom half into a slit in the concrete floor.

"Don't even think about it." The voice was Kerrigan's, and

it came from ground level. They slowly turned to face the man. His arm was outstretched, a pistol pointed directly at Travis. Kerrigan kept the gun centered on Travis's chest as he skirted the edge of the loading dock and climbed the stairs at the far end. He reached the concrete platform and walked to within a few feet of them. "Throw the gun on the ground and kick it over here," Kerrigan said, motioning to the gun Travis had tucked in his belt.

"It's empty," he replied, his hand moving for the gun.

"I didn't ask if it was empty. I simply told you to drop it and kick it over to me." His voice was vile, full of contempt. "And if you so much as twitch while it's in your hand, I'll kill you. I'm quite aware of your skill level with weapons."

Travis gingerly removed the Glock from his waistband with two fingers and dropped it in front of him. He kicked it the short distance between the two men and it stopped against Kerrigan's right foot. Kerrigan bent down and picked it up, keeping Travis in his sights. He snapped the clip out and took a quick glance inside. He raised an eyebrow. It was empty.

"Why didn't you do what I hired you to do?" he asked Samantha. "Just find the diamonds and tell me where they are. Simple. But no, you had to keep the location secret."

"I don't trust you," she answered. "I don't think you have an honest bone in your body. Giving you access to that diamond formation is dangerous."

"What you think doesn't matter. What does matter is that you tell me exactly how to find the formation."

"Fuck you, Kerrigan."

Kerrigan cocked the hammer on the pistol and raised it to target McNeil's head. "I wouldn't be so cocky, you little bitch. I'll kill him *now*. And you'll have his blood on your hands for the rest of your life."

Samantha was trembling. She knew Kerrigan would kill Travis just to make his point, and that was not an option. Yet neither was giving the fox the key to the chicken coop. "I brought some with me," she said quietly, undoing a couple of buttons on her blouse and reaching inside. She withdrew the small suede pouch from her bra, opened the drawstring and let the stones fall into her left hand. She held them up for him to see. "I picked these up in less than two hours."

Kerrigan studied the stones from a distance. Putting them under a microscope wasn't necessary for him to realize the value of what she held in her hand. The size and shape of the stones spoke for themselves. They were priceless. The gun wavered slightly as his pulse picked up. He watched as Samantha replaced the stones in the pouch and slid it back into her bra.

"I think I'll take those as well," he said, holding out his free hand. "Now!"

Samantha began to reach for the diamonds, then stopped. "Let him go; then I'll give you these—and the location." She moved closer to him, almost daring him to go for the stones.

"Oh, you'll give me both, you stunned bitch. As for letting this fellow go, I don't think so. He's too dangerous to have milling about."

She was within arm's length of Kerrigan, her blouse still unbuttoned and the pouch visible. The first sounds of police sirens cut through the stifling Cairo heat. Time was waning. It was Kerrigan who made the first move. Simultaneously, he squeezed the trigger and grabbed for the diamonds. Travis was ready. He threw himself against the wall as Kerrigan's finger tightened on the trigger. The bullet blew by his neck with millimeters to spare, hot air actually singing the tiny hairs on his nape. Travis crashed into the wall, his shoulder hitting the button for the steel door. It started to close, the two halves rising from the floor and dropping from the ceiling.

Samantha lost the diamonds. Kerrigan's grab for the pouch was more accurate than his shot at Travis's head. His finger caught the clasp on her bra and ripped it off along with the diamonds. He fell back for a second, slightly off balance. Travis made one vain attempt at leveling Kerrigan before the man could take aim with the pistol. Travis lunged out from the wall, spinning as he moved, his right leg kicking up and out. His foot hit Kerrigan directly in the chest, driving the man back toward the closing doors. Kerrigan stumbled, hit the bottom part of the door as it rose, then fell backwards through the narrow horizontal crack. A second later, the two halves of the door slammed together, Kerrigan on one side, he and Samantha on the other. The sounds of the police sirens were louder, closing by the second.

"Let's go," Travis yelled, grabbing her and jumping from the elevated loading dock to the ground. They landed in a run, heading straight for Adel Hadr's Chevrolet. They covered the distance with no sign of the police. He gunned the ignition and headed for the exit, still blocked by Kerrigan's Mercedes. He veered off at the last possible second, aiming for a small gap in the trees that bordered the exit. The Chevy hit the curb hard, sending it airborne for twenty feet and heading directly at the trees. The car hit the soft earth, sending dirt and sand flying and causing him to momentarily lose control of his steering. For a second the car careened sideways toward a sixty-foot tree, Travis fighting for control. He floored the gas pedal, sending torque to the rear wheels and driving the car forward even faster. The force of the power to the wheels straightened the car at the last possible second, propelling it between two trees. Both side mirrors were ripped off as the Malibu scraped its way through the narrow gap. Then they were free.

The car crashed onto the access road to the main highway. Travis spun the wheel hard left to counteract the skid, then straightened it out as the car came under control. He slowed to a reasonable speed and moved into the proper lane. A moment later, the first of many police cars came racing past them, heading for lot E. He stayed at the posted speed limit, entered the freeway traffic and took a deep breath. His shoulder hurt from crashing into the wall, but it was better than taking a bullet in the skull.

"How about we get out of Cairo now?" Samantha said, her head resting against the side window. "This city is dangerous."

He drove with the traffic, no faster, no slower, and stopped at the outskirts of the city for gas. They dusted themselves off as best as possible and bought food at the convenience store attached to the service station. He also picked up a small shovel. They paid for the gas with the last of their money and left Cairo, heading into the desert. Two hours out, Travis pulled onto a seldom-used side road and drove a few miles off the highway. He stopped at a low point in the desert, where it was impossible for passing vehicles to see them. He opened the trunk and dragged out Alain's body. Samantha watched as he dug a grave, his muscular body methodical and rhythmic. Twenty minutes later he stepped from the shallow grave and rolled Alain in. He covered his friend with sand, then knelt on the ground, staring at the individual grains of sand. Samantha joined him.

"I knew him for a long time," Travis said as she knelt beside him. "We went through a lot together. In my business, it takes a lot before you really trust someone."

She didn't respond, just touched his elbow. They knelt in silence at the graveside for a few minutes. He finally stood up and helped her to her feet. They didn't speak as they headed back to the highway that led to Israel and the end of the nightmare that Cairo had become. It wasn't an awkward silence, just a necessary one. Mile after mile of sand passed by, each dune melding into the next, desolate and devoid of life. Such a wonderful climate, yet the land was totally useless without water. The sun alone was not enough. Perhaps she had been the sun all these years, standing alone in her victories, not knowing she needed another person to take away the desolation of her successful life. She needed water, and without it her life would always mirror the vast wasteland that surrounded her. And for the first time in her life, she knew exactly who that water was. She eventually stretched out on the front seat and drifted off, her head resting on Travis's thigh. It was comfortable, reassuring.

Patrick Kerrigan slammed his suitcase shut and answered the knocking at his hotel door. It was the bellboy for his luggage. He waved at the suitcases and followed the boy out into the corridor. They took the elevator to the main floor and he checked out as they loaded his bags into the waiting limo. He had to get out of Cairo before they tied the Mercedes at the university back to him. The Mercedes with a body in the front seat, a single bullet through its head.

The Cairo police were on a rampage. Two of their officers had been found dead, stuffed into the trunk of their squad car, and they wanted answers. They wanted someone other than the dead bodies littering the campus to be held accountable. And the only person left who fit that description was Patrick Kerrigan. His options were simple. Leave Cairo within the next hour or rot in an Egyptian jail. The limo driver nodded when he told him there was an extra one hundred dollars if they could make his plane. Despite the traffic, the driver made exceptional time, depositing Kerrigan by the front doors twenty minutes before his flight was scheduled to depart. The driver smiled at the tip and Kerrigan made a mad dash for the airline counter. Six people were in line and he offered each one twenty dollars to let him crash the line. Six takers. He gave the ticket rep the confirmation number he had received over the Internet only thirty minutes prior, and she handed him a boarding pass. She checked the luggage with an urgent sticker attached to it and he headed for boarding gate thirty-two. A metal detector surrounded by police stood between him and the gate. He approached it, his boarding pass in his right hand.

"Mister," the official paused as he read the name on the pass, "Kerrigan." The entire bevy of guards had their eyes pasted on him. "You are picking a very interesting time to leave Cairo."

"Interesting?" Kerrigan asked. "Why interesting?"

"We've had a very nasty disturbance at the university today," the man replied, looking intently at the passport Kerrigan had handed him along with the boarding pass. "A foreigner was spotted leaving the area just after the trouble. You fit the description."

"Sorry, gentlemen. I've been at my hotel all morning, but I never turned the television on. Must have missed all the action."

"I see. What sort of business brought you to Cairo, Mr. Kerrigan?"

He did not like the way this was going. It was time to take a risk, one that could go either way. "My business is somewhat confidential," he said, looking a bit embarrassed. The guard just stared at him, waiting. "I sell ladies' lingerie. To the women of Cairo who wish to be more western. It's not a job that I would want other men to know about." He motioned to the group of police and soldiers that hovered nearby.

The man stared at him for a moment, then grinned. "Ladies' underwear." Kerrigan nodded. The man turned to the group and spoke in rapid Arabic. They all began to laugh. The guard held up the boarding pass and passport and Kerrigan took them back. "I hope you sold lots of panties, Mr. Kerrigan."

Kerrigan was pressed to catch the flight. He walked at a brick pace until he was out of sight of the police, then broke into a fast jog. He made the gate just as they were closing the door. The ticket agent ripped his boarding pass in half and ushered him onto the ramp. Ten minutes later, the plane was pushed back from the terminal and taxiing onto the runway. He breathed deeply as the pilot hit the throttle and the engines roared to life. They bounced down the runway; then came the smooth sensation of becoming airborne. He relaxed fully into the business-class seat and accepted a drink from the flight attendant.

Christ, that had been close.

Close all around, he thought. Egypt was one country he would never visit again. He had miraculously escaped a horrific life in a Cairo jail, but he had also lost Samantha Carlson. And with her, he had lost the location of the diamonds. He sipped his drink, his thankfulness for evading capture in Cairo slowly turning to rage. Samantha Carlson. She had gone up against him and she had won. McNeil and his small band of mercenaries had managed to wipe out Mugumba's troops and kill Liam O'Donnell and his entire team. He cursed himself for failing to pull the trigger when he'd had McNeil in his sights. That was stupid. He had used the man for bait while trying to extract the location from Carlson, but it had backfired. If he had shot the man, she probably would have caved. The long quest would have finally been over. But hindsight was twenty-twenty, and he had screwed up. He mulled over his options as the plane clipped through the high-altitude clouds en route to London.

Garret Shaw, his ace in the hole. Shaw had never failed him. Where O'Donnell was professional and efficient, Shaw was lethal. There was no hesitation, never a mistake. Once his Washington connections ferreted out Carlson, and they would, Garret would get the assignment. With or without Travis McNeil, she was dead. Tortured first to reveal the formation, then killed without remorse.

He felt a warm glow creep down his spine, and it wasn't from the free alcohol.

TWENTY-SIX

The peninsula that cradled the sleepy town of Lindos jutted into the Mediterranean Sea, a tiny appendage on the island of Rhodes. Sandy beaches rimmed the scrub-covered rocky hillside that rose from the sea. Whitewashed houses encircled the hill about halfway up, a band of white against the paramilitary browns and greens that dominated the landscape. The aging acropolis shared the hilltop with the Castle of the Knights, a monolithic medieval structure capped with turrets. An ancient defense to repel ancient intruders, stark against the deep blue of the Greek sky. The sky mirrored the era when the castle was necessary, a defense against marauding hordes, but modern times had overtaken Greece. Now tourists littered the beaches and shallow waters of the leeward coves, their bronze bodies glistening in the afternoon heat.

Samantha stepped onto the balcony of her room at the Lindos Mare, a four-star resort that peered down on Vlicha Bay. She watched a hotel employee, dressed in crisp white linen, serve drinks to the well-heeled guests reclined on chaise lounges at the pool. He smiled each time he delivered a libation, his white teeth in contrast to the darkness of his tanned skin. And then he smiled again as his clients tipped him generously, especially the women. A noise in the room behind her caused her to turn. Travis swept aside the frail curtain covering the patio doors and walked onto the balcony. He looked rested.

They had left Adel Hadr's car on a quiet residential street in Mage after crossing the border from Egypt into Israel. The Israeli border guards were suspicious, but their American passports eventually allowed them access to the Jewish state. They were broke, but not without resources. Samantha had slipped one diamond into her pants pocket when they first arrived in Cairo, and that forethought had paid dividends—fifty thousand dividends. And at that price they had demanded American dollars in cash. The diamond merchant couldn't capitulate quickly enough, understanding the incredible value he held in his hand. They took the money and kept moving.

Israel was too hot for them. Security was heightened by a recent rash of Palestinian uprisings, and soldiers were everywhere, constantly checking personal papers and, in their case, passports. It was just a matter of time before they were detained for being in the wrong place at the wrong time. Travis found a small charter airline that would fly them from Tel-Aviv to Nicosia. Once on Cyprus they purchased new clothes and baggage, two wedding rings, and then chartered another flight to Rhodes, the jewel of Greece. Just another husband and wife enjoying a late-spring vacation on the Mediterranean. They checked into a suite at the Lindos Mare and immediately slept, Travis on the pullout and Samantha in the king-size bed. Morning brought a clear blue sky and both of them felt rested and safe.

"It's beautiful," she said as he padded across the balcony in his bare feet. "So calm and peaceful."

"The travel brochures say that Lindos is the best Greece has to offer. Sun, sand, and a castle." He looked across the bay at the heavily fortified Castle of the Knights. "I don't imagine it was always so peaceful here."

"No, I'm sure not," she said quietly.

Travis pulled a cigarette package from his loose-fitting shirt and struck a match. He lit the smoke and puffed deeply. He leaned against the rounded edges of the balcony and looked to her. A slight breeze stirred the air on the patio, lifting her hair back from her face for a moment. He caught her profile and tried to memorize it, every detail of her intricately carved features. Every strand of hair as it hung suspended against the forces of gravity. Then the air swirled about, changing direction, and her hair fell back against the edge of her cheeks. A solitary strand touched her face and she gently brushed it away. Even the motion of her hand seemed ethereal. "So what do we do now, Dr. Carlson?" he asked, forcing himself to concentrate on their situation and not just on the beautiful woman who stood so close to him.

"I've been thinking about that," she answered, turning away from the vista and looking at him. "Remember back in Cairo when we thought Kerrigan might have been involved in the Cranston Air Flight 111 crash?" He nodded and she continued. "We both know that he's not going to just go away. He's going to hunt us down, or have some of his hired killers hunt us down, and kill us. So we have to do something. Maybe, if he did have something to do with the Cranston Air crash, and we could find some proof, we could hand that proof over to the Federal Aviation Administration or the FBI. They may take care of him for us if they think he brought down an airliner and killed hundreds of people."

He straightened. "How do you prove it?"

"Most of the information about the crash is public knowledge. Whatever I need should be on the Internet. Our room has a high-speed connection."

"There's bound to be a huge investigation when an airliner crashes and kills more than two hundred people, but no one has pointed a finger at sabotage yet. What makes you think that you can find proof where they couldn't?"

"I'll be looking at it from the other end. They see a plane crash and try to find a reason. I see a man with a motive and work backwards."

"Okay, maybe it's not such a long shot," he said, grinding his cigarette in the ashtray. "Just remember to put that proxy thing on the computer. I don't feel like having to deal with Kerrigan any sooner than possible."

"No shit," she said, instinctively rubbing her arm where the bullet had cut through her flesh only three days ago.

"Let's see that," he said, moving closer to her and gently turning her shoulder so he could look at the wound. It was covered with a scab and healing well with no signs of infection. "It looks good," he said.

She nodded and walked into the living room, her skin still tingling from his touch. She powered up the computer Lindos Mare supplied in each of their upscale rooms and set to work building the proxy. It took a few minutes and she tested it to ensure it was active. The diagnostics were fine and she started a search on the web for Cranston Air Flight 111. The results were staggering: 7507 hits. She hadn't expected that many. It didn't take long to sort through the jumble and hone in on a few key sites. An hour later she signed off and gathered the pages she had printed from the Laser-Jet. She left the room, searching for Travis.

Stairs led from their ocean-view suite to a series of stucco arches adjacent to the freshwater pool. She wandered through the tangle of chairs and plants in the lobby lounge and through one of the arches. The pool was almost deserted. A man and woman floated in the calm waters, bobbing up and down together with the gentle waves generated by a lone lap swimmer. The swimmer's stroke was efficient and his body cut through the water like a shark, leaving only a small wake. She watched as he reached the edge closest to her and stopped. He stood up, snapping his head back to clear the water from his hair. It was Travis. She just stood there, expressionless, and waited for him. He pulled himself from the pool and grabbed a nearby towel.

"Well," he said, his breathing rhythmic, not rushed. "Did you find anything interesting?"

"Come up to the room; I want to show you something." There was a strange tone to her voice and he gave her a quizzical look. He fell in beside her and they made quick time back to the room. She walked across the living room, dropped the handful of pages from her hand onto the coffee table, then continued to the double French doors leading to the bedroom. She turned to face him. She reached up and grasped the top button on her shirt. A small flick of her index finger and her thumb undid the button. She continued, undoing each button with a simple fluid motion. She let the shirt slide off her shoulders and onto the ceramic floor. She wore no bra. A thin white rope encircling her thin waist held up her cotton pants. She pulled it and the knot came free. She slipped out of her thong panties and stood in the doorway, waiting.

He glided slowly toward her, his eyes moving up and down her body. He felt his breath coming quicker, shallower. He had seen her at the jungle pool in the Congo, but that was from a distance, both emotionally and physically. This was up close and personal. She was perfect in every way, her body what every man dreams of but rarely finds. He brushed against her, his hands tracing her figure from her hips up across her flat stomach to her firm breasts. He stopped, his eyes staring deeply into hers.

"Is this really what you want?" he asked. He had to be sure.

"Yes, Travis. I want you more than you could imagine."

"That's a good answer," he said. He could hardly control his breathing now. She didn't speak and he tilted his head slightly and kissed her. She responded with the ferocity of a tiger, her arms reaching up and over his shoulders, her fingers grasping his hair, her lips pushing against his with an intensity he'd never felt. He picked her up and walked the short distance to the bed, falling with her onto the soft mattress. She slipped his bathing suit off and they made love with a passion that had built from the first day they met. A passion fueled partly by mutual respect and partly by the dangers they had faced together, but mostly by an incredible physical attraction to each other. The spark ignited long-simmering desires, and both partners strove to please and be pleased. They fell back onto the sheets afterward, drenched with sweat and feeling satisfied.

They spoke quietly for a while about nothing, just small talk. An hour later Travis had drifted off but Samantha couldn't sleep, and after a few more minutes she slipped out from under the covers and donned a bathrobe. She walked into the kitchen, every nerve in her body heightened from her wonderful experience with the man she had wanted for so long. The floor felt cool to the balls of her feet and sent tiny shivers up her legs and into her spine. They traveled slowly and she could feel every synapse as the sensation moved from nerve to nerve. It reached the base of her skull and sent the message in a thousand directions, flooding her brain with sensuous tingles. She reached out and touched the countertop to steady herself. Wow, Travis, she thought. You are some kind of lover.

Samantha opened the fridge and poured some orange juice into a tall glass. She walked over to the coffee table and picked up the pages that held the information on Cranston Air Flight 111. She began to read, noting the details of the doomed plane. The McDonnell Douglas MD-11 departed JFK at 21:18 ADT on September 2, 2002. It was destined for Geneva, Switzerland. That made sense, she figured, as most of the contraband diamonds that reach the market do so through Switzerland. And even though these were not necessarily contraband, they were certainly undervalued. And that was why Kerrigan wanted them to land in Switzerland, or not land at all.

The plane carried 215 passengers and fourteen crew members to their deaths that evening. Fifty-three minutes after takeoff, the pilots noticed a strange smell in the cockpit. Three minutes later, smoke was visible, and the crew sent the international urgency signal "Pan Pan Pan" to the Moncton air traffic control. She set the pages down for a moment, thinking. If Kerrigan had planted someone on the plane to disable it, fifty-three minutes certainly gave him or her enough time to set his or her plans in motion. She read on. Halifax air traffic control cleared the flight to proceed directly in for an emergency landing. The aircraft was fifty-eight nautical miles southwest of the airport. But as she continued, it became apparent that something else had intervened, keeping the plane from making a direct approach to the airport.

The pilot cut his altitude from 32,900 feet to 19,800 in less than six minutes. He continued to descend as the plane cut in over the eastern landmass. Once away from the ocean, the pilot nosed the plane down even quicker, cutting an additional 8,000 feet from their altitude in under two minutes. She sat back for a moment, trying to envision the panic that must have gripped the passengers as the plane lost altitude so quickly. Then the pilot banked the plane sharply to the left, away from Halifax. Now, that did not make sense. The cockpit is filling with smoke, the oxygen masks are operational, visibility must be almost zero, yet the pilot steers his plane away from the closest runway. She traced the path of the plane with her finger as it continued to descend and head back out over the Atlantic. At 22:25, Flight 111 had reached 10,000 feet. At almost precisely that point, both the Flight Data Recorder—the FDR—and the Cockpit Data Recorder—the CDR—quit working. Six minutes later, the plane crashed into the six-foot swells of the frigid Atlantic Ocean. No one survived.

A slight pressure on her shoulder startled her, and she twisted her neck to look behind her. It was Travis, a warm smile etched on his face. He leaned over and gently kissed her on the forehead. "What are you up to?" he asked, lighting a cigarette.

"Just having a look at the Cranston Air disaster."

"See anything interesting?"

"Two things strike me as odd," she said. "The pilots had clearance to land in Halifax, yet at an altitude of under 12,000 feet they turned away from the airport and headed back out to sea. Perhaps they wanted to dump their fuel before trying to land."

He shook his head. "Naw, they could dump their fuel over land with no problems. That Jet A fuel would evaporate before it hit the ground. Does it tell you their fuel burn prior to crashing?"

She looked over the data for a minute. "Yes. They had 65,300 kilograms of fuel on board at takeoff and had burned 11,000 kilograms when the FDR stopped functioning six minutes before they crashed."

He nodded. "Not a problem to dump 54,000 kilograms of fuel at 12,000 feet. There was no reason for the pilot to head back out over water. And he would have known that."

"So you have to ask why he did it," Samantha said.

"It's a good question. What else did you find? You said two things struck you as odd."

"The FDR and the CDR both stopped recording six minutes before the plane hit the water. Why?"

"Show me the details on the equipment," he said, stubbing out his cigarette and sitting beside her. She scrolled back through the data until she came to the section dealing with the instrumentation.

"Ah, an L3 Communications, model F-1000," he said. He ignored the screen and talked directly to her. "This recorder uses compression techniques to store data, almost foolproof. There's no way this baby goes down unless there's a power failure, and even then there are two backup power systems in place." He looked back at the data on the monitor. "And the CDR is also an L3. The model 93-A100-81 uses a continual thirty-minute loop recording system. You said the initial distress call was made at about 22:11 and the plane crashed at 22:31?" She nodded. "Then there's no reason why all the data shouldn't be there. Again, only a power outage to the recorder would cause that."

"It does mention a power stoppage just before both the recorders failed."

"Anything on the condition of the wiring?"

"Yes, right here." She pointed at the screen. The investigation had revealed charred wires and burnt insulation in two places. One was about three feet inside the bulkhead that closed the cockpit off from the passenger section. The other was a few yards back, in the passenger compartment.

"Can you get a plan of the MD-11 showing the wiring sequence?" he asked. Samantha shrugged her shoulders and started looking for one. The web site she was in held the crash details but little else. She exited it and went to McDonnell Douglas, the manufacturers of the plane. Again, nothing. "Try these guys," he said, pointing to the electrical contractors who supplied the wiring harnesses for the McDonnell Douglas planes. Samantha found the web site and pulled up the information on the MD-11. The wiring plans were there.

"Bingo," she said. "Each wiring harness has a part number. McDonnell Douglas must use this schematic to order the harnesses they need for construction or repairs."

"Check this out," he said, tracing his finger back from the bulkhead. "You said there was evidence of burnt wiring a few yards from the bulkhead. There's an intersection of harnesses right here. Even the backup systems come together at this point. They all use separate harnesses, but if something happened at precisely this point, it could take out all the power, even the backup. What seat number is this under?"

She pulled up the seating plan of the plane and he noted the row number. The window seat was directly over it. "Christ," Samantha said suddenly. "There's an access panel immediately above this junction. All the passenger sitting in that seat would have to do is drop a piece of carry-on luggage over it, slice through the carpet and open the hatch. It's only six inches square."

"So if the passenger sitting in that seat knew exactly what he or she was doing, he or she could effectively kill the power supply to the cockpit. Or even worse," he paused for a moment, "overload it to cause a fire inside the bulkhead and then cut the power."

"I think we should get our hands on the passenger manifest and find out who was sitting in that seat," she said, signing on to the Cranston Air web site. A list of the passengers who had been killed in the crash was posted, but not the seats they had occupied. Samantha poked around for a while, trying to find a back door into the confidential Cranston Air files. Travis bored of the tedious work and got up to stretch his legs.

He walked over to the balcony doors and into the afternoon sunshine. Lindos was spectacular, drenched in sun and history. And suddenly his life was as it should be. He had feelings for Samantha that he had never felt before, an insatiable desire to be with her and to know every nuance of what made her so special. He was in love. The great warrior, ever vigilant against letting anyone too close, had finally peeled away the veneer and allowed someone in. And it felt good. He walked back into the suite, lightly touching her shoulder as he moved into the kitchen. He grabbed a cold beer from the fridge, picked up his cigarettes and went back to the balcony. He cracked open the beer and lit a smoke.

So many years of denying himself the luxury of a normal life. So many times pulling back from what might have been the right woman, but never the right time. The memories of his mother, Mary Lambert, before Joe McNeil had destroyed his childhood, still remained locked in his mind. Happy memories. He felt them flooding out as he slipped in the key and unlocked the recesses that held young Travis's pictures and words. He smiled as his mother's face came back to him, healthy and happy. So glad to be with him. At the ballpark with a foot-long hot dog loaded with mustard. On the beach, helping him load the pail with sand to make turrets for the sand castle. In the kitchen, baking Christmas cookies and shortbread. And he suddenly realized that beneath the tough shell he had built, that of the consummate Navy SEAL, lay a gentle and understanding man. A man capable of loving, and accepting love. And then he knew that he and Samantha could make it together despite the atrocities he had suffered. He ground the cigarette out and reentered the hotel suite.

Samantha was still hunched over the computer, staring at the monitor. She turned as he entered the room. He walked over to her, and without speaking lifted her from the chair. He cradled her in his arms and moved into the bedroom. She didn't speak, just smiled.

The afternoon passed and evening swept over the rocky crags and into Lindos. The temperature dropped from over eighty to sixty-two degrees. Samantha wrapped a light shawl around her shoulders and joined Travis in the foyer. They locked the room and strolled through muted shades of twilight to the elegant restaurant that served the evening meal. They ordered shellfish and selected a '99 Assyrtiko Boutari from the wine list to complement the entrée. Conversation came easily and he found himself recounting some of the high points of his early childhood to Sam, something he had never done before. After dinner they settled in with coffee, and she filled him in on what else she had found on the Internet that afternoon.

"The passenger sitting above the access panel to the electrical harnesses was Garth Graham. He was an American, lived in Providence, Rhode Island. That's not a big place and it was pretty easy to find him in the Providence phone book."

"Where the hell did you find a phone book for Providence? We're in Greece."

"You don't use the Internet much, do you?"

"You haven't stripped down many AK-47s, have you?" he countered.

"I don't give my men numbers," she shot back. "Anyway, I

got his address from the phone book, then called in a land title search on his house. The registry office e-mailed this back." She slipped a single leaf of folded paper from her pocket and handed it to him.

"Holy shit, he paid off his mortgage two weeks before the flight."

"Over two hundred thousand dollars. So I thought I'd try one more thing."

He waited for a moment as she took a sip of her coffee. "The coffee's good, isn't it?"

"Sam, you've got something. Stop pissing around and tell me."

"Okay, okay. Kerrigan gave us one thing before we left New York that no one has," she said. He shrugged his shoulders and motioned for her to continue. "He gave us an account number and the codes to access the money for our expedition. Remember?"

"So—he used the same account to pay Garth Graham two hundred thousand dollars." He smacked the table with his fist as Samantha nodded. "Lord thundering Jesus, we've got him."

"Lord thundering Jesus? Where'd *that* come from?"

"I learned it from a Canadian from Newfoundland. Newfies, they call them."

"That's nice. But no, we don't have him. When I left the account, it purged all the past transactions. Kerrigan must have had it set up to do that. And now he'll know that someone was looking at his account."

"Can he find us?"

"No. He had it set up with cookies, but I've got a cookie cruncher on this machine. We're safe."

"Excuse me. What the hell are cookies, and a cookie cruncher?"

"You *are* a dinosaur. Cookies are identification tags that can be transferred to the hard drive of the user entering a web site or a secure site. A cookie cruncher is a program that eats the cookies—kills them dead, so to speak."

"So the proof is gone from the online banking, but the bank must have records."

"Offshore bank, Travis," she countered. "Not covered by the banking statutes that mainland banks have to contend with. In other words, the bank doesn't have to tell."

"So where are we? We know Kerrigan paid this Graham two hundred thousand to tamper with the wiring on the plane. Chances are pretty good that this guy didn't know exactly what messing with the wiring would do. Kerrigan probably told him it was harmless."

"If Graham knew Kerrigan was involved with gems, it would be easy enough for him to think whatever it was he attached to the wiring was just a small box of illegal diamonds to be picked up by someone else later."

"Possibly. There're lots of explanations and Kerrigan's devious enough to think of every possible one. Anyway, whatever it was Kerrigan designed worked exactly as it was programmed to. It started two fires, one right at the seat and the other at the next junction box along the line, three feet into the cockpit. Then the FDR and CDR fail when Kerrigan's little tool shuts down the power. With the cockpit power gone, they're flying blind. No instruments, no visibility."

"And that explains why they turned away from the airport, Travis."

"I don't see that."

"The data recorders were still functioning at 22:22. That's when they turned away from Halifax. The pilot still had instruments, still had control of the plane. Then, four minutes later, the power to the cockpit was cut off. By that time, they were already too far from the airport to recover."

"Christ, he thought of everything. So the pilot knew he was in trouble, but his professional opinion was that they had enough time to circle, dump the fuel and make a controlled descent into Halifax. Then wham! Kerrigan kills them all. Fucker!"

The guests at the next table glanced over at Travis. He

shrugged his shoulders at them and turned back to Samantha. "I still don't see why the investigators never found this."

"They did. All this information came from their investigation. Like I said before, they saw a plane crash and looked for a reason. We saw the cause and looked for how he did it."

So Kerrigan was even more of a monster than they had envisioned. That he had slaughtered at least two mining expeditions was horrific. And the guilty finger was beginning to point to him as the cause of a plane crash that had taken 229 lives. He had tried to kill them in the vile jungles of the Congo and on the streets of Cairo. Tried and failed. Now a trail of dead bodies lay strewn across the Congo and amidst the chaos that defined Cairo. Travis had seen the carnage of battle many times, never enjoying it. But this was senseless slaughter at its worst—lives for diamonds. Kerrigan had to be stopped. But with the power his vast wealth gave him, he was almost invincible, at least on American soil. The authorities would be reluctant to press charges against such a rich and upstanding citizen without definitive proof. And what they had on Kerrigan was anything but definitive. Circumstantial at best.

Two thoughts swirled in his mind. First, that Samantha was right, Kerrigan would hunt them down and kill them. And second, no one was going to stop him. So for the sake of self-preservation, it was up to them to bring Kerrigan down.

But how?

TWENTY-SEVEN

New York was cloudy and dull, intermittent rain falling on the medley of buildings that made up the world's most famous skyline. Taxis did a brisk business as they kept the Wall Street business execs dry. Street vendors rolled out the canopies and shutters, and Central Park had a reprieve from the masses as they stayed indoors. Moods matched the weather and tempers flared. The city needed the rain, but after two weeks of late spring sunshine, New Yorkers were happy to have a taste of summer, and the overcast skies were not welcome.

A white limo moved with the traffic in south Brooklyn, heading from JFK toward the Manhattan Bridge. The car entered the bridge and rose above the East River, giving its passenger a panoramic view of the city. The Statue of Liberty was visible briefly through the spans of the Brooklyn Bridge, then gone as the car descended off the bridge and into Manhattan. Eight blocks shy of ground zero, the limo pulled over to the curb. Patrick Kerrigan instructed his driver to pick him up in two hours and slammed the door. He strode quickly to the building entrance, irritated by the dampness creeping into his bones. If he'd wanted rain, he thought, he would have stayed in London. He caught the executive elevator to the sixty-third floor and rejoined the corporate world of Gem-Star.

"Welcome back, Mr. Kerrigan," the receptionist greeted him.

"Thank you, Anne. Is there anyone here to see me?"

"Yes, sir. Mr. Shaw has been waiting in your office for twenty minutes."

Kerrigan nodded and walked down the hall, saying the perfunctory hellos to his staff as they greeted him. He reached his corner office, entered and closed the door behind him. Garret Shaw sat in an easy chair close to the window. He set the *New York Times* on the coffee table next to the chair when Kerrigan entered. An idle cigarette burned in an ashtray beside the paper, smoke curling lazily through the stagnant office air. Kerrigan gave Shaw a disapproving glance.

"I've asked you not to smoke in my office," Kerrigan said icily.

"Funny, I always seem to forget that." Shaw reached over and ground out the cigarette, snapping it in half. "I get bored when I have to wait for people."

"Traffic was bad from JFK. The rain slows things down." Kerrigan reined in his tone, remembering he was talking to the most cold-blooded killer he had ever met. Getting on the wrong side of Garret Shaw was not only stupid, it was fatal. "Do you want coffee?"

Shaw nodded and Kerrigan called through to his secretary. A few moments later she appeared with an insulated pot of hot coffee and two cups, then disappeared with equal efficiency. Kerrigan offered his guest cream and sugar but Shaw declined. "I took these off Ms. Carlson two days ago," he said to the assassin, dumping the small satchel of rough diamonds on the table. "But things did not go well in Cairo."

"What happened?"

"O'Donnell's dead." Kerrigan watched Garret for any sign of emotion. Nothing. "His entire team is wiped out. McNeil killed them all."

"Single-handedly?" Shaw asked, raising an eyebrow. "Impressive. How many men did O'Donnell have with him?"

"Seven, including O'Donnell himself. McNeil did have one other guy with him in Cairo, but he's dead."

"So it's just McNeil and Carlson," Shaw said thoughtfully. "I think that we should review the cost of taking care of these two, considering Mr. McNeil's apparent skill levels."

"I've already thought of that," Kerrigan snapped. "I'll pay you a million up front, today in fact, and an additional four million if McNeil is eliminated and Samantha Carlson delivered to me alive and well."

"Five million dollars. That's a very generous offer."

"I'm a generous man."

"No, you're not," Shaw snarled, rising from his chair. "That's the last thing you are." Shaw waved his arm at the extensive trappings that furnished the corner office. "You're ruthless, no different from me, except you don't pull the trigger or stick the knife in. You pay people like me to take care of your dirty work while you reap the rewards. And the payoff for finding Samantha Carlson alive must be huge. I'm sure the five million has very little to do with killing McNeil. The treasure is the woman." He moved quietly about the room as he spoke.

"What's your point, Garret?"

"I want five million up front and another five for bringing her in. Ten million or I walk out of here an unhappy man. And I don't think you want to make me unhappy."

Kerrigan shrugged his shoulders in deference. "Five, ten, the amount is not that important to me. If it were, I'd be pissed off at you. But you're right; the girl is worth that, and more. I agree to your terms." Kerrigan walked over to his wall safe and opened it. He took stack after stack of cash from the safe, then closed the door and slid the picture back in place. He handed the pile of money over. "Five million dollars."

Shaw placed the cash in a valise. "Any idea where they were heading when they left Cairo?"

"Israel, I imagine." Kerrigan sat down at his desk. "Now if that's all you need, a lot of work seems to have piled up while I've been gone."

"I'll keep you up to date."

Shaw's Audi was parked a couple of blocks north of Kerrigan's building and the rain picked up as he walked, falling at a steady pace by the time he reached the parking garage. He left the garage, then Manhattan. He drove north on I-87, through the Bronx and Yonkers, then past Scarsdale and toward the east bank of the Hudson River. He cut north again on the number nine, a minor roadway that paralleled the jagged edge of the river. He slowed to the speed limit at Tarrytown, then again at the entrance to Sleepy Hollow. He cut off the main drag at one of the entrances to Rockefeller State Park, then took a quick right into a secluded driveway. Two sweeping turns through dense, but well-manicured vegetation led to the main house. It was a character home almost two centuries old, but painstakingly restored to its original beauty.

Shaw switched off the engine and left the Audi in the driveway. He entered the house through the unlocked front door, calling out for his groundskeeper. The man heard Garret and came loping over from the flowerbed he had been attending to. Shaw handed him two hundred in cash and told him to take the rest of the day, and tomorrow, off.

He watched the gardener leave in his older model Ford truck, then returned to the house. With the gardener gone, he was alone. He dumped the contents of the valise on the table. It spilled over onto the floor, all the cash in hundreds. Five million dollars. He thumbed a few of the wads, then quickly bored with the exercise. Money held little fascination for him, but what it bought was wonderful. Like the house. He had wanted to be closer to Kerrigan than his home base in Los Angeles, but he hated the congested feeling Manhattan gave him. He didn't mind large cities, in fact he rather enjoyed them, but New York was too much. He decided on Sleepy Hollow because of its name. It was sexy, dangerous. He found out afterward it had been North Tarrytown until as recently as 1996. But that was of no matter; he still liked the quaint village, and the natives seemed to accept him. Just another New Yorker trying to escape the rat race.

He told anyone who asked that he was an editor for a book publisher with offices in Manhattan. He often carried briefcases jammed with blank paper, and never wore a suit. They believed him. But Shaw was no Ichabod Crane. He was the Headless Horseman. The specter of death that rode about, killing at will. And his world was not limited to Sleepy Hollow and the Old Dutch Church. His world was global. All the resources that modern technology could provide were within his grasp. Any weapon or communication device he wanted was his for the asking. He had the connections, and he had the money. And what he didn't have, Kerrigan did.

Shaw's tenure as a counter-terrorist squad commander had given him access to a vast resource base, but it was Kerrigan's moles inside the CIA and NSA who could ferret out the most discreet information. That, plus his wealth, made Kerrigan a very dangerous man. For seven years, he had taken orders from Kerrigan and the two men had a reasonably trusting relationship. As trusting as can be had, considering the nature of his business. He had seen the vast amounts of money Kerrigan skimmed off the unproductive Gem-Star properties and he wanted a piece of the action. Mostly for the money, but also to be an equal partner and not just a hired gun. But Kerrigan had consistently shut him down, something no other person on the planet dared do. It pissed him off. The thought of killing Kerrigan had passed through his mind numerous times, but he really had no interest in doing it. The thought of ripping him off, however, was intriguing.

Shaw knew Kerrigan had connections to other men similar to himself—men who killed people. And he knew that if he stole from Kerrigan, he would have to kill the man. The CIA and NSA contacts were too good. They could track him no matter where he hid. They would eventually find him, and then the assassins would come. So it all came back to business as usual. Kerrigan gave him a target and he sniffed him out, usually with the help of the moles, and then eliminated the victim. Easy, and very profitable. An idea came to him and he put a call through to Kerrigan's private line.

"Have your men watch Israel for a large diamond or a small quantity of lesser-carat roughs coming onto the market. They may have brought more out with them than you took from Carlson. They may need cash. Credit cards are out of the question. McNeil would never use a credit card when someone is looking for him."

"Excellent idea," Kerrigan said. "I'll have my sources get on it. Anything else?"

"Nothing we didn't cover earlier today. I'm heading for Israel tomorrow. Call me on my cell phone when you have something."

"Okay."

He replaced the phone in the cradle and poured himself a drink of bourbon. He sipped it slowly, relishing the way it gently burned as it went down. Great bourbon. And a great life. After all, he was about to make more money killing one person than most people could make in a lifetime. Free enterprise. He loved it.

The only obstacle was his adversary. Travis McNeil. This was a man not to be taken lightly. He knew Liam O'Donnell and what O'Donnell had been capable of. The man had survived situations that had buried many others, yet McNeil had taken out him and his entire team. And that was after McNeil had wiped out an entire platoon of crack Congolese troops on their own turf. No, this guy was not be trifled with. When they met, as they would, his strike would be quick and decisive. Travis McNeil would never know what hit him.

TWENTY-EIGHT

Samantha was up before the sun, jogging on the deserted beach as the first rays of dawn poked over the flat expanse of the Mediterranean. The sky lightened as pastel colors merged with the last darkness of night, chasing the stars behind a veil of undulating orange. The sun's crown thrust above the horizon, a beautiful arc of burning amber. Then it rose, quickly, and Samantha looked back to the beach as the intensity began to hurt her eyes. A solitary figure was jogging toward her. He moved with alacrity, every motion of his powerful legs bringing him closer to her. She recognized the silhouette—Travis.

He pulled up a few yards from her and slowed to a walk. She felt the sand between her toes and the new warmth of the sun as he closed the last few feet. He slipped his hand around her waist and pulled her close. She could feel his chest moving rhythmically, and his breath felt hot as he kissed her. They remained entwined for a few moments; then he backed off and took her hand. They walked casually back toward the hotel.

"You like to jog in the morning?" he asked her.

"Sometimes. It clears my head, lets me think better." She paused. "Not every morning, though."

"That's good, because I hate this shit. Nothing before coffee is my motto."

"Nothing?" she asked.

He looked like a kid staring at the loaded tree on Christmas morning. "I could make exceptions, shall we say, every day." She didn't respond, just squeezed his hand and angled for the light surf straying onto the beach. The water slithered across the sand and over their toes, wiping out their footprints. She looked back and frowned.

"Is that what life is like? Once you move on, everything you did in your life is wiped out, forgotten? That's sad."

"Everyone leaves an impression. Some greater than others. But the people we touch during our lives are our legacy. We live on in them. Our friends, our kids, the people we meet in our business lives. You don't have to be written up in a history text to have been successful in life. Even though you'll most likely be a footnote in lots of geology texts."

"Is that really important? In the overall scheme of things, what does my proficiency in geology matter?"

"It has to matter. It has to mean something that you're one of the best in the career you chose. Look at your father. He was a very successful man. I'm sure he won awards, wrote articles, published his theses. And you love him and respect him. Your mother, too. She was an extremely accomplished woman. She lives on in you. People who make a positive influence on you are remembered."

He was right. Society placed a measuring stick on your life, judging you by the degrees you held and the money in your bank account. But what really mattered was how you treated the other people you interacted with over the course of your life. The shoe salesman, the dentist, your corner grocer, your spouse. If each person who touched your life was enriched by it, *that* was success. She stopped walking and hugged him, looking into his eyes.

"Think you can wait fifteen minutes for that first coffee?" she asked.

Two hours later, he set his croissant back on the plate and sipped his coffee. He looked out over the view of Vlicha Bay, thinking about what Samantha had just said. "Okay, I agree that our best plan is to destroy Kerrigan's reputation. But do you think contacting Davis Perth is safe? You don't think the CEO of Gem-Star knows what Kerrigan is up to?"

"It's a guess, but no, I don't think he does. Kerrigan has hidden the past expeditions, including ours, from Gem-Star. If Davis Perth were in the know, he wouldn't have done that. I think we're okay to approach him. The problem is, how? He's always off sailing somewhere. And we can't leave a voice mail."

"No shit. But we have to find him if we want to discredit Kerrigan. We can talk to Davis Perth and tell him what Kerrigan is up to. That should take care of Kerrigan's job. He'll still be wealthy, but I don't see how we can change that."

"There's no way. I'm sure he's got money spread all over the planet in numbered accounts, real estate, safety deposit boxes, God knows what else."

"What about his professional reputation? He deals in precious stones, Sam. That must be a relatively small community."

"It is, but I have no idea how to make him look bad." She sat quietly, gently running her finger around the rim of her coffee cup, thinking.

"Aw, this is frustrating," he said after a minute of silence. "He keeps getting away with murder, and he keeps getting richer. He'll probably take those stones he grabbed from you in Cairo and sell them. What did you say they were worth? Twenty million?"

"Probably closer to twenty-five," she said, then stopped, her eyes wide. "That's it. That's how we can get him." She left the balcony and powered up the computer. She logged on and searched for Antwerp, then diamond sights. Seven hits. She checked each one carefully, looking for a sight recently added to the list. She found one, then studied the inventory the sight would offer.

"Bingo. A new sight was added to the Antwerp schedule two days ago. It goes in ten days from now and features forty-one diamonds. Thirty-two stones, eight shapes and one cleavage. It's exactly what he took from us in Cairo, less one shape, one cleavage and four macles. This is definitely Kerrigan. He's selling the diamonds."

"Okay, that's great. We know where he'll be in ten days, but what can we do about it?"

"I have some contacts in Antwerp," she answered, her mind racing. "I may be able to get in on this sight."

"What good will that do?"

"The Diamond Purchasing and Trading Company often invites world-class field geologists to the sights. An additional expert opinion is always welcome. If we can get something put together in the next few days, we may be able to destroy him professionally."

"How?"

"A member of the World Federation of Diamond Bourses, of which Kerrigan is one, automatically loses his membership if he goes into bankruptcy or attempts to defraud another member at a sight. He's then disbarred and his name is sent worldwide on green slips to every Bourse and Club. That ex-member will never trade in precious stones again."

"And we can do that to him?"

"Perhaps," she said. "We need two things. First, I need an invitation to that sight. And my name has to be kept under wraps until the exact moment the sight begins. That way, Kerrigan has no advance notice that I'll be there."

"He *will* be there, won't he?"

"Oh, yes, he'll be there. We'll be eye to eye."

"What's the other thing you need?"

"Some hardware. What I plan to do is steal the real diamonds and replace them with fakes. Paste of the highest quality and barely discernable, but paste. We leave with the real stones and he's left with his reputation in ruins."

"Okay. What do you need to produce the fake diamonds?"

"I'll take my own proportion analyzer, eyepiece and mini-microscope with me. So I'll need a case to keep the equipment in. And the case is how we can duplicate the gems. Here, take a look." Samantha took a piece of hotel stationery and drew a rough sketch of a case. She noted the dimensions as about four inches high by twelve inches long and nine inches deep. She drew another box inside the first one, about an inch smaller all around. She lightly shaded in the area between the two boxes.

"The larger case is the exterior shell and the inner box will contain the instruments. The shaded space in between is ultra-light rubber padding. Or so they'll think. In reality, the padding will be a special mixture of polymers that can form around objects and then harden once given the correct catalyst. The clasp will not only open the outer case, but if you turn it one more twist, you have access to the padding." She drew as she spoke, now adding two small holes to both the top and bottom sections of the case. "These holes will provide a means of injecting the catalyst and the liquid zircon."

"You're going to duplicate the diamonds right at the sight," he said softly. "You put the originals in the top and bottom compartments, inject the catalyst to form the casts, then pour in the gunk to form the fakes. Unbelievable."

"You forgot one step. After I form the fake diamonds, I have to coat them with a light greenish colorant so they look exactly like the originals."

"Will it work?"

"If we can find someone to modify a standard manufacture box in time, yes. If not . . ."

"We're in luck." He grabbed the phone. "I know exactly the person. This guy can make anything work. Especially if it eventually blows up." He finished dialing and looked at her. She was just staring at him. "He's a munitions expert," he explained, "but he can do shit like this. No problem."

"Where is he?"

"London, England. At least the last time I talked to him . . ." He held up a finger as the line to the European continent connected. "Basil, Travis McNeil. How the hell are you, old boy?"

Samantha listened for a few minutes, then tired as they yapped on about what they'd been up to for the last year. The overall tone was good, though. McNeil was excitedly explaining to his colleague what they needed, and by his tone, Sam was pretty sure this Basil fellow was saying he could do it. She strode onto the balcony and took in the view. The late-morning surf was almost nonexistent, the waves just a ghost of what they could be. Nature could be so calming.

He popped out from the hotel room and gave her the thumbs up. She listened as he detailed exactly how he knew Basil, and why the man was so trustworthy. Travis was talkative and she let him ramble on, inserting an occasional comment to keep things moving. But her mind was elsewhere—in Antwerp. She kept thinking about what lay ahead of them and hoping she hadn't overestimated her abilities. The success of duplicating the diamonds and destroying Kerrigan's reputation fell directly on her shoulders. And it was a heavy burden.

She looked to the sea and breathed in the warm salt air. They were going on the offensive. They were going after Kerrigan, and that was good.

TWENTY-NINE

"Watching for a large diamond to hit the Israeli market was a brilliant idea, Garret," Kerrigan said, giving his assassin the jeweler's name. "He purchased a twenty-eight carat stone four days ago in Rafah, a border town on the Egypt-Israeli line. His shop is on the Jewish side. My NSA man found the connection because he put it on the auction block right after he bought it. Sold it to some other Jewish jeweler in Tel-Aviv."

"Excellent." Shaw's voice was cool, complacent. "I'm sure there's a redeye every Monday night directly to Tel-Aviv. I should be in Rafah in about sixteen hours. Let's hope the trail hasn't gone cold."

"I have faith in your abilities," Kerrigan said. "Let me know the minute you find them."

Garret Shaw hung up and then redialed. He talked to the ticket agent at United Airlines and purchased a business-class ticket from JFK to Tel-Aviv, departing in three hours. He packed a suitcase and left his home in Sleepy Hollow for the Big Apple. Traffic was average and he made good time, checking in at the ticket counter almost an hour early. Good for him; he usually arrived ten minutes before the flight departed. He boarded the plane and settled in. He was unarmed, but that didn't bother him. He had to get through Israeli customs, and bringing a gun through that level of security was foolish. He could always find a gun when he needed one, especially in Israel. There was no problem when the whole area was a powder keg and everyone was armed. Pick a victim, kill him and take his weapon. Simple.

A seasoned traveler, he slept for most of the flight, waking up an hour out of Tel-Aviv. He thanked the flight attendant as she offered coffee, then watched the daily news on the TV monitor. He declined the light breakfast and reset his watch to local time. It was almost six o'clock Tuesday evening Tel-Aviv time; the seven-hour time difference plus the nine-hour flight duration had cost him almost an entire day. He cleared Israeli customs without a hitch and found a car-rental booth. Twenty minutes later he left Tel-Aviv behind and headed south into the semi-arid hills that bordered the Mediterranean. Eighty miles in Israel was not quickly driven, and it was closing in on midnight when he finally arrived in Rafah. He found an inn with a vacancy and registered under a false name. The plane flight had refreshed him and he wasn't yet tired. Shaw dumped his suitcase in the room and returned to his car.

The town was quiet this late at night and it didn't take him long to find the jeweler's house. The street was narrow with inlaid cobblestones that bounced the rental car no matter what speed he drove. Shaw's vehicle crept down the darkened lane at a crawl. He checked the name Kerrigan had given him as he pulled up in front of the shop—Moshe Kandel. The windows in the off-white single-story building were dark and shuttered. He eased off the brake and glided down the road to the end of the block. He turned the corner and cut the ignition and lights. A lane separated Kandel's house from the row of similar homes backing up to it. He slipped into the shadows of the alley and moved quietly, counting the houses until he reached the sixth one. A solitary light flickered behind thick curtains. Shaw hugged the dark recesses and reached the back door. He donned a thin pair of leather gloves, slid a thin metal instrument into the lock and worked the tumblers. They clicked into position and he silently opened the door.

The house was small but nicely furnished. He was in the kitchen, a room that stood as a testament to what remodeling can do. Sub-zero appliances sat on Italian tiles and the cabinets were lacquered maple. He could vaguely see some of the living and dining rooms, which were equally upgraded. The jewelry business must be booming. The room with the light was to his right and he stole down the hall. A sliver of light appeared beneath its door. He slipped a small mirror from his shirt pocket and slid it beneath the door. The lone occupant of the room sat on a bed, reading from a heavy text. Shaw gripped the door handle, took one breath in and twisted the handle. Before the man could swivel his head to see what was happening, Shaw was on the bed and had a hand clasped over the man's mouth. Shaw stared into terrified eyes.

"Are you alone?" Shaw asked quietly. The man nodded slightly. "Are you Moshe Kandel?" Again, the man nodded. "I'm going to take my hand off your mouth. If you make any noise other than to answer my questions, I'll break your neck. Do you understand?" A terrified nod.

He relaxed the pressure on Kandel's face and sat back. He eyed the man intently for a full minute, taking in his features. An ultra-orthodox Jew, Kandel wore the usual beard and mustache. His face was gaunt, his cheekbones pronounced over the deep hollows of his cheeks. His eyes, filled with abject fear, flickered as he stared back. This man would not be a problem.

"I'm going to ask you a few questions, not many. If I think you've answered them correctly, I'll leave. I will not hurt you. However, if you lie, I will kill you."

Kandel's lips and mouth were dry, but he said, "I understand."

"You bought a diamond a few days ago. A large diamond. What did the people who sold it to you look like?" Kandel accurately described McNeil and Carlson. "What did you pay them for it?"

"Fifty thousand American dollars."

"Cash?"

"Yes, cash."

"Did either of them say where they were going?"

"No."

"How were they dressed?"

"The man wore light-colored khaki pants and a loose white shirt. The woman wore jeans and a bright red shirt. Both had sandals on."

"Any luggage?"

"Not that I saw. It may have been in the taxi."

"Anything else you want to tell me?" The man shook his head and Garret backed up to the bedroom door. "I know where you live, Moshe Kandel. I can find out where your family lives anytime I want. And if you tell anyone I was here tonight, I will return and I will kill you and every one of your family members I can find. Is that clear?"

"Yes, yes, very clear. I will tell no one." He nodded emphatically.

Shaw eased the door shut and left the house. His mind was racing as he returned to the car and started back to the hotel. Fifty thousand dollars, cash. They were wearing sandals, not shoes, and the woman had on a bright shirt. Two things were perfectly clear to him. They were not staying in either Egypt or Israel. Carlson would have chosen more subdued tones in her clothing to meld in with the whites, grays and blacks the orthodox community favored. But they were going somewhere hot, and not on foot. Sandals were not built for walking long distances. And they had cash. What could they do with fifty thousand dollars in cash?

He grinned as he drove. Charter an airplane is what they could do, and what they would do. A private flight would allow them to leave the country without their passports being scanned at the airport. He stopped at a deserted corner and slipped out his map of Rafah. A tiny airstrip serviced the settlement, and he reversed direction, heading for it. There was no control tower, and only one tin and adobe building offering gas and limited mechanical services. Nine privately owned airplanes lined the runway and nowhere was there mention of charter services. Garret left the airstrip and returned to his hotel. He was finished in Rafah. The nearest major center was Tel-Aviv, and after a few hours of sleep, he would drive back to the city of over a million people. One of the charter services would identify McNeil and Carlson and he would be on their tail. He felt sure of it.

Although he was well rested from the overseas flight, he still managed four hours of sleep. The night manager was just ending his shift as Shaw paid his bill in cash and left in the rental. He made good time on the early-morning roads, reaching Tel-Aviv just after eight o'clock. He stopped at a convenient restaurant and had breakfast as he got his bearings. Ben Gurion International Airport was twelve miles southeast of the city on the highway to Jerusalem. A private airstrip bordered Ben Gurion and shared the international airport's restricted airspace. Twenty minutes, tops, would have him at the airport.

Wednesday mornings were business as usual across the board at all the charter companies flying small aircraft out of Tel-Aviv. The first company he approached was small, and the counter man was also the pilot. He guaranteed Shaw that he had not seen or flown a couple matching their description in the past week. The man did provide Shaw with the names of three charter companies that would be most likely to charter an aircraft on short notice for cash. Shaw zeroed in on the three companies and hit pay dirt at the second counter.

"Yes, I remember them well," the charter rep said. "Very polite and they paid cash. I asked for a premium rate for the short notice and he didn't even balk. Just paid it."

"Where did they charter to?"

"Cyprus. Nicosia."

"Could you arrange a plane to take me to Nicosia? It's imperative I reach them quickly. A relative has died and they must be present at the reading of the will." He smiled at the rep. "A very wealthy relative."

"I understand. I'm sure one of our pilots could get you there this afternoon."

"I would prefer the same pilot, just in case he overheard something that would help me find them quicker. The name of a hotel, anything . . ." He added an additional five hundred dollars to the rate the man had quoted him.

"The pilot's on his day off, but I'm sure we could arrange something."

At almost precisely noon, Garret Shaw and Ari Cohen, the pilot who had flown McNeil and Samantha to Cyprus, were cleared for takeoff. The Beechcraft King Air 200 could accommodate four passengers, leaving Shaw with ample space in the rear of the aircraft. He waited until they were about halfway through the flight before moving up front to engage Ari Cohen in conversation. The twin engines were muffled but the noise level in the cockpit was high. Shaw realized that even if his pilot had tried to listen in on what McNeil and Carlson were saying as they relaxed in the passenger cabin, it would have been impossible. Even so, the man may know something.

It turned out that he did. After yelling over the engine noise for a half hour, he finally jogged the man's memory. The pilot remembered the woman saying she had always wanted to see the Acropolis. That term was used in one country and one only—Greece. Shaw settled back, wishing the flight were over and he could get on with locating the charter that flew them into Greece. He checked his watch. They would be in Nicosia before the charter companies closed for the day. He should be able to ferret out which one had flown them to Greece quite easily. Nicosia was not a major center. Shaw worked his timetable through in his head. It was Wednesday afternoon. On Thursday morning, he would have Ari fly him to Greece. Which island, he didn't know, but that would come. If they were in Athens, it would take some time to find them. But if they had opted for a quieter spot, that would make things easier.

So much easier.

THIRTY

Second to perfect weather, room service at the Lindos Mare was the most predictable thing on the island of Rhodes. Every day at precisely eleven o'clock, the maids showed up to clean the room, change the linen and restock the minibar. Travis and Samantha left the room and sat by the pool, soaking up the midday sun and sipping on the dark roast coffee the resort brewed for its guests. Travis offered to rub some suntan lotion on Samantha, despite the fact that she was already glistening brown and didn't need it. She humored him and lay on her stomach in the chaise lounge as he slowly massaged the oil onto her back.

"How's Basil doing with the box?" he asked, knowing Samantha had talked to their London connection earlier in the day.

"Excellent. He found a standard box at a lapidary shop that he can modify. He's already replaced the foam padding with the material to mold around the diamonds. Drilling the holes through the box was tougher than he expected—it's made with high-quality steel. He's having trouble trying to figure out how the box can hold the liquid zircon."

Travis squeezed a few more drops of lotion on her back. "Does he think he can have it ready in time?"

"Today is Thursday and we need the box by Sunday at the latest. He needs one day to get the zircon and the catalyst from a chemist in London. Then another day or two to perfect storing the liquid zircon and catalyst in separate chambers and injecting them into the molds." She counted on her fingers. "That takes us to Saturday or Sunday. It's going to be tight."

"He'll get it done; he always does." Travis undid her bikini top and let the ties drop onto the chaise lounge.

"Don't get any ideas. This is a public area."

"The oil's not going on evenly with the strap in the way," he protested, a grin on his face. "Did you call Adel Hadr?"

"Yeah. He was glad to hear his car was still in one piece. He's driving down to Rafah tomorrow with a friend to pick it up. He told me to tell you that nothing's to happen to me. He seems to think I need you for protection."

"I don't think so. You can take care of yourself."

Samantha turned a bit to face him. "I would have been dead so many times I can't even count them if it weren't for you, Mr. McNeil. I owe you more than I've ever owed anyone."

"Is that any part of the reason you're sleeping with me?"

"Zero." She laughed at his hurt look. "You just happen to be this Crocodile Dundee meets Rambo kind of guy. That's a bonus."

"Okay, then we're even. I was, and I emphasize *was*, getting paid to keep you alive. You now get that service for free."

"Another bonus," she said, relaxing onto the pool chair. "What time is our flight to Athens?"

"Two o'clock," he answered, working his way down to her buttocks with the oil. "I reserved on an inter-island airline that flies sixteen-seaters. We have an hour from the time we arrive in Athens until our flight to Rome leaves."

"How long in Rome?" she asked.

"Two hours. We have to switch airlines, but two hours should be enough."

He had found a way around using a credit card to book the flights to Rome and London. After spinning a story about having their wallets stolen off the beach while snorkeling, he'd offered another hotel guest cash to put their flights on his credit card. The man had agreed, okay with a chance to help such a nice young couple. They had paid cash for the inter-island flight. That left their passports as the only possible way for someone watching the area electronically to pick up on their movements. And that was a distinct possibility. It bothered him, but there was no other way of crossing international borders and getting to London in time to pick up the box from Basil. He glanced at his watch. It was closing in on eleven-thirty, and the cleaning staff should be finished. Since they were checking out, the maids would probably only refill the bar fridge. He tied a bow in Samantha's bikini top and they returned to their suite.

"Let's try Davis Perth once more before we leave," Samantha said as she finished packing. She snapped her suitcase shut and dialed the New York number for Gem-Star. Again she was informed that Mr. Perth was sailing in the South Pacific and incommunicado. When pressed for the CEO's projected return date, his private secretary was tight-lipped. The best Sam could get from her was to try back in a few days. She hung up and shrugged. "I'm not getting a warm fuzzy from that bitch," she said. Reaching Davis Perth and cutting off Kerrigan's ties to the United States was important in alienating the man. And it wasn't going well.

They checked the suite to ensure they had everything, then checked out, paying cash for the tab. The island was small, just forty miles long by twenty-five miles wide, and they still had almost two hours until their flight left. Paradisi, the town next to the airport, was on the windward side of Rhodes, and they asked the cab driver to take the seaside road rather than the shortcut inland. The drive was spectacular.

The Mediterranean was a shimmering veil of teal, its color alternating between luminescent blue and tortoise green.

The shoreline was rocky and barren for long stretches, punctuated with sandy alcoves, sheltered and private. Mostly the shoreline was void of people, just the sea and sand. Samantha snuggled close to Travis as they drove, wishing their visit to Rhodes was for different reasons.

The taxi crested the northeast tip of the island and continued along the windward side of Rhodes. The surf was more prominent here, whitecaps rolling in relentlessly on the rocky, scrub-infested shores. Paradisi was only a few miles down the coast and they pulled up to the airstrip twenty minutes before their flight was due to depart. Travis paid the driver and tipped him well, thanking him in Greek for the safe journey. The baggage handler for Delphi Airlines stowed their luggage in the underbelly of the twin prop plane and they were just about to board when Travis felt a hand on his shoulder. He turned, instinctively grasping the wrist just above the hand and twisting. He stopped the motion as he recognized the man. It was the pilot who had ferried them across to Nicosia a few days prior.

"Sorry about that," he said as the pilot grimaced in pain and rubbed his wrist. "It's Ari, right?" The man nodded. "I thought you said you seldom flew as far as Greece."

"Very seldom. But I have some very exciting news for you two."

"What would that be?" Samantha asked.

"It's good news and bad news. I just flew in with a man who is trying to locate you. I initially flew him to Nicosia, and when we found out from the other charter service which island you had flown to, he hired me to fly him over immediately." He turned to face Samantha as he spoke. "He told me that your Uncle Everett had passed away in New York six days ago. They're holding off reading the will until he finds you. One provision of the will is that you be present. He thinks you're in for a large inheritance."

"Uncle Everett is dead?" Samantha said haltingly. "This man, what did he look like?"

"White guy, quite tall, over six feet. He's about thirty-five to forty with short blond hair, military style. Very muscular."

"What did you tell him? About us?"

"Just that you were staying at the Lindos Mare. You must have just missed him. I only landed twenty minutes ago. He rented a car and I saw him drive off, that way." He pointed inland, away from the coastal highway they had taken.

"Thanks, Ari. We'll contact the hotel and give them a forwarding address so he can reach us." Travis watched the man depart, then searched out a phone and called the hotel. He told them that they were to release no information to the man who was about to show up, especially their telephone logs. The hotel manager assured him that their privacy was guaranteed. The man would be provided with no information whatsoever.

They boarded the plane and buckled in. The flight was about half full and left on time. They rose to a cruising altitude of six thousand feet, leaving Rhodes behind, a jewel amidst the sparkling brilliance of the Mediterranean. Travis glanced over Samantha's shoulder and out the small window. How had he allowed them to get so close not only once, but twice? They had stayed too long in Cairo and that mistake had cost Alain Porter his life. Three days in Lindos had given Kerrigan's network enough time to track them and send in an assassin. But how? They hadn't used credit cards or showed their passports other than for entry into Cyprus, then Greece. The ports of entry were tiny and unsophisticated. He could scarcely believe that the border guards had entered their names into a computer at any point. The only way that happened was at major border crossings or international airports that were equipped with bar scanners. No, Kerrigan had tracked them some other way.

He felt a familiar sensation tingle along his spine as the danger levels heightened. If they had driven directly from Lindos Mare to the airstrip, they would have arrived earlier and been waiting when Kerrigan's man chartered in. They wouldn't have recognized him, but he surely would have known who they were. There was one positive aspect to this, he thought. They knew what Kerrigan's man looked like.

And in that, another thought occurred to him. Knowing how capable they were at protecting themselves, Kerrigan had sent only one man after them. Who the hell was this guy?

Travis mentally calculated the time frames. By the time the hired killer reached Lindos, found out they had left and returned to the airstrip, it would be too late for him to fly into Rome and intercept them. That gave them clear passage to London. But Travis was positive Kerrigan would track their movements from Rhodes to London in no time, so they would have to disappear quickly and stay invisible for three or four days. The logistics were getting ugly. They needed Basil's magic box in their hands and working in a maximum of four days. That would be difficult. And they needed Davis Perth. Without the CEO of Gem-Star on their side, Kerrigan had the United States to turn to for refuge when things heated up. And if Kerrigan still had a free reign after they humiliated him in Antwerp, then all was lost. His financial empire would still be standing and he would eventually find them.

Travis stared out the window at the beauty of the Mediterranean Sea, and saw nothing. He preferred a fair fight, not this. Things that were far beyond their control would decide their destiny, and he knew that it was the uncontrollable variables that often killed a mission. And if this mission were to die, so would he and Samantha.

THIRTY-ONE

Garret Shaw was ready to reach out and snap the woman's neck, but he controlled the urge and asked her the same question again. "Did they leave a forwarding address?"

"I'm sorry, sir, the hotel is unable to give out any information on our guests."

"Could I speak with the manager, please?" He managed to keep civility in his tone, but his anger was building quickly. The desk clerk informed him that the manager would only reiterate what she had told him, then left to find her boss. A few minutes later she reappeared with a well-dressed, dark-skinned man in tow. He greeted Shaw and stated Lindos Mare's policy, just as the woman had.

"This couple is not who they appear to be," Shaw started, withdrawing a false set of identity papers from his vest pocket. They identified him to be a field agent with the Central Intelligence Agency, operating out of Langley, Virginia. The hotel manager scrutinized the ID for a minute, then handed it back. "They are wanted in the United States for treason and espionage. They are extremely dangerous and will kill on a moment's notice to stay outside the reach of justice. You and your staff are quite lucky no one died while they were here."

The manager was trembling as he responded. "I really wish I could help, sir. If you request that the local police get involved and they obtain the proper warrants, I would be glad to help you. Until then . . ."

Shaw snapped the leather ID holder shut and nodded to the man. "I understand," he said. "Thank you for your assistance." He left the hotel and began the drive back to the airstrip. Something wasn't right with the way the hotel staff had reacted to him. They were intimidated, almost scared. Usually when he pulled out the CIA identification, people were intrigued, stimulated by his presence. Somehow they knew he was not CIA. He slipped his cell phone out and checked to see if he was in a service zone. It was roaming, so he dialed Kerrigan's New York number and waited. Eventually it clicked through and rang.

"Did you locate them?" Kerrigan asked. His office phone had caller ID.

"Just missed them. They were on the Greek island of Rhodes at a hotel called the Lindos Mare. I suspect I missed them by only a few hours at the most. I think the hotel staff are covering for them. I'd like to go back and persuade them to tell me what they know."

"No." Kerrigan's voice was crystal clear. "Keep on their tail. I'll have my Washington connections dredge up whatever information the Lindos Mare may have. Whatever clues they left will be electronic, not personal. Is there an airport on the island?"

"Just an airstrip, no control tower. I'm heading back there now."

"Excellent. It would appear you were correct about them chartering out of Israel. Nice work. You'll find them. Keep your cell phone on; I'll call you the minute I've got something."

"Okay. When are you leaving New York for Antwerp?"

"Next Monday, via Brussels. Antwerp doesn't have an international airport. The sight is set for Wednesday. I'll phone you with a number once I'm checked into my hotel."

Patrick Kerrigan pushed his finger down on the disconnect button. He let it up and listened for a dial tone. He punched in a number that took him directly into the bowels of the CIA in Langley. A familiar voice answered.

"I need you to hack into the electronic records for a hotel in Greece," he said.

"Not a problem. What's the name of the hotel?"

"Lindos Mare. It's on Rhodes."

"I'll call you when I have something." The line went back to a dial tone. Kerrigan repeated the same request to his contact at the NSA, then leaned back in his chair. Time was on his side. McNeil and Carlson were on the run, scared and helpless. They had no access to money or credit without triggering an electronic signal that would pinpoint exactly where on the globe they were. Instantaneously. And they couldn't survive without money. At some point they would surface, and when they did Garret Shaw would be there. Faceless and without remorse.

A small percentage of him wanted Samantha Carlson, and the location of the diamonds, right now. But the greater part of the whole was willing to wait. She would surface in due time, and with her would come the greatest diamond mine in history. Hell, the thirty-odd stones he had taken from her in Cairo would generate in excess of twenty million dollars at the sight next week. Yes, patience was acceptable. Prudent even.

He rose from his chair and walked across to his wall safe. He opened it and took the small suede pouch from inside. The diamonds spilled onto his open palm. They were beautiful. And nothing could stop him from getting them to the Antwerp market. Rumor had it that Davis Perth might be arriving back from his South Pacific sailing expedition sometime next week, but that was pure conjecture. Oftentimes Davis didn't show for a month or two after he was expected back. If Davis did arrive, he would have to come up with some lame excuse for heading to Antwerp, but that wasn't difficult. Davis was absent from the office so often, he didn't question what his president was up to. And that was good, Kerrigan thought, because if the idiot ever knew, he would be quite shocked.

Kerrigan placed the stones back in the safe and spun the dial. It was still early morning in New York and the day was looking to be a good one. He called a friend and set a lunch date, then rang his secretary for some coffee. Yes, this would be a good day.

THIRTY-TWO

Basil Abercrombie stared back at Samantha. He was a tall, gangly man with long dark hair that hung straight, emphasizing his oval face. His facial features were well proportioned, but he was not handsome. Not even close. He had poor-people teeth, crooked with gaps in places and overlapping in others. His dress was sloppy and his shirt hung down over his loose trousers.

"Wow," Basil said, his accent thick Cockney. "You weren't shitting me. She's fucking gorgeous."

"Thank you. I think," Samantha replied.

Basil grinned, his eclectic mixture of teeth between his thick lips. The kettle began to whistle and their host jumped up from his chair and hustled into the kitchen. Samantha glanced around the Regent's Park flat, amused and intrigued by what she saw. There was no theme to Basil's decorating; it just all melded together somehow, like much of London. The sofa and chairs were overstuffed and covered with a fuzzy velvet-like material that showed every bit of dirt and dust. The coffee and end tables were Victorian, hand carved and probably worth a bundle at the local antique dealer. Same with the dining-room suite that sat crammed against the far wall. The windows were covered with sheers but allowed in enough filtered sunlight to placate the twenty or thirty plants scattered about. The walls were covered with framed art, original oils of the English countryside. Thick throw rugs lay underfoot, atop polished hardwood flooring. Basil returned from the kitchen with a tray. On it was a teapot, three cups, and milk and sugar. None of the cups matched. He set the tray on the coffee table.

"So what the hell is going on, Travis?" he asked, sitting back and waiting for the tea to steep.

"We're in a bit of a predicament," Travis began, running through exactly where they were with Kerrigan, the diamonds, and the latest in a string of people assigned to kill them. Basil carefully poured the tea, added milk and sugar according to his guest's tastes, and handed out tea biscuits. He also listened without interrupting. Travis finished with a warning of sorts. "I'm not sure we're all that safe here. I was stupid enough to call your number from our suite on Rhodes."

"Oh, you know me. Too paranoid to have a normal phone circuit. The one into the house is patched through a satellite network and is totally untraceable. It'll come up with a different number and area code each time you called. None of them remotely close to where we are."

"I'm impressed, Basil," Samantha said.

"How are things going with the box?" Travis asked.

"Good on the box, not so good on the synthetic diamonds. Here, come with me and I'll show you." Basil took his tea and headed for the basement. At the bottom of the steep stairs, he pulled a string and a lone bulb flickered on, revealing a small, cramped dugout with earthen walls and floor. The air was damp and smelled musty. He crouched low to keep his head from hitting the ceiling joists while he moved to the far corner of the hole. A lone shelf, covered with paint cans and stacks of old newspapers, clung to the wall. Basil fiddled with a paint can, then pushed on the shelving unit. A section of the wall swung in and he disappeared into the darkness. A moment later, light flooded the secret doorway and he popped his head back out and waved them in. Samantha trailed Travis into the room and stared, her mouth agape.

She was surrounded by a state-of-the-art laboratory. Beakers, burners, centrifuges, isolation chambers, and a hundred pieces of equipment she had never seen before. Three long benches provided the working space for various ongoing experiments, and she noticed the metal box sitting near the end of the closest bench. She walked over and picked it up, scanning the exterior for signs it had been tampered with. She saw none. She set the box down on the counter and watched Basil as he retrieved a metal container from a small blast furnace in the distant corner.

"This is your zircon," he said, opening the thick latches on the heavy box and taking out a piece of silver metal. The chunk was translucent, with varying shades of blue cutting through it. "Zirconian silicate, specific gravity between 4.2 and 4.86 with a hardness of 7.5. Commonly referred to as Matura diamonds, as it's the closest thing to real diamonds that occurs naturally. And," he dropped it on the bench with a thud, "totally fucking useless."

"What are you talking about? You said it yourself; it's the closest thing to a real diamond."

"I can't keep it in a liquid form," Basil said. "The melting temperature of zircon is 1852 degrees Celsius. Usually you can find some sort of solvent-catalyst to reduce the melting temperature, but not here. I tried tungsten, no luck. Then tantalum, tungsten's periodic-table neighbor with a less stable carbide. I managed to get the temperature down to 1472 degrees Celsius. That's the best I could do."

"Holy shit," she said quietly. "I could never touch the box, let alone carry it, at that temperature."

"I do have another idea, one that I know will work," he said, picking up a second container from the bench and handing it to her. "Cubic zirconia."

Samantha shook her head. "No way. You can fool some yokel in a bar with cubic zirconia in an expensive setting, but we're talking the top diamond experts in the world. They'd laugh at the attempt, then ask for the real diamonds back."

Basil grinned at her. "What are the major differences between real diamonds and cubic zirconia?"

"Density is the greatest. Cubic zirconia is almost double the density of a natural diamond. You can measure the density by dropping the stones in methylene iodide. The diamond will take at least twice as long to float to the bottom of the jar."

"Not a problem. What else?"

Samantha stared at the man for a minute, trying to decide whether or not to take him seriously. Anyone related to geology or chemistry knew that cubic zirconia was the closest simulant to real diamond ever produced. Given the right circumstances, it was difficult to tell them apart. But there were a handful of clues that consistently revealed the forgery. And density was the greatest. Yet this ragtag of a man, with a chemistry lab in the basement of his London flat, was telling her that density was not a problem. Any chemist who could alter the density of cubic zirconia to mirror that of real diamond was brilliant, and destined to be very rich.

"All right, we'll skip over the density issue. How about its refractive index?"

"That is a little trickier, but I think I have it figured. Next?"

"Thermal conductivity."

"Piece of fucking cake."

"Thermal conductivity tests are completely reliable. You can't alter the nitrogen levels in the cubic zirconia enough to make the fake stone cool like a diamond."

"Yes, I can."

"No, you can't."

"Yes, I fucking can."

"No, you *fucking* can't!" She was shouting now.

Basil's face sported a huge grin and he turned to Travis. "I fucking love this woman."

"Yeah, me too." Travis stood up from the stool he'd been sitting on. "Basil, why don't you take a few minutes and tell Sam exactly how you're going to do all these wonderful things."

Basil nodded. "The problem with pure zirconia is that the cubic arrangement of atoms is stabilized by either calcium oxide or yttrium oxide. That lowers the symmetry of the crystal enough to cause double refraction, high density, heat retention, and increase its reflection coefficient. Look here, Sam, and you'll see what I've done to alter the chemical makeup of the . . ."

Travis retreated to the stairs and climbed back to the main floor. He had no idea what they were talking about, nor did he care. Chemistry wasn't his strong suit. He poured another cup of tea and added a touch of milk. He lit a cigarette and sipped on the English staple. Time was ticking as they approached the day Kerrigan would present the diamonds at the Antwerp sight. It was midmorning Friday, and both Samantha and he were well rested after flying into London from Rome the previous evening, and finding a private bed and breakfast in Whitechapel. The Antwerp sight was set for next Wednesday. The rate at which Basil was moving along with the box was encouraging. Travis knew the man well enough to feel confident that he would have it ready for Sunday or Monday at the latest. But that only took care of one part of bringing Kerrigan to his knees. They desperately needed to speak with Davis Perth, to try and convince the man that the president of his company was a remorseless murderer.

There was an option that precluded Davis Perth, but he didn't like it. Contacting the FAA and the FBI and detailing exactly what they knew about the Cranston Air 111 crash was risky at best. Travis was positive Kerrigan had friends in high places, and moles in low places. Both agencies would deal with the information through the proper channels, which would mean slowly and methodically. They would demand to meet with Sam and him, and that would open them up to Kerrigan again. No, it was much better if they could convince Perth to take care of that end of things for them. He was a man of influence and that would fast-track an FBI investigation. He jerked around, startled, as Sam and Abercrombie came up from the basement. They were both smiling.

"My head hurts," Samantha said lightly. "Is it safe to take a walk?"

"Sure." He ground out his cigarette and followed her to the door. "You going to be here?" he asked, and Basil nodded. They left the flat, walking hand in hand up the hill toward some shops they had seen when the taxi dropped them off earlier. The day was pleasant for late spring, the sky clear with only an occasional hint of cloud. Walk-up townhouses lined both sides of the street, some well kept with new wrought-iron railings and ornate Victorian moldings, others in ratty condition with peeling paint and cracked windows. They reached the crest of the hill and began peering through the windows into the various shops. Samantha broke the silence.

"Now he," she said, referring to Basil, "is an interesting fellow. Where and how on God's green earth did you meet him?"

"Absolute luck, nothing else," he said. "I was in London catching a bit of R&R between SEAL assignments and I stopped in at a pub for a drink. While I was enjoying a pint of lager and lime, this guy gets in an argument with a group of skinheads. All six of them pulled knives on him. Well, it was an obvious injustice that had to be taken care of."

"So you relieved the skinheads of their knives?"

"God no, that would be dangerous. I just happened to have a gun with me. I pulled it out and threatened to shoot them. They left."

"And the guy you saved was Basil."

"Yup. He'd had a few too many pints, and I helped him home. When he found out what I did for a living, he insisted I have a look at his setup in the basement, so I did. I came back the next morning to make sure he was all right. He didn't even remember showing me the room. He was freaked that I knew what he had down there. It was awkward at first, but we've developed a great friendship over the years."

"Whom does he work for? That equipment is worth hundred of thousands of dollars, maybe over a million."

"The British Government. Only two people in the secret service know who he is. One deposits checks into his Swiss accounts, and the other fields requests from various departments and passes them along for Basil to work on."

"He's absolutely brilliant. In three days, he managed to figure out how to modify the chemical makeup of cubic zirconia to match that of real diamonds almost to a tee. There is one downside to his work that would make it useless on the world market, but that won't affect us."

"What's that?"

"By altering the molecular bonding, he weakened the structure. It's far too brittle to ever withstand a sharp blow. It would just shatter."

"That won't be a problem?"

"Not at all. The tests the experts in Antwerp will run on the fake diamonds don't involve hitting them with a hammer. They'll test for heat conductivity, density, refraction index and a few other subtle things. Basil's modified cubic zirconia should test very well."

"I don't get it," he said, stopping in front of a fish-and-chip store. "You want them to discover that Kerrigan brought fake diamonds to the sight, but now you're telling me that Basil has perfected this to the point where they won't be able to tell the difference. How does that destroy Kerrigan's professional reputation?"

Samantha rolled her eyes. "You've got to learn to listen, Travis. If I were to exchange the real diamonds with standard cubic zirconia, the experts would just laugh. The fakes have to be as close to authentic as possible. It has to look like Kerrigan really thought he could get away with it."

"And what happens if the fakes actually fool all the experts? He walks."

"Hardly." She grinned. "*I'll* hit one of them with a hammer. By accident, of course."

They continued until they reached a corner pub. It looked quaint and quiet and they opted for a beer, even though it wasn't quite noon. It was a victory drink, of sorts. After all, it was starting to look like they might have a shot at derailing Patrick Kerrigan.

THIRTY-THREE

Garret Shaw stood in the middle of Trafalgar Square, marveling at the number of pigeons that called the infamous square home. They were everywhere. From the tip of Lord Nelson's cap to the thousands of tiny alcoves in the monolithic National Gallery, they found places to nest. He looked around the open-air aviary, thinking that trying to find one particular pigeon was akin to his task of locating McNeil and Carlson in London. They had effectively vanished into the historic city without a trace. Kerrigan's moles in the NSA and CIA had picked up their flights out of Athens and Rome within minutes of customs swiping their passports through their computers. Kerrigan had passed the information along to him, but he physically couldn't catch up with his prey. They had landed at Heathrow three days ago, late Thursday evening. Since then, nothing.

He pulled his mobile phone from his vest pocket and checked the signal. The battery was charged and the phone was roaming properly, but no call from the U.S. Damn it. He needed some sort of direction if he was to find them—direction that had to come from Kerrigan. He pulled his macintosh up around his neck against the cool spring air that had descended on London late the previous evening. It was cold and he was tired. Tired of searching the haystack for two needles that were proving themselves to be very worthy foes.

The assassin dialed Kerrigan's New York number and listened to it ring. Kerrigan answered on the third ring.

"Anything new?" Shaw asked.

"About two hours ago, my CIA connection managed to pull the phone logs from their hotel room on Rhodes. Three of the calls were to Gem-Star."

"What?" Shaw said. "Why are they calling you?"

"They're not calling me, you fool. They're looking for Davis Perth."

"What do they want with Davis?"

"They must have figured out we're acting independently of Gem-Star. Davis would be interested in their story. We've got to find them before they can reach him."

"When's he back?"

"When I found out they had phoned here looking for him, I called him on his satellite phone. He's docking in Nuku'alofa on the island of Tonga tonight to restock, heading for Samoa tomorrow. He's completely out of the picture for at least three weeks."

Shaw was puzzled. "If he has a satellite phone, he's reachable."

"I'm the only person with the number," Kerrigan said.

"Three weeks is an eternity. They'll be fish food long before that. What else did you get from the phone logs?"

"They made four other calls, all over the globe. One each to Switzerland, Russia, Canada and Australia. My guy is getting names and addresses on each one."

"Don't bother," Shaw said, walking through Trafalgar. "They made four calls to different area codes, but not one to London. Then they left Rome for London and disappeared. The four calls were all to London, Patrick. Whoever they called is using a scrambler to bounce the signal off a satellite."

The transatlantic line was quiet for a few moments, save for the controlled breathing of the New York party. "They are proving to be quite resourceful, Garret."

"Yes, they are. You're leaving for Antwerp tomorrow morning?"

"Yes. I land at Brussels about six in the evening, Belgian time. Antwerp is less than an hour from Brussels."

"All right. If you get anything on them, let me know right away. This waiting is starting to piss me off." He hung up just as he reached the north end of Trafalgar Square. He skirted the National Gallery and headed up one of the numerous side streets leading past Leicester Square into Soho. The area was seedy, and darkened taverns and strip joints littered both sides of the street. He chose a particularly raunchy-looking pub called the Rat and Parrot and left the cool afternoon weather outside.

The bar was exactly what he'd expected. A few tables empty, a few occupied. It was dark and smoky and smelled of stale beer. Every eye in the place was on the stranger as he approached the bar. He ordered a malt whiskey and downed it in one swallow. He asked for the best lager they had on tap and sipped contentedly on it for a few minutes. When he ordered another, he asked the bartender if anyone in the pub could provide him with a few joints and maybe some crack cocaine. He was convincing enough that the man gave a nod to a table near the dartboard. Three men were hunched over their pints, talking in low tones.

"I understand you gentlemen may be able to help me," Shaw said as he approached them. All three were large, muscular men. Two were black with close-cropped curly hair, the third white with long stringy hair that needed shampoo and water. All three wore long coats.

"What the fuck do you want?" one of the black men asked him. His tone was uncivil, nasty at best.

"Drugs. I'm in from the States and I need something. Crack would be nice."

"You look like a fucking cop," the white guy said.

"Well, I tell you what. Why don't all three of you take me out and pat me down? If I'm a cop, you can do me, if not, you can sell me something. How does that sound?"

The three men looked about, nodding and generally agreeing that the proposal sounded okay. One asked, "You got cash?"

Garret pulled out some English pounds and American dollars. "Whichever you prefer."

They left the dive and returned to the street. One of the two black guys pointed to an alley about halfway up the block. They reached it and turned in. It was narrow and wound in from the main street, cutting off any view passersby might have. They reached a spot bordered on both sides by brick buildings and no windows. A gun appeared in the white guy's hand.

"Okay, stupid, let's have the cash." He grinned at his buddies as Shaw offered up his money. "Fuck, you are one dumb ass. What makes you think we'd do anything but take your money and cut you up a bit?" Blades in both black men's hands reflected the dim light from the alley. "Stupid fucking Americans."

"Stupid fucking Brits," he said, his right hand shooting out and grabbing the wrist that held the pistol. He snapped it, breaking every bone in the lower forearm. With his free hand he wrenched the pistol from the man's hand and leveled it at the two remaining thugs. "Now, what were you saying?" He let go of the wrist and the man dropped to the ground, writhing in the dirt of the alleyway. Shaw kept the gun pointed at one man's head. He cocked the trigger.

"What the fuck am I supposed to do with you three? Kill all of you? That would probably make the headlines in those stupid rags you call newspapers. And all those witnesses in the bar. I'm just not sure."

The man with the gun pointed directly at him spoke, quietly and with newfound respect. "I think we've made a mistake here, sir. We actually meant to give you the proper amount of drugs for your money. We forgot. How about we give you your money back and call it a day?"

"You want to take your friend and leave?" Both men nodded. Garret pretended to think on it for a minute. "Okay. Return the money and get the hell out of here. And don't say a
word to anyone. Got it?"

A minute later, he stood in the deserted alley, the gun
dangling at his side. That was all he had wanted. Breaking
the man's wrist was a cheap price to pay to obtain a gun. He
tucked the pistol into his belt and made his way back toward Trafalgar Square and the side street where his rental
car was parked. God help McNeil when he found him. One
of these six bullets had his name on it.

THIRTY-FOUR

Monday morning brought showers to London, bringing out the umbrellas and quick tempers. Even the clerk in the grocery store at the end of Basil's block was in a blue mood. She dumped the eggs and bacon into a bag and scarcely acknowledged Samantha and Travis as they paid. They left the store and hurried back to Basil's flat. By the time they arrived, they were both drenched.

"I told you to take the brelly," their host chided them as they shook off inside his front door. "Now you both smell like wet dog."

"Now there's something I've never been accused of," Travis said. "I'll cook up some breakfast if you two want to go over the box again. We should be leaving for Heathrow in about an hour, Sam. Flying into Belgium is international from London and we should be at least an hour or two in advance."

Samantha listened intently as Basil went back over the operation of the box. He had worked out the last few snags and it was completely operational. She was amazed at the work he had done in such a short time.

"I eliminated the need for drilling holes in the exterior of the box by encasing the liquid cubic zirconia in these corrugated steel pieces that line the inside of the box. Thirteen of fourteen are filled with the zirconia to make the diamonds, the last one has the catalyst to make the liquid solidify."

"And that catalyst is tinged with green, right?"

"Yes. It will coat the outside of the zirconia with an ultrathin layer that should resemble the natural color of the rough diamonds. A spectrometer could easily note the color differences, but you don't think they'll have tested the originals by the time you get to see them."

"I'm sure of that. Color is mostly discernable by the naked eye, and the preliminary inspection of the rough doesn't get technical enough to require a spectrometer reading."

"Okay. All you have to do is take the original diamonds and place them in the padding between the outer and inner boxes. They will create exact molds of their shapes. Then remove the diamonds, close the case and turn this handle the opposite way you would to open it. That releases the liquid cubic zirconia into the molds. Now, this is very important. Once you're sure the molds are filled, release the catalyst and let it set for at least six minutes. Eight would be ideal."

"What happens if I don't have six minutes?"

"Your fakes will not have hardened. If you open the case too soon and they're not hardened all the way through, they'll crack from the cool air hitting their surface. You cannot open the case until a minimum of six minutes after you inject the catalyst. Got it?"

"Got it."

"Once you've created the fake diamonds, drop them on the table and put the originals back into the molds. You'll have to put each one back in the same mold it formed, so remember the exact order you put them in."

"Holy shit, this is getting difficult," she groaned.

"You think stealing twenty-five million dollars in diamonds from a highly guarded room in the diamond headquarters of the world should be easy?" he asked. "I don't think so."

Samantha laughed. Basil was right. She would be inside the very heart of De Beers, the company that controlled the diamond flow worldwide. And inside that building was a small locked room where only authorized personnel were allowed. Inside that room was a handful of rough diamonds that were so spectacular, De Beers had agreed to hold an unscheduled sight just for them. Unheard of. And she was going to steal them. Abercrombie's comment *did* put things in perspective.

Travis had breakfast on the table when they were finished. They had just helped Basil clean the dishes when the taxi pulled up. Travis loaded their luggage into the cab and came back in for Samantha. She was talking to Basil, saying good-bye, and he decided one more time to try Davis Perth in America. He dialed the main number to Gem-Star and waited. Finally the answering service picked up. It was four A.M. in New York and the office was not yet open. He asked for Davis Perth and readied to hang up.

"Who's calling, please?" came the unexpected reply.

He had one shot at this, and he wasn't about to screw it up. "It's Senator Watson from Oregon, ma'am. It's imperative I speak with Mr. Perth immediately."

"One moment, please." Light music filtered into his ear as he sat waiting, praying that the next voice he would hear would be Davis Perth.

"Senator Watson." The voice was strong, authoritative. "Davis here. What can I do for you at this hour?"

Travis felt his palm go sweaty and his breath become shallow. On the phone he had the man who could forever sever Kerrigan's ties to the United States. Whatever assets Patrick Kerrigan had inside American borders would be seized or frozen. He would be unable to return home, pending criminal charges that would include killing 229 innocent people on Cranston Air Flight 111. Davis Perth was the man who could make these things happen—if he believed what he was about to hear. Travis took a deep breath and began.

"Mr. Perth, this is not Senator Watson. My name is Travis McNeil and this call concerns Patrick Kerrigan. . . ."

THIRTY-FIVE

Knightsbridge was bordered by Hyde Park on the north and by some of the most valuable London real estate on the other three sides. It featured a bevy of shops and restaurants catering to the well-heeled crowd that didn't mind spending a small fortune for clothes or lunch. Harrods, the bastion of British department stores, occupied a large chunk of Brompton Road, an appendage that gracefully curved from Knightsbridge toward the Natural History Museum. Set in this upper-end community of gentlemen in top hats and nannies pushing prams was a small restaurant aptly named the Queen's Ransom. A visitor only had to glance at the prices to see where the eatery got its name. Seated at a table for two near the rear was a single American—Garret Shaw.

Halfway through the rack of lamb, his cell phone rang. Every eye in the restaurant turned to view the culprit, the offender who had disobeyed the cardinal rule of the establishment. All cell phones were to be turned off, no exceptions. Shaw ignored the stares and answered the call.

"This is an acquaintance of Patrick Kerrigan," the voice said. "Am I talking with Mr. Shaw?"

"You are. What can I do for you?"

"Mr. Kerrigan knew he would be unable to receive phone calls for part of today and gave me your number in case his cellular telephone went directly to his voice mail. I work in a rather, shall we say, sensitive area, Mr. Shaw. I'd rather not reveal my name or exactly where I work. I would, however, like to pass on some information that I know Mr. Kerrigan would consider important."

Shaw checked his watch and subtracted the time difference. Kerrigan's flight to Belgium would just be departing JFK. He would be unreachable for seven to eight hours. Two plus two came together quickly and Shaw realized he was speaking with one of Kerrigan's moles. "Go ahead, sir," he answered.

"Mr. Kerrigan had feelers out for McNeil and Samantha Carlson. Am I talking to the right person about this?"

Garret sat bolt upright in his seat. "Yes, please continue."

"I just received confirmation that both their passports were entered into the British customs computer less than ten minutes ago. They are boarding a flight for Brussels, leaving Heathrow in fifty-two minutes."

"You're positive?"

The man assured him he was and gave him the airline name, flight number and terminal. Shaw thanked him and pushed the end button. He grabbed the nearest waiter.

"Get me my bill in less than thirty seconds, or I'm not paying it," he said, pushing the man toward the front desk. He glared back at every person who continued to stare at him, and eventually they all turned away. His bill arrived and he paid it, almost running from the restaurant to his car. He slammed it into gear and headed for Heathrow. He checked his watch again. Forty-seven minutes. He swerved in and out of traffic, cursing the British for driving on the left. Three times, he swung into the left lane only to get jammed in behind a slow driver. He finally stayed put in the right lane and went with the flow. The traffic was heavy coming around Earl's Court, but thinned out as he hit Kensington High

Street and headed west. He kept checking his watch and swearing under his breath. Time was running out. He took the exit ramp onto the A4 and floored it. The motorway was moving well and he began to relax as he edged the speedometer up over eighty.

Finally, Heathrow loomed ahead and he took the short-stay car park lane for Terminal Two. The access road was clear and he accelerated to over seventy miles an hour down the final stretch. The car threatened to leave the pavement as he made the turn into the dropoff area, but he controlled the skid and slid into an open spot. He took nothing with him, but locked the car and slipped the keys in his pocket. If he made the plane, someone would eventually find a bag of clothes and a gun, but since he had rented the car under an assumed name, the trail would lead nowhere. If he missed the plane, he would simply come back and leave.

He leaped over the concrete dividers and sprinted toward Terminal Two. He was scarcely breathing hard as he entered the terminal and glanced around for the Lufthansa counter. He spotted it a hundred yards to the right and again broke into a run. There was no lineup and he approached the first ticket agent, slipping his credit card from his pocket.

"I need a first-class seat on Flight 972 to Brussels, please," he said, watching the woman enter the information into the computer in slow motion.

"That flight departs in eleven minutes, sir. The ticketing is most likely closed."

"Please check. Quickly."

"Oh, I'm sure that we stopped ticketing that flight . . . Well, I'll be darned. It hasn't been closed off yet. I have availability in first class or coach, whichever you prefer—"

"First class. No baggage. Just get me the ticket." He saw the look she gave him and he added, "Please."

Four minutes later he grasped the ticket and ran for the gate. He reached the bank of metal detectors that separated the general airport population from the ticketed passengers.

A line at least thirty people deep snaked back from the door. He skirted the edge of the line and jumped in front of the first person. He flipped out an American one-hundred-dollar bill and told the man he had three minutes to catch his plane. The man politely let him in, and took the bill.

He walked through the detectors at a satisfactory pace, then broke into a run on the other side. Gate thirty-six was at the far end of the corridor and he dodged passengers and flight crews as he sprinted through the crowded passageway. He reached his gate and handed his ticket to the agent. She looked startled at his lateness, checked the ticket, then turned to check the status of the airplane. Through the window they could both see the retractable sleeve moving back from the doorway.

"I'm sorry, sir, but the flight is already disengaged from the bridge. I'm sure we have a later flight. . . ."

"Get on the radio and ask the pilot to have the bridge reattached, please," he said, his eyes steel blue and penetrating into her very soul.

She stared at him for a moment, then picked up the two-way radio that fed into the cockpit. She spoke directly to the pilot, then nodded and shut down the radio. "There is no way the pilot can do that, sir. If he does, they will lose their position in the takeoff queue and that will result in a huge delay. He was very firm, sir. I am sorry."

He stared at her for a minute, then looked out the window. The plane was pushing back, away from the terminal. In a few minutes it would taxi onto the runway, be cleared for takeoff and leave for Brussels. With Travis McNeil and Samantha Carlson on board. He ground his teeth and clenched his fists, mangling his ticket and boarding pass without even noticing. He had been within seconds of getting them—seconds. He finally left the gate and began the return journey back to his car. He stopped at the Lufthansa counter and exchanged the crumpled ticket for a flight departing for Belgium first thing Tuesday morning.

He had been so close. So very close.

THIRTY-SIX

The plane jerked slightly as it pushed back from the gate, then rolled smoothly as the ground crew maneuvered it into taxiing position. It turned and taxied onto the apron, taking its proper slot for takeoff. Six minutes later, the wheels left the ground and Lufthansa Flight 972 was en route to Brussels.

Samantha accepted a *London Times* newspaper from the flight attendant, but set it in her lap as she watched London fall away. She recognized the twists in the Thames and found the Parliament buildings and Big Ben before the plane rose into the underbelly of a cloudbank, obscuring her view. She turned to Travis.

"You were on the phone with Davis Perth for quite a while. Do you think he took what you said seriously?"

Travis flipped the tray down and set his paper on it. "I think so," he said slowly. "He was mighty pissed off at first when he found out I wasn't Senator Watson. Especially since it was four in the morning."

"How did you know Perth knew Senator Watson, let alone that he'd take a call from the man in the middle of the night?"

"That was easy. His company is active in Oregon and there's a picture in the Gem-Star lobby of Perth and Watson opening a new mine. Anyway, a midnight call from a senator is not one you turn down."

"I take it he got over the deception."

"Eventually. He listened to what I had to say. Asked a lot of questions about the Cranston Air thing. That seemed to really get him."

"No kidding. The guy running his company murders 229 people to keep the value of some diamonds a secret. That would piss me off if I owned the company."

"Yeah, that's a good point. He had no idea about our expedition and I got the feeling he didn't know about the others either. He wasn't a happy man."

"But was he mad enough to sic the FBI on Kerrigan?"

"I don't know. We'll have to wait and see."

The plane had reached cruising altitude, and the flight attendants moved through the cabin, serving drinks. Samantha had a rum and Coke, something she almost never did when flying. Travis settled for coffee, and they sipped on their drinks for a few minutes in silence. Samantha spoke first.

"You ever been to Antwerp?" she asked casually.

"No. Never had a reason to until now. Never stole millions of dollars in rough diamonds. Until now, of course. You're a bad influence."

"Yeah, right, me. I'm the bad influence. I don't think so." She laughed. She'd had her share of interesting situations, but nothing like what he had seen in his life. "It's a very different city. Rubens was from Antwerp—painted all of his masterpieces in the city. He built his own home, a beautiful house and garden with a gorgeous courtyard. But the whole city is flat and it rains a lot. Check out the trees when we get there. Every side, not just the north, is covered with moss. I think Antwerp has the least number of sunny days of any European city."

"It sounds depressing."

"God, no. It's beautiful. You'll see."

"And De Beers is there."

"Oh, yes, Travis. De Beers is there," she said, envisioning the monolithic company. The heart of the world diamond cartel was in London, but the Antwerp office was crucially important to them. The rough diamonds that poured into Belgium were cut and polished by some of the best craftsmen in the world, then sent ahead to the world market. Antwerp represented a link in De Beers's chain that, if severed, would severely impact the monopoly they held. And at the heart of what held Antwerp out as such a cherished link were the diamond sights. "De Beers is definitely in Antwerp," she added. "In some ways, De Beers *is* Antwerp."

Flight 972 landed in Brussels slightly ahead of schedule and they caught an inter-city bus into Antwerp. McNeil didn't want to risk using a credit card for a car rental, even though he was positive Kerrigan's people had already picked up their movements when their passports cleared British and Belgium customs. The bus was actually quite enjoyable, one of the large luxury cruisers usually reserved for long-haul trips. Samantha stared out the window, watching a narrow band of rippled water that paralleled the road as it swept north toward Antwerp. Windmills dotted the fields, their blades rising above the new summer growth. An occasional farm, surrounded by trees in full foliage, broke the monotony of the tidal basin that was northern Belgium. The farmland gave way to houses first, then to the commercial bustle of Antwerp's port. They entered the city from the south, the driver cutting off the Autoweg at Koning Albert Park and slowing as he maneuvered through the slower traffic.

The city was typical European, with narrow cobblestone streets lined with three-story, centuries-old brick buildings. Flemish was the dominant language on the ornate signage that identified businesses and guild houses. Numerous humpback bridges spanned the River Schelde as it snaked its way through the heart of the city, each ancient and sturdy in its stone construction. Houses and shops lined the waterway, and life was in full bustle as their bus pulled into the central station. They asked the driver for directions to a reasonably priced hotel close to the diamond district. He jotted down an address for a mid-range hotel on Appelmansstraat, close to the Andimo Building, home of De Beers's Belgium office. It wasn't far and they opted to walk.

"We must be running out of money," she said as they cut through a square with a central fountain.

"Actually, no, we're just fine there. I borrowed a few thousand from Basil before we left London. The guy's loaded; he won't miss it."

"We have to pay him back," she said. "Somehow."

"I have an idea," he said, pointing down Appelmansstraat to number thirty-one. "I'll tell you later." The Alfa Empire Hotel, complete with a tacky vertical sign and glassed-in lobby, stood out like a sore thumb amidst the restored historical ambience that bordered it on either side. Travis just shrugged his shoulders and headed for the lobby. "Maybe it's better inside."

It was. The rooms were acceptable and had private baths. It was far from a five-star hotel, and they felt comfortable that Kerrigan wouldn't be sleeping next door. Samantha dragged out the phone book and looked up the main switchboard number for De Beers. She dialed the number, explained who she was, and asked the receptionist if it would be possible to get the names of the current directors. The woman was surprisingly accommodating and read off a few names. Samantha stopped her at the fifth name, Peter Van Housen. She asked to be put through to his local number, and waited as the phone rang. It eventually went to his voice mail, and she hit zero. The recording stopped and a different woman answered.

"Mr. Van Housen's office, Stephanie."

"Hello, do you speak English?" Samantha asked. Her Flemish was nonexistent.

"Yes, how can I help you?"

"I'm looking for Mr. Van Housen. Could you put me directly through to him, please?"

"I'm sorry, but that is quite impossible. Mr. Van Housen is on holiday this week. Could I be of some assistance?"

Samantha thought quickly. Peter Van Housen was her ticket to an invitation to Wednesday's sight. She knew the man well from several meetings in different cities over the past five years. He represented De Beers in the capacity of international marketing, and in the course of his daily duties met with geologists, cutters, buyers and competitors on a regular basis. She respected his abilities, and knew that he held her in the same capacity.

"Could you please contact Mr. Van Housen at home and let him know that I'm in Antwerp?" She gave the woman her name.

"That would be highly irregular, Ms. Carlson." The woman sounded uncertain.

"Please call him. I know Peter well, and I think he'd be very disappointed if he knew I had visited Antwerp and was unable to contact him."

The secretary capitulated and asked Samantha to hold while she tried the director's home phone number. Two minutes later, she took Sam off hold, apologized profusely for not putting her directly through, and patched the line across to Van Housen's home. It rang twice and a familiar voice picked up.

"Samantha Carlson, is that really you?"

"Hi, Peter. It's me. I just arrived in Antwerp a couple of hours ago and thought I'd look you up. I hope I'm not bothering you by having your office ring you at home."

"God, no. I would have been furious if they hadn't put you through. Listen, I'm on an international call on the other line. Would you like to pop over and have a drink, maybe dinner?"

"That sounds wonderful. I've got a friend with me, if that's okay?"

"Of course it is. My address is twenty-two Ambiorixlei, in Schoten. Just give the taxi driver the house number and he'll know where it is. See you in an hour?"

She agreed and hung up. She turned to Travis, a grin on her face. "I know this guy pretty well. I'm feeling a lot better about getting an invite to the sight."

He clutched her close to him and kissed her. He felt the urgency and unabashed desire in her lips as she kissed him back. She slid her hands up and began to unbutton his shirt, then his pants. "Do we have enough time?" he asked quietly.

"The guy's on holiday, Travis. He's at home and expecting us. Where is he going?"

"God, I love your attitude," he said, working his own magic on her buttons.

Forty minutes later, Samantha hailed one of the many black Mercedes cabs that cruised about the city in search of paying customers and gave the driver the address. He headed north, weaving through the back streets and giving his passengers the scenic route. He spoke some English and tried to point out landmarks and important buildings as they passed. Eventually he merged onto a main thorough-fare to cross the Albert Kanal, then angled east and into Schoten. The upscale neighborhood was anything but Euro-pean. The houses were huge and surrounded by estate-size lots, covered with mature fir and birch trees. The roads were still cobblestone, but gone was the congestion of the city, re-placed by a tranquil country setting. Samantha had to keep reminding herself she was in the heart of a city in the most populated country in Europe.

"What are these houses worth?" Samantha asked the driver.

"If you have to ask, you can't afford them," the man replied. "Anyone who lives here is either very wealthy, or a foreign national working in Belgium. Or both."

They turned onto Ambiorixlei and then through the brick-pillared gates of number twenty-two. The house was deep brown, with brick stretching across the exterior of the main floor. Dormers punctuated the steeply sloped roofline and the white trim was freshly painted. The Mercedes rattled ever so slightly as it pulled slowly up the long, sweeping cobblestone drive. They had just come to a stop when the front door opened and a middle-aged man walked out to greet them. He was well-dressed and very fit for his age, his hair still brown with no signs of gray. He clasped Samantha's hand and shook it vigorously. His complexion was pale and looked white against her tanned skin. She greeted him cordially and introduced him to Travis.

"I'm pleased to meet any friend of Samantha's," Peter Van Housen said warmly as he shook Travis's hand. He insisted on paying the taxi driver and waved them into the house.

The home was furnished with a masculine hand, the furniture dark leather with silver studs on its arms. The heavy tables were highly polished. Coats of arms decorated one wall of the foyer and original oils graced the formal living room. Van Housen motioned for them to be seated. The leather was soft and warm to the touch.

"I noticed a brass plaque on one of the brick pillars in front of the house," Travis said, interested. "It said Villa T'luipeerd. What exactly does that mean?"

"All the houses in this area have names," Van Housen said, relaxing in an armchair. "This one is Leopard Villa."

"It makes that look a little out of place," Samantha said, pointing at a stuffed beaver tucked away in the far corner of the room.

"Ah, my beaver. I bought this house from an executive with General Motors. He and his wife were Canadian. I made the mistake of telling them I liked it and when they left Belgium, they left me the beaver. It does make an interesting conversation piece."

Samantha nodded. She was interested in how Peter had ended up in Antwerp, and the next half an hour was spent tracing his movements for the past year or two. Finally, Van Housen asked Samantha what had brought them to Antwerp.

"We're just taking some time to see a bit of Europe," she said. "Antwerp seemed like a nice place to visit. And . . . I noticed De Beers has a sight set for Wednesday morning. Now that would be interesting to sit in on."

"Are you kidding?" Van Housen sat upright in his chair. "It would be an honor to have you at the sight, Sam. We don't get enough field geologists in Antwerp. Too many cutters and polishers, and not enough gatherers. Do you really want to take it in?"

"Absolutely."

He reached for the phone that sat on the table next to his chair. "Then consider it done." He began to dial.

"Peter, do me a favor?"

"Anything, Sam."

"Just tell your people that a geologist will be attending. Don't use my name." When he looked bewildered, she went on to explain. "Diamonds might be a girl's best friend, but the business is still run predominantly by men. Sometimes guys get their shorts in a knot when a woman is peeking over their shoulder. But once I'm face to face with them, it's usually okay."

He finished dialing. "As you wish, Sam." Someone answered and Van Housen spoke in fluent Flemish. He was on the line for a minute, then hung up. "That's arranged. Now, how about some dinner?"

It was well after nine in the evening when they finally poured themselves into a cab and headed back to their hotel. Peter Van Housen had been the consummate host, entertaining them with stories and plying them with food and liquor. The truth be known, both of them were fairly smashed when they left. They fell into bed together and Travis was asleep within seconds, leaving Samantha alone with her thoughts. And the one thought that kept recurring to her was that she was going to get her chance at Kerrigan. One chance, and only one.

But could she pull it off?

THIRTY-SEVEN

Patrick Kerrigan deplaned in Brussels, hailed a cab and stretched out in the backseat. He gave the driver his hotel name in Antwerp and watched the man's expression light up. Brussels cabbies liked nothing better than fares to Antwerp—they were a license to print money. It was bordering on dusk and Kerrigan had lost all of Monday to the flight and time difference. He hadn't slept at all on the plane and drifted off intermittently as his ride cruised through the Belgian countryside. He woke as they entered Antwerp, and twenty minutes later, the cab pulled up in front of the city's only five-star accommodation, the Radisson SAS Park Lane Hotel.

His room was reserved and the desk clerk had a message for him from a Mr. Shaw when he checked in. He settled into the suite, then called Garret on the number his hired killer had left. It was prefixed with a London area code.

Shaw answered immediately. "Hello, Patrick. McNeil and Carlson are in Belgium."

"What?" Kerrigan was stunned. "Where in Belgium, and when did they get here?"

"They flew into Brussels this afternoon. Probably arrived about three o'clock or so."

"They flew into Brussels? What the hell are they up to?"

"No idea. I missed getting on the plane by seconds. One of your moles called from Washington. They couldn't contact you, so they tried me."

"Shit. My guess is they're coming to Antwerp. But why?"

"Maybe the diamonds you got from them in Cairo were not all they had. They could be in Antwerp to dump off some rough to a cutter."

"Perhaps," Kerrigan said slowly, "but I don't think so. No, they're up to something."

"I'm on the next flight from London. It leaves tomorrow morning."

"Okay, you know where I'm staying. I'll see you when you get here." He hung up and paced the room.

Samantha Carlson was a major fucking headache. A headache that refused to go away. And with McNeil in tow, she was dangerous. All this two days before the private sight he had arranged at De Beers. He briefly contemplated whether the two could be connected, then discarded the idea. De Beers had set the sight at his request and had arranged for two Saudi princes as potential buyers for the entire lot, but his name had not been associated at any time. There was no way Carlson could have linked him to the sight. Of that he was positive.

Room service arrived with fresh coffee and pastries. He poured some coffee into the fine china that accompanied the urn and stirred in some cream. He watched as the cream dissipated in the coffee, lightening the color. The world was a bit like that, he thought. Every person who was added into the mix changed things a bit, altered the original. Some more so than others. And some in very distinct ways. He had committed some actions that could be construed as atrocities. Bringing down Cranston Air Flight 111 was horrific, but necessary. Killing the geologists didn't bother him in the least. They had been hired to perform a specific task, and when they double-crossed him by keeping the location of the diamonds secret, he had no choice. Eliminating people who stood in his way wasn't a major concern to him, nor was it the highlight of his life.

But Samantha Carlson was different. Killing her was going to be fun. A simple death was too good. He would make her suffer, torture her until she screamed to be put down, like a wounded dog. But even then he would refuse. He would make the pain linger until he was satisfied she had suffered enough. Then, and only then, would he kill her.

Perhaps her trip to Antwerp was a blessing in disguise. She was close by and Shaw was on his way in from London. They would slip up somehow, and Shaw would pounce. Once McNeil was out of the way, she would be helpless. His pulse quickened as a surreal vision of Samantha Carlson at his mercy ran through his mind.

Soon, he thought. Very soon.

THIRTY-EIGHT

Tuesday dawned clear in Antwerp, a rarity in a city that generally languished under cloud cover. The parks were jammed with families, the squares bustled with activity and the sidewalk cafes did a robust business. Antwerp worshipped the sun on the few days it chose to show itself. Travis and Samantha were caught up in the adrenaline and spent some of the day outside their hotel room, touring and taking in the city's history. Being spotted by Kerrigan was a concern and they kept a low profile, spending most of the time in the back of a cab. Belgian chocolate, world-famous for its rich texture and taste, was plentiful and Samantha tried a few different stores. They found a quaint restaurant specializing in mussels and opted for an early dinner.

The conversation varied, but consistently came back to Kerrigan and what would happen tomorrow morning. The sight was to begin at ten o'clock and Samantha was set to arrive only a couple of minutes before ten. She would meet both the seller and the buyers, then have an opportunity to grade the diamonds before the buyer's agents made an offer. It would be precisely ten o'clock when she locked eyes with Patrick Kerrigan.

"You going to be okay?" Travis asked, finishing off the last of his mussels and ordering another Stella Artois.

"Don't worry about me. Just make sure you're there to take the case after I come out of the room."

"I know, take the case and casually get the hell out of there—with the diamonds. If the security's as tight as you think it is, they'll search it on the way out. But I don't think they'll find the section where the diamonds will be hidden. Basil's work is absolute perfection."

"I just hope Basil's little contraption works. If it doesn't, I'll look like a complete idiot. Worst-case scenario lands me in jail for attempted theft."

"You'll do fine, Sam. You're a woman of many talents."

"Theft was never high on my list."

"If you get the diamonds and replace them with the cubic zirconia, Kerrigan is finished. He'll never trade in precious stones again."

"Travis." She looked at the table as she spoke, afraid to make eye contact in case he gave her the wrong answer. "After this is over, would you consider getting out of this lunatic line of work you're in? I've got more than enough money. Not just to live on, but for us to start a business or something. You know, something not so dangerous."

He reached across the table and cupped his hand under her chin. He gently lifted it and her eyes met his. He smiled. "Yes" was all he said.

They paid their bill and left the restaurant. They were close enough to the hotel to walk, and with twilight setting in, Travis thought they would be safe without taking a cab. The walk was refreshing and half an hour later they locked and bolted the hotel-room door. Samantha checked out Basil's box for the final time and Travis powered up the computer and logged on to the Internet. Sam had already programmed a proxy into the machine, effectively blocking it from sniffers. Travis opened and closed a few web sites and was getting bored when he had an idea. Learn more about geology. He pulled up the American Institute of Professional Geologists and began to poke around. Eventually he made his way to the awards section. He noted that every year, the AIPG selected a member who was without peer and awarded him or her with a silver-plated geologist's hammer. He scrolled back, reading the brief bios of the recipients over the past few years. He hit 1994 and stopped in his tracks. David Samuel Carlson had been the board's unanimous choice that year for his selfless devotion to the discipline. Samantha's father.

"Hey, look at this," Travis said. "Check out the 1994 winner of the AIPG fellow of the year."

Samantha set the box on the table and sauntered over. She leaned on his shoulders and read off the winners until she hit 1994. "My dad won it that year. I knew they'd picked him once but I didn't know what year. David Samuel Carlson," she read off the screen. "He always hated David, much preferred Sam."

"Not your average trophy. The winner gets a silver hammer."

Samantha stared at the screen. What had he said? The winner gets a silver hammer. Her knees went weak and she collapsed to the floor. He turned quickly in his chair, then was on his knees helping her up. His lips were moving, asking her if she was okay. Some part of her brain sent a reply— she needed water. He picked her up and set her on the couch, then hurried off to find some. He returned a few seconds later. She drank deeply, almost trancelike. He was close, staring at her, talking to her. She cut him off, asked him a question.

"What was the name of the hotel we stayed at in Butembo?"

"The Queen Anne. Why?"

"Could you do me a favor and get the telephone number for the hotel?" He just stared at her. "Please," she added. He dialed the international directory, and after a few minutes jotted a number down on the pad of paper beside the phone. He held it up for her to see. "Dial it, please." He nodded and handed her the phone as he dialed the number.

"What's wrong, Sam?" he asked quietly.

"Let me make this call first, Travis." She held up her finger. Someone in Butembo had picked up. "Could I speak with Martine Abouda, please?" A few moments of silence. "Hello, Martine, this is Samantha Carlson. Do you remember me? I stayed at your hotel a few weeks ago." She was silent as he confirmed that he knew who she was. "Martine, when I introduced myself to you I remember you said something rather odd to me. You said that I don't look like Sam Carlson. Why did you say that?"

He watched the remaining color drain from her face as she listened to the answer. "Could you please check your records and see exactly when Mr. Carlson stayed at your hotel." Again, silence as the man dug up the old records. "I see. Thank you very much." She hung up. Tears pooled in the corners of her eyes and she stared ahead at nothing.

"What's going on?" he asked, moving beside her and holding her. She was shaking.

"When we were in the Congo, in Butembo, the manager of the hotel said I didn't look like Sam Carlson. He said that because he had already met Sam Carlson. My father had stayed at the hotel."

"What? When?"

"Just over two years ago. Two years and three months, minus a couple of days. Dad stayed at the Queen Anne before heading into the Ruwenzori."

"What are you saying?"

"The hammer. The geologist's hammer we found at the foot of the diamond formation. D.S.C–1994. It never clicked until now, because Dad never called himself David. But that hammer, the one we found in the Congo, was given to my father by the AIPG in 1994. And my father stayed at the Queen

Anne just before he died. Travis, Kerrigan sent another expedition to the Congo, one that we didn't know about. And my father was in charge of it."

"Oh, my God," he whispered softly. "After your father finished with the expedition, he met your mother in Morocco. They were killed in a plane crash taking off from Casablanca."

"That bastard," she seethed. Gone was the timid woman with the tears. In her place was a woman consumed with anger. She stood up, the room whirling. Her arms lashed out, smashing the lamp and a vase. She grabbed the phone and hurled it at the wall. It missed the window and bounced off the painted stone, pieces flying about the room. Travis grabbed her and held her close. Her fists were clenched, her eyes afire, her lips contorted into a vicious sneer.

"That bastard," she said again, this time with sorrow. "He killed my parents."

THIRTY-NINE

The mood over the breakfast table was somber. After talking with the hotel manager in Butembo, Travis and Samantha had spent three hours reconstructing the last few weeks of her parents' lives. There was no doubt Kerrigan had initiated the sequence of events that had culminated in the fatal plane crash off the coast of Morocco. Before he left on the fated trip, her father had talked to her about his upcoming expedition, but never with any clarity that would allow her to pinpoint his exact target. She had remained in the dark, without really thinking about it, for the two years since the crash. All she knew was that her mother had met her father in Casablanca and they were to fly into London—and that they had never arrived. And her life had forever been changed.

But there had been clues that she had either ignored or failed to see—clues that now pointed to Kerrigan as the architect of her parents' deaths. The Manhattan meetings before he left New York, his interest in laser ablation, malaria pills, and his reputation inside the geological community. Kerrigan made no bones about going after the best, and her

father was the best. Then there was the timing. They had calculated that Kerrigan had sent three teams, including theirs,
into the jungle. But that left a huge gap between the first and
second. There was no such gap; there was an additional expedition. The one her father had led. He had located the
same vein that she had, and he had refused to divulge to
Kerrigan where it was, probably for the same reasons she
had refused. Finding his hammer at the formation and con-
firming he had stayed at the Queen Anne just before
trekking into the Ruwenzori was merely the concrete proof.
Kerrigan had killed her parents.

Samantha poked at her breakfast, tired and despondent.
Travis looked awful, his face readily showing the lack of
sleep. He drained a fifth cup of coffee and waved for the
waiter to bring another. "I'm so sorry, Sam," he said.

"I know you are," she replied, reaching across the table
and taking his hand. "You are so special to me." Tears welled
up in her eyes and a solitary droplet spilled down her
cheek. "I've got to stop taking this whole thing so personally
and remember that getting Kerrigan isn't just for me, it's for
every person with a loved one on that plane. And for the
families of the expedition members he murdered. And
more."

"It's time to go. You ready?"

She nodded. "Let's do it."

They checked out of the hotel and piled their luggage
into a waiting cab. The sky had clouded over and Antwerp
seemed drab, almost devoid of energy. Gone were the children skipping on the cobblestone squares, replaced by a
light drizzle of rain that muted the colors and highlighted
the gray stone the city's architects had loved so dearly. They
drove on in silence, both knowing that this was it.

Kerrigan snapped his briefcase shut and glanced across the
hotel suite at Garret Shaw. The man was tinkering with a
gun, polishing it. Killing time, Kerrigan thought. And time
was something that Travis and Carlson were running out of.

He was sure they were in Antwerp but he wasn't sure why. That bothered him, but not enough to alter the plans he had in place. Shaw had spent all of Tuesday calling the local hotels, trying to locate them, with no luck. Not surprising, as Travis would surely have checked in under an assumed name. But this was Wednesday morning and De Beers awaited. The phone rang just as he stood up with his briefcase and umbrella. He waved Shaw off and answered it himself. It was Langley.

"I've got them," the voice from deep inside CIA headquarters said. "One of the numbers I had a tracer on got a hit."

"Which one?"

"An Antwerp number called the Queen Anne hotel in Butembo last night."

"Where in Antwerp did the call originate from?" Kerrigan asked, angry that it had taken the man this long to call, but hesitant to tear a piece off of him.

"The Alfa Empire Hotel, on Appelmansstraat."

"Thank you." He hung up and turned to Shaw. "The Alfa Empire on Appelmansstraat. It's not far from here."

"Fuckers. That was one of the first ones I called yesterday. The bastards at the front desk lied when they told me no one matching that description had checked in."

"Don't worry about it. Get over there and take care of them. Now."

Shaw slid the pistol into his waistband, grabbed a jacket and was gone. Kerrigan stood in the center of the room, thinking. Samantha Carlson had arrived in Antwerp the same day he had. Coincidence? He was beginning to think not. Then she called the hotel in Butembo where both she and her father had stayed. Why? Was there any way she could have linked her father to him? Next to impossible. But still, if she had somehow figured out that Samuel Carlson had led the spring expedition two years ago, she would be on the warpath. Especially if she extrapolated that logic one step further to the plane crash he had engineered. The stupid bastard. If her father had just told him where the damn diamonds were, he and his wife could have lived. But no, he refused, and in doing so had signed his own death warrant. A slight adjustment to the plane's stabilizers had caused it to crash into the Atlantic, killing everyone on board.

Possibly, he reminded himself, was the key word. There was no proof to tie him to the Casablanca incident. He began to relax. Shaw was on his way to their hotel, and soon McNeil would be dead and Carlson would be in his hands. And he had wanted to tell her about her father anyway. Perhaps she already knew, and if she did, so what? It would just take away the element of surprise. He would still have the enjoyment of describing to her in the tiniest detail exactly how he had killed her parents. This twist wasn't a problem. He would still have his way with the bitch.

He left the suite, his briefcase in one hand, umbrella in the other. A taxi was at the curb and he slipped into the backseat. A twisted smile came to his face as he thought about the day that lay ahead. Twenty-five million dollars in uncut diamonds would pass from his hands, through De Beers, to some fabulously wealthy Saudi princes. De Beers would take their cut and he would pocket over twenty million. Then Shaw would call on his cell phone and inform him McNeil was dead and Carlson was captive. And then the real fun would begin. Yes, this was going to be a very good day indeed.

Shaw cursed under his breath as his taxi glided up to the lobby of the Alfa Empire Hotel. Exiting the front doors right in front of him were McNeil and Carlson. He thought briefly about taking McNeil out right there on the sidewalk. He nixed the idea—too many witnesses. He chose instead to have his driver follow their taxi. It wasn't a long drive. The cab pulled up in front of the Andimo Building, home of the De Beers Antwerp office. Shaw sat in stunned disbelief as McNeil and Carlson paid the fare and disappeared into the building. He dialed Kerrigan's cell phone number, but the call went directly to voice mail. The building must be screened to prevent cellular calls from entering. He got out of the cab and stood on the sidewalk, trying to decide what to do.

Kerrigan was already in the building, of that he was sure. And so was Carlson. This was not a coincidence. He checked his watch. It was three minutes to ten. There was no way he could just walk into De Beers, unannounced and unexpected, and be ushered through to the inner sanctum in order to warn Kerrigan. Whatever was going to happen inside was going to happen. There was nothing he could do to stop it. But when they came out, that was a different story. He moved across the street to a cafe, chose a corner table and ordered a coffee. His targets would eventually walk out that door, and when they did . . .

FORTY

Samantha and Travis cleared the first level of security on the third floor and entered De Beers's Antwerp offices. The furnishings were opulent, the interior design tasteful and muted, matching the early summer day outside. Persian carpets overlaid Italian marble floors and original oils hung intermittently throughout the reception area. The teak wood accents and the gilt-edged lighting added an exclusive ambience. They were welcomed by a fashionably dressed receptionist, fluent in unaccented English, and led through a series of rooms and hallways to a highly secure wing of the floor. The decorating here was stark in comparison, the walls an off-white and the furniture simple. Nowhere to hide diamonds.

A director of the Antwerp office introduced himself to Samantha and Travis, then led them deeper into the labyrinth of grading rooms. In one of the larger rooms, bench after bench, covered with white paper, sat next to south-facing windows. Piles of diamonds sat on each table, carefully sorted according to size, color, quality and shape. They passed the largest of the sorting rooms and entered an anteroom adjacent to the private sorting chamber. Four men were already in the room: a De Beers employee, two Saudi princes, and an American. Patrick Kerrigan. He turned to see the newcomers, and froze.

"Mr. Kerrigan, this is the world-renowned geologist we mentioned would be helping to grade the diamonds at the sight. May I introduce Dr. Samantha Carlson. Dr. Carlson, this is Patrick Kerrigan, a regular client and president of Gem-Star, based out of New York."

Kerrigan's eyes showed surprise, but no emotion as he took the outstretched hand. Samantha's fury boiled precariously close to the top. She stared into the very soul of the monster who had taken her parents from her. The man who had killed countless others, innocents who stood in his warped way. And she loathed him. She had never felt true hate like she felt as she gripped his cold hand. She squeezed, her grip equally as strong as his, perhaps stronger. Then she relaxed, releasing his hand and letting it slip from her grasp. This was not the time or manner in which to hurt Kerrigan. That would happen soon enough.

"I'm pleased to meet you, Dr. Carlson," Kerrigan managed to grind out.

"Likewise."

The De Beers director introduced her to both the Saudi princes and she shook their hands. "Dr. Carlson, the diamonds are already in the sight room." He pointed at the small metal box she carried. "We'll have to examine that case before we can allow you in the room. Standard procedure, of course."

"Of course," she answered lightly, handing it to the nearby employee. He opened it, removed and checked each piece of instrumentation, then carefully scrutinized the box itself. Satisfied it was a standard carrying case filled with the usual geological tools, he returned it to her. "Thank you, Dr. Carlson."

The director waved to the door and she entered, closing it behind her. The room faced south, with a large window that allowed ample sunlight in. Even with the typical Antwerp cloud cover, the room was bright. A table covered with white paper sat facing the window. On the paper sat the diamonds—the diamonds Kerrigan had taken from her in Cairo. She moved to the table and set her box down as she seated herself. She opened it and removed the microscope first, then the proportion analyzer and finally the eyepiece. As she worked, she noted every inch of the room. She was looking for the camera she knew was there somewhere. Then she saw it. Slightly behind her, to the left, was a section of wall a fraction of a shade lighter than the surrounding area. The stream of filtered sunlight reflected off the cover at a slightly different angle, revealing the tiny square. She shifted slightly to place her body between the diamonds and the camera, then got to work.

With her left hand, she worked the proportion analyzer and the eyepiece, carefully judging each stone, taking her time as she went. With her right hand, she twisted the clasp on the box in the reverse direction and it popped open. One after another she carefully placed the rough diamonds into the soft black rubber between the inner and outer shells of the box. She positioned twenty-one on the upper side of the box, then snapped it shut and flipped it over. She opened the bottom and inserted the final twenty stones. She snapped it shut for a few seconds, then opened both the top and bottom and let the stones fall back on the table. Forty-one perfect molds stared back at her, all vacant and ready for the cubic zirconia. She snapped the case shut and twisted the handle slightly as Basil had shown her. The liquid zirconia flowed from its storage tubes into the rubber that lined the case. It settled out in the indentations, filling them. She waited the required two minutes, then released the catalyst by twisting the handle in the opposite direction. Now she needed at least six minutes for the catalyst to harden the zirconia. She turned her attention back to the real diamonds, which lay on the paper in front of her.

She was four minutes into the hardening time when the

door behind her opened. She turned abruptly from her instruments, glaring at the intruder. It was the De Beers employee who had checked her case.

"What do you want?" she snapped at him, her tone bordering on uncivil.

"We were wondering how much longer you will be, Dr. Carlson," the man said, taken aback by the tone in her voice. Behind him, Samantha could see Kerrigan starting to move for the door.

She got to her feet and faced the man, blocking the entrance to the room. "Grading diamonds takes time, sir," she said. "You have allowed me the professional courtesy of examining these stones; now please give me privacy while I analyze them." The employee moved back. When he was outside the door, she grasped the handle and pushed. The door closed. She waited a moment for Kerrigan to rip it open, but that didn't happen. She moved to the table and resumed examining the real stones. She checked her watch. It was just six minutes. Basil had said eight would be better. She relaxed into the chair and placed another stone on the proportion analyzer.

A full nine minutes from first injecting the catalyst, Samantha opened the case and let the stones fall out on the table. She gasped as they landed close to her and away from the real ones. They were perfect. The color was identical to the rough greenish tinge that covered the diamonds she had taken from the kimberlite pipe in the Congo. Their shapes were without flaw. She quickly examined one with her instruments, marveling at how the modified zirconia now simulated the exact molecular structure of diamond. Christ, Basil was good.

She now had two piles of diamonds. The fakes were closest to her and hidden from the camera, the real ones sitting out in plain sight. One by one, she took a real diamond, exchanged it for a fake and placed the real stone in the correct mold in the case. Time was wearing on and she knew placing the wrong stone in a mold would be disastrous. She finally came to the last diamond and slipped it into the only remaining mold. It fit perfectly. She snapped both the bottom and top of the case shut and stood up. She walked to the door and opened it. Two Saudi princes, one director of De Beers and one employee, McNeil, and Kerrigan all stared at her from the anteroom.

"Gentlemen," she began. "I'm afraid the news is not good. The diamonds are fakes."

"Impossible!" Kerrigan shouted. "You know damn well those stones are real."

Every eye turned to look at him. "And how would she know that, Mr. Kerrigan?"

He swallowed, hesitated. "Because she just examined them, of course."

The De Beers director was stone-faced. He picked up a phone on a nearby table. "Please have three of our best gemologists come to the executive room," he said. "Immediately." He turned to the employee. "Please check Dr. Carlson's instrument case. Carefully."

Scant seconds later, three men dressed in white lab coats appeared at the door. The director explained to the men the situation, and asked them to closely examine the stones to determine authenticity. The three men piled into the sight room and began their examination.

"Mr. Kerrigan, I don't have to tell you what this means if Dr. Carlson is correct," he said.

"Of course not," Kerrigan fumed. "*If* the diamonds were fakes, my membership to the World Federation of Diamond Bourses would be revoked. But they are not. They are real. Very real." He stared directly at Samantha as he spoke. The lifelessness had left his eyes, and she saw the epitome of hate growing from the depths of his mind and manifesting itself in his stare. She had never seen such evil, and after a few moments she looked away.

Time passed until a full fifteen minutes had elapsed. The De Beers employee completed a thorough check of Samantha's instrument case, declared it was fine and handed it back to her. A tense silence enveloped the anteroom, with Samantha and Kerrigan exchanging hateful glances as they waited for the verdict. The door to the sight room opened and the three experts filed out. One of them spoke for the group.

"We're not sure," he said, hesitantly. "Some of the tests are conclusive—they appear to be real diamonds. But others are not so clear. There's more than a shadow of doubt as to their authenticity."

The director looked grim. "It's either diamond, or it's not. You're the experts. Which is it?"

"We dropped the stones in question into methylene iodide alongside real diamonds and watched how quickly they sank to the bottom," one of the gemologists said. "They dropped at exactly the same rate. Therefore the density is identical, eliminating cubic zirconia, strontium titanate, YAG and GGG."

A second gemologist continued, "We ran a thermal conductivity test and sent pulses of power through the stones. The stones registered as diamond on the calibrated scale."

"At that point, we were convinced they were diamond," the third man said. "But a final test has us wondering."

"You measured the reflection coefficient," Samantha interjected.

"Yes." The man turned to her. "Is that how you knew?" She nodded and he continued. "In cubic zirconia, the refractive index changes faster with the wavelength than with diamond. We measured the difference in the infrared spectrum and found substantial differences from where a true diamond should measure. The readings were closer to cubic zirconia."

Samantha made a slight motion to Travis. Then she set the instrument case on the table. He gathered it up and excused himself under the intent of leaving the building to have a cigarette. After he was gone, Samantha addressed the room.

"Gentlemen, there *is* one test that is quite easy to perform that would conclusively prove whether the stones are genuine or fake."

"What is that, Dr. Carlson?" the director asked.

"Let me show you." Samantha reentered the sight room and waited until the gemologist, the director, both Saudi princes and Kerrigan had all followed her in. "It's quite simple, really. If this is a molecularly modified form of zirconia, it will fail this test miserably." She turned abruptly, picked up the small microscope from the desk and brought the base down on one of the stones. A series of gasps escaped from the onlookers. She left the microscope sitting for a moment, then lifted it up. Scattered on the table was a pile of broken zirconia. "As I said, the test is rather simple."

"What the fuck did you do with my diamonds?" Kerrigan exploded.

"Mr. Kerrigan, De Beers is a respectable establishment. Foul language is not acceptable. Another outburst and I will insist you leave immediately." The De Beers director was very serious.

Kerrigan could barely control his rage. Through clenched teeth he managed to snarl, "Where are my diamonds?"

"On the table, Mr. Kerrigan. Exactly where they were when I entered the room."

Kerrigan turned to the director. "She did something with the diamonds. These are not the same ones I brought to the sight."

The director motioned to the employee. "The photographs, please." The younger man produced a full set of high-quality digital photographs printed on a color laser printer. The quality was impeccable. The photographs were placed on the table and the diamonds arranged so they sat beside the photo that had been taken when they first arrived. Careful examination revealed that the stones were identical.

"These are the stones, Mr. Kerrigan," the director said. He picked up the microscope and brought it down on another of the forgeries. It smashed, as the first one had. "I think you owe us an explanation."

"She switched them," Kerrigan said defiantly. "She has the diamonds."

"We searched her instrument case and found nothing," the director said, turning to Samantha. "Would you object to a search, Dr. Carlson? A very, shall we say, intense search of your person?"

"I would and I do. However, to protect the De Beers name, I'll allow it." She left the room with the employee as the director called for a female security officer to meet them in the security office.

"We shall see, Mr. Kerrigan," the director said after Samantha had left the room. "You had better pray that she has them, or your days dealing in precious stones are over. This is not something De Beers takes lightly."

"She has them," Kerrigan spat back at him. "Somewhere, somehow, she has them."

The search did not take long. The female officer peered into the anteroom and shook her head. Moments later, a vilified Samantha Carlson entered. She smiled at Kerrigan. "What a terrible mistake, Mr. Kerrigan. Trying to defraud De Beers."

The Saudi princes had had enough. They bowed politely to the director and left. Samantha thanked the man for allowing her to sit in on the sight, and he thanked her emphatically for preventing a complete disaster. She took one last glance at Kerrigan as she left. He was arguing with the director, but the man looked disgusted and was shaking his head. She felt partially vindicated. Kerrigan's reputation was in tatters. His high-income years had just come to an abrupt halt, but that still didn't take care of the immense wealth he had already accumulated. And he could use that money to live out the remainder of his life in style. It wasn't right. He deserved to suffer hell on earth.

And then, as she left the De Beers building, an idea hit her. Perhaps there *was* a way to mete out justice and punish the man on the level he truly deserved. She reached the sidewalk and looked for Travis. He was nowhere to be seen. Sam checked her watch, noting that almost twenty minutes had passed since Travis had left the executive sorting room. As she scanned the faces that passed her on the street, a police car careened around a corner and came to rest in front of Antwerp's main train station. Its blue light was flashing and the officers leapt from the car and hustled into the massive building. Another car followed suit, then another. As she watched, the wide street outside Central Station filled with police and emergency vehicles, all with their flashing lights on.

She drew a deep breath. Travis.

FORTY-ONE

Travis picked up the instrument case and excused himself as Samantha led the men into the examining room. The hallway was clear and he walked nonchalantly back through the maze, encountering three security checks en route. He showed his visitor's pass, allowed the guards to check his clothing and the box, then strode to the elevator and pressed the ground-level button. He exited on the main floor, still clutching the small metal box containing Samantha's geological instruments and the diamonds.

The muted sunlight was stronger than the interior lighting, and it took a second or two for his eyes to adjust. Despite his sight being blurred for a moment, he still picked out the man across the street immediately. The man altered his position slightly to shield his face from Travis's line of sight, but it was too late. He matched perfectly the description of the man the pilot had flown to Rhodes. Travis clipped the small box that held the diamonds onto his belt to give him two free hands, turned left and started toward the cavernous structure of Antwerp's Central Station. Safety in numbers.

He reached the station and entered through the main doors. A short hallway with an arched roof ended with a staircase leading down into a massive chamber. Columns and windowed arches lined the walls and the floor was a sweeping mosaic of squares with inlaid diamond shapes. Towering over the door was a huge fan-shaped window centered with a tower clock. He wasted no time and dove into the mass of people milling about the station as they waited for trains to arrive or depart.

Through the steady stream of people coming and going, Travis spotted the man enter the station, move to the side of the arched hallway and hug one of the columns, almost obscuring himself from view. Travis held his position inside a throng of people checking the arrivals board. A group of tourists found the information they needed and moved toward the tracks, exposing Travis for a moment. He risked a quick glimpse over his shoulder and then started walking. His tail had spotted him and was on the move.

Travis traversed the open hall and entered the ticketing area of the station. The roof and walls were closer here, with no vantage point for his tail to spot him from above. The space was more confined and the passengers closer together, both sheltering him and allowing his shadow to close in without being spotted. He saw a doorway with a small stairway sign on it and angled toward it. The door opened to his touch and he left the crowds for the quiet of the stairs. He started up and had just reached the second floor when the door opened and closed below him. It was an educated guess that the person entering below him was Kerrigan's man. Travis tried the door handle on the second floor landing—locked. He continued up. At the third level, the stairs stopped. A solitary locked door was the only way out other than retreating down. He heard cautious footsteps from below and knew that that route was gone. He looked to the door.

It was a fire door of heavy metal construction, but the lock was on the handle alone, no deadbolt. Travis slipped his lock-picking tool from his belt and went to work. Seconds later the tumblers clicked and he swung open the door. The space behind the door was dark, but he entered and closed the door behind him, locking it. He moved ahead slowly, feeling his way down the pitch-black hallway. The stones were old and rough to the touch, never having been exposed to the elements. An occasional glimmer of light shone through tiny cracks in the mortar, but not enough to give him any visual sense of where he was or what lay ahead. The narrow passage curved as it continued, and he sensed that it was following the roofline at the top of the station's grand entrance. He heard a noise behind him and looked back. For a brief second there was light in the hall, then nothing. His adversary was through the door and coming.

He kept moving, one step at a time. His senses of touch and sound were heightened by the lack of visual stimulation, and he could hear the gentle scraping of the person behind him as he felt his way through the narrow hall. Travis's hand suddenly hit something solid. He put both hands ahead of him and felt the obstacle—a door. He swiped his hands across the flat surface, looking for and finding the handle. It was locked. He slipped the slender metal tool out again and went to work, this time totally blind. A few moments later, the handle turned and he opened the door.

Light flooded into the narrow passageway and he moved quickly to get out of the exposed doorway. He clicked the door shut behind him and glanced about. He stood atop a tiny catwalk that overlooked the entrance hall. He estimated the distance to the floor at fifty feet. Beside him was a stone railing and ahead the clock that centered the giant fan-shaped window he had seen from below when he entered. He moved cautiously along the catwalk toward the clock, then stopped. He looked back at the door.

It was an out-swing door. If he stayed at the door, he could wait for the man to open it about halfway, then slam it shut.

It might stun his attacker, perhaps knock his weapon from his hand, if he had one. He looked ahead to the clock, then back again. He made his decision and moved back to the doorway, positioning himself on the side with the hinges. Then he waited.

Fifty feet below him, the crowds moved about their daily schedule, totally unaware of the drama playing out in the rafters of the old building. Travis watched a family enter the train station and move together toward the tracks. Two small children clutched their parents' hands for security amid the noise and confusion. He found himself wanting what they had. The simplicity of a normal life, with children and a future that extended further than the next five minutes. A scratching sound from inside the door brought him back to reality. His tail was inches away, separated only by the metal fire door.

He steeled himself, driving his heels against the stone pillars that bordered the catwalk. He angled his body so his shoulder was at ninety degrees to the door. The handle slowly turned, then stopped. The door opened a crack. He didn't move a muscle, waiting for the man to commit. The door suddenly flew open and a hand with a pistol in it appeared. Travis pushed with all the strength his legs could muster and threw his weight into the door. His momentum was greater than the man coming through the opening, and the door slammed back into its jamb. The extended arm was caught as the door slammed shut and the finger automatically squeezed the trigger. A single shot rang out through the cavernous room, echoing like thunder. The bullet smashed into one section of the huge glass fan above the front door, showering people inside and out with shards of sharp glass. Screams split through the air as panicked crowds ran for cover.

Travis heard his opponent yell in agony as the door partially crushed his right arm. The gun clattered to the catwalk and Travis made a grab for it. The door opened again, this time with the man barreling through and hitting him full force in the chest. For the first time, Garret Shaw and Travis McNeil were eye to eye. A millisecond passed as the men took stock of each other, then both tried for the gun. It sat on the catwalk, only a few feet from them. Travis's hand touched the metal first, but Shaw hit the pistol away just as Travis tried to grab it. The gun hovered at the edge of the catwalk for a moment, then plunged to the floor below. Travis spun to face his attacker, his hands already coming up in self-defense.

Too late. A well-placed fist smashed into his jaw, knocking him sideways. He twisted to avoid the next blow, but again, too late. Shaw anticipated the open body shot and took it. He drove his fist into Travis's kidney, doubling him over in pain. Another shot, then another. Travis couldn't get up, couldn't get a chance to go on the offensive. The blows that were now raining down on him would soon be lethal. Once his limited defense was gone, the man would snap his spine or neck.

Travis reached down and grabbed the metal box that held the diamonds and wrenched it off his belt. With all his strength he threw a wild roundabout punch, leading with the box. He felt it hit flesh and for a brief second the blows stopped. He rolled and dragged himself to his knees, seeing the blood pouring from a nasty gash on his attacker's head. He threw a straight rabbit punch at Shaw's face and felt the pain shoot through his hand and arm as it hit.

Shaw staggered back, his senses almost gone from the shattering blow to his temple. He saw the metal box coming at his face but couldn't stop it. Again and again. For a second Shaw teetered on the edge of the catwalk, unable to stop the relentless pummeling. One last blow and he felt gravity begin to take over. He reached the point of no return and clutched for the stone rail as he fell. He missed, then was airborne for a couple of seconds. His body hit the stone floor with a sickening sound.

Travis took a quick look over the edge and disappeared back into the dark hallway. He moved quickly now, his footing sure and his hands steady. He clipped the box back onto his belt and smoothed out his hair with one hand while keeping the other against the wall. He reached the door to the stairwell and opened it, glancing about. No one had responded to the fight on the catwalk yet and he raced down the stairs. He heard the familiar sound of sirens as police closed in on the station. He had to get out of the stairwell and in with the masses before the police came, or the game was up. He'd be charged with murder and the diamonds would surely be found, exonerating Kerrigan.

He reached the door leading to the main station and opened it a crack. Police were pouring in the front doors, guns in hand. He quickly opened the door, slipped through and merged in with the other bystanders trying to stay out of harm's way. He slowly migrated to the nearest exit, moving neither slowly nor quickly. At the door, an ambulance worker grabbed him as he walked from the building. He was speaking Flemish and pointing at Travis's face.

"I don't speak Flemish," he said. "Just English."

"Yes, yes. I speak the English. You face is with blood. You are hurt."

"I'm okay, just a bit shaken. There are many more people inside hurt much worse." He pointed at the door. "You should get in there and help them."

The man nodded that he understood and disappeared into the station. Travis unclipped the metal box from his belt and took a minute to wipe the blood off his face, using the metal as a crude mirror. He angled across the street toward De Beers. The sidewalks were crowded with office workers and pedestrians who had stopped to watch all the action outside Central Station. He politely made his way through the crowd, watching for Samantha as he approached De Beers. At first he didn't see her—she was partially hidden behind a tall man. Then their eyes locked and they both smiled. He closed the distance and hugged her close to him.

"That wouldn't be your handiwork over there, would it?" she asked.

"Hey, some guy was crawling around the rafters of the building. He fell off. How could I have anything to do with that?"

"I don't believe you, Mr. McNeil." They linked arms around each other's waists and began to walk away from the station. She glanced up at him. "I've got an idea of what we can do with Kerrigan. We need to find the nearest pharmacy."

FORTY-TWO

Patrick Kerrigan stormed out of De Beers and into the crowds watching the commotion at the station. He ignored the excitement and flagged down a passing cab. He gave the driver the name of his hotel and settled into the back-seat. What a mess.

She'd switched the real diamonds and replaced them with highly accurate forgeries. She must have duplicated them before he took them from her in Cairo. But why? He was completely in the dark. She had taken a shot at him and it had hurt. He knew full well what the repercussions would be. His career was finished. His name would be blacklisted in every establishment worldwide that dealt in legitimate precious stones. He would be a social pariah—again. It wasn't enough that his ex-wife had screwed him; now Samantha Carlson had as well.

Shaw had probably taken out McNeil by now. The confusion at the station may have had something to do with Mc-Neil's death, but he didn't care. Right now, he just wanted to get back to his hotel, have a drink and think of what to do with Carlson when he finally got her in his hands. The audacity of the bitch. Showing up at his sight. Then fucking everything up. Christ, he was furious.

The taxi pulled up outside the Park Lane Hotel. He paid his fare and entered the lobby. The desk clerk waved to him with a message. Davis Perth in New York. Now what the fuck did Davis want with him? The stupid, rich asshole. He should just stay on his sailboat and leave the office stuff to someone who knew what he was doing. The elevator opened at his floor and he entered the quiet hotel suite. He poured a drink of scotch and calculated the time difference to New York. It would be about seven o'clock in the morning. He placed a call to Perth, expecting his secretary to answer. He was mistaken.

"Good morning, Patrick," Davis said once Kerrigan had identified himself. "How are things in Antwerp?"

"Very well, thank you. I thought you wouldn't be back for another few weeks?"

"Oh, some part broke on the boat and it was going to be three weeks to have it manufactured and shipped over, so I just came back to New York. What are you doing in Belgium?"

"We had some rough I wanted to get graded. What better place than Antwerp?"

"Yes, of course. We've got a meeting with the Securities Commission tomorrow, Patrick. Is it possible for you to be at the meeting?"

"I hate those pricks, Davis. Why don't you handle them this time?"

"Because that's what I pay you for. I don't like them either. The meeting is set for two in the afternoon. Please make it back." The line went dead.

Kerrigan hung up the phone and poured another drink, this one a double. Things were just getting worse. The Securities Commission were Doberman Pinschers, and they weren't scared to take a bite out of your ass. And it had only been four months since the last face-to-face meetings with the pricks. Usually it was six months, almost to the day. Then he stopped. Something was wrong. These guys were diarists. They probably made notes of when they crapped each day. There was no way they would be two months early.

Kerrigan placed a call to his CIA connection and asked him to check around and see if anything was going on behind the scenes. He didn't have long to wait. The return call came back inside five minutes.

"Jesus, Patrick. What have you done?"

His knees began to tremble as he spoke. "What do you mean? What's wrong?"

"The FBI and the FAA have both issued warrants for your arrest. They aren't saying what for, but you've been placed on the top of their most wanted list. You must have really fucked someone over."

"Warrants?" Kerrigan steadied himself by sitting in the armchair close to the phone. "They've issued warrants?"

"Yes. If you set foot in the United States, you're going to jail."

"Okay, I understand. Thank you." He let the phone slip from his hand onto his lap. He sat motionless for a minute until the phone began to beep. He replaced it in its cradle and cupped his head in his hands. What had happened? If the FAA was involved, it could very well be that someone had finally connected him to the Cranston Air disaster. But whom? And how?

He placed another call, this time to Lufthansa. They had a flight for Tunisia leaving in three hours and he booked a seat. He needed a country that the United States did not have an extradition treaty with, and Tunisia would work just fine. He packed his bags and called the front desk to send up a porter. He spent the five minutes waiting for the porter downing another scotch. He gave the room a quick once-over, then took the elevator down with his baggage. He had the desk clerk total his bill and handed over a platinum card. After a few swipes on the machine, the clerk apologized to Kerrigan.

"I am sorry, sir, but our machine must be malfunctioning.

Your card is being rejected. I've been asked to phone the bank. I'm sorry, but I must comply."

"Do as you wish. As you say, the machines must be down."

The clerk dialed a central number for the Visa center, spoke to the representative, then hung up and addressed Kerrigan. "They have instructed me to destroy the card, sir. Do you have another?"

Kerrigan stared at the man. His platinum card had a one-hundred-thousand-dollar limit. He pulled another card from his wallet and handed it over. Three swipes and a phone call later, the clerk destroyed the second card.

"I'll pay cash," Kerrigan said, withdrawing a wad of bills and paying the tab. He left the hotel knowing that the far-reaching tentacles of the FBI were in motion, and that he had limited time to transfer his assets to safe havens. He instructed his taxi driver to find a Credite Suisse Bank. The man knew of one and drove him straight there. He told the driver to wait and entered the bank. Fifteen minutes later, a distraught Patrick Kerrigan exited the bank. All his accounts were frozen. At best, he was limited to the offshore accounts in the Bahamas and Cayman Islands. And those would follow suit soon. He had to think. He had over one hundred thousand dollars in cash, tucked in a hidden compartment of his carry-on baggage. There was no way to access the two accounts that weren't frozen without actually visiting the Caribbean, and that was too dangerous right now. He had to get to Tunisia and lie low for a bit.

He ordered the driver to the international airport in Brussels and sank into the leather seat, watching the countryside. The longer he thought about it, the more it all started to come together. Samantha Carlson. Somehow, she had figured out his complicity in the Cranston Air crash and had relayed that information to the FBI. And they had bought it. The Bureau had then issued the warrants for his arrest, terminated his charge cards, and frozen his accounts, both national and international. Christ, she had screwed him and screwed him good.

The only avenue left to him was to flee. And his options were very limited. The United States had powerful connections worldwide, and that meant only a handful of countries would be safe. He cursed her as the taxi sped toward Brussels. He cursed her and he hated her like he had never hated anyone before.

FORTY-THREE

The phone rang and Samantha picked it up. She handed the phone over to Travis and went back to wrapping a small package for the post. She covered the bubble wrap with brown paper and addressed it. She slipped it and a letter into her handbag. He waited as the hotel operator connected the overseas line.

"Is this Travis McNeil?"

"Yes."

"This is Davis Perth. We spoke two days ago."

"Yes, of course I remember. What can I do for you, Mr. Perth?"

"Please, call me Davis. And the question would be more like, what can we do for you?" he said. "I gave an accurate account of what you told me on the phone to the director of the FBI. He happens to be a personal friend and golfing buddy. He contacted the FAA. It seems that the FAA knew exactly what downed that airliner, but they never released that information to the press. They also knew about the payment to Garth Graham, but they didn't know who had paid him. They were keeping what they knew under wraps until something else came up. Something like Patrick Kerrigan's involvement."

"So they believed us that Kerrigan was the mastermind?"

"Absolutely. They've drawn the net in on him already. Warrants have been issued for his arrest. His credit cards are useless and all his accounts worldwide are frozen. The man is finished."

"Excellent. Thanks, Davis. Without you getting the FBI to lend a high-ranking ear to all this, he would have walked."

"He may still," Davis Perth cautioned. "He's reserved a seat on Lufthansa to Tunisia. It departs Brussels in less than two hours. The U.S. consulate in Brussels can't work through diplomatic channels fast enough to stop him."

"Then I've got to go. Samantha came up with an idea that might just work. Talk to you later." He turned to an inquisitive Samantha Carlson. "I'll tell you in the taxi what's going on. Let's go."

Kerrigan sat in the business-class passenger's lounge, relaxing now that he had cleared customs and immigration. The ticket agent had been excellent, considering his predicament. The credit card authorization he had initiated from his hotel room an hour earlier had been rejected, leaving him without a ticket. The plane was almost filled, but the agent managed to find him a business-class seat when he produced the cash. Now he was just a few minutes from boarding, and freedom. A sharp prick on the back of his left hand caused him to open his eyes and jerk upright. To his right was Samantha Carlson, and to his left was Travis McNeil. They both clamped their hands over his, holding him tight to the arms of the chair.

"Thinking about leaving, Mr. Kerrigan?" McNeil asked.

"I don't think that's such a good idea," Samantha added. "Since you're a murdering son of a bitch."

"Fuck you, Carlson. You've done enough damage. You're not stopping me from getting on that airplane."

"You're the one who's done the damage. I loved my parents, and a day doesn't go by that I don't think of them. And you killed them. Just like you murdered every person on Cranston Air Flight 111."

"Not to mention the expeditions you sent into the jungle, knowing full well that you were going to kill them once they found the diamonds," said Travis.

Kerrigan was twitching slightly, and his sight was blurring. He shook his head to try to clear the cobwebs. McNeil was grasping at his coat. He pulled away, talking loudly to attract the attention of the gate personnel. An airline rep appeared and Kerrigan lurched forward into her arms. He tried to talk, but his speech was slurred, incoherent. The Lufthansa employee looked to Travis and Samantha for help.

"Our uncle is mildly handicapped," Samantha explained. "If you could help him to his gate and onto the plane, it would be greatly appreciated.

"Of course, miss," the agent said, grasping Kerrigan and steadying him. She led him toward the row of gates leading to the planes. "Where is your ticket, sir?" Kerrigan managed to pat his chest and the woman removed his ticket from the vest pocket. She looked at it and led him away. "You're at gate forty-one, and they are just starting to board."

Travis and Samantha watched as the woman led Kerrigan to the plane. They returned through the metal detectors and left the section reserved for ticketed passengers. They threw the business-class tickets they had just purchased in the garbage, went to the main doors and jumped in a cab.

"I hope he enjoys the flight," she said cheerfully.

"I don't think he'll remember much of it. How much curare did you put on that needle?"

"Quite a bit. He's going to be in a trance for quite a while. Curare is a powerful muscle relaxant. Pretty good idea, eh?"

"Very good." He gave her a long, loving kiss.

"Remember when I asked you if you'd consider quitting what you do and maybe starting a business?"

"Yes, I remember."

"Do you remember what you said?"

"I said yes, and I meant it."

"Okay, then let's figure out what we should do. You like to dive, right?"

"Scuba?" he asked and she nodded. "Yup, I love to dive."

"Then we could set up shop somewhere really warm, with white sand beaches and underwater reefs and run a dive shop."

"But I also like to ski," he said, frowning insincerely.

"Okay. We'll run a dive shop for five months, and a skiing operation for five months. How does that sound?"

"That's only ten months."

"We need two just for us." The taxi pulled into Antwerp and she asked the driver to find a post office. He did, and she deposited a letter and a small package, then rejoined Travis in the backseat.

"You're probably the kind of guy who hates the thought of marriage," she said.

"I used to. I'm not so sure anymore." He grinned at her and she knew. He was sure.

FORTY-FOUR

The flight attendant gently nudged the passenger in 4B. He had slept for the entire flight and the pilots were just beginning their final approach into the airport. He snorted a couple of times, then opened his eyes. They were unfocused, teary.

"Sir, we're going to be landing soon. You have to put your seat back in an upright position."

"Oh, yes, of course. Did you say we're almost there?"

"Yes, sir. We're just beginning our final descent right now."

"I must have slept through the entire flight."

"You did, sir."

"That makes buying a business-class ticket seem like a waste," he said. The attendant smiled.

Patrick Kerrigan handed over the small airline pillow and blanket. He moved his seat back to the proper position and ran his hands over his hair. The attendant reappeared with a glass of water and he accepted it. He took a long drink and relaxed. He had slept well on the flight and felt refreshed. Slowly, however, he began to recall the incident at the Brussels airport. McNeil and Carlson sitting on either side of him. Then nothing. No recollection of anything until now. He shook his head slightly, trying to stir his memory. Something else had happened at the airport. What was it? McNeil's voice, then a pinprick on his hand. His left hand. He looked down at the back of his hand, and balked. Between his second and third knuckles was a tiny red mark.

He began to sweat. The vague memory of McNeil and Carlson was real. They had been at the airport. But what had they wanted? He had made his flight and escaped. They had failed to stop him. His breathing began to slow and he felt the initial adrenaline rush dissipate. He settled back into the first-class seat and closed his eyes. Whatever they had tried, it hadn't worked.

He felt the tires touch down on the runway. He was safe. Safe from the FBI and Interpol, and aside from the CIA mounting a covert operation to return him to the United States, safe from any law enforcement agency. And the chances of the CIA sending in a team on such a high-risk mission was just about zero. It would take time to rebuild his fortune but it could be done. It would be done. He had enough cash with him to get set up in Tunisia and finance a quick trip to Sierra Leone. He still had ties to small mining sites in that hellhole that would move him back to millionaire status within months. And once he was back on his feet financially, he'd take care of Samantha Carlson.

The ground crews attached the bridge to the plane and the flight attendants opened the door. The business-class passengers began to deplane and Kerrigan fell in line. He smiled at the attendant as she thanked the passengers for flying Lufthansa.

"Welcome to Cairo, sir," she said pleasantly to Kerrigan as he passed.

He stopped dead in his tracks and the passenger behind him almost walked into him. He turned to the attendant. "What did you say?"

"Welcome to Cairo." She looked puzzled at his expression.

"This flight wasn't to Cairo, it was to Tunisia. What the hell are we doing in Cairo? Was the plane detoured?" He was panicking now.

"Sir, this flight is a regularly scheduled one that flies direct from Brussels to Cairo. If you check your ticket, you'll see——"

Kerrigan watched as the woman spoke to him, her lips moving, telling him his life was over. He staggered back against the flow of passengers and sat down hard in a first-row business-class seat. He looked at the back of his left hand, at the tiny red mark. McNeil and Carlson had been at the airport, all right. They had drugged him and they had switched his ticket. And now he sat on the runway in a city where the police wanted him for murdering two of their men. That bitch.

The passengers finished filing out of the plane and a group of heavily armed police marched through the bridge and encircled his seat. He looked up and saw unabashed hatred in the officers' eyes as they stared down at him.

"Patrick Kerrigan?" one of them asked. He simply nodded. "You are under arrest for the murder of Abdullah Minghas, and complicity in the murder of two Cairo police officers."

Kerrigan stood up and faced the man. "Do I even get a trial?"

"You have had your trial. You have been found guilty and sentenced to life in prison." The police officer leaned close to Kerrigan and spat in his face. He whirled Kerrigan around and snapped a pair of handcuffs on him. They were far too tight. He spun the prisoner around to face him again. "We have a very special part of our jail reserved for you. I do not think you will like it."

Kerrigan put up no resistance as they grabbed him and pushed him roughly through the airport and toward a waiting car. He had lost everything. His position in society, his reputation, his wealth and now his freedom. And she had taken it from him.

"Damn you to hell, Samantha Carlson."

The sun was bright in his eyes as they shoved him into the car. Then the door closed and the light was gone. It was the last time in his life he would feel the warmth of the sun.

EPILOGUE

Basil Abercrombie watched the postman turn and climb the stairs to his stoop. The metal flap on his door opened and two letters dropped through, followed by a small package. The flap clicked shut and the postman retreated from the door. Basil set his tea on the table and walked over to the door. He picked up the mail and returned to the couch. He ignored the letters and scanned the package. It was addressed to Abe Lisab. Cute. The return address was some street in Antwerp, Belgium. The person who had packaged it and put it in the post was Samuel Travis. He chuckled lightly as he ripped the wrapping apart and spilled the contents onto the table.

Twelve greenish stones fell to the wooden surface. He sat back, staring at the diamonds. Travis had promised he would repay the few thousand pounds he had borrowed and he had come through. Basil knew that the value of the stones, even on the black market, was in excess of three million pounds. But what was more important was the knowledge that they had pulled it off. They had gone into De Beers and stolen the diamonds back. His little box had worked.

He scooped the rough into a small brown envelope and sealed it. He stood in the middle of his flat and looked about. Somehow, it didn't matter anymore. It wasn't him. He picked up the phone and booked a flight to Barbados. He slipped the diamonds into his pocket and left the flat, locking the door behind him. He dropped the key in the first trash bin he passed and kept walking.

With the money he already had stashed in the bank and the newfound wealth in his pocket, he felt confident of one thing. If Travis could land a babe like Samantha, so could he. And what better place than Barbados?

Mail arrived seldom in Kigali, and overseas mail was a real event. The postman knocked on the door and hand-delivered the letter from Belgium directly to Hal and Mauri. Their four children looked on excitedly as Hal opened the letter. He read it aloud.

Dear Hal and Mauri,

Travis and I have had quite the adventure since we last saw you in the Congo. I hope you arrived home safely and had no problems with the soldiers. I know how resourceful you are, Hal, and I'm confident you will be standing in your living room reading this with Mauri and the kids.

Thanks again for your services during the gorilla expedition. We wouldn't have seen so many primates without your expert guidance. You're the best.

You really must try this little hole in the wall we found. It's the last place you would ever think of looking. It's about halfway down the west side of Ridge Street and the front of the shop is covered with shrubs and vines. Very tropical and tough to see. But once you're inside, the menu is unbelievable. I think you'll find it very rewarding.

Say hi to the kids for me.
By the way, Travis and I are getting married.
All my love,
Samantha

Hal finished reading and the kids went off to play. Mauri started to prepare lunch and Hal sat in his easy chair. He reread the letter again, smiling as he did. Tomorrow he would leave on an adventure—a very profitable adventure.

The letter was a map. A map to the diamondiferous formation deep in the Ruwenzori Mountains. He would travel to the last target Samantha's expedition had looked at. He knew the exact location. Then he would carefully examine the western ridge for a hole. Once he found the hole, he would find the diamonds. And then things would change. He would pay off every important person he had ever blackmailed. That would ensure his safety. Then he would take the wealth from the vein and slowly distribute it to the needy of Kigali. He would make life so much better for so many.

The last thought he had before he folded up the letter and slipped it into his shirt pocket was that he would buy Mauri a new house, one with running water and a proper bathroom. And bedrooms for the children. He withdrew the letter from his pocket and kissed it lightly.

"Thank you, Doctor Sam," he said quietly. "Thank you."

COLD BLOODED

ROBERT J. RANDISI

NYPD Detective Sergeant Dennis McQueen has his hands full with a very bizarre case. A series of dead bodies have been found, all frozen—killed by various methods, but disposed of in the same manner. Just a coincidence, or is there a serial killer at work?

Things heat up when McQueen is sent to investigate a body found in the rubble of a fire and meets FDNY Fire Marshal Mason Willis. Willis is investigating it as an arson, but the medical examiner's report makes it obvious that this is a case for McQueen. McQueen and Willis have no choice but to work together. Will even the combined efforts of the NYPD and the FDNY be able to stop the killer…or killers?

- -

Dorchester Publishing Co., Inc.
P.O. Box 6640   _5574-0
Wayne, PA 19087-8640 $6.99 US/$8.99 CAN

Please add $2.50 for shipping and handling for the first book and $.75 for each additional book. NY and PA residents, add appropriate sales tax. No cash, stamps, or CODs. Canadian orders require an extra $2.00 for shipping and handling and must be paid in U.S. dollars. Prices and availability subject to change. **Payment must accompany all orders.**

Name: _____

Address: _____

City: _____ State: _____ Zip: _____

E-mail: _____

I have enclosed $_____ in payment for the checked book(s).

CHECK OUT OUR WEBSITE! **www.dorchesterpub.com**
_____ Please send me a free catalog.

★ RAYMOND ★
DUNCAN
PATRIOT TRAP

Neal McGrath is not a spy. He's a university professor visiting Havana to research a book. Before he left the States, though, an old colleague from the CIA pressured him for a favor—get in touch with Elena Rodriguez, a beautiful and mysterious woman from Neal's past. But one meeting with Elena is enough to trap Neal in a life-and-death game of international conspiracy.

Elena now works for Cuba's top-secret intelligence agency, the Ministry of Interior, and the information she possesses can sway governments—or get her killed. Neal offers to help her any way he can, all the while struggling to make sense of events that draw him and Elena ever deeper into Cuba's cutthroat world of power and lies, where only one rule is clear: Survive any way you can.